用字正典

序

這本《用字正典》是李端老師的嘔心之作。

李端老師是我們認識的英文老師中最有學養、英文造詣也是最佳的其中一位。卅年前，他以第一名的成績考入台大外文研究所，旋即受教於李本題老師。李本題老師亦是我在外語學校的恩師，英文、語法、修辭及文學素養可謂已達登峰造極的地步。我個人教學的態度就深受李本題老師的影響。得知李端老師亦是李本題老師的門生時，我頓時感到很親切。

數年前，我經由友人吳乃作老師的介紹認識李端老師。與他寒暄未久，即知李端老師是一位中英文學養俱佳的好老師，我隨即請求他擔任常春藤的資深編審。或許是師出同門的關係，他爽快答應了。未久，他就與本人伙同本社其他中外編輯群投入叢書編輯行列。他的筆譯及英文撰寫工夫連老外都佩服，然而他仍一本謙遜和善的態度善盡編審職責，這種精神令我感佩，對我而言，李端老師不啻是亦師亦友。

一年半前，李端老師特別提出要撰寫《用字正典》的構想，期望對台灣所有欲學好英文的學子盡一份力量。我當然表示支持。計劃展開時，我親自目睹到他以極為嚴謹的態度廣泛蒐集資料，逐一求證關鍵英文字的用法，並不時與我的好友 Bruce Bagnell（目前執教於台大外文系）諮商，以求這本《用字正典》的精確性及實用性。

這本《用字正典》歷經李端老師及中外編輯的用心校對及編排終於付梓成書。我相信這是一本好書，值得親愛的讀者細心品味。

[illegible]

于台北寓書齋

自序

英語《用字正典》這本書特別針對華人在用英語表達時易犯的錯誤而撰寫。

在學習英語的過程當中，我認為最大的困難不在於字彙多、詞藻廣或文法規則龐雜，因為這些問題都可以逐步加以解決。我想最大的障礙在於中文的『包袱』。由於華人習慣於中文的語法，再加上喜用『英漢字典』，所以在寫或說英文時很容易造出或講出『中文式』的英文。這種情形可以說比比皆是，而且不乏有人犯了這類錯誤一輩子而不自知。有鑑於此，特別撰寫本書。

本人才疏學淺，動筆之初甚感惶恐。幸有賴世雄教授及美籍教授 Bruce Bagnell 從旁指正，本書才得以完成。賴教授治學甚為嚴謹。他常言英文是他的『愛人』，我則半開玩笑說英文是我的『敵人』。不過，在做學問的這條路上，『由愛生恨』或『因恨而愛』是可以殊途同歸的。

李端

用字正典

A a

A

a (n)

He is male chauvinist to the core. (✗)
He is a male chauvinist to the core. (✓)
(他是十足的大男人主義者。)

單數可數名詞之前需置 a 或 an。

As for cooking, I'll give her A for effort. (✗)
As for cooking, I'll give her an A for effort. (✓)
(她的烹調手藝並不怎麼樣。)

Mr. Smith would like to buy a SUV. (✗)
Mr. Smith would like to buy an SUV. (✓)
(史密斯先生想買一部休旅車。)

英文字母或縮語開頭如為母音, 用 an。

I'm afraid you have to wait a hour or two. (✗)
I'm afraid you have to wait an hour or two. (✓)
(恐怕你必須等候一兩個小時。)

若干 h 開頭的單字 h 並不發音, 需用 an 搭配其後的母音。這一類的字還有: heir, honest, honor, hourly 等。

Miss Wang is on the phone. I doubt whether you know such a person. (✗)
A Miss Wang is on the phone. I doubt whether you know such a person. (✓)
(有一位王小姐來電，我懷疑你認識這一個人。)

對不認識的人士, 必須說 a Mr./Miss。

aback

I was taken back by her loose talk. (✗)
I was taken aback by her loose talk. (✓)
(她大放厥詞令我嚇了一大跳。)

be taken aback 意為『某人嚇了一大跳』。be taken back 兼指某 (購買) 物被拿回去退換或比喻某人被帶回到舊時光。如: If you don't like the shirt, it can be taken back. (如果你不喜歡這件襯衫，可以拿回去退換。) I am taken back to my salad days whenever I hear this old song. (每當我聽到這首老歌，我就想起從前少不更事的日子。)

abandon

Quite a few people believe the death penalty should be abandoned. (✗)
Quite a few people believe the death penalty should be abolished. (✓)
(不少人士認為應該廢除死刑。)

abandon 是指放棄計劃、活動或做某事之企圖。如: Doctors often persuade those who smoke to abandon the habit. (醫師經常勸抽煙人士戒除這種習慣。)
abolish是指廢除法令、傳統或某種制度。

On the ground are piles of abandon cars. (✗)
On the ground are piles of abandoned cars. (✓)
(地面堆滿了廢棄車輛。)

abandon 不能作形容詞, 需用 abandoned, 即『被拋棄的』。

ABC's

The book is about the ABCs of nature. (✗)

The book is about the ABC's of nature. (✔)

(這本書是介紹大自然的基本知識。)

以美式用法而言，說某學科的基本知識要用 the ABC's of..., 但在英式用法中 the ABC of...也是正確用法。

abide

If you join the army, you have to abide its rules. (✗)

If you join the army, you have to abide by its rules. (✔)

(如果你從軍，就必須遵守其規定。)

abide sth (用於否定句) 表『(不能) 忍受某物』, 如: I can't abide those rules. (我無法忍受那些規定。) abide by sth 是『遵守規定/則等』。

ability

Logic helps develop your ability of thinking. (✗)

Logic helps develop your ability to think. (✔)

(邏輯有助於培養你的思考能力。)

the/sb's ability to do sth 為英文的習慣用法。

How can I improve my ability of writing? (✗)

How can I improve my writing ability? (✔)

(我該如何才能增進我的寫作能力？)

reading/writing/teaching/acting ability 為固定用法。

Your ability of English leaves much to be desired. (✗)

Your ability in English leaves much to be desired. (✔)

(你的英文能力有待加強。)

ability in + 學科/語文 (能力), 如: The test is designed to assess the students' ability in listening comprehension. (這個測驗是為評估學生的聽力而設計的。)

Peter has shown his abilities for a leader. (✗)

Peter has shown his abilities as a leader. (✔)

Peter has shown his leadership abilities. (✔)

(彼德已展現其領導能力。)

abilities as + 身分, 表『當……的能力』。

able

An epidemic like this is able to claim thousands of lives. (✗)

An epidemic like this is capable of claiming thousands of lives. (✔)

An epidemic like this can claim thousands of lives. (✔)

(像這樣的疫情是能夠要走幾千條人命的。)

論能力時, be able to 需用人當主詞。如: He was able to write poems at the age of seven. (他七歲時便能寫詩。) 至於 be capable of (doing) sth 或 can + V 則用人或物作主詞皆可。

A small child is able to make big trouble. (✗)

A

A small child is capable of making big trouble. (✔)
A small child can make big trouble. (✔)
(年紀小的孩子也可能闖大禍。)

be able to 表某人具有……之能力。be capable of (doing) sth 或 can + V 除表能力外兼具有『有……的可能性』之含意。

Please read it aloud. I am not able to hear you. (✗)
Please read it aloud. I can't hear you. (✔)
(請唸大聲點，我聽不見。)
She is not able to decide what to buy. (✗)
She can't decide what to buy. (✔)
(她無法決定該買什麼。)

感官動詞 (see, hear, smell) 和心智活動的動詞 (understand, decide, remember) 恆搭配 can/can't 使用。

In my country, you are not able to buy cigarettes or alcohol until you are 18. (✗)
In my country, you can't buy cigarettes or alcohol until you are 18. (✔)
(在我國你必須年滿十八歲始得購買煙酒。)

有關法令或規定, 需用 can/can't 或 be (not) allowed to. 如: Teenagers are not allowed to stay out late at night. (青少年不准深夜在外逗留。)

above

Above two thousand people staged the rally. (✗)
Over two thousand people staged the rally. (✔)
(超過兩千人參加了該集會遊行。)

表『超過時』, above 一般不與數字連用, 需用 over。但 above 可與表度量衡的數字連用。如: I'm afraid the child is well above 90 kilos. (恐怕這孩子早已超過九十公斤。)

I'm sure the man is over suspicion. (✗)
I'm sure the man is above suspicion. (✔)
(我肯定這名男子沒有嫌疑。)

above suspicion/criticism/reproach 沒有嫌疑/無可非議/不能指責, 為固定用法。

abroad

The artist is very famous at home and in abroad. (✗)
The artist is very famous at home and abroad. (✔)
(這位藝術家在國內外均享有盛名。)

abroad 是副詞, 其前不可置介系詞。唯一的例外是 from abroad, 如: My dad is fresh from abroad. (我老爸剛從國外回來。)

Keep in touch when you go abroad. (✗)
Keep in touch when you are abroad. (✔)
(你出國時要保持聯絡喔。)

go abroad 是指 (搭機) 出國的動作, 此時保持聯絡不合情理。be abroad 是人在國外時的狀態, 此時保持聯絡才合情合理。

absent

There are two absent students today. (✗)
There are two students absent

A

today. (✔)
(今天有兩名學生缺席。)

absent表『缺席/不在的』時一般不直接修飾名詞, 大都接在 be 動詞之後。two students absent 即 two students who are absent之略。不過在英式用法中, absent可直接修飾少數幾個字。如: He is an absent father. (他是一個經常不在家, 即不克盡父職的父親。) 這句話的美式說法是: He is an absentee father.

abuse

John becomes abused when he gets drunk. (✗)
John becomes abusive when he gets drunk. (✔)
(約翰一喝醉酒就開始謾罵。)

abused 是『被虐待的』, 如 an abused child 就是一個受虐的小孩。abusive 是『謾罵的』或『虐待人的』, 如an abusive parent 就是指虐待兒女的父或母。

accent

Mayumi speaks English with strong Japanese accent. (✗)
Mayumi speaks English with a strong Japanese accent. (✔)
(真由美講英文帶著濃厚的日本口音。)

accent 是可數名詞, 其前需置 a 或 an.

accept

I cannot accept such a person. (✗)
I cannot stand such a person. (✔)
(我無法接／忍受那種人。)

accept只能用於接受事物, 即建議、忠告或邀請。如: I accepted her proposal then and there. (我當場接受了她的提議。) stand 表『忍受』, 可用人或事物作受詞。

access

Besides the Net, students should have an access to a good library. (✗)
Besides the Net, students should have access to a good library. (✔)
(除了網路之外，學生也應善用圖書館。)

have/get/gain access to sth 是指某人有機會或權利進入/利用某物。其中access是不可數名詞, 其前不可加 an。

accident

In fact, the birth of our third child was by accident. (✗)
In fact, the birth of our third child was an accident. (✔)
(事實上，我們生第三個孩子完全是個意外。)

by accident 是副詞片語, 只能修飾一般動詞, 不能作為 be 動詞之補語。如: I found out the secret by accident. (我意外/偶然地發現這個祕密。) 表沒有料想到的『意外』, 應該說 sth is/was an accident。

She cut her finger carelessly. (✗)
She cut her finger by accident. (✔)
(她不小心割到手指。)

carelessly 表『粗心大意地』, 如: He often drives carelessly. (他經常開車粗心大意。) by accident 表『意外地』。

It is not an accident that Nick has three divorces. (✗)
It is no accident that Nick has three divorces. (✔)

(尼克離婚三次絕非偶然。)

It is no accident that...意為『某事的發生絕非偶然』。此為固定用法, 不可將 no 拆成 not an。

accompany

I'll accompany you to go to the market. (✗)

I'll accompany you to the market. (✔)

(我陪你去市場。)

accompany sb = go with sb, 所以使用該動詞無需再接 to go。

according

According to us, the problem is just the tip of the iceberg. (✗)

In our opinion, the problem is just the tip of the iceberg. (✔)

(依照我們的看法，這個問題只是冰山之一角。)

according to + 他人 (不可接 me 或 us)。提出自己的意見時, 需用 in my/our opinion。

account

Charge her meal on my account. (✗)

Charge her meal to my account. (✔)

(把她這一餐記在我的帳上。)

charge sth to sb's account 意為『將……記在某人的帳上』。on sb's account = for the sake of sb 表『為了某人的緣故』。如: Don't do it on my account. (不要為了我的緣故做這件事情。)

accurate

It happened sometime in April. I can't remember the accurate date. (✗)

It happened sometime in April. I can't remember the exact date. (✔)

(這件事情發生在四月間，我記不得正確日期。)

accurate 是『正確無誤的』。是針對所說或所寫的內容沒有錯誤而言。The data may not be accurate. (資料也許並不正確。) exact 是『精確的』或『確確實實的那一個』。

accuse

The man was arrested and accused of arson. (✗)

The man was arrested and charged with arson. (✔)

(這名男子遭到警方逮捕並被控縱火。)

be accused of + 罪名　用於非正式的指控/責, 即口頭上說某人犯了某種罪。如: Tom was accused of theft. (湯姆被指控偷竊。) be charged with + 罪名 = be indicted for + 罪名, 則是正式控告某人犯下某種罪, 進入司法程序。

ache

Sometimes taking a hot bath can help relieve your ache and pain. (✗)

Sometimes taking a hot bath can help relieve your aches and pains. (✔)

(有時候泡個熱水澡有助於緩和身體的種種痠痛。)

aches and pains 指身體的種種疼/痠痛, 為固定用法, 不可用單數形式。

act

It was an action of wisdom when you decided to quit. (✗)

It was an act of wisdom when you decided to quit. (✔)

(你已決定洗手不幹，真是明智之舉。)

act 是指『特殊的』舉/行動, 如 an act of courage/kindness/foolishness/heroism/generosity 即是一樁勇敢/仁慈/愚蠢/英勇/慷慨之舉。action是指『一般的』舉/行動, 較為籠統, 如: We believe the authorities should take action. (我們認為主管當局應採取行動。)

It's a human fault rather than an action of God. (✗)

It's a human fault rather than an act of God. (✔)

(這是人禍而非天災。)

an act of God 指的是天災, 為固定用法。

Stop being childish! Behave like your age. (✗)

Stop being childish! Act your age. (✔)

(別幼稚了！舉止成熟點。)

act your age 為英語慣用法。Behave like your age.這句話不通, 應該說 Behave like a grown-up/gentleman/lady.

actually

His novels have been selling like hot cakes. Actually, he is very well-off now. (✗)

His novels have been selling like hot cakes. As a matter of fact, he is very well-off now. (✔)

(他的小說大賣了一陣子。事實上，他現在富足的很。)

actually 主要是用來解釋誤會。如: My neighbors think I am well-off, but actually I am quite poor. (我的鄰居都以為我很有錢, 不過事實上我相當貧困。) as a matter of fact 主要是用來拓展先前的一句話。另外, in fact 則兼有上述兩種用法。

adapt

Lisa has difficulty adapting new surroundings. (✗)

Lisa has difficulty adapting to new surroundings. (✔)

(麗莎很難適應新環境。)

adapt (oneself) to sth 意為 (使自己) 適應某物

The movie is adapted for a best-seller. (✗)

The movie is adapted from a best-seller. (✔)

(這部電影改編自一本暢銷小說。)

be adapted for sth 意為『被改編成……』。如: The novel has been adapted for the stage. (這本小說已被改編成舞台劇。) be adapted from sth 意為『改編自……』

add

Add some sugar into your coffee, if you like. (✗)

Add some sugar to your coffee, if you like. (✔)

(如果你喜歡，可以加點糖在你的咖啡裏。)

add sth to sth 意為將某物加入某物, 是固定用法。

The dragon dance will add up the festive atmosphere. (✗)

A

The dragon dance will add to the festive atmosphere. (✔)
(舞龍可增加節慶的歡樂氣氛。)

add up 是把數字加在一起 (以求總數), 如: please add up these figures. (請把這些數字加在一起。) add to = increase 是『增加』的意思。

addicted

He admitted he was addictive to drinking. (✗)
He admitted he was addicted to drinking. (✔)
(他承認他有酒癮。)

addictive 是指煙酒或藥物會使人上癮的。如: Smoking is highly addictive. (抽煙極容易使人上癮。) be addicted to + N/Ving 是指某人有……之癮或沉迷於……。

adoptive

I was brought up by my adopting parents. (✗)
I was brought up by my adoptive parents. (✔)
(我是被養父母撫養大的。)

adopt sb 表『領養小孩』, 如: You can become parents by adopting a child. (你們領養個小孩就可當父母了。)
adoptive 是『領養的』, 所以養父母的說法是 adoptive parents。adopted 是『被領養的』, 因此養子/女是 adopted children。

advanced

The retired colonel is advancing in years. (✗)
The retired colonel is advanced in years. (✔)
(這名退休上校已經年邁。)

be advanced in years 是指某人已經年邁, 為固定用法。advancing years/age 則用來描述某人『年事漸高』。如: We should take his advancing age into account. (他的年事漸高, 我們也該列入考慮。)

advice

Let me give you an advice. (✗)
Let me give you a bit of advice. (✔)
(讓我給你一個建言吧。)

advice 為不可數名詞, 所以既不能置 an 於前也不能加 s 在後。不過, 我們可說 a bit/piece/word of advice.

advise

Many dietitians advise to eat more fruit. (✗)
Many dietitians advise eating more fruit. (✔)
Many dietitians advise people to eat more fruit. (✔)
(很多營養師建議人們要多吃水果。)

給予忠告或建議要用 advise, 句型如下: advise sb to do sth 或 advise + N/Ving.

affair

We don't want any foreign countries to interfere in our internal affair. (✗)
We don't want any foreign countries to interfere in our internal affairs. (✔)
(我們不希望任何外國來干涉我們的內政。)

A

單數的 affair 可指個人的『私事』或與某人的『曖昧』關係。如: My private life is my own affair. (我的私生活是我的私事,用不著你管。) He had an affair with his secretary. (他跟他的祕書有染。) 但指國家的重大事務,如外交、內政等時恆用複數形的 affairs, 如: foreign affairs.

affect

Smoking will definitely influence your health. (✗)
Smoking will definitely affect your health. (✓)

influence 是指影響事物的後續發展, 如: Don't let others influence your decision. (不要讓別人影響你的決定。) affect 是指對事物的改變或產生 (負面) 的影響。

afford

I can't afford losing face. (✗)
I can't afford to lose face. (✓)
(這張臉我可丟不起。)

can/can't afford + to V, 表『付 (買)/承受不起……』, 為固定用法。

afraid

My mother is old and ill; therefore, I am afraid of her. (✗)
My mother is old and ill; therefore, I am afraid for her. (✓)
(媽媽又老又病,我很擔心她。)

be afraid of 是指害怕某人/物。媽媽既老又病, 有什麼好怕她的? be afraid for = be worried about, 是為……擔心/憂心意思。

Since you are here, he is afraid of coming. (✗)
Since you are here, he is afraid to come. (✓)
(既然你人在這兒,他是不敢來的。)

be afraid to do sth 是指不敢或極不願意做某事。

A: Will the typhoon come? B: I'm so afraid. (✗)
A: Will the typhoon come? B: I'm afraid so. (✓)
(甲:颱風會來嗎?)(乙:恐怕會吧。)

I'm so afraid.是『我很怕。』答非所問。I'm afraid so.是接近 "Yes." 的回答。

after

Don't worry. They'll be back after a week. (✗)
Don't worry. They'll be back in a week. (✓)
(不用擔心。他們一星期後就回來。)

當我們從現在 (說話時) 講到過了一段時間之後的未來, 需用 in a day/two weeks/three years.
after + N 主要是以事件或活動為主, 如 after work (下班後); after the war (戰後); after two days' rest (休息兩天之後)。

John became a successful businessman after two years. (✗)
John became a successful businessman two years later. (✓)
(兩年後約翰成為一個成功的生意人。)

當我們從更早的過去提到過了一段時間之後的過去, 需用 a week/two months later。

A

after all

Don't be too harsh on him. He is a child, above all. (✗)
Don't be too harsh on him. He is a child, after all. (✓)
(不要對他過於嚴苛。他畢竟只是個孩子。)

above all 意為『最重要者』，作副詞片語用, 如: Above all, you should wear warm clothes. (最重要的是, 你要穿保暖的衣服。) after all 是『畢竟』的意思。

again

I'll have to write the letter over and over again because it is missing. (✗)
I'll have to write the letter all over again because it is missing. (✓)
(這封信我必須重寫一遍，因為遺失了。)

over and over again = again and again = time and again 都是『一而再』的意思, 如: I've told you over and over again not to oversleep. (我一而再地告訴你, 不要睡過頭了。) all over again 是『重來一遍』的意思。

This bike costs again as much as that one. (✗)
This bike costs as much again as that one. (✓)
This bike costs twice as much as that one. (✓)
(這部腳踏車是那部腳踏車的兩倍價格。)

as much/many/large again as = twice as much/many/large as 意為『是……的兩倍(大)』。

age

My father went to college in the age of 45. (✗)
My father went to college at the age of 45. (✓)
(我老爸四十五歲時上大學。)

in an/the age of...是指『在……的時代』，如: We are living in the age of technology. (我們現正生活在一個科技的時代。) 指『在幾歲時』需用 at the age of + 數字。

How old did you start smoking? (✗)
At what age did you start smoking? (✓)
(你多大年紀開始抽煙？)

how old 是形容詞片語, 只能搭配 be 動詞來用, 如: How old are you/is he? (你/他多大年紀？) at what age 是副詞片語, 可以修飾其它一般動詞。

When I was at your age, I used to like jazz a lot. (✗)
When I was your age, I used to like jazz a lot. (✓)
(當我在你這個年紀時，我很喜歡爵士樂。)

at your/his/her age 是副詞片語, 不能作 be 動詞的補語。用法如: At his age he can be very rebellious. (在他這個年齡是可能很叛逆的。) be sb's age 表『在某人的年紀時』。

People like my age tend to become more conservative. (✗)
People of my age tend to become more conservative. (✓)
(像我這種年齡層的人會有較為保守的傾向。)

people like my/your/his age 沒有意義, 因為 people 和 age 怎麼會『像』呢？people/boys/girls of your/my/his age 方是正確的用法。這裏的"of"表『屬於』，即屬於……的年齡層之意。另有 be of an age + 不定詞也有『屬於』之意, 如: The boy is of an age to know better. (這個孩子按年齡應該懂事了。)

A

aged

I have two children, aging 12 and 15. (✗)

I have two children, aged 12 and 15. (✔)

(我有兩個孩子，分別是十二歲和十五歲。)

aged + 數字表『年齡為……』。aging 可當名詞或形容詞, 意為『老化』或『老化的』, 如: The aging process comes slowly but surely. (老化的過程來得很慢但絕錯不了。)

These toys are designed to target children aged 7 and 10. (✗)

These toys are designed to target children aged between 7 and 10. (✔)

These toys are designed to target children aged 7 to 10. (✔)

(這批玩具是鎖定七至十歲的兒童而設計的。)

children aged 7 and 10 是指七歲和十歲的兒童(即跳過中間八歲、九歲的兒童), 顯然不合理 aged between A and B = aged A to B 是指介於 A 和 B 的年齡層。

agent

Jane is applying for a job at a real estate agent. (✗)

Jane is applying for a job at a real estate agent's/agency. (✔)

(阿珍目前正在應徵一家房地產仲介公司的工作。)

agent 指的是經紀人或從業人員, 如: a travel agent 就是一名旅遊從業人員。agent's 或 agency 指的是一個公司或機構, 如: a news agency 就是一家報社。

ago

The war had ended well over 50 years ago. (✗)

The war ended well over 50 years ago. (✔)

(這個戰爭早在五十多年前結束。)

ago = before now, 是以現在 (說話時) 為基準的若干時間以前, 恆搭配過去簡單式。

Have we met ago? (✗)

Have we met before? (✔)

(我們以前有見過面嗎？)

ago 不能單獨使用。其前需有明確的一段時間, 如: a week/two days ago。before 有兩種用法: (1) 籠統的以前 (可搭配現在完成式或過去簡單式), 如: I (have) never heard of the man before. (我之前從未聽說過這個人。) (2) 某個過去時間的以前 (常搭配過去完成式), 如: The patient had died two hours before the doctor came. (醫生來時病人已經死亡兩個小時。)

agree

My father did not agree with my brother studying abroad. (✗)

My father did not agree to my brother studying abroad. (✔)

(我老爸並不同意我哥哥出國讀書。)

agree with sb/sth 是指同意某人的看法或意見。如: My father does not agree with my mother about everything. (老爸和老媽對事情的看法不曾相同。) agree to 則是同意 (某人的) 建議或做法, 有『贊成』或『准許』之意。

As a matter of fact, coffee does not agree to me. (✗)

As a matter of fact, coffee does not agree with me. (✔)

A

(事實上，咖啡不適合我的體質。)

食物 + agree with + 某人表該食物適合某人的體質。

The date and the site need to be agreed to. (✗)
The date and the site need to be agreed on. (✔)
(日期和地點需要大家同意後決定。)

agree on + 共同決定的事物

At that time, we both had to agree to difference. (✗)
At that time, we both had to agree to differ. (✔)
(在那個時候我們必須接受彼此的歧見。)

agree to differ/disagree 就是接受或容許彼此不同的看法, 為固定用法。

ahead

A clever and hard-working person like him is sure to go ahead. (✗)
A clever and hard-working person like him is sure to get ahead. (✔)
(像他這麼精明又勤奮的人一定會有成就。)

go ahead 是請人繼續做某事, 如: Go ahead. I won't interrupt you again. (繼續做吧。我不會再干擾。) 或表同意別人的想/做法, 如: If you want to move out, then go ahead. (如果你想搬出去住, 那請便。) get ahead 是指在事業或學業上有成就。

aid

The war-torn country is trying to seek humanitarian aids from the UN. (✗)
The war-torn country is trying to seek humanitarian aid from the UN. (✔)
(這個飽受戰爭蹂躪的國家正設法尋求聯合國的人道援助。)

aid 當『援助 (金錢或物資)』時為不可數名詞, 如 economic/medical/foreign/international aid (經濟的/醫療的/外國的/國際的援助)。aid 作『輔助器/教材』時為可數名詞, 如 a hearing aid (助聽器); audio-visual aids (視聽輔助器材)

aim

These measures are aiming at reducing the crime rate. (✗)
These measures are aimed at reducing the crime rate. (✔)
(這些措施的目的就是要降低犯罪率。)

aim at sb/sth 是 (用槍) 瞄準某人或某物, 如: The hunter is aiming at a boar. (這名獵人正瞄準一頭野豬。) be aimed at (doing) sth 表『為……之目的』。be aimed at sb 表『以某人為對象』, 如: The TV commercial is aimed at housewives. (這一則電視廣告針對的是家庭主婦。)

air

Jack enjoys putting on air. (✗)
Jack enjoys putting on airs. (✔)
(傑克喜歡裝腔做勢。)

air 作『空氣』解時為不可數名詞, 如: I need some fresh air. (我想出去透透氣。) 作『態度』或『樣子』解時為可數名詞, 如: He came back home with a triumphant air. (他帶著得意揚揚的姿態回家。) put on airs 意為『裝腔做勢』, 恆用複數。另外 air 還可當動詞作『表達』的意思, 如: air one's opinions/views/concerns (表達某人的意見/看法/關切)

aircraft

All the aircrafts are grounded because of the heavy fog. (✗)
All the aircraft are grounded because of the heavy fog. (✔)
(因為濃霧所有的飛機都停飛。)

aircraft 表飛機或直昇機等『飛行器』, 單複數同形。

alarm

The burglar ran away empty-handed after he touched the alarm. (✗)
The burglar ran away empty-handed after he triggered the alarm. (✔)
(這名竊賊觸動警報系統後即雙手空空跑掉。)

trigger/set off an alarm 觸動警報系統

alike

The Lord of the Rings is a film that appeals to young and old both. (✗)
***The Lord of the Rings* is a film that appeals to young and old alike. (✔)**
(《魔戒》是一部老少咸宜的電影。)

A and B alike = both A and B 既 A 且 B

alive

Hussen was captured lively. (✗)
Hussen was captured alive. (✔)
(海珊被活捉了。)

lively『活潑的』, 為形容詞, 如: Tom is a lively child. (湯姆是個活潑的孩子。) alive 意為『活生生的』也是形容詞。be buried/burned/captured alive (被活埋/活活燒死/活捉) 為固定用法。

The man in question is still living and kicking. (✗)
The man in question is still alive and kicking. (✔)
(我們所提到的人仍然健在。)

living 作為形容詞時通常置於名詞之前。如: living death (行屍走肉般的生活); living things (生物); living expenses (生活費)。alive and kicking (健在) 為固定用法。

all

He was so hungry that he ate all the chicken. (✗)
He was so hungry that he ate the whole chicken. (✔)
(他非常飢餓竟然吃下一整隻雞。)

在單數可數名詞之前應該用 the whole/entire + N 來表達整體或全部。all 經常搭配代名詞使用, 如: She ate it all. (她全部吃下去了。)

allow

Mary and Bill are coming to dinner tonight, so be sure to allow them when buying food. (✗)
Mary and Bill are coming to dinner tonight, so be sure to allow for them when buying food. (✔)
(瑪麗和比爾今晚來我們家吃飯, 所以買菜時務必要考慮到他們兩位。)

allow sb to + V 表『容許某人做某事』, 如: My parents won't allow me to stay out overnight. (我父母不准我在外過夜。) allow for sb/sth = take sb/sth into consideration 表『考慮到某人/物』。

almost

Those who signed up were almost women. (✗)

Those who signed up were mostly women. (✔)

(報名參加者幾乎都是女人。)

almost (幾乎) 是『幾近於』的意思。所以 almost women 是不通的說法 (除非他們都在進行變性手術)。mostly 是『十之八九』的意思。

alone

Only words cannot express my gratitude. (✗)

Words alone cannot express my gratitude. (✔)

Mere words cannot express my gratitude. (✔)

(光是文字無法表達我的感激之情。)

表達『光是/單憑...』需用 N + alone 或 (a) mere + N。另外, 原錯誤句是一個很奇怪的說法, 其意為: 只有文字不能表達我的感激之情 (其它方式則可?)

along

We are having a great time in a theme park. Want to come together? (✗)

We are having a great time in a theme park. Want to come along? (✔)

(我們在一家主題樂園玩得很開心。要不要一道來 ?)

come together 是指兩個或更多人一起來, 如: You both can come together. (你們兩個可以一起來。)。come along 是指某人 (順便) 一道過來。

I knew all alone that he was a spy. (✗)

I knew all along that he was a spy. (✔)

(我一直都知道他是個間諜。)

all alone 是『十分孤單』的意思, 如: She is all alone in the world. (她舉目無親無故。) all along 是『一直』或『自始至終』的意思。

aloud

Read it loudly so that I can hear. (✗)

Read it aloud so that I can hear. (✔)

Read it out loud so that I can hear. (✔)

(唸大聲點我才聽得見。)

loudly 是『很大聲地』, 幾近於製造噪音, 這個用法相當於副詞的 loud, 如: Don't talk so loud/loudly. (不要這麼大聲說話。)。aloud 或 out loud 是指聲音大到可以讓人聽得見。

already

They have already too many guests. (✗)

They already have too many guests. (✔)

They have too many guests already. (✔)

(他們的客人已經太多了。)

When I arrived, the teacher already was in the classroom. (✗)

When I arrived, the teacher was already in the classroom. (✔)

(當我到達時，老師已經在教室裏。)

This industry already has gone downhill. (✗)

This industry has already gone downhill. (✓)

(這種產業已經走下坡了。)

already在句中的位置: (1) 置於一般動詞之前或句末。(2) 置於be動詞之後。(3) 置於have/has 和 pp.之間。

also

Turn off the TV, and turn off the computer also. (✗)

Turn off the TV, and turn off the computer too/as well. (✓)

(關掉電視，也關掉電腦。)

also 不可置於句末。置於句末需用 too/as well。

My uncle has also a villa around here. (✗)

My uncle also has a villa around here. (✓)

(我的叔叔在這兒附近也有一棟別墅。)

The little boy also can turn a somersault. (✗)

The little boy can also turn a somersault. (✓)

(這個小男孩也能翻觔斗。)

The king also was a philosopher. (✗)

The king was also a philosopher. (✓)

(這位國王也是一個哲學家。)

also在句中的位置: (1) 置於一般動詞之前。(2) 置於助動詞之後。(3) 置於be動詞之後。

alternative

Why don't you try alternate medicine? (✗)

Why don't you try alternative medicine? (✓)

(為什麼不試試另類療法呢？)

alternate 除了當動詞表『輪流』或『交替』外, 也可作形容詞用。如: I go and visit my grandfather on alternate Sundays. (我每兩個星期去探望我的阿公一次，都在禮拜天。) alternative medicine (另類療法) 為固定用法。

although

Although we all did our best, but we lost the game. (✗)

Although we all did our best, we lost the game. (✓)

We all did our best, but we lost the game. (✓)

(雖然大家全力以赴，不過我們還是輸掉這場比賽。)

although 和 but 不能並用, 需擇一使用。

I can't stay. I'll have a coffee, although. (✗)

I can't stay. I'll have a coffee, though. (✓)

(我不能留下來。不過，我可以喝杯咖啡再走。)

置於句首時 although = though, 皆為連接詞, 表『雖然』。另 though 亦可作副詞用, 置於句末表『不過』, although 則無此用法。

altogether

A few rare animals may be extinct all together. (✗)

A few rare animals may be extinct altogether. (✓)

A

(有些稀有動物可能會完全絕種。)

all together 是『一起』的意思。『一起絕種』實際上不可能。其用法如: It's been a long time since we were all together. (我們已經很久沒有大家在一起了。) altogether = completely, 是『完全』的意思。

amateur

Mr. Jones is an amateurish photographer. (✗)
Mr. Jones is an amateur photographer. (✓)
(瓊斯先生是一位業餘攝影師。)

amateurish 是形容詞, 意為『非專業的』, 恆用來形容事物, 如: The accusation is described as crude and amateurish. (這項指控被形容為既粗糙又不夠專業。) an amateur golfter/painter/musician/photographer, 即一位業餘高爾夫球員/畫家/音樂家/攝影師, 為固定用法。

amend

Two articles need to be mended. (✗)
Two articles need to be amended. (✗)
(有兩個條款需要修正。)

mend 意為『修理/補』, 如: It is never too late to mend. (亡羊補牢, 猶未晚也——諺語。) amend 通常是指對『法令、條款』的修正。

I hope you can make amend for my loss. (✗)
I hope you can make amends for my loss. (✓)
(希望你能彌補我的損失。)

make amends for = make up for = compensate for 表『彌補……』之意。

amid

The chairman was forced to step down among a wave of opposition. (✗)
The chairman was forced to step down amid a wave of opposition. (✓)
(主席在一片反對聲浪中被迫下台。)

among 表『在三個或以上的具體人或事物當中』, 如: A new mayor will be elected from among the three candidates. (新市長將從三位候選人當中選舉產生。) amid 表『在較為抽象的情緒反應或笑鬧聲中』。

amount

There has been a growing number of traffic recently. (✗)
There has been a growing amount of traffic recently. (✓)
(最近的交通流量一直在持續增加。)

a...number of + 複數名詞
a...amount of + 不可數 (單數) 名詞

A big amount of money has been invested in the semiconductor industry. (✗)
A large amount of money has been invested in the semiconductor industry. (✓)
(已經投下大量資金在半導體產業。)

a large 或 small amount/number 為正確用法, 不可用 a big 或 little amount/number。

amuse

The party was a huge success. All the people really amused themselves. (✗)
The party was a huge success.

All the people really enjoyed themselves. (✔)
(這個派對極為成功，所有人都樂在其中。)

amuse oneself是指做一些娛樂或消遣的事情，如: How do you amuse yourself in your free time? (你閒暇時做何消遣？) enjoy oneself 是指玩得很開心。

amusing

I took my children to an amusing park last Sunday. (✗)
I took my children to an amusement park last Sunday. (✔)
(上個星期天我帶孩子到一處遊樂園區。)

amusing 意為『有趣的; 好玩的』, 如: The story he told is really amusing. (他講的故事真的很好玩。) an amusement park (遊樂公園) 為固定用法。

angle

It's an obtuse angle, not a sharp one. (✗)
It's an obtuse angle, not an acute one. (✔)
(這是一個鈍角不是銳角。)

銳角的正確說法為 an acute angle。sharp 是『尖銳的』, 專指器物, 如 a sharp knife, 即是指一把尖刀。

another

Falling in love is one thing; getting married is the other. (✗)
Falling in love is one thing; getting married is another. (✔)
(談戀愛是一回事，結婚是另一回事。)

the other 是指兩者的『另一』。如: I have two computers. One is a desktop; the other is a laptop. (我有兩部電腦, 一部是桌上型的, 另一部是筆記型的。) another 是指三者或以上的『另一』。one thing 和 another 為表『……是一回事; ……是另一回事』的固定搭配。

I don't like beef noodles. Let's eat another. (✗)
I don't like beef noodles. Let's eat something else. (✔)
(我不喜歡牛肉麵。咱們吃點別的吧。)

指不同的事物或人時, 需用 something/someone else。

George traveled from a country to another by bike. (✗)
George traveled from one country to another by bike. (✔)
(喬治騎單車到各國旅行。)

from one + N to another = from N to N 是正確用法, 如: The tradition will be passed down from one generation to another. = The tradition will be passed down from generation to generation. (這種傳統將會一代代的被傳下去。)

answer

I rang the doorbell, but nobody responded. (✗)
I rang the doorbell, but nobody answered. (✔)
(我按了門鈴，可是沒人來應門。)

respond 特指採取行動或措施來反應或以書寫的方式來回應, 如: Thousands of viewers responded to our questionnaire. (好幾千名收視者回答了我們的問卷。) 『應門』的說法是 answer (the door)。

A

I wrote her a letter but she has not answered back. (✗)
I wrote her a letter but she has not answered (it). (✔)
(我寫了一封信給她，可是她至今尚未回信。)

回信的英文是 answer (a letter); 回電是 call back;接電話是 answer the phone。answer back = talk back 是『頂嘴』的意思, 如: I hate children who answer back. (我討厭會頂嘴的孩子。)

The dog answers the name of "Hero." (✗)
The dog answers to the name of "Hero." (✔)
(這隻狗的名字叫『英雄』。)

人/動物 answer to the name of...本指某人或動物對某一個名字有回應, 引申為『名字叫……。』

I am going to answer for the job ad. (✗)
I am going to answer the job ad. (✔)
(我準備要回那一則徵人的廣告。)

answer for = be responsible for 是『對……負責』的意思。如: You'll have to answer for the consequences of this decision. (你將必須對此決定的後果負責。) 表回覆一則徵人的廣告, answer an/the ad 方是正確的用法。

anticipate

I anticipate to be of service to you. (✗)
I anticipate being of service to you. (✔)
(我期望能為你效勞。)

anticipate + Ving = expect + to V, 如: I expect to be of service to you.

antique

It must be an old shop for they sell a variety of curios. (✗)
It must be an antique shop for they sell a variety of curios. (✔)
(那一定是家古董店，因為他們賣的是各式各樣的古器物。)

an old shop 是指一家 (百年) 老店但賣什麼並不清楚。a secondhand shop 是一家專賣二手貨的店。an antique shop 則是一家古董店。

anxious

Our company keeps losing money, and the boss is very anxious. (✗)
Our company keeps losing money, and the boss is very nervous. (✗)
Our company keeps losing money and the boss is very worried. (✔)
(我們的公司一直在虧損，因此老闆很憂心。)

anxious 特指對未來不可知的事情表示焦慮不安, 如: I'm anxious about the exam results. (我對考試的結果感到焦慮不安。) nervous 是指對即將要發生或面臨的事情感到緊張, 情緒無法放鬆, 如: I'm very nervous about the upcoming exams. (我對即將來臨的考試備感緊張。) worried 可指對已 (或未) 發生的事情表示憂心。公司虧損既成事實, 不能用 anxious 或 nervous。

I am anxious to get a copy of her new novel. (✗)
I am impatient to get a copy of her new novel. (✔)
I can't wait to get a copy of her new novel. (✔)
(我迫不及待想要擁有一本她的新小說。)

表『迫不及待』想做什麼, 需用 be eager/keen/impatient/longing/dying to + V 或 can't wait to + V。

any

To tell you the truth, I don't have any friend here. (✗)
To tell you the truth, I don't have any friends here. (✓)
(說真的，我在這裏一個朋友也沒有。)

在否定句或疑問句中, any 需接複數的可數名詞或單數的不可數名詞, 如: "Do you have any money with you?" "No, I don't even have any coins." (『你身上有帶錢嗎？』『沒有, 我連銅板都沒有。』)

Don't worry. Any idiots can do that. (✗)
Don't worry. Any idiot can do that. (✓)
(不同擔心。但何一個白痴都能做那件事。)

在肯定句中 any 表『任一』限接單數名詞。

Any time cannot be wasted. (✗)
No time can be wasted. (✓)
(任何時間都不能浪費。)

Any 及相關字 (anybody, anyone, any thing 等) 不可置於否定句之句首。需用 No + 名詞的形式。

anyone

Anyone should avoid making these mistakes. (✗)
Everyone should avoid making these mistakes. (✓)
(任何人都應該避免犯這些錯誤。)

指涉全體人員時應該用 everyone 或 everybody。強調個人 (即不管他/她是誰), 可用 anyone 或 anybody, 如: Anyone can make such mistakes. (任何人都有可能犯這種錯誤。)

Some of my colleagues own two or three cars, but I don't have anyone. (✗)
Some of my colleagues own two or three cars, but I don't have any (one). (✓)
(我有幾個同事同時擁有兩三部車，而我一部也沒有。)

anyone/anybody = any person 專門指人。any one 或 any 兼指人和事物。另外 I don't believe anyone of them. 是錯誤的句子。應改為: I don't believe any (one) of them. anyone 不能接 of..., 但 any (one) 可以。

anywhere

Boys of this type are anywhere. (✗)
Boys of this type are everywhere. (✓)
(這種類型的男孩到處都是。)

everywhere 是『到處』的意思, 指『在/到每個地方』。anywhere 是『在/到任何地方』, 比較有選擇性。如: You can go anywhere you like. (你可以去你喜歡的任何地方)。即: 你可以選擇去哪裏, 不必『到處』去。

Mere talking won't get you everywhere. (✗)
Mere talking won't get you anywhere. (✓)
(光說不練對你們於事無補。)

not get sb anywhere 指對某人沒有任何幫助, 於事不能有所進展, 為慣用法。

A

apart

My two daughters were born five years between. (✗)
My two daughters were born five years apart. (✔)
(我這兩個女兒出生相隔五年。)

four days/three weeks/two years apart 即(時間) 相隔四天/三週/兩年, 為慣用法。

The twin brothers are worlds away in terms of personality. (✗)
The twin brothers are worlds apart in terms of personality. (✔)
(這一對雙胞胎兄弟性格迥異。)

worlds/poles apart 表『有極大的差異』, 為習慣用法。

apologize

I would like to apologize for her. (✗)
I would like to apologize to her. (✔)
(我想向她道歉。)

apologize to sb for sth, 表『因某事向某人道歉』, 如: I would like to apologize to him for being late. (因為遲到, 我想跟他道歉。)

appeal

Though written for young children, the book appeals for adults as well. (✗)
Though written for young children, the book appeals to adults as well. (✔)
(雖然這本書是為兒童寫的，成年人也趨之若鶩。)

appeal for sth 是『呼籲/請求……』的意思, 如: The government is appealing for calm/unity. (政府正呼籲大家要冷靜/團結。) appeal to sb 是『對某人有吸引力』的意思。另外, appeal to sth 是『訴諸……』, 如: President Bush decided to appeal to arms. (布希總統決定訴諸武力。)

appear

Typhoons often appear between July and September. (✗)
Typhoons often occur between July and September. (✔)
(颱風經常在七到九月之間出現／發生。)

appear 是指人或物出現 (被看見), 較適合用在具體的名詞上, 如: Venus appeared in the evening sky. (金星出現在傍晚的天空。)。颱風或地震這類事件用 occur 方是正確。

appetite

Don't destroy your appetite by eating snacks before a meal. (✗)
Don't spoil your appetite by eating snacks before a meal. (✔)
(不要在餐前吃點心以免破壞食慾。)

destroy 是『破壞殆盡』, 即破壞到不可收拾的地步。食慾如果遭到這樣的破壞, 以後吃東西就完全沒有味口。這多可怕啊！spoil/ruin one's appetite 才是正確的說法。

applause

After the performance, the leading actor and actress reappeared on the stage amid a thunderous applause. (✗)
After the performance, the leading actor and actress reappeared on the stage amid thunderous applause. (✔)
(戲演完之後，男女主角在掌聲如雷的鼓

諫下，重新出現在舞台上。)

applause (鼓掌) 為不可數名詞, 所以不能說 an applause 或 a(n)...applause。但可以說 a round of applause (一陣鼓掌聲)。

applicable

My older sister is majoring in applicable linguistics. (✗)

My older sister is majoring in applied linguistics. (✓)

(我老姐目前主修應用語言學。)

applicable 是『適用的』, 如: These rules are not necessarily applicable to foreigners. (這些規定未必適用於老外。) 應用的學科一律用 applied, 如 applied physics/mathematics/psychology, 即應用物理學/數學/心理學。

apply

My younger brother is now applying to a scholarship. (✗)

My younger brother is now applying for a scholarship. (✓)

(我的老弟正在申請獎學金。)

apply to + 機關/學校/公司是指向某機關/學校/公司申請 (某物) 或應徵 (某職位)。如: I applied to three universities but was not accepted by any of them. (我向三所大學申請入學但都未蒙錄取。) apply for + 事/物是應徵 (某職位) 或申請 (某物)。另外, apply to + 人/物也可表適用於某人或某物, 如: What applies to me does not apply to you. (適用於我的未必適用於你。)

They have applied for a divorce. (✗)

They have filed for a divorce. (✓)

(他們已申請離婚了。)

apply for sth 的用法見於之前說明。file for sth 表某人正式 (向法院) 申請離婚或破產等, 為固定用法。

Why don't you apply some suntan lotion on your skin? (✗)

Why don't you apply some suntan lotion to your skin? (✓)

(何不在你的皮膚上塗點防曬乳液?)

apply sth to sth 表『將某物塗抹在某物上』。

appointment

I'm supposed to see a dentist at three. Looks like I'm unable to make the appointment. (✗)

I'm supposed to see a dentist at three. Looks like I'm unable to keep the appointment. (✓)

(我應該在三點鐘去看牙醫。看來我是無法履約了。)

make an/the appointment 是預約去見某人 (尤指醫生、律師等)。而 keep an/the appointment 是指『履約去見某人』。

Mary has made an appointment with Jane, her cousin. (✗)

Mary has arranged to meet Jane, her cousin. (✓)

(瑪麗已經跟表妹阿珍約好要見面。)

make an appointment with 只能接醫生、律師、商業人士等。約親友見面需用 arrange to meet/see sb。

appreciate

I would appreciate if you could come and pick me up. (✗)

I would appreciate it if you could come and pick me up. (✓)

(如果你能開車來接我，我會很感激的。)

A

appreciate 作『感激』或『欣賞』解時均為及物動詞，需接受詞。如: His boss does not really appreciate him. (他的老闆並不真正欣賞他。) appreciate 唯一『不及物』的用法是作『升值』解時，如: The euro has appreciated for two consecutive weeks. (歐元已經連續升值了兩個星期。)

approach

The plane was approaching to the airport when we encountered unexpected turbulence. (✗)

The plane was approaching the airport when we encountered unexpected turbulence. (✓)

(當我們遭遇到突如其來的亂流時，飛機正朝機場接近中。)

approach＋人/物即是『朝某人/物接近』，不需加 "to"。但作名詞時，approach 可接 "to"，如: We should adopt/take a more flexiable approach to the problem. (對於這個問題，我們應該採取更富彈性的方式來處理。)

appropriate

Write clearly and logically. Look, these sentences are not appropriate. (✗)

Write clearly and logically. Look, these sentences are not relevant. (✓)

(寫作的時候思想要明確，概念要合乎邏輯。你看，你這幾個句子根本是不相干的。)

appropriate 意為『適當的』，是指適合某種場合或目的，如: Jeans are not appropriate on formal occasions. (在正式的場合穿牛仔褲並不合適。) relevant 是與主題有關的。

approve

I don't approve sending our parents to a nursing home. (✗)

I don't approve of sending our parents to a nursing home. (✓)

(我不贊成將我們的父母送到安養院。)

approve sth 是『正式批/核准某物』的意思，如: Congress has approved the budget. (國會已批准該預算案。)。approve of sth 是『贊成/同意』某事的意思。

apt

Children of this age are easy to make mistakes. (✗)

Children of this age are apt to make mistakes. (✓)

(這個年齡的孩子容易犯錯。)

easy (容易的) 針對事物而不針對人，如: These questions are easy to answer. (這些問題很容易回答。) be apt to = tend to = be inclined to 表『有……之傾向』的意思。

area

Many industries have moved into the electronic area. (✗)

Many industries have moved into the electronic arena. (✓)

(許多產業已經跨入電子領域。)

area 是有關『地區』最籠統的一個字。arena 本意為『競技場』，引申為任何『角逐的領域』。如: enter the political arena, 即『進入政界』的意思。

arise

A new difficulty happened when we tried to solve the problem. (✗)
A new difficulty arose when we tried to solve the problem. (✔)
(當我們試著解決問題時，又有新問題發生了。)

happen/occur/take place 是指事件的『發生』。difficulty/problem/issue/question 的『發/產生』限用 arise。

arithmetic

Arithmetics is a branch of mathematics. (✗)
Arithmetic is a branch of mathematics. (✔)
(算術是數學的一分支。)

arithmetic 不可加 "s", mathematics 恆有 "s", 此為固定用法。

arm

Susan wouldn't stop crying until her boyfriend took her under his arm. (✗)
Susan wouldn't stop crying until her boyfriend took her in his arms. (✔)
(蘇珊直到男友把她緊緊抱在懷裏才停止哭泣。)

take/hold sb in your arms 即將某人緊緊抱在懷裏, 為固定用法。under your arm 是指把某物挾在腋下, 如: Helen was carrying a book under her arm. (海倫將一本書挾在腋下。)

Keep that guy at an arm's length. (✗)
Keep that guy at arm's length. (✔)
(跟那個傢伙保持距離。)

keep sb at arm's length 意謂『跟某人保持適當距離』, 為固定用法, 不可加"an"在 arm's 之前。但 cost sb an arm and a leg 這個片語則需置入"an", 如: It will cost an arm and a leg to buy a house like this. (要買像這樣的一棟房子是需要花很多錢的。)

arouse

Rachel's strange look arose our suspicions. (✗)
Rachel's strange look aroused our suspicions. (✔)
(瑞秋奇怪的表情引起我們的懷疑。)

arose 是 arise 的過去式, 為不及物動詞, 其後不可直接接受詞, 但 arise from (起源於) 可接受詞, 如: Our misunderstandings arise from the lack of communication. (我們之間的誤會起源於缺乏溝通。) arouse one's sympathy/suspicious/curiosity 表『引起某人的同情/懷疑/好奇』為固定用法。

arrival

At his arrival in Taipei, he went straight to the Grand Hotel. (✗)
On his arrival in Taipei, he went straight to the Grand Hotel. (✔)
(一抵達台北，他就直接前往圓山大飯店。)

on/upon sb's arrival 表『某人一抵達 (某地)』, 為固定用法。

Early arrival may get the best seats. (✗)
Early arrivals may get the best seats. (✔)
(早到的人可以取得最好的座位。)

arrival 表『抵達』時, 通常是不可數的名詞。作『抵達的人或物』解時, 是可數名詞。

A

art

Do you like modern arts? (✗)
Do you like modern art? (✔)
(你喜歡現代藝術嗎？)
If you don't like the sciences, you may pick up the art. (✗)
If you don't like the sciences, you may pick up the arts. (✔)
(如果你不喜歡理科，你可以選文科。)

art (藝術) 作為抽象名詞時不可數, 如: Renaissance art (文藝復興時代的藝術)。作為人文學科時是可數名詞且恆用複數。

artificial

In fact, it is an artificial disaster. (✗)
In fact, it is a man-made disaster. (✔)
(事實上，這是一樁人禍。)

artificial和man-made這兩個字都可表『人造的』, 但很容易產生混淆。要之, artificial所強調的是『由人造 (非天然) 的材料所形成的』, 如: artificial flowers/pearls/limbs, 即人造花/珍珠/義肢。另外, artificial亦可表『由人力的干預所形成的』, 如: artificial insemination/intelligence/respiration, 即人工授精/智慧/呼吸。man-made 強調的是『人類製造或人工開挖的』, 如: a man-made lake, 即是一個人造湖。

as

As other species of apes, this species does not eat meat. (✗)
Like other species of apes, this species does not eat meat. (✔)
(就像其它種類的猿猴一樣，這種猿猴是不吃肉的。)

as (像) 作為連接詞時, 其後需接子句, 如: As his wife does, Peter enjoys reading Chinese classics. (就像他老婆一樣, 彼德也喜歡閱讀古典的中國作品。) like是介系詞, 其後接名詞 (片語) 即可。另外, 如果我們把句子改寫成這個樣子: As other species of apes do, this species does not eat meat. 文法正確但意思完全改觀。其意為:『就像其它種類的猿猴是吃肉的, 這種猿猴不吃肉。』

as if

David talked as if an authority. (✗)
David talked as if he were an authority. (✔)
David talked like an authority. (✔)
(大衛講話的口氣好像是個權威似的。)

帶有假設語氣的as if/though (好像) 其後需接子句。like 是介系詞, 接名詞 (片語) 即可。

as it is

Mr. Hopkins is, as it is, a walking dictionary. (✗)
Mr. Hopkins is, as it were, a walking dictionary. (✔)
(哈普金先生可以說是一部活字典。)

as it is 表『依目前的狀況』或『事實上』, 往往用來與『過去的期望』對照, 如: We hoped she might recover soon, but, as it is, her health is worsening. (我們本希望她能很快康復, 可是事實上, 她的病情卻在惡化中。) as it were = so to speak 是『比方』的說法。如原句把人比喻做字典, 因為人畢竟不是字典。

as from/of

Since today, everyone will be

required to wear a mask at work. (✗)
As of/from today, everyone will be required to wear a mask at work. (✔)
(從今天開始將要求每個人上班時戴口罩。)

since 表『自從』時, 恆接一個過去的時間或事件, 且主要子句限搭配現在完成式, 如: It hasn't rained since the beginning of this month. (自從這個月初以來就沒有下過雨。) as from/of 通常接現在或未來時間, 表『今後』或從『未來某個時間以後』。

ash

According to his will, his ash is to be scattered at sea. (✗)
According to his will, his ashes are to be scattered at sea. (✔)
(按照他的遺囑，他的骨灰要撒在海上。)

ash 作為一般的『灰燼』解時兼有可/不可數的用法, 如: Watch your cigarette ash! (注意你的煙灰!) 或 The house was burned to ashes. (這棟房子已被燒成灰燼)。但指『骨灰』時, 恆用複數形的 ashes。

ashamed

Being poor is nothing to be shameful of. (✗)
Being poor is nothing to be ashamed of. (✔)
(貧窮並不是什麼可以引以為恥的事情。)

shameful 意為『可恥的』, 通常指『行為』。be/feel ashamed of sb/sth 是『以某人/事為恥』。shamless 則為『無恥的』, 通常指人。如: That shameless person should be ashamed of his shameful behavior. (那一個無恥的人真應該以自己的可恥行為引以為恥。)

asleep

I was so tired that I fell sleepy amid the speech. (✗)
I was so tired that I fell asleep amid the speech. (✔)
(我非常疲倦以致於在聽演講時睡著了。)

feel (felt、felt) sleepy 是感到『很想睡覺』的意思, 如: As soon as the old man sat in his armchair, he felt sleepy. (這個老人一坐到扶椅上就覺得很想睡。) fall (fell、fell) asleep = begin to sleep 是『睡著』的意思。

The baby is asleep soundly. (✗)
The baby is sound asleep. (✔)
(這名嬰兒睡很熟。)

用英文表達『睡得很熟』可以說 (1) sleep soundly (其中 sleep 是動詞) 或 (2) be sound/fast asleep (其中asleep是形容詞)。

aspect

We all enjoy declicious food, but we often forget the healthy aspect. (✗)
We all enjoy delicious food, but we often forget the health aspect. (✔)
(我們都喜歡美食，但卻經常忘記健康的一面。)

the health/safety/security aspect 指『健康/安全的一面』, 為固定用法。另外, healthy 通常用來形容人或動物的健康。

In this aspect, we are in complete agreement. (✗)
In this respect, we are in complete agreement. (✔)
(在這方面，我們的看法完全一致。)

提及剛說過的內容時, 限用 in this/that respect, 即指『在這/那方面』。

A

assure

He assured me his help. (✗)
He assured me of his help. (✔)
He assured me that he would help me. (✔)
(他向我保證一定會幫助我。)

assure sb of sth 意為『向某人保證一定可獲得某物』, 為固定用法。另外, assure sb 之後亦可接 that 子句。

You may rest assure that everything will turn out all right. (✗)
You may rest assured that everything will turn out all right. (✔)
(你放心好了，事情都會有很好的結果。)

rest assured that...指『某人大可放心, ……』, 為固定用法。

asylum

The dissident is now looking for asylum in the United States. (✗)
The dissident is now seeking asylum in the United States. (✔)
(這名異議人士目前在美尋求庇護。)

seek (political) asylum 意為『尋求 (政治) 庇護』, 是固定用法。不可用 look for 取代 seek。

at

Since 1948 Israel has never been in peace. (✗)
Since 1948 Israel has never been at peace. (✔)
(自從一九四八年以來以色列從沒有和平過。)

in peace = peacefully 是副詞片語, 意為『和平地』或『不受干擾地』, 如: They came in peace. (他們帶著善意而來。) 或 I just want to have my meal in peace. (我只是想要不受干擾好好吃頓飯。) be at peace/war/rest/work, 即在和平/戰爭/休息/工作的狀態, 是形容詞的用法。

You may reach me by 2331-7600. (✗)
You may reach me at 2331-7600. (✔)
(你可以打 2331-7600 這支電話找到我。)

告訴他人電話號碼時, at + 電話號碼為美式用法; on + 電話號碼為英式用法。

A: "What time is the concert?"
B: "It's 7:30." (✗)
A: "What time is the concert?"
B: "It's at 7:30." (✔)
(甲：演唱會幾點開始？)
(乙：七點半。)

針對某一事件/活動發生的時刻應該 It's at + 時刻。如對方問『現在幾點?』, 才可答 It's + 時刻, 如: A: "What time is it?"B: "It's 7:30."。

athletic

Several athletic reporters are writing for the sports magazine. (✗)
Several athletics reporters are writing for the sports magazine. (✔)
(目前有幾位體育記者為這家運動雜誌寫作。)

athletic 是形容詞, 意為『體格健壯並愛好運動的』。因此 athletic reporters 是指上述這一類型的記者。athletics 指的是『有關各種運動項目』, 所以體育記者應說 athletics reporters。

atmosphere

The exhaust emissions will definitely

worsen the pollution of atmosphere. (✗)
The exhaust emissions will definitely worsen the pollution of the atmosphere. (✔)
(汽機車排放的廢氣絕對會使大氣污染更形惡化。)

指大氣(層)時應該說the atmosphere。指氣氛(氛圍)時，常用 a(n) + Adj. + atmosphere 或 an atmosphere of + N，如：A tense atmosphere filled the banqueting hall. = An atmosphere of tension filled the banqueting hall. (整個宴會廳充滿著緊張的氣氛。)。

attempt

Someone made an attempt to the mayor's life. (✗)
Someone made an attempt on the mayor's life. (✔)
(有人企圖殺害市長。)

make an attempt to + V 意為『企圖做……』，如：He made an attempt to resist arrest but failed. (他企圖拒捕但失敗了。) make an attempt on sb's life 是『企圖殺害某人』的意思。

attention

May I have your attentions, please? (✗)
May I have your attention, please? (✔)
(請大家注意好嗎？)

attention 作為『注意(力)』解時是不可數的名詞。若指對異性『獻殷勤』，則常用複數形的 attentions，如：I'm fed up with his attentions. (我受不了他對我直獻殷勤。)

Children usually have a short attentive span. (✗)
Children usually have a short attention span. (✔)
(通常兒童的專注力不能持久。)

attentive 是形容詞，意為『專注(聽講)的』，如：an attentive audience 就是指一群專心聽講的聽眾。這個字只能形容人不能形容事物。attention span 是指『專注的一段時間』，為固定用法。

audience

The TV show attracted millions of spectators. (✗)
The TV show attracted an audience of millions. (✔)
(這場電視表演吸引了數百萬名觀眾。)

spectator 通常是指到現場看比賽或其它活動的觀眾，如：The spectators at the boxing match are all very excited. (這場拳擊比賽的觀眾都亢奮得很。) audience 本身是集合名詞，專指一群看電影/視或聽演講等的觀眾。另外，專指看電視的觀眾還可以用 viewer(s) 這個字。

author

I'd like to become an author. (✗)
I'd like to become a writer. (✔)
(我想當作家。)

author 專指已有作品發表或出版的作者『本人』，通常需用形容詞(片語)加以限定，如：He has become a famous author. (他已經成為一個名作家。) 或 She is the author of 16 best-sellers. (她是十六本暢銷書的作者。) 單指作家的『身分』時用 writer 這個字。

authority

None of us dare question his

authorities. (✗)

None of us dare question his authority. (✔)

(我們當中沒有人敢質疑他的權威。)

authority 作『權威/勢』解時是不可數的抽象名詞。作『權威人物』解時是可數的普通名詞, 如: Mr. Murphy is an authority on pathology. (莫非先生是病理學的權威。) 指『主管當局』時恆用 the authorities, 如: The health authorities have adopted drastic measures to fight against SARS. (衛生主管當局已經採取強硬措施來對抗 SARS。)

average

Amy's performance tonight is above the average. (✗)

Amy's performance tonight is above average. (✔)

(阿美今晚的表演可謂水準以上。)

be above/about/below average 意為『水準以上/左右/以下』, 是固定用法, 無需加冠詞。至於 the/an average, 通常要接名詞或 of + 名詞於其後, 如: The average temperature in Taipei last month is 28℃. (台北上個月的平均氣温是 28℃。) 或 I spend an average of 2,000 dollars on books per month. (我平均每月花兩千塊錢買書。)

avoid

The government has taken action to avoid the spread of bird flu. (✗)

The government has taken action to prevent the spread of bird flu. (✔)

(政府已採取行動以避免會禽流感繼續擴散。)

avoid 是『避開』或『刻意不去做某事』的意思, 如: Avoid the partk after dark. (天黑後避開那個公園。) Try to avoid exposing your skin to the sun. (儘量避免將你的皮膚暴露在陽光下。) prevent + N 或 prevent sb/sth from Ving 是『阻/防止某事發生』的意思。

awake

Before the alarm clock went off, I was already widely awake. (✗)

Before the alarm clock went off, I was already wide awake. (✔)

(在鬧鐘響之前我早已完全清醒。)

be wide awake = be completely awake 是『完全清醒』的意思, 固定用法。

award

The reward for this year's best actor went to Tom Cruise. (✗)

The award for this year's best actor went to Tom Cruise. (✔)

(今年的最佳男主角獎由阿湯哥獲得。)

reward 是『酬勞』的意思, 如: He was given a reward for helping the police solve the crime. (他因幫助警方破案而獲得一筆酬勞。) award 是某人表現傑出獲頒的『獎項』。

away

The wedding is only two weeks to come. (✗)

The wedding is only two weeks away. (✔)

(婚禮只剩兩個星期就到了。)

three weeks/two days away (再過三星期/兩天就到了) 為固定用法。

B b

B

baby

The doctor was talking to a woman who was having a baby. (?)
The doctor was talking to a woman who was expecting a baby. (✔)
(醫生正在跟一名孕婦講話。)

having a baby 可兼指『懷孕的』和『正在生孩子』。為避免混淆應使用 expecting a baby 或 pregnant 來表『懷孕的』。

back

Once you marry that guy, there will be no going backward. (✗)
Once you marry that guy, there will be no going back. (✔)
(你一旦跟那傢伙結婚就無法回頭了。)

no going/turning back 意為『無法回頭』是一種比喻的說法,為固定用語。backward 作副詞時純指方向上的『向後』, 如: I glanced backward to see what happened. (我向後看了一眼以瞭解發生什麼事。)

Don't speak ill of others behind their back. (✗)
Don't speak ill of others behind their backs. (✔)
(不要在別人的背後說人家的壞話。)

behind one's back(s), 意為『在某人的背後』, 需配合單複數變化使用。

I've got a photo of that rock star with his autograph in the back. (✗)
I've got a photo of that rock star with his autograph on the back. (✔)
(我已得到那位搖滾明星的照片，背面還有他的親筆簽名呢。)

on the back (of sth) 是指『在某物的背面』。in/at the back (of sth) 通常是指在書本或報紙的最後幾頁, 如: Refer to the index in the back for technical terms. (專業術語請參閱書後的索引。)

bad

You cannot imagine how bad I need the money. (✗)
You cannot imagine how badly I need the money. (✔)
(你無法想像我多麼需要那筆錢。)

need/want sth badly 是『非常需/想要某物』的意思, 為固定用法。

bag

They all believe the election is in a bag. (✗)
They all believe the election is in the bag. (✔)
(他們都認為勝選在握。)

be in the bag = be certain to be won or achieved, 意為『一定贏得或成功』, 是固定用語。

baggage

How many baggages do you have? (✗)
How many pieces of baggage do you have? (✔)
(你有多少件行李？)

baggage 或 luggage (英式用法) 是『行李』的集合名詞, 不可數。要表達件數時需用 a piece/two pieces of baggage.

Don't forget to go to the baggage's claim. (✗)
Don'g forget to go to the baggage claim. (✔)
(不要忘了去領取行李。)

機場領取行李處的固定用語為 baggage claim (美式用法) 或 baggage reclaim (英式用法), 不需加's

bail

The suspect was released on a bail. (✗)
The suspect was released on bail. (✔)
(這名嫌犯已交保候傳。)

bail 是『保釋金』, 為不可數名詞。

balance

You ought to get a balance between work and play. (✗)
You ought to strike a balance between work and play. (✔)
(你應該工作與玩樂之間取得一個平衡。)

strike a balance (between...) 是在兩者之間取得一個平衡, 為固定用法。

The US government is based on the principle of check and balance. (✗)
The US government is based on the principle of checks and balances. (✔)
(美國政府立基於制衡的原則。)

checks and balances 是指行政、立法和司法機關的互相制衡, 恆用複數形式。

The importance of a balance diet cannot be overemphasized. (✗)
The importance of a balanced diet cannot be overemphasized. (✔)
(飲食均衡的重要性再怎麼強調也不為過。)

balanced 是形容詞, 常用來修飾名詞, 如: a balanced budget 即是『平衡的預算』。

ban

The ban is likely to be cancelled at the end of the year. (✗)
The ban is likely to be lifted at the end of the year. (✔)
(該禁令年底可望解除。)

impose/lift a ban (on sth) 是 (針對某件事情)『頒佈/解除禁令』的固定說法。

bankrupt

The company has declared bankrupt. (✗)
The company has declared bankruptcy. (✔)
(這家公司已宣告破產。)

bankrupt 通常作形容詞, 如 go bankrupt 就是『破產』的意思。bankrupt 作名詞時意為『破產人士』, 是可數名詞, 如: As a bankrupt, I am unable to pay the debts. (淪為破產人士, 我無力償債。)『宣告破產』需用名詞形式的 bankruptcy 來作 declare 的受詞。

bar

My son was admitted to a bar at the age of 22. (✗)
My son was admitted to the bar at the age of 22. (✔)
(我兒子二十二歲就當上律師。)

B

be admitted to a bar 可以解釋為『獲准進入一家酒吧』。the bar 是指『律師業』，所以 be admitted to the bar = become a lawyer，即成為律師之意。

bare

He is so drunk that he can bare stand. (✗)

He is so drunk that he can barely stand. (✓)

(他醉到幾乎連站都站不穩。)

bare 是形容詞，意為『光禿禿的』或『沒有遮蔽的』，如：The baseball landed on his bare head. (那顆棒球掉落在他光禿禿的頭上。) barely = hardly = scarcely，意為『幾乎不』，是副詞，因此能夠修飾動詞。

bargain

John made a fortune and married a beautiful woman in a bargain. (✗)

John made a fortune and married a beautiful woman in the bargain. (✓)

(約翰發了財還娶個美嬌娘回家。)

in/into the bargain = in addition 表『除此之外』的意思。另外，bargain 也表『廉價品』，如：Many bargain hunters went to the computer fair. (許多尋找便宜貨的人去逛電腦展。)

base

Our subsidiary company is based on Malaysia. (✗)

Our subsidiary company is based in Malaysia. (✓)

(我們的子公司設置在馬來西亞。)

be based on 是『根據……』或『以……為基礎』的意思，如：The movie is based on a best-seller. (這部電影是根據一本暢銷書改編。) be based in + 地方是『設立於某地』的意思。

basic

Irene is learning the basic of computer programming. (✗)

Irene is learning the basics of computer programming. (✓)

(艾琳正在學習電腦程式設計的基本知識。)

basic 是形容詞，意為『基本的』，不能充當名詞使用。the basics (恆用複數) 才是名詞的正確用法。所以 the basics of sth = the basic knowledge/fact of sth。

basis

They are all employed on a full-time base. (✗)

They are all employed on a full-time basis. (✓)

(他們都是以專職的方式被僱用。)

base 作名詞時，專指具體 (可見) 的基礎，像擺放東西的『基座』或『軍事基地』，如：The statue is placed on a solid base. (這尊雕像被安放在一個穩固的基座上。) basis 專指『抽象』的基礎，如 on a daily/weekly/monthly/part-time basis 是指按天/週/月計算或以兼職的方式。

bath

I'll make a bath for you. (✗)

I'll run a bath for you. (✓)

(我來幫你放洗澡水。)

B

英文中沒有 make a bath 的說法。放洗澡水是 run a bath。洗澡是 take a bath (美式用法) 或 have a bath (英式用法)。另外如要講『你的洗澡水放好了。』可說 Your bath is ready.

battery

The battery is useless. You need to recharge it. (✗)

The battery is dead. You need to recharge it. (✔)

(這顆電池沒電了。你需要將它再充電。)

The battery is useless.是說這顆電池不能再使用,因此充電也無濟於事。所以該接著說 You need to change it. (你需要更換電池了。) 至於電池沒電正確的用字是 dead (美式用法) 或 flat (英式用法)。

be

I started to be angry when I sensed that she would stand me up. (✗)

I started to get angry when I sensed that she would stand me up. (✔)

(當我隱隱約約感覺到她會放我鴿子時,我就開始生氣起來。)

be angry 是生氣的『已然』狀態。如: Mary was angry when I came in. (當我進門時, 瑪麗 (早就) 在生氣。) get/become/grow angry 則表由『未然』進入『已然』的動作。如: Mary got angry when I came in. (當我進門時, 瑪麗就生氣了。) 這個『氣』擺明是『衝』著我來。

bear

Since my brother is well over 30, he would like to get married and bear children. (✗)

Since my brother is well over 30, he would like to get married and have children. (✔)

(我哥哥都三十好幾了,所以他想娶妻生子。)

生孩子是女人的專利, 所以男人不能 bear/give birth to children。但是男人可以 have/beget children (按: beget 是典雅的用字, 較少使用)。

beat

Peter can win anyone at chess. (✗)

Peter can beat anyone at chess. (✔)

(下西洋棋彼德可以贏任何人。)

win (贏) 可以接比賽、戰爭、獎項或獎金為受詞, 甚至不接受詞, 但不可以某人作受詞, 如: You win (the game/money).就是『你贏了 (這場比賽/獎金)』。贏了/打敗某人應說 beat/defeat sb。

A couple of drinks make my heart jump faster. (✗)

A couple of drinks make my heart beat faster. (✔)

(兩三杯酒下肚後就會使我心跳加速。)

sb's heart jumps 是指某人受到驚嚇或遇到意外時, 心臟好像快跳出來似的。如: When a truck sped alongside me, I felt my heart jump. (當一輛大卡車從我身旁呼嘯而過時, 我覺得心臟都快跳出來似的。) 單純的『心跳加速』用 beat faster 方是正確。

B

I'm beaten, and I really need a rest. (?)

I'm beat, and I really need a rest. (✔)

(我累壞了，真的需要休息一下。)

be beaten 是『被打敗』的意思。be beat (此處的 beat 作形容詞) =be exhausted = be very tired 是『疲憊不堪』的意思。

before

If you want to come, let us know before. (✗)

If you want to come, let us know before you do. (✔)

If you want to come, let us know beforehand. (✔)

(如果你們要來，要事先讓我們知道。)

before 是『從前』的意思, 用法見於前 (ago 條)。beforehand = in advance 是『提前』或『事先』的意思。

beginning

At the beginning, I didn't particularly like Mandy, but later I found myself growing attached to her. (✗)

In the beginning, I didn't particularly like Mandy, but later I found myself growing attached to her. (✔)

(起初我不並特別喜歡小曼，可是後來我不知不覺地已迷戀上她。)

at the beginning 通常要接 of 所引導的片語, 用來表達一個『明確的』開始。如: At the beginning of the movie, there is a war scene. (在這部電影的開始有一個戰爭的場面。) in the beginning (不接 of) = at first = initially 用來表達『起初』這個較為籠統的開始。

behave

I think he behaves rudely to his children. (✗)

I think he behaves rudely toward his children. (✔)

(我認為他對待孩子的方式很粗魯。)

behave toward(s) = treat 是『對待某人』的意思。towards 是英式的用法。

behavior

How do you explain her eccentric behaviors? (✗)

How do you explain her eccentric behavior? (✔)

(你如何看待她的古怪行為？)

behavior 為不可數名詞, 恆用單數。

Your behavior is like an idiot. (✗)

Your behavior is like an idiot's. (✔)

You behave like an idiot. (✔)

(你的言行舉止像白痴一樣。)

英文的語言邏輯: 某人可以像白痴 (因白痴也是人), 但行為是『物』不能像白痴, 因無法對應。上列正確的兩個例句中, your behavior 可以和 an idiot's (省略 behavior) 對應。you 可以和 an idiot 對應。

behind

He swore to find out the truth on the back of the rumor. (✗)

He swore to find out the truth behind the rumor. (✔)

(他揚言要找出謠言背後的真相。)

on the back of sth 是指具體之物的背面。the truth/motive behind sth 是指某事/物背後的真相/動機, 為固定用法。

believe

I believe in George this time because he seems to be telling the truth. (✗)
I believe George this time because he seems to be telling the truth. (✔)
(這回我相信喬治，因為他好像在說真話。)

believe in sb/sth 是相信某人/物之存在, 如: I believe in God/ghosts. (我相信上帝/鬼魂之存在。) believe sb 是相信某人所說的話。另外 believe in sb 也有『信賴某人(的能力/人格)』的意思, 如: We want a President that we can believe in. (我們要的是一個能夠信賴的總統。)

Quite a few people still believe capital punishment. (✗)
Quite a few people still believe in capital punishment. (✔)
(現今仍有不少人主張死刑。)

believe sth 是相信某事/物是真的, 如 I believe nothing she says. (我不相信她說的任何一句話。) believe in sth 是相信某事/物有益或有效, 所以有『主張』的意思。如: As far as losing weight is concerned, I believe in taking exercise. (就減肥而言, 我主張運動。)

Can you believe in your eyes? (✗)
Can you believe your eyes? (✔)
(你能相信你的親眼所見嗎？)

can/could (not/hardly) believe your eyes/ears, 即『能/不能相信自己的親眼所見或親耳所聞』, 常用於否定或疑問中, 為固定用法。

I deeply believe that nature will bite back. (✗)
I firmly believe that nature will bite back. (✔)
(我深信大自然將會反撲。)

deeply believe 是『中文式』的說法, 英文無此說法。要說『對某事/物深信不疑』, 正確的說法是 firmly/sincerely/strongly/truly believe (that)...

belong

The dictionary belongs to that shelf. (✗)
The dictionary belongs on that shelf. (✔)
(這本字典應歸位在那個書架上。)

belong to sb 是『屬於某人』的意思, 如 The encyclopedia belongs to me. (這套百科全書屬於我。) belong on/in 是(該)歸位在某個地方的意思。

Please go back where you belong to. (✗)
Please go back where you belong. (✔)
(請回去你所屬的地方吧。)

belong here/there/where (不加 to), 是固定用法。

belongings

When you get off, don't forget your personal belonging. (✗)
When you get off, don't forget your personal belongings. (✔)
(下車時，不要忘記你們隨身的東西。)

B

belongings 指某人的財物或隨身的東西，恆用複數。belonging (不可數名詞) 則見於 sense of belonging 這個片語，是『歸屬感』的意思，如：I have no sense of belonging working there. (在那裡工作我沒有歸屬感。)

below

It's raining now. Come and stand below my umbrella. (✗)

It's raining now. Come and stand under my umbrella. (✓)

(下雨了，站進來我的雨傘下。)

below sth 是指在某物的下方，位置並不確定，如：I could hear loud voices in the market below my window. (我可以聽窗戶下的市場人聲鼎沸。) under sth 是『直接在某物之下 (受其保護)』之意。

Can you imagine it being 25 degrees under zero outside? (✗)

Can you imagine it being 25 degrees below zero outside? (✓)

(你能想像外頭現在零下二十五度嗎？)

below zero/freezing 意為在零度/冰點以下，是固定用法。

beneath

To use four-letter words would be below a gentleman. (✗)

To use four-letter words would be beneath a gentleman. (✓)

(罵三字經有失紳士身分。)

beneath sb = not worthy of sb, 即有失某人身分。

beneficial

Vitamins are beneficiary to our health, but we should use caution when taking them. (✗)

Vitamins are beneficial to our health, but we should use caution when taking them. (✓)

(各種維他命對我們的健康有益，不過在服用時需謹慎。)

be beneficial to sb/sth 是對某人/物有益的意思，為固定用法。beneficiary 是『受益人』的意思，如：Nick is the sole beneficiary of his father's will. (尼克是他父親立下遺囑的唯一受益人。)

benefit

The new medicine will benefit from untold millions of patients. (✗)

The new medicine will benefit untold millions of patients. (✓)

Untold millions of patients will benefit from the new medicine. (✓)

(這種新藥將造福不知幾百萬的病人。)

benefit sb 是指『某物使某人獲益』，即造福某人之意。反過來 benefit from sth 是『某人從某物中獲益』。

beside & besides

Besides the young, handsome son, the woman seems like an old maid. (✗)

Beside the young, handsome son, the woman seems like an old maid. (✓)

B

(與年輕瀟灑的兒子相形之下，這婦人簡直就像老媽子。)

Beside the young, handsome son, the woman has three beautiful daughters. (✗)

Besides the young, handsome son, the woman has three beautiful daughters. (✔)

(除了這個年輕瀟灑的兒子之外，這婦人還有三個漂亮的女兒。)

Besides a good companion, the dog can carry out duties. (✗)

Besides being a good compainion, the dog can carry out duties. (✔)

(除了是很好的伙伴外，狗也能執行任務。)

beside是介系詞,意為『在……之旁』或引申為『與……相較』, 即 beside = compared with。besides是介系詞兼副詞,意為『除……之外』, 即 besides = in addition (to)。

best

She has become the most known anchorwoman on TV. (✗)

She has become the best known anchorwoman on TV. (✔)

She has become the most famous anchorwoman on TV. (✔)

(她已成為電視台最為有名的女主播。)

the best known = the most famous 均表『最為有名的』,為固定用法。

better

She knows better than trusting him with money matters. (✗)

She knows better than to trust him with money matters. (✔)

(她不致於笨到將金錢事務託付給他。)

know better than + 不定詞, 意為『不致於笨到……之地步』,是常用句型。有時候也可用 know better (省略 than + 不定詞) 來表達同樣的情況, 如: Everyone thinks it was a mere accident, but I know better. (每個人都認為這只是一起意外, 不過我可不這麼認為。)

It's not better than a robbery to demand such a high price. (✗)

It's no better than a robbery to demand such a high price. (✔)

(價錢要得這麼高不啻為搶劫。)

be no better than = be as bad as, 意為『簡直就是……』,用於較『負面』的情況。

between

In my country, children between three to five go to kindergarten. (✗)

In my country, children between three and five go to kindergarten. (✗)

(在我國三至五歲的兒童上幼稚園。)

(年齡)介於……和……之間,正確的用法是 (aged) between...and...

Between you and me, we have collected $2000 for charity. (✗)

Between us, we have collected $2000 for charity. (✔)

(由於共同努力，我們己為慈善機構募到二千美金。)

Between us, our boss is a gay. (✗)

Between you and me, our boss is a gay. (✔)

(不要告訴別人，我們老闆是個男同志。)

B

兩者或以上共同的努力或擁有, 用 between us/them, 至於表『不要告訴別人』則需用 between you and me 或 between ourselves.

beware

Be aware of the dog! It might bite. (✗)

Beware of the dog! It might bite. (✓)

(要提防那隻狗！牠可能會咬人。)

be aware of = know, 是『知道』或『瞭解』的意思, 如: None was aware of the seriousness of the matter. (當時沒有人知道這件事情的嚴重性。) beware of 是叫人要『要提防某人或某物』的意思, 常用於祈使句。

bible

The bible is also valuable in terms of literature. (✗)

The Bible is also valuable in terms of literature. (✓)

(就文學的觀點而言，聖經也是很有價值的。)

指基督教的聖經 (版本) 時, 需用 a/the Bible (恆用大寫形式)。I'd like to buy a hardback Bible. (我想要買一本精裝本的聖經。) 作為一般可供參考的『有價值書籍』則用 a/the bible, 如: The anatomy book has been a bible for medical students. (這本解剖學學用書一直被醫學院學生奉為圭臬。)

big

There is a big possibility that the politician will stage a comeback. (✗)

There is a strong possibility that the politician will stage a comeback. (✓)

(那名政客捲土重來的可能性極大。)

The virus poses a big threat to human life. (✗)

The virus poses a serious threat to human life. (✓)

(這種病毒對於人的生命構成極大的威脅。)

雖然中文可講可能性『很大』,但英文只能說 a "strong possibility"。這是英文的『慣用』, 我們不能硬拗。同理, 極大的威脅是 a serious (非 big) threat。

bit

Before I go to work, I usually watch a bit TV news. (✗)

Before I go to work, I usually watch a bit of TV news. (✓)

Before I go to work, I usually watch a little TV news. (✓)

(上班之前我通常會看一點電視新聞。)

a bit/little + 形容詞, 如: I'm feeling a bit/little tired. (目前我覺得有點累了。) a little/a (little) bit of + 名詞, 如: The child could eat a little/a (little) bit of food now. (現在這個小孩可以稍微進點食了。)

You are a little bit too young to be a soldier. (✗)

You are a little too young to be a soldier. (✓)

You are a bit too young to be a soldier. (✓)

(你想當兵年紀還稍嫌太年輕點。)

a bit/little too...為固定用法。如用 a little bit too...即是『無謂的重複』。

B

blame

Martha and I got divorced, and she blamed on me. (✗)
Martha and I got divorced, and she blamed it on me. (✓)
Martha and I got divorced, and she blamed me for it. (✓)
(瑪莎同我離婚並把這事兒歸罪於我。)

blame sth on sb = blame sb for sth, 即將某事歸罪於某人,是固定用法。

I wonder who is to be blamed for these ridiculous mistakes. (✗)
I wonder who is to blame for these ridiculous mistakes. (✓)
(不知道誰該對這些烏龍事件負責。)

be to blame (for sth)是指某人該 (為某事) 負責, 為習慣用法。

blind

Suddenly the TV screen went blind. (✗)
Suddenly the TV screen went blank. (✓)
(電視螢幕上的畫面突然不見了。)

go blind 是指某人因疾病或意外導致眼睛瞎掉, 如: The accident made him go blind in one eye. (那起事故使他瞎了一眼。) 指 (電視等) 畫面的突然消失, 用 go blank, 即一片空白之意。

blink

It all happened in the flash of an eye. (✗)
It all happened in the blink of an eye. (✓)
(這一切都是在一瞬間發生的。)

『在一瞬間』的英文表達方式為 in the blink of an eye = in the twinkling of an eye = in a twinkling = in/like a flash.

blow

The hijackers threatened to explode the plane. (✗)
The hijackers threatened to blow up the plane. (✓)
(劫機者揚言要炸掉飛機。)

explode 是指『炸彈』的爆炸或引爆, 如: The bomb failed to explode. (這枚炸彈沒有爆。) 炸掉某物需用 blow up sth.

blue

Whenever you feel the blue, try singing a song. (✗)
Whenever you feel blue/get the blues, try singing a song. (✓)
(每當你感到憂鬱時，試著唱首歌吧。)

『感到憂鬱』的正確英文說法是 feel blue 或 get the blues.

board

There is a doctor on board of the plane. (✗)
There is a doctor on board the plane. (✓)
(機上有一名乘客是醫師。)

on board = aboard 可作介系詞使用, 其後直接接交通工具即可。

B

boast

Our school boasts of a library of 200,000 volumes. (✗)

Our school boasts a library of 200,000 volumes. (✔)

(我們學校擁有一座藏書二十萬冊的圖書館。)

boast of/about sth 是『吹噓』某事或某物, 通常以『人』作主詞, 如: He always boasts of his swimming skills. (他總是吹噓自己的游泳技能。) boast sth 是以擁有某物自豪, 常以『地方』作主詞。

boggle

Her behavior completely boggles me. (✗)

Her behavior completely baffles me. (✔)

Her behavior completely boggles my mind. (✔)

(她的行為完全使我無法理解。)

baffle sb 或 boggle sb's/the mind 是『使某人無法理解』的意思, 為固定用法。

bone

I know from the bottom of my heart that my brother was framed. (✗)

I know in my bones that my brother was framed. (✔)

I know deep down that my brother was framed. (✔)

(我打從心底知道我弟弟是被陷害的。)

from the bottom of sb's heart = sincerely, 是『誠懇地』或『由衷地』的意思, 如: I thank you all from the bottom of my heart. (我由衷地感謝你們大家。) 指某人對某事『心知肚明』需用 know deep down 或 know in sb's bones (that)...。

book

The flight is already fully ordered. (✗)

The flight is already fully booked. (✔)

(這班飛機的機位早已被訂一空。)

order 是『訂購』或『點菜』的意思, 如: The model is out of stock, but we can order one for you. (這個機種目前缺貨, 不過我們可以幫你訂一台。) 訂機位或餐廳需用 book。

border

The boundary has been a bone of contention between the two countries. (✗)

The border has been a bone of contention between the two countries. (✔)

(國界的問題一直是兩國爭執之所在。)

boundary 通常是指州/縣界, 國界宜用 border。

born

I was born in a single-parent family. (✗)

I was born into a single-parent family. (✔)

(我出生在一個單親家庭。)

be born in + 地方/年代, 如: My younger sister was born in Tokyo in 1980. (我妹妹於一九八〇年在東京出生。) be born into + 特殊的家庭。

B

He was born an athlete. (✗)
He was a born athlete. (✓)
(他是天生的運動員。)

He was born an athlete.是說『他出生時就是運動員。』這顯然不合理。He was born to be an athlete. (他出生就是注定要當運動員。)這合理。He was born an orphan. (他生下來就是孤兒。) 這也合理。a born athlete/musician/artist 是強調某人天生就是一塊運動員/音樂家/藝術家的料。

bound

The train is bound to I-lan. (✗)
The train is bound for I-lan. (✓)
(這班火車開往宜蘭。)

be bound to + V = be certain to + V, 是『一定……』的意思, 如: Your teacher is bound to find out about it. (你的老師一定會發現的。) 另外, be/feel bound to + V = be/feel obliged to + V, 是『有義務……』的意思, 如 I feel bound to tell her the truth. (我覺得有義務告訴她真相。) be bound for 是『前/開往』的意思。

It seems that a child's curiosity knows no bound. (✗)
It seems that a child's curiosity knows no bounds. (✓)
(小孩子的好奇心似乎是沒有止境的。)

know no bounds (恆用複數)意為『沒有止境/界限』, 為固定用法。

brand

What brand is your car? (✗)
What make is your car? (✓)
(你的車子是什麼廠牌？)

一般貨物的廠牌用 brand, 如:What brand of detergent do you use? (你使用何種廠牌的清潔劑?) 機器或汽車的廠牌用 make。

break

You could be sued for break of contract. (✗)
You could be sued for breach of contract. (✓)
You could be sued for breaking a/the contract. (✓)
(你要是違約可能會挨告。)

『違約』的說法有 (1) (a) breach of contract (其中的 breach 為名詞) (2) break a/the contract (其中的 break 為動詞)。

breakfast

What time do you usually have the breakfast? (✗)
What time do you usually have breakfast? (✓)
(你通常幾點吃早餐？)

三餐 (breakfast, lunch, dinner)指『事件』時, 不加 a/the/this/my 於其前。但指『內容』時則可加a/the/this/my於其前, 如: It's an American breakfast. (這是美式的早餐。)

breathe

I have a stuffy nose, so I cannot breath properly. (✗)
I have a stuffy nose, so I cannot breathe properly. (✓)
(我鼻塞所以呼吸有點困難。)

breath 是『呼吸』的名詞形式, 如: take a

deep breath (深深吸一口氣)。動詞的形式是 breathe。

B

bribe

Jack was accused of bribe. (✗)
Jack was accused of bribery. (✔)
(傑克被指控行賄。)

bribe 當動詞時為『賄賂某人』的意思, 如: He tried to bribe the judge. (他想要賄賂法官。) bribe 作名詞時指用來行賄的金錢或禮物, 如: The officer admitted taking a bribe. (這名員警承認收賄)。專指賄賂的行為用 bribery。

bring

Our electronics industry brings a lot of foreign exchange. (✗)
Our electronics industry brings in a lot of foreign exchange. (✔)
(我們的電子產業賺進不少外匯。)

bring 是『帶來』的意思。bring in 是『賺進』的意思。

broke

Now I'm completely broken. Could you lend me some money? (✗)
Now I'm completely broke. Could you lend me some money? (✔)
(我現在可是身無分文。能借點錢給我嗎？)

broken 是『破碎的』, 如: Be careful not to step on the broken glass! (小心不要踩到碎玻璃！) broke 是指個人或公司『身無分文』或『破產』。

build

The robber is medium build and about your height. (✗)
The robber is of medium build and about your height. (✔)
(搶匪的體型中等，身高跟你差不多。)

build 作名詞時是指某人的『體格/型』。of medium/average build 是屬中等體型。

built-in

The body has a built-in ability to heal itself. (✗)
The body has an inbuilt ability to heal itself. (✔)
(身體有一種天生自然的痊癒能力。)

built-in 表『內建/置的』, 主要用來說明機械或儀器中的『裝置』, 如: The gadget has a built-in camera. (這個玩意兒內建有一個小相機。) inbuilt 或 in-built 則專門用來說明某人/物『天生自然』的特質。

bulk

Despite its big, the Mercedes handles like a small car. (✗)
Despite its bulk, the Mercedes handles like a small car. (✔)
Despite its (big) size, the Mercedes handles like a small car. (✔)
(儘管車身龐大，這部賓士車操作起來像小汽車一樣輕鬆自如。)

big 是形容詞, 不能作名詞用。表人/物的體型『龐大』應該用 bulk 或 size。

bumpy

The entire journey was a choppy ride. (✗)

The entire journey was a bumpy ride. (✓)

(整個旅程都是行駛在顛簸的路上。)

choppy 表水面『波濤洶湧的』, 如: Our boat was sailing on the choppy water. (我們的船正行駛在波濤洶湧的水面上。) bumpy 表路面或旅程『顛簸難行的』。

byword

"Shorty" is a byword for the duke. (✗)

"Shorty" is a nickname for the duck. (✓)

(『矮冬瓜』是這位公爵的綽號。)

be a byword for sth (非 sb) 表某人/物『是某種特性/點之別名或代名詞』, 如: "Rolex" is now a byword for quality. (『勞力士』是品質保證的一個代名詞。) nickname 是稱呼某人的『綽號』或『暱稱』。

A Quick Note

Cc

C

cake

I need a towel and a soap. (✗)
I need a towel and a cake of soap. (✓)
(我需要一條毛巾和一塊肥皂。)

soap (肥皂) 一般為不可數名詞, 需加『單位』於其前。『一塊肥皂』的說法是 a cake/bar of soap.

calculated

It must be a calculating crime. (✗)
It must be a calculated crime. (✓)
(這必定是一起蓄意犯罪。)

calculating 是『精打細算的』, 如: Mr. Li is a calculating businessman. (李先生是一位精打細算的生意人。) calculated 是『事先計劃好的』或『蓄意的』。

caliber

It takes a man like your caliber to complete the mission. (✗)
It takes a man of your caliber to complete the mission. (✓)
(需要有你這種才幹的人才能完成這個使命。)

caliber 本指『槍/砲的口徑』, 引申為『人的才幹』。of your/his/my caliber 為固定用法。

call

Mary called in to say sick this morning. (✗)
Mary called in sick this morning. (✓)
(今天早上瑪麗打電話進來稱病。)

call in sick 是『打電話進來請病假』, 為固定用法。

calm

The countryside will provide a calm environment. (✗)
The countryside will provide a peaceful environment. (✓)
(鄉間將可提供一個靜謐的環境。)

calm 是『平靜的』之意, 尤指在一陣動亂之後平靜。如: The city is calm again after yesterday's riots. (經過昨天的暴動之後, 這個城市回歸於平靜。) 『安靜的』需用 peaceful。

cameraman

The scandal has attracted a host of photographers. (✗)
The scandal has attracted a host of cameramen. (✓)
(這件醜聞吸引了不少攝影記者前來。)

photographer 是指專業或業餘的『攝影師』, 與新聞工作無關。cameraman 是指為電視台工作的『攝影記者』。

camp

The Boy Scouts are pitching a camp by the river. (✗)
The Boy Scouts are pitching camp by the river. (✓)
(這批童子軍正在河邊紮營。)

『紮營』的正確說法是 make/pitch/set up camp。『拔營』的正確說法是 break/strike camp, 均不需加冠詞。但如果指一個特殊的營區/地則需加冠詞, 如: a refugee/

concentration camp, 即一個難民/集中營。

can

I can drink like a fish when I was young. (✗)

I could drink like a fish when I was young. (✔)

(我年輕時酒量很好。)

can 表『現在的能力』; could 表『過去的能力』。至於『未來的能力』可以用 will be able to 來表達, 如: We will be able to travel to outer space in the near future. (在不遠的將來我們將能夠到外太空去旅行)。

cancel

The meeting will be cancelled until further notice. (✗)

The meeting will be postponed until further notice. (✔)

(這個會議將延到進一步通知為止。)

be cancelled 是『被取消』的意思。會議一旦被取消, 進一步的通知就沒有意義。所以應該用 be postponed (被延期)。

cancer

The actress died of a breast cancer. (✗)

The actress died of breast cancer. (✔)

(那位女演員死於乳癌。)

die of breast/lung/stomach/cervical cancer (均不加冠詞), 即表死於乳/肺/胃/子宮頸癌。至於大寫的 Cancer 為可數名詞, 是十二星座之一的『巨蟹座』, 如: He is a Cancer. (他是巨蟹座。)

candlelit

We are planning to enjoy a candlelight dinner together. (✗)

We are planning to enjoy a candlelit dinner together. (✔)

(我們計劃共進一個燭光晚餐。)

candlelight 是名詞, 意為『燭光』, 如: They were having dinner by candlelight. (他們在燭光下共進晚餐。) candelit 是形容詞, 意為『有燭光的』, 可修飾名詞 dinner。

cap

Make sure you put the cover back on the pen. (✗)

Make sure you put the cap back on the pen. (✔)

(務必將筆蓋套好。)

cover 是指書籍的『封面』或其它東西的『覆蓋物』, 如 a drain cover 就是指下水道的蓋子。鋼筆或原子筆的筆蓋是 cap。

capacity

The diva is singing to a capacious audience. (✗)

The diva is singing to a capacity audience. (✔)

(這位歌唱天后正在對滿座的聽眾獻唱。)

capacious 是『寬敞的』, 用來形容地方, 如: The car has a capacious trunk. (這部車子有很寬敞的後行李箱。) a capacity audience/crowd 是『爆滿的』聽眾/群眾, 為固定用法。

captivate

Her radiant smile caputred me. (✗)

Her radiant smile captivated

C

C

me. (✔)
(她那燦爛的笑容深深地吸引著我。)

capture是『捕捉/獲』的意思,如: The stray dog was captured finally. (這隻流浪狗終於被捕捉了。) captivate = attract sb very much, 是『深深地吸引某人』的意思。

car

We went to the wedding by a friend's car. (✗)
We went to the wedding in a friend's car. (✔)
(我們搭乘朋友的車子去參加婚禮。)

表『以搭車的方式』用 by car 或 in a car.

career

My father is a professional soldier. (✗)
My father is a career soldier. (✔)
(我父親是一名職業軍人。)

professional (職業的) 通常是相對於 amateur (業餘的) 而言, 如: a professional boxer 即是一名職業的拳擊手。career 是強調其終身為業的意思。軍人可以幹一輩子, 拳擊手總不能打一輩子吧!

carry

Birds, wild or domestic, can take disease. (✗)
Birds, wild or domestic, can carry disease. (✔)
(野鳥或家禽都可能傳播疾病。)

carry disease 是指動物或人類為某種疾病的帶原者 (carrier), 會造成該疾病的散佈。

With a credit card, you don't have to bring much cash. (✗)
With a credit card, you don't have to carry much cash. (✔)
(有一張信用卡你就不必帶很多現金。)

bring是『帶來』的意思。carry是攜帶 (在身邊) 的意思。

case

That was a case in the past, but things are different now. (✗)
That was the case in the past, but things are different now. (✔)
(從前是真的有那回事,可是現在情況改觀了。)

a case = an instance, 可指一個事例、案例或病例。如: a case of robbery 就是一樁搶案。a case of cholera 就是一個霍亂的病例。the case = the situation = true, 是『真有其事』的意思。

My mother is very frugal, and my older sister takes after her in that case. (✗)
My mother is very frugal, and my older sister takes after her in that respect. (✔)
(我媽媽非常節儉,而在這方面我老姊跟她很像。)

in this/that case = if this/that happens, 意為『要是這/那樣的話』, 多多少少有『假設』的味道。如: In that case, I'll take over. (要是那樣的話, 我就來接管。) in this/that respect 是指『在這/那方面』, 即之前提過的實際情形。

cash

I'd like to pay by cash. (✗)
I'd like to pay cash. (✔)

I'd like to pay in cash.
(我想付現金。)

『付現金』的正確說法是 pay cash 或 pay in cash。『以信用卡付帳』是pay by credit card;『以支票付帳』是 pay by check。

cast

The majority of citizens will throw their ballots for the incumbent mayor. (✗)
The majority of citizens will cast their ballots for the incumbent mayor. (✔)
(大多數的市民會把選票投給現任的市長。)

throw 一般是指投擲器物。投票需用 cast a/one's ballot/vote。

casual

I feel most comfortable in usual wear. (✗)
I feel most comfortable in casual wear. (✔)
(我穿便服時感到最舒適。)

『便服』的說法是 casual clothes/wear。

casualty

The bombing caused a heavy casualty. (✗)
The bombing caused heavy casualties. (✔)
(這個爆炸事件造成重大的傷亡。)

指重大事故的『傷亡人數』時多用複數形的 casualties。

catch

The shoplifter was caught in the spot. (✗)
The shoplifter was caught on the spot. (✔)
The shoplifter was caught in the act. (✔)
(那名商店的小偷當場被逮了。)

當場被逮的說法是 be caught on the spot/ in the act。

causal

There is a casual link between smoking and lung cancer. (✗)
There is a causal link between smoking and lung cancer. (✔)
(吸煙與肺癌有明顯的因果關係。)

a casual link 是一種『偶然的關聯』。a causal link 是一種『因果關係』。

cause

For this cause I've changed my major. (✗)
For this reason I've changed my major. (✔)
(基於這個理由我才轉系。)

cause是造成某個事件的直接原因, 如: The cause of most car accidents is speeding by drivers. (大部分的車禍的原因是開車者超速。) reason 是事後提出解釋的理由。

The management wanted to know the cause for the strike. (✗)
The management wanted to know the cause of the strike. (✔)
(公司高層想要知道罷工的原因。)

C

C

習慣上英文說the reason for sth, 如: Tell me the reason for your frequent absences. (請告訴我你經常缺課/曠職的理由。) 不過, the cause of sth 是『發生某事的原因』之固定說法。然而 也有 cause for alarm/concern/optimism/pessimism 之說法, 即驚慌/擔心/樂觀/悲觀的理由或必要。如: There is no cause for alarm. (沒有必要驚慌嘛。)

Air pollution is the most important cause of acid rain. (✗)
Air pollution is the major cause of acid rain. (✔)
(空氣污染是酸雨形成的主要原因。)

中文可以說『最重要的原因』, 英文卻不可說 the most important cause。正確的說法是 a/the chief/major/primary cause。

celebrate

The poem sings the joy of being young. (✗)
The poem celebrates/sings of the joy of being young. (✔)
(這首詩歌頌青春的喜悅。)

詩歌『歌頌』某物需用 celebrate sth 或 sing of sth, 不過後者是較為古典的說法。

celebration

The festival is alive with celebrities and other activities. (✗)
The festival is alive with celebrations and other activities. (✔)
(這個節日充滿著許多慶祝和其它活動。)

celebrities 是『名人』, 與 other activities (其它活動) 不能對應, 需用 celebrations (慶祝活動) 才貼切。

certain

There are certainly things we need to discuss. (✗)
There are certain things we need to discuss. (✔)
(是有一些事情我們需要討論一番。)

a certain + 單數 N 表『某一』; certain + 複數 N 表『某些』。certainly 是副詞, 表『的確』, 通常置於被修飾的動詞或形容詞之前。所以如果說: There certainly are things we need to discuss. 意思就是『的確有些事情我們需要討論一番。』

I know for certainty that the thief is hiding in here somewhere. (✗)
I know for certain that the thief is hiding in here somewhere. (✔)
(我篤定這個小偷藏身在這裡面某處。)

know/say for certain (有把握知道/說出) 為固定用法。如要用 certainty, 則必須說 I know with certainty that...。

challenged

A new law has been enacted to protect the physically challenging. (✗)
A new law has been enacted to protect the physically challenged. (✔)
(有一條保護身體殘障者的新法令已經被制定出來了。)

challenging 是形容詞, 意為『具有挑戰性的』, 如: The task is at once challenging and rewarding. (這件工作既富挑戰性且同時具有回饋性。) the physically/mentally challenged (身/心障礙者) 是現今美語用來代替 the handicapped 較委婉的說法。

chance

You did have a chance, but you destroyed it. (✗)
You did have a chance, but you blew it. (✓)
(你原本有機會，可是你把這機會毀了。)

毀掉一個機會的說法是 blow/ruin/spoil a chance。

This will increase your chances to win the election. (✗)
This will increase your chances of winning the election. (✓)
(這將增加你獲得勝選的機率。)

當 chance = opportunity (機會) 時, 其後可接不定詞片語, 如: I had no chance to introduce myself. (我沒有機會作自我介紹。) 不過, 當 chance = possibility (可能性; 機率) 時, 其後需接 of + Ving/N。

I've lost a lot of money in the stock market, so I don't want to take the chance. (✗)
I've lost a lot of money in the stock market, so I don't want to take any chances. (✓)
(我在股票市場已經賠了不少錢，所以我不想再冒險了。)

take the chance = use the opportunity, 即『利用機會』的意思, 如: You should take the chance to get to know more people. (你應該利用這個機會多認識一些人。)。take a chance/chances 是『冒險』的意思。

The chance is that there will be a boardroom reshuffle soon. (✗)
The chances are that there will be a boardroom reshuffle soon. (✓)
(很可能最近董事會要改組。)

(the) chances are that = it is likely that 表『很可能……』。這個說法恆用複數形的 chances。

change

The villa has changed hand several times. (✗)
The villa has changed hands several times. (✓)
(這棟別墅已經數度易主了。)

change hands 意為『換手; 易主』為固定用法。類似的用法如: change shifts (換班); change trains/buses (換車), 恆用複數形。

We need a change of personnel to boost morale. (✗)
We need a change in personnel to boost morale. (✓)
(我們需要調整人事以提振士氣。)

a change of sth 是『完全改變或取代』的意思, 如: The general staged a coup because he thought the country needed a change of government. (這名將軍發動政變, 因為他認為該國需換新政府。) a change in sth 是做『局部改變或調整』。如果人事全換, 何來士氣可提升？

She had a change of mind about their marriage. (✗)
She had a change of heart about their marriage. (✓)
(她對他們的婚事改變了主意。)

『改變主意』的英文有兩種說法: (1) have a change of heart (2) change one's mind。

I need some small changes to buy something from the vending

C

machine. (✗)

I need some small change to buy something from the vending machine. (✓)

(我需要一些銅板來買自動販賣機的東西。)

change 作『零錢/銅板』解時為不可數名詞, 如: Keep the change. (零錢不用找了。)

character

These two social movements are similar in their objectives but different in characters. (✗)

These two social movements are similar in their objectives but different in character. (✓)

(這兩個社會運動在目標上相近可是在本質上卻不相同。)

character 作『本質』、『性格』或『品德』解時, 一般為不可數名詞或採單數的用法。作『特殊的人物』或小說、戲劇裡的『角色』時則為可數名詞, 如: He used to sow his wild oats, but he is a reformed character now. (他從前放蕩不羈, 如今可是浪子回頭一個了。)

characterize

The ruling party is characterized as sheer conservatism. (✗)

The ruling party is characterized as (being) too conservative. (✓)

(執政黨被形容為過於保守。)

be characterized as (being) + 形容詞表『被形容為……』。be characterized by + 名詞表『具有……之特徵』, 如: The ruling party is characterized by sheer conservatism. (執政黨的特徵就是極度保守主義。)

charge

There is no service fee added. (✗)

There is no service charge added (✓)

(沒有另加服務費。)

fee 通常指你必須付給專業人士或某機構的費用, 如: an annual fee (年費) 或 a registration fee (註冊費)。a service/delivery charge 即『服務費/運費』, 為固定用法。

The man was arrested by a charge of murder. (✗)

The man was arrested on a charge of murder. (✓)

(這個男子因殺人罪名被逮捕。)

on a charge of sth 意為『以……之罪名』, 是固定用法。

My wife charged the cosmetics by Visa. (✗)

My wife charged the cosmetics on Visa. (✓)

(我老婆用威士卡支付化粧品的費用。)

charge sth (on sth) 表『以某家信用卡支付某物』, 為美式英語的用法。

charity

It is supposed to be a charitable event. (✗)

It is supposed to be a charity event. (✓)

(這應該是一場慈善活動。)

charitable 是『慈善的』, 通常用來形容機構或團體, 如: a charitable institution/group 就是一個慈善機構/團體。至於為了做慈善而舉辦的活動一律用 charity。a charity event/concert/ball 即是一個慈善活動/音樂會/舞會。

charm

The new drug works like charm. (✗)
The new drug works like a charm. (✔)
The new drug works like magic. (✔)
(這種新藥功效神奇。)

charm 作『魅力』解時為不可數名詞, 如: She is a woman of great charm. (她是一個極有魅力的女人。) 作『護身符』或『咒語』解時, charm 是可數名詞。

cheap

The repairman did not come cheaply, but he really did a great job. (✗)
The repairman did not come cheap, but he really did a great job. (✔)
(請這名修理工人花了不少錢，不過他所做的也確實令人滿意。)

not come cheap = cost or charge a lot, 意為『需花很多錢』, 是固定用法。

The rents for office buildings around here are very cheap. (✗)
The rents for office buildings around here are very low. (✔)
(這兒附近辦公室大樓的租金都很便宜。)

cheap/expensive 主要是對商品而言。修飾 prices, costs, rents, wages, fees 等應該用 low/high 才正確。

check

Please find enclosed a check of $200. (✗)
Please find enclosed a check for $200. (✔)
(隨函附上一張兩百美金支票，請查收。)

a check for + 金額為固定用法。

cheek

The little girl has a rosy cheek. (✗)
The little girl has rosy cheeks. (✔)
(這個小女孩臉頰很紅潤。)

臉頰有兩邊, 所以應該用 cheeks 才對, 否則只紅一邊不很奇怪嗎? 另外, 表『無禮/沒品』恆用單數的 cheek (主英式用法), 如: He had the cheek to call me a liar. (他居然如此沒品, 說我是騙子。)

chill

Among the symptoms of pneumonia are high fever, chill, and muscle pain. (✗)
Among the symptoms of pneumonia are high fever, chills, and muscle pain. (✔)
(肺炎的症狀包含有發高燒、畏寒和肌肉疼痛。)

『畏寒』的症狀通常用複數形的 chills。單數形的用法見於 catch a chill = catch a cold, 即『感冒著涼』之意。

choice

I have no choice but take your advice. (✗)
I have no choice but to take your advice. (✔)
(我別無選擇，只好聽取你的勸告。)

have no choice but + 不定詞 = cannot (choose) but + 原形動詞, 表『不得不

C

……』的意思。

The restaurant serves choosy steak. (✗)
The restaurant serves choice steak. (✓)
(這家餐廳供應上選的牛排。)

choosy 是形容詞，意為『挑剔的』。choice 也可作形容詞，意為『上等/選的』。如: We serve choice steak because customers can be very choosy. (我們供應上等的牛排,因為顧客有時很挑剔。)

C

choose

At the book fair there are tens of thousands of books to choose. (✗)
At the book fair there are tens of thousands of books to choose from. (✓)
(在書展時有上萬種書讓你從中選擇。)

choose from 是『從中選擇一些』的意思。這個 from 不能少, 否則你便要選出上萬本的書, 豈不荒唐!

circle

Henry is very active in the literary circle. (✗)
Henry is very active in the literary circles. (✓)
(亨利在文藝界非常活躍。)

the academic/literary/political/scientific circles (恆用複數) 是學術/文藝/政治/科學界的固定說法。

I think our discussion has come a full circle. (✗)
I think our discussion has come full circle. (✓)
(我想我們討論了老半天又回到原點了。)

come/go/turn full circle 表『繞了一圈又回到原點』。

circumstance

Under no circumstance will I agree to this marriage. (✗)
Under no circumstances will I agree to this marriage. (✓)
(我絕不同意這門婚事。)

under/in no circumstances 表『絕不』, 恆用複數形。至於單數的用法, 如: He is a victim of circumstance. (他是一個受環境擺佈的可憐蟲。)

citizenship

The official has double citizenship. (✗)
The official has dual citizenship. (✓)
(這名官員擁有雙重國籍。)

『擁有雙重國籍』的說法是 have/hold dual citizenship/nationality。double 表『兩人份的』, 如: We want a double bed. (我們要一張雙人床。)

claim

The earthquake deprived thousands of lives. (✗)
The earthquake claimed thousands of lives. (✓)
(那次地震奪走數千條人命。)

deprive sb of sth 通常是指『剝奪某人的權利』, 如: The criminal was deprived of his civil rights. (這名罪犯被褫奪公權。) 天災人禍『奪走人命』的英文說法是 claim lives/victims。

Don't forget to go to the baggage place to pick up your bags. (✗)

Don't forget to go to the baggage claim to pick up your bags. (✔)

(不要忘了到提領行李處提領你的包包。)

機場『提領行李處』的英文說法是 baggage claim (美式用法) 或 baggage reclaim (英式用法)。

classic

Your romance is a classical example of "opposites attract." (✗)

Your romance is a classic example of "opposites attract." (✔)

(你們的戀情可以視為『不是冤家不聚頭』的一個典範。)

a classical example 是一個『古典的』例子, 如: *The Iliad* is a classical example of epic poetry. (《伊利亞德》是古典史詩的一個例子。) a classic example/case = a typical example/case 即一個典型 (有代表性) 的例子。

Joyce's *Ulysses* has been regarded as an all-time classical. (✗)

Joyce's *Ulysses* has been regarded as an all-time classic. (✔)

(喬哀思的《尤利西斯》被奉為空前最佳的經典鉅著。)

classical 是形容詞, 不能當名詞用。classic 可作名詞, 表『經典鉅著』。

clean

You'd better come cleanly about the crime. (✗)

You'd better come clean about the crime. (✔)

(關於這個罪行你最好從實招來。)

come clean (about) 是『說出真相』或『坦承不諱』的意思, 為固定用法。

The cat is by nature a cleanly animal. (✗)

The cat is by nature a clean animal. (✔)

(貓天生就是一種愛乾淨的動物。)

按照現代英文的用法, cleanly 作副詞意為『以乾淨的方式 (即不造成污染)』或『乾淨俐落地』。如: The fuel burns cleanly. (這種燃料燃燒得很乾淨。) The player hits the ball cleanly. (這名選手揮棒擊球乾淨俐落。) cleanly 作形容詞用表『愛乾淨的』屬舊式的用法。

I cleanly forgot about the party. (✗)

I clean forgot about the party. (✔)

(我把那派對的事忘了一乾二淨。)

clean 作副詞時等於 completely, 即『完全地』的意思。clean forget 為固定用法。

clear

She has a clean conscience because she did not do anything wrong. (✗)

She has a clear conscience because she did not do anything wrong. (✔)

(她沒做錯任何事，所以她心安理得。)

have a clear conscience 或 sb's conscience is clear 是指某人『心安理得』，為固定用法。

The shoe shop is having a clear sale. (✗)

C

The shoe shop is having a clearance sale. (✔)
(這家鞋店正在舉辦清倉大拍賣。)

a clearance sale (清倉大拍賣) 為固定用法。

I think you need to clear your position. (✗)
I think you need to clarify your position. (✔)
(我想你需要澄清你的立場。)

clear 當動詞時意為『清理』, 如: Mom is clearing the table. (老媽正在清理餐桌。) clarify = make clear 是『表明』或『澄清』的意思。

climate

Thailand is known for its hot weather and spicy food. (✗)
Thailand is known for its hot climate and spicy food. (✔)
(泰國以炎熱的氣候和辛辣的食物聞名。)

weather 是『天氣』, 指某地一天的氣象變化。climate 是『氣候』, 指某地長時期規律的氣象型態。另外, climate 也見於下列比喻的用法: economic/political/social/moral/intellectual climate, 即經濟/政治/社會/道德/知識氣候。如: Small businesses can hardly survive in the current economic climate. (在目前這種經濟氣候下小型企業幾乎無法生存。)

clock

Everyone is working against a clock. (✗)
Everyone is working against the clock. (✔)
(每個人都在趕時間工作。)

against the clock = against time 是『趕時間』的意思。另外 around the clock 則表『全天候』。During the peak season, we often have to work around the clock. (在旺季時我們常常須全天候工作。)

close

The kidnapper closed the child in a room. (✗)
The kidnapper shut/locked the child in a room. (✔)
(綁匪將那個孩子關在一個房間裡。)

一般的關門可以用 close 或 shut, 如: Don't forget to close/shut the door behind you. (出去時別忘了關門。) 但把某人關 (鎖) 在某地則需用 shut/lock sb in...。

Be sure to close the computer before you leave. (✗)
Be sure to turn/switch off the computer before you leave. (✔)
(離開前務必要把電腦關機。)

開啟電器設備要用 turn/switch on。關掉電器設備則用 turn/switch off。

I was so angry that I came close to hit him. (✗)
I was so angry that I came close to hitting him. (✔)
(當時我生氣到差點想揍他。)

come close to + Ving (這裡的 to 是介系詞) 意為『差一點就……』。

Tom is running ahead, with Jack closely behind. (✗)
Tom is running ahead, with Jack close behind. (✔)
(湯姆跑在最前頭，傑克緊跟在後。)

作副詞時, close 表『距離方面』的接近, 如:

Stand closer or you'll get wet. (站進來一點以免淋溼。) closely 表『關係方面』的接近，如: The two problems are closely related. (這兩個問題密切相關。)

cloth

The suit is made of a woolen cloth. (✗)
The suit is made of woolen cloth. (✓)
(這套西裝是用羊毛布料製成。)

指『布料』時cloth為不可數名詞，如: linen/cotton/woolen/silk cloth 就是亞麻/棉/羊毛/絲質布料。a cloth 是指一塊用來擦拭的布，如: The waitress wiped the table with a cloth. (女服務生用一塊抹布擦拭餐桌。)

clothes

She has only a few clothes in her wardrobe. (✗)
She has only a few items of clothing in her wardrobe. (✓)
(她衣櫥裡只有幾件衣服而已。)

clothes 之前不可用 a few, several, a number of 或 two/three 等明確數字修飾，但可以說 many clothes。衣服計件時可用 a piece/an article/an item of clothing 或 three pieces/articles/items of clothing 來表達。

I'm sopping wet. I've got to have my clothes altered. (✗)
I'm sopping wet. I've got to have my clothes changed. (✓)
(我全身溼透了，非換衣服不可。)

alter something 表『修改某物』。因此, I've got to have my clothes altered. 是說『我非把我的衣服拿去修改不可』。change sth 表『換掉某物』，如: change clothes/tires 就是『換衣服/輪胎』。

coincidence

It's not an advance arrangement; it's a pure coincidence. (✗)
It's not an advance arrangement; it's pure coincidence. (✓)
(這並非事先安排。這純是巧合。)

coincidence 可作為可數名詞或不可數名詞。指『純為巧合』時，用 pure/sheer coincidence (不加 a 於前)。需加 a 的用法如下: What a coincidence to meet you here! (在這兒遇見你真巧啊！)

collaboration

The military would like to thank the police for their collaboration. (✗)
The military would like to thank the police for their cooperation. (✓)
(軍方想要向警方感謝他們的合作。)

collaboration 的『合作』專指在科技、工業、醫學或藝文領域的『共同開發』，如: The new drug is a collaboration between the two medical colleges. (這種新藥是這兩所醫學院共同開發的。) 一般的『合作』用 cooperation。

college

My father did not go to a college. (✗)
My father did not go to college. (✓)
(我老爸並沒有讀大學。)

『讀大學』的英文是 go to college 或 be at college，均不需加冠詞。需加冠詞的情況如: I want to go to a good college. (我想上一所好大學。)

color

C

The tie has the same color as the suit. (✗)

The tie is the same color as the suit. (✔)

(領帶和西裝的顏色相同。)

描述顏色時, 英文習慣用 be 動詞而非 have, 如: What color is your car? (你的車子什麼顏色?) It's black. (是黑色的。)

The hostess was dressed in green color. (✗)

The hostess was dressed in green. (✔)

(女主人穿著一襲綠色的衣服。)

英文不習慣用顏色的名稱, 如 green/red/black/yellow 等來形容 color, 直接用該顏色的名稱即可。唯一的例外是描述一種『不純』的顏色時, 如: a light brown color (淡褐色); a bluish-gray color (藍灰色)。

colored

I need a few pieces of color paper. (✗)

I need a few pieces of colored paper. (✔)

(我需要幾張色紙。)

color 作為形容詞意為『彩色的』, 專指以自然顏色呈現的狀態, 如: a color picture/TV 就是指彩色照片/電視。colored 作為形容詞時是指有一種或以上顏色 (黑白除外) 的。另外 colorful 是指『顏色鮮艷的』, 如: colorful costumes (顏色鮮艷的戲服) 或指『多彩多姿的』, 如: a colorful life (多彩多姿的一生)。

comfort

Can you live without modern comfort? (✗)

Can you live without modern comforts? (✔)

(沒有現代生活的舒適設備你能過活嗎?)

指『身心舒適』時 comfort 為不可數名詞, 如: Everyone hopes to live in comfort. = Everyone hopes to live a comfortable life. (每個人都希望過個舒舒服服的生活。) 但指舒適的設備或用品時, 如電視、電話、冷氣等, 則恆用複數形的 comforts。

commemorate

A statue was erected to memorize the martyr. (✗)

A statue was erected to commemorate the martyr. (✔)

(曾經豎立一座雕像來紀念這位烈士。)

memorize 是『背好』或『熟記』的意思, 如: I have memorized some of Yeats' poems. (我已經背好葉慈的幾首詩。) 紀念某人或某事件需用 commemorate。

comment

The President's speech has provoked strong comments from the media. (✗)

The President's speech has provoked strong comment from the media. (✔)

(總統的演說引發媒體措詞強烈的評論。)

comment 作為一般的意見批評時可視為可數或不可數名詞, 如: He's not supposed to make any comment(s). (他不應該發表意見。) 但作為媒體的評論時則恆用為不可數名詞。

Stop arguing! I can't hear the baseball comment. (✗)
Stop arguing! I can't hear the baseball commentary. (✓)
(不要再爭吵了！我聽不見棒球的轉播。)

電視或收音機實況轉播的『評論』需用 commentary。這位『評論者』則稱為 commentator。

common

There is almost nothing in common between the father and his son. (✗)
The father and his son have almost nothing in common. (✓)
The son has almost nothing in common with his father. (✓)
(這一對父子幾無共同之處。)

have sth/nothing in common (with sb) 表 (與某人) 有/無共同之處, 為固定用法。

company

Joy is not coming—she has a company. (✗)
Joy is not coming—she has company. (✓)
(喬伊不來了，她家裡有客人。)

company 作『公司』解時是可數名詞, 如: It is a multinational company. (這是一家跨國公司。) company 作『伙伴』、『朋友』或『客人』解時為不可數名詞。

A man is known by the company he has. (✗)
A man is known by the company he keeps. (✓)
(觀其友知其人—諺語。)

have company 是指 (臨時) 有客人。花一段時間與某人相處/交的說法是 keep sb company 或 keep company with sb。相反的情形就是 part company (with sb), 如: They have parted company. (他們已經拆夥/分手了。)。

compare

Life has often been compared with a journey. (✗)
Life has often been compared to a journey. (✓)
(人生經常被比喻為一趟旅程。)

比較兩種事物時可用 compare sth with/to sth, 如: Compared with/to ours, your house seems like a palace. (與我們的相較, 你們的房子就像一座宮殿一樣。) 但作『比喻』時只能用 compare sth to sth。

comparable

Your salary is comparative to that of a senior engineer. (✗)
Your salary is comparable to that of a senior engineer. (✓)
(你的薪水不輸一位高級的工程師。)

comparative 意為『從事比較的』, 如: She is working on comparative literature/linguistics. (她目前從事比較文學/語言學的研究。) be comparable to/with sth 是『可與某物相比的』。

compensate

Lack of intelligence can often be compensated by diligence. (✗)
Lack of intelligence can often be compensated for by diligence. (✓)
(勤往往可以補拙。)

compensate for sth 是『彌補』某物的意思。compensate sb for sth 是因某事『賠償』某人的意思, 如: The company will compensate you for your loss. (該公司會賠償你的損失。)

C

compensation

Only Belgium pays unemployment compensations indefinitely. (✗)

Only Belgium pays unemployment compensation indefinitely. (✓)

(只有比利時無限期支付失業補助金。)

作『賠償/補助金』解時, compensation 是不可數名詞。作『補償』的作用/行為解時, 則兼有可/不可數的用法, 如: One compensation of losing my job is that I can spend more time with my family. (失去工作的補償之一就是我可以花較多的時間陪陪家人。)

compete

It looks like we are able to compete with the international marketplace. (✗)

It looks like we are able to compete in the international marketplace. (✓)

(看來我們已有能力在國際市場競爭。)

compete with sb 是『與某人競爭』的意思, 如: The fact is that we have to compete with quite a few companies.(事實上我們必須和很多家公司競爭。)compete for sth 是『為了得到某物而競爭』, 如: Many companies are competing for the contract. (許多家公司正在競標。) compete in somewhere 是『在某個場合競爭/角逐』的意思。

competent

I believe our prices are competent enough. (✗)

I believe our prices are competitive enough. (✓)

(我認為我們的價格有足夠的競爭力。)

competent 是指『能勝任的』, 如: Mary is a competent secretary. (瑪麗是一位稱職的秘書。) competitive 是指『有競爭性的』或 (價格)『有競爭力的』。至於另一個形容詞 competing 是指『參與競爭的』, 如: Some of the competing nations are from East Africa. (有些參賽國來自東非。)

complain

My daughter was complaining about a toothache last night. (✗)

My daughter was complaining of a toothache last night. (✓)

(我女兒昨晚直吵著說牙痛。)

對一般情況的『抱怨』或『訴苦』可用 complain about/of sth, 如: She kept complaining about/of being sexually harassed. (她一直抱怨被性騷擾。)『訴說』病痛時限用 complain of sth。

complete

Please send your complete form to us. (✗)

Please send your completed form to us. (✓)

(請把填寫好的表格寄來給我們。)

complete 作形容詞時意為『完整/美的』, 如: The dinner wouldn't be complete without the dessert. (要是沒有這道甜點, 這個晚餐就不算完美。) completed 是『已被完成的』或『被填寫完畢的』。

C

complementary

In Western countries, acupuncture is a type of complimentary medicine. (✗)

In Western countries, acupuncture is a type of complementary medicine. (✔)

(在西方國家，針炙算是一種輔助療法。)

complimentary 是『恭維/奉承的』, 如: complimentary remarks (恭維/奉承的話) 或『免費的』, 如 a complimentary copy 就是『免費的贈本』。而 complementary 是『輔助的』或『互補的』, 如: Mr. and Mrs. Kim are an interesting couple: they have complementary personalities. (金氏夫婦是一對有趣的夫妻: 他們的性格互補。)

comprehensible

The medical jargon is barely comprehensive to us. (✗)

The medical jargon is barely comprehensible to us. (✔)

(這些醫學術語我們幾乎無法理解。)

comprehensive 是『全面的』或『廣泛的』之意, 如: We offer a comprehensive range of services. (我們提供全面性的各種服務。) comprehensible = understandable 即『可以理解的』。

compromise

They would not compromise the number of working hours. (✗)

They would not compromise on the number of working hours. (✔)

(在工作時數方面他們是不會妥協的。)

compromise on sth 是指『在某方面妥協』。compromise sth 是『連累』或『損及』某物的意思, 如: You'll compromise your reputation by doing so. (你這樣做會損及你的名譽。)。

compulsory

Military service is compulsive in some countries. (✗)

Military service is compulsory in some countries. (✔)

(服兵役在有些國家是強制／義務性的。)

compulsive 意為『強迫性的』, 乃因心/生理因素所造成的狀態, 如: compulsive drinking/gambling/overeating 就是指自己無法控制的『強迫性』喝酒/賭博/暴飲暴食之行為。至於 compulsory 是因法律規定而帶有『強制性』或『義務性』的, 如: compulsory education 就是指『義務教育』。

concentrate

You have got to be concentrated to learn better. (✗)

You have got to concentrate to learn better. (✔)

(你必須專心才能學得更好。)

concentrate 作為『專心』解時沒有『被動』的用法。作為『濃縮』解時則有『被動』的用法, 如: The fresh fruit juice will be concertrated and canned. (這種新鮮果汁將被濃縮後製成罐頭。)

concern

Many social workers have voiced their concerns over child abuse. (✗)

Many social workers have voiced their concern over child abuse. (✔)
(許多社工人員都對虐待兒童的現象表示憂心。)

C

express/voice concern over sth 是對某事表示憂慮或關心。這個用法的 concern 為不可數名詞。若表『關心的事項』, concern 則為可數名詞, 如: One of our main concerns is how to narrow the gap between the rich and the poor. (我們主要關心的事項之一就是如何縮小貧富之間的差距。)

concerned

The report is concerned about the safety of drinking water. (✗)
The report is concerned with the safety of drinking water. (✔)
The report concerns the safety of drinking water. (✔)
(這篇報告的內容有關飲用水的安全問題。)

be concerned about sth/sb = be worried about sth/sb, 表『對某事/人擔憂』, 如: I'm concerned about your health. (我擔心你的健康狀況。) be concerned with sth/sb = concern sth/sb, 表『與某事/人有關』。

concerning

Concerning the merger plan, we are now evaluating it. (✗)
Regarding the merger plan, we are now evaluating it. (✔)
(關於這個合併計劃案，我方正在評估中。)

concerning 表『關於』通常接於名詞之後, 如: He has written several articles concerning the damage of the ozone layer. (他寫了好幾篇有關臭氧層破裂的文章。) 置於句首引介一個新話題時, 不可用 concerning, 需用 regarding, with regard to, as regards 或 as far as...is concerned。

conclusion

For conclusion, you are what you do. (✗)
In conclusion, you are what you do. (✔)
To conclude, you are what you do. (✔)
(總而言之，你的作為代表你的為人。)

寫文章或發表演講下『結論』時需說 in conclusion 或 to conclude。

condition

Mr. Richardson, though advanced in years, is in excellent physical conditions. (✗)
Mr. Richardson, though advanced in years, is in excellent physical condition. (✔)
(理查森先生雖然年事已高，身體狀況極佳。)

作『狀況』解時 condition 為不可數名詞, 如: What kind of condition is your car in? (你的車況如何?)。作『條件』或『環境』解時恆用複數形的 conditions, 如: We hope the management will provide better working conditions. (我們希望廠方能提供較好的工作環境。)。

conduct

He was released on parole because of his good conducts at the prison. (✗)
He was released on parole because of his good conduct at

the prison. (✔)
(他因在獄中表現良好而假釋出獄了。)

conduct = behavior (行為) 是不可數名詞, 沒有複數形。

confetti

Since college diplomas are being handed out like confetties, they are like something you get dirt cheap. (✗)
Since college diplomas are being handed out like confetti, they are like something you get dirt cheap. (✔)
(既然大學文憑如此大量地頒發，這些文憑就不值錢了。)

confetti 本指在慶典或婚禮大量灑下的『糖果』或『五彩碎紙』。這個字沒有複數形 (其實它本身是 confetto 複數形式, 但作單數使用)。like confetti 表『大量地』, 是一個固定片語。

confidence

Nancy and her sister-in-law spent the entire evening exchanging confidence. (✗)
Nancy and her sister-in-law spent the entire evening exchanging confidences. (✔)
(南西和她的小姑整晚都在互吐心事。)

confidence 作為『信心』或『信任』解時為不可數名詞, 如: I have absolute confidence in your abilities. (我對你的能力絕對有信心。) 或如: Public confidence in the government is at an all-time low. (民眾對於政府的信任可謂空前的低。) 作為『秘密』或『心事』解時, confidence 是可數名詞。share/exchange confidences 是『分享秘密』或『互吐心事』的意思。

confirm

You should make a call to conform your booking. (✗)
You should make a call to confirm your booking. (✔)
(你應該打電話去確認一下你訂的機位。)

conform = comply, 是指行動上的『配合』或『符合』, 如: There will be penalties for those who refuse to conform. (拒絕配合的人將給予懲罰。) confirm 是『證實』或『確認』的意思, 如: The rumor is not yet confirmed. (這個傳聞尚未獲得證實。)。

conflict

The whole region has been devastated by arm conflict. (✗)
The whole region has been devastated by armed conflict. (✔)
(這整個地區由於武裝衝突而受到重創。)

armed/military/violent conflict (confrontation) 是武裝/軍事/暴力 衝突, 為固定用法。

confront

Almost every day we confront with a few new problems. (✗)
Almost every day we confront a few new problems. (✔)
Almost every day a few new problems confront us. (✔)
Almost every day we are confronted with a few new problems. (✔)

(我們幾乎每天都要面對一些新的問題。)

confront 有『面對』和『使面對』的意思。要之, 面對問題/困難需待解決的句型如下: (1) sb confront sth (2) sth confront sb (3) sb is confronted with sth。

C

congratulation

We have received more than a thousand letters of congratulations. (✗)

We have received more than a thousand letters of congratulation. (✓)

(我們收到一千多封的祝賀信。)

congratulation 作為『祝賀的性質』解時為不可數名詞。但作為『祝賀用語』時限用複數形的 congratulations (on sth), 如: Congratulations on your being promoted! (恭喜你升官了!)

conscious

The injured woman still had consciousness when the ambulance arrived. (✗)

The injured woman was still conscious when the ambulance arrived. (✓)

(救護車到時這名受傷的婦女仍有意識。)

have consciousness 為極不自然的說法。表『有意識狀態』通常的說法是 be conscious。不過,『失去意識』要說 lost consciousness;『恢復意識』要說 regain/recover consciousness。

consecutive

It has been snowing for three continuous days. (✗)

It has been snowing for three consecutive days. (✓)

(已經連續下了三天的雪了。)

continuous 是『繼續不斷的』, 通常指的是過程或活動, 不與時間名詞連用, 如: Education is a continuous process. (教育是百年大計。) consecutive 是一個接一個的『連續不斷』, 常與時間名詞連用。

consequence

The death rate has been significantly reduced as a consequence of improved nutrition and medical care. (✗)

The death rate has been significantly reduced as a result of improved nutrition and medical care. (✓)

(由於營養和醫療的改善, 死亡率已大幅下降。)

consequence 通常指『負面的』結果, 如: Many people have died as a consequence of the epidemic. (這個疫情結果造成很多人死亡。)『一般的』結果用 result。

conserve

The government called on the public to preserve water during the drought. (✗)

The government called on the public to conserve water during the drought. (✓)

(政府呼籲大眾在乾旱期節約用水。)

preserve sth 是『保存』某物以免變質或喪失的意思, 如: We use the refrigerator to preserve food. (我們使用冰箱來保存食物。) conserve sth 是『節約使用』某物的意思。

consider

Stephen is considering to buy a notebook computer. (✗)

Stephen is considering buying a notebook computer. (✔)

(史帝芬正在考慮買一部筆記型電腦。)

consider + Ving 是正確用法。

Considering all things, we'll delay going abroad. (✗)

All things considered, we'll delay going abroad. (✔)

(全盤考慮之後，我們要暫緩出國。)

all things considered 為慣用語。

considering

To consider her age, she's very learned. (✗)

Considering her age, she's very learned. (✔)

(要是考慮到她的年齡，她算很有學問了。)

considering + 名詞/that子句 = If we take... into consideration, 表『要是考慮到……』之意, 為固定用法。

consist

The panel is consisted of four experts. (✗)

The panel consists of four experts. (✔)

(這個小組由四位專家組成。)

『由……組成』的說法是 consist of = be composed of = be made up of。

The beauty of the poem consists of its vivid imagery. (✗)

The beauty of the poem consists in its vivid imagery. (✔)

(這首詩之美在於它的意象活潑生動。)

consist in sth = lie in sth 表『在於……』之意。

consistent

Parents should adopt a persistent attitude in educating their children. (?)

Parents should adopt a consistent attitude in educating their children. (✔)

(父母在管教孩子時應採取一貫的態度。)

persistent 是『持續的』之意, 如: Her persistent cough just won't go. (她的咳嗽不斷就是好不了。) 或如: I am sick of the persistent rain. (這種陰雨綿綿的天氣真叫人討厭。) consistent 意為『一貫的』或『前後一致的』。

conspire

It seems everything is conspiring with me. (✗)

It seems everything is conspiring against me. (✔)

(似乎每件事情都在醞釀對我不利。)

conspire with sb 是『與某人共謀/串通』之意, 如: He was conspiring with a teller to steal money from the bank. (他當時正與一名行員患通竊取銀行的錢。) conspire against sb 本是指『策劃不利於某人或某政權』之舉動, 引申為『醞釀不利於某人之狀況』。

C

constantly

The copy machine constantly breaks down. (✗)

The copy machine is constantly breaking down. (✓)

(這台影印機老是當機。)

當 constantly = again and again 時, 恆搭配進行式。

construction

The dam is now under a construction. (✗)

The dam is now under construction. (✓)

(水庫目前正在興建中。)

construction 意為『興建』時為不可數名詞。但若作為『建築物』解時則為可數名詞, 如: The new theater is an impressive construction. (這家新戲院是一棟令人印象深刻的建築物)。

Most of our customers are constructive workers. (✗)

Most of our customers are construction workers. (✓)

(我們大部分的顧客是建築工人。)

constructive是指『有建設性的』或『有助益的』, 如: We welcome any constructive criticism. (我們歡迎任何有建設性的批評。) 至於『建築工人』應說construction workers, 『建築工地』應說 a construction site。

consult

Why don't you consult with a dictionary? (✗)

Why don't you consult a dictionary? (✓)

(你為何不查本字典呢?)

consult with sb 是『與某人商量』的意思, 如: As to when and how to pay the debts, I have to consult with my business partners. (至於何時及如何償債, 我必須跟我的合夥人商量。) consult sb 是『請教某人』的意思, 如: You had better consult a lawyer before signing the contract. (在簽約前你最好先請教律師。) consult a dictionary/map 是『查閱』字典/地圖的意思。

consumable

Staplers and paper clips are consumer goods. (✗)

Staplers and paper clips are consumable goods. (✓)

Staplers and paper clips are consumables. (✓)

(訂書機和迴紋針都是消耗品。)

consumer goods 是指個人或家庭使用的『消費品』, 如: Food and clothing are consumer goods. (食物和衣服是消費品。) 至於公司或機關使用的『消耗品』要說 consumable goods 或 consumables。

contact

Please contact with me at your convenience. (✗)

Please contact me at your convenience. (✓)

(你方便時請與我聯絡。)

contact sb (不需加 with) 表『與某人聯絡』, 是及物動詞的用法。contact 作為名詞時則經常搭配 with, 如 keep/stay in contact with sb (與某人保持聯絡)。lose contact with sb (與某人失去聯絡)。

Please give an emergency

contactable number. (✗)
Please give an emergency contact number. (✔)
(請留一個緊急聯絡電話號碼。)

contactable 意謂 (某人)『可以被聯絡上的』, 不能用來形容事物, 如: A cell phone makes you contactable wherever you are. (不管你人在哪, 手機總是讓別人能夠隨時聯絡上你。) a contact number/address 是『可以用來聯絡的』電話號碼/地址。

content

You may take a look at the table of content. (✗)
You may take a look at the table of contents. (✔)
(你可以看一下目錄。)

content 指書本、電影或演講的『內容』時為不可數名詞, 如: The film has little content. (這部影片沒什麼內容。) 但指書本的『目錄 (表)』或裝在盒/箱子或瓶罐或包包裡的東西時, 恆用複數形的 contents, 如: The cop is rummaging through the contents of the trunk. (這名警察正在翻找後行李箱裡面的東西)。

continent

The biologist specializes in the fauna and flora of the North America continent. (✗)
The biologist specializes in the fauna and flora of the North American continent. (✔)
The biologist specializes in the fauna and flora of continental North America. (✔)
(這名生物學家專攻北美洲的動植物。)

continent 是名詞, 意為『大陸』或『洲』, continental 為其形容詞。英文的順序一般是形容詞 + 名詞, 所以『歐陸』的說法是 the European continent 或 (不加 the) continental Europe。

continual

The artist has been trying to present the continual flow of time in concrete terms. (✗)
The artist has been trying to present the continuous flow of time in concrete terms. (✔)
(這位藝術家一直嘗試用具體的形式來呈現時光不停的流逝。)

continual 和 continuous 都是動詞 continue 的形容詞。其間的不同是 continual 表『一再的』, 即有間斷的『持續』, 如: I've had enough of her continual nagging. (她一再的嘮叨, 我真的受夠了。) 而 continuous 則表『連續不斷的』。『時光之流』總不能間斷吧!

contract

The singer is still under the contract to a record company. (✗)
The singer is still under (a) contract to a record company. (✔)
(這位歌手和一家唱片公司的合約還未滿。)

『約期未滿』, 即『還要履約』的英文說法是 be under (a) contract to sb。

contrary

Despite all evidence on the contrary, he believed his eyes. (✗)

Despite all evidence to the contrary, he believed his eyes. (✔)
(儘管所有證據都是相反的，他仍相信自己親眼目睹的一切。)

on the contrary 表『正好相反』, 是用來表達相反意見或反駁別人的副詞片詞, 如: "You think I'm a good swimmer? On the contrary, I'm a lousy one." (『你以為我很會游泳嗎? 正好相反, 我游得很爛。』) to the contrary 通常接於名詞之後, 表『相反的』, 作形容詞片語用。

C

contrast

Cats usually look neat and clean. On the contrary, dogs mess up everything and never learn to tidy themselves. (✗)
Cats usually look neat and clean. By contrast, dogs mess up everything and never learn to tidy themselves. (✔)
(貓通常看起來既乾淨又整齊。相形之下, 狗總是製造髒亂也不會打理自己。)

on the contrary 是用來反駁前一句話藉以表達相反的意見。形成『對照』或『對比』時應該用 by/in contrast 或 on the other hand。

control

The dictator wanted to control over the people's lives. (✗)
The dictator wanted to control the people's lives. (✔)
The dictator wanted control over the people's lives. (✔)
(這名獨裁者想要控制人民的生活。)

control 作為動詞時是及物的用法, 不需加 over。但 control 作為名詞時則需加 over 或其它介系詞再接受詞。

My car lost control and crashed onto a traffic island. (✗)
My car went out of control and crashed onto a traffic island. (✔)
(我的車子失控撞上安全島。)

lose control (of sth) 是指人們 (情緒) 失控或無法掌控車輛、機器等, 如: He lost control and began to call me names. (他一時情緒失控, 然後就開始咒罵我。) The driver lost control of the vehicle on the muddy road. (在這泥濘的道路上, 車子不聽司機使喚了。) 至於車輛或機器本身的『失控』要用 go/get out of control。

convenience

You may pay me back for your convenience. (✗)
You may pay me back at your convenience. (✔)
(你可以在你方便的時候償還給我。)

for sb's convenience 表『為了某人的方便』, 如: For your convenience, just give us a call and we'll handle everything. (為了您的方便, 你只要撥個電話, 我們一切都幫您搞定。)『在某人方便時』應該用 at sb's convenience。

The limousine is equipped with a variety of modern convenience. (✗)
The limousine is equipped with a variety of modern conveniences. (✔)
(這部大型豪華轎車裝有各式各樣的現代設備。)

convenience 作『方便』或『便利』解時，是不可數名詞。但作能使生活舒適的『設備』解時則為可數名詞且常用複數。

convenient

There are several convenient stores nearby. (✗)
There are several convenience stores nearby. (✔)
(附近有幾家便利商店。)

『便利商店』的正確說法是 convenience store。convenience food 是指已經烹調好，要吃時只需加熱的『方便餐』，有別於從麥當勞或肯德基買到的 fast food。

Are you convenient at two o'clock? (✗)
Is two o'clock convenient for you? (✔)
(兩點鐘你方便嗎？)

convenient 這個形容詞並不能修飾人，只能修飾事物。對某人方便的句型是 it/事物 is convenient for sb (to do sth)。

cook

The cooker put too much MSG in the soup. (✗)
The cook/chef put too much MSG in the soup. (✔)
(廚師在湯裡頭放了太多味精。)

cooker (主英) = stove (主美) 是指烹飪的『鍋爐』。廚師的說法是 cook (一般) 或 chef (餐廳的大廚)。另外，MSG 為 monosodium glutamate 的縮寫，是『味精』的學名。

My mom is cooking a fruit salad. (✗)
My mom is making a fruit salad. (✔)
(我老媽正在做一道水果沙拉。)

cook sth 指的是需要動用電鍋/瓦斯爐來『烹煮某物』，如: Dad is cooking dinner for us tonight. (老爸今晚為我們做晚餐。) 做沙拉/三明治/生魚片時，用 make salads/sandwiches/sashimi。

cooking

I'd like to buy some cooking books. (✗)
I'd like to buy some cookbooks. (✔)
I'd like to buy some cookery books. (✔)
(我想買幾本食譜。)

『食譜』的正確說法是 cookbook (主美) 和 cookery book (主英)。cooking 作為形容詞時意為『烹調的』，主要用來修飾設備或器材，如: cooking facilities/utensils 就是指烹調設備/器具。

cope

She found it difficult to cope with the customer. (✗)
She found it difficult to deal with the customer. (✔)
(她發現這名顧客很難應付。)

cope with 專指『應付』問題或困難。可兼指『應付』人物或問題是 deal with 或 handle。

corner

My sister sat on the corner reading. (✗)
My sister sat in the corner reading. (✔)
(我妹妹坐在角落裡閱讀。)

C

on the corner 通常是指在街道的角落上, 而 at the corner 則是在角落附近, 如: She was standing on/at the corner waiting for her boyfriend to pick her up. (她站在街角上/附近等候男友開車來接她。) in the corner 是在室內的『角落裡』。

Don't cut corner in doing anything. (✗)
Don't cut corners in doing anything. (✔)
(做任何事情不可敷衍了事。)

cut a/the corner (主央) 是『抄捷徑』的意思。cut corners 是指做事情時『敷衍了事』或『偷工減料』。

corresponding

An increase in a nation's money supply, without a constrasting growth of economy, tends to result in inflation. (✗)
An increase in a nation's money supply, without a corresponding growth of economy, tends to result in inflation. (✔)
(一個國家貨幣供給額的增加，要是沒有相對的經濟成長，就會有通貨膨脹之虞。)

contrasting (相對的) 表『對照』或『相反』之意, 如: Those contrasting views were taken into consideration. (那些相對的觀點都被列入考慮。) corresponding (相對的) 指的是『相關/配合的』。

could

Could you start the car after the collision? (✗)
Were you able to start the car after the collision? (✔)
(撞車之後你車子發得動嗎？)

could 表平時 (非一時) 的過去能力, 如: I could remain awake for two days when I was younger. (就在幾年前我還能夠連續兩天不睡覺。) 這個用法的 could 也可代之以 was/were able to。不過若指過去的單一事件則限用 was/were able to 或 managed to。

The two sisters can't be more different in personality. (✗)
The two sisters couldn't be more different in personality. (✔)
(這一對姊妹個性大不相同。)

couldn't be + 比較級為固定用法, 如: Booking online couldn't be simpler. (網路訂位最為簡便。)。

count

His promises never count anything. (✗)
His promises never count for anything. (✔)
(他的承諾一文不值。)

count 當動詞時可表『計算』或『有重要性』, 如: Count me in. (算我進去/一份。) What really counts is your attitude toward life. (重要的是你對人生態度。) 另外 count for something/nothing 就是表『有/沒有價值』的意思。

countless

The word is a countless noun. (✗)
The word is an uncountable noun. (✔)
(這個字是一個不可數名詞。)

可數名詞是 a countable noun, 不可數名詞是 an uncountable noun。countless 是『數不清的』, 如: I've told you countless times. (我已經告訴過你無數次了)。

course

I'm taking a course of history. (✗)
I'm taking a course in history. (✔)
I'm taking a history course. (✔)
(我正在修一門歷史課程。)

『一門課程』籠統的說法是 a course of study。但具體的說法是 a course in + 學科或 a(n) + 學科 + course, 如一門英文課程就是 a course in English 或 an English course。至於 the course of history 是指『歷史的進展』, 如: A great person can sometimes change the course of history. (一個偉人往往能改變歷史的進展)。

court

There is a golf court over there. (✗)
There is a golf course over there. (✔)
(那邊有一個高爾夫球場。)

『球場』的英文有下列不同的說法: (1) a basketball/tennis court (籃/網球場) (2) a golf course (高爾夫球場) (3) a baseball/football field (棒/足球場)。

cover

Everyone was running for a cover when it began to pour. (✗)
Everyone was running for cover when it began to pour. (✔)
(下傾盆大雨時大家都跑去找地方躲。)

cover 作『蓋子』或書的『封面』解時是可數名詞。作『被子』解時恆用 the covers, 如: She crept under the covers and turned out the light. (她爬進被窩裡然後熄燈就寢。) cover 作『躲避處』解時為不可數名詞, 如: run for/take/seek cover 表『(跑去) 找地方躲』。break cover 表『自躲藏處竄出』, 如: The hunter was waiting for the fox to break cover. (這名獵人正在等候狐狸從其躲藏處竄出)。

coverage

The election campaign has received an extensive media coverage. (✗)
The election compaign has received extensive media coverage. (✔)
(這個選舉活動獲得媒體廣泛地報導。)

coverage 意為 (新聞或電視)『報導』, 是不可數名詞。

craft

Many crafts sailed into the harbor seeking cover from the impending typhoon. (✗)
Many craft sailed into the harbor seeking cover from the impending typhoon. (✔)
(許多小船駛進港口躲避即將進來的颱風。)

craft 作為『船隻』或『飛行器』解時單複數同形, 即 one/two/many craft。但作為『手工藝(品)』解時其複數形是 crafts, 如: It is a display of traditional crafts. (這是一項傳統手工藝品的展覽)。

C

crafty

As a novelist Henry James is a very crafty man. (✗)

As a novelist Henry James is a great craftsman. (✔)

(作為小說家亨利詹姆士是個大師。)

a crafty man 是一個『狡滑人物』。a craftsman 除可指一名『手工藝匠』之外也可指一位『藝術大師』。

cramp

I got stomach cramp this morning. (✗)

I got stomach cramps this morning. (✔)

(今天早上我的胃絞痛。)

get (stomach) cramps (恆用複數) 是指『胃絞痛』。get (a) cramp 是指『抽筋』, 如: I got (a) cramp in my left leg after swimming for 20 minutes. (游了二十分鐘後我的右腿抽筋了。)

crash

My car went out of control and crashed head-on with another car. (✗)

My car went out of control and crashed head-on into another car. (✔)

(我的車子失控就一頭撞上另一部車子。)

crash into sth 是指車輛或飛機『撞上某物』, 為固定用法。

A truck crashed into a pedestrian this morning. (✗)

A truck ran down a pedestrian this morning. (✔)

(今天早上有一輛卡車撞上一名行人。)

crash into 限用於撞上某物。車輛『撞上某人』需用 hit/run down sb。

credible

There is no creditable evidence for these allegations. (✗)

There is no credible evidence for these allegations. (✔)

(目前並沒有可信的證據來支持這些指控。)

creditable 是『值得讚賞的』之意, 如: Their performance was highly creditable. (他們的演出值得高度讚賞。) 而 credible = believable 是『可信的』之意。

crew

The plane crash killed all the passengers and crews. (✗)

The plane crash killed all the passengers and crew. (✔)

(該班機失事造成全體乘客和機組人員喪生。)

crew 是一個集合名詞, 表在飛機或船上服務的全體機組人員或水手。這個字本身就是複數形式, 不可再加"s"。作主詞時需接複數動詞, 如: The crew are fifteen in all. (水手總共有十五位。)

crime

It took the police years to find out the crime. (✗)

It took the police years to find out about the crime. (✔)

It took the police years to solve the crime. (✔)

(這個犯罪事件警方花了好幾年才破案。)

將某個犯罪事件『破案』的說法是 find out about/solve a crime。

Our town has a very low criminal rate. (✗)
Our town has a very low crime rate. (✔)
(我們的鎮上犯罪率相當低。)

crime rate/figures/wave 即『犯罪率/數據/暴增』皆為固定用法。criminal 作為名詞時是『罪犯』之意, 如 a convicted criminal 就是一名『已被定罪的罪犯』。另外, criminal 也可作形容詞, 如 a criminal act/offense 就是一件『犯罪的行為』。a criminal court 是指一個『刑事法庭』。

crisis

We need a person that is good at crises management. (✗)
We need a person that is good at crisis management. (✔)
(我們需要一位擅長危機處理的人。)

crises 是『危機』的複數形, 不過『危機處理』的固定說法是 crisis management。另外, a crisis of confidence 是所謂的『信心危機』, 如: The plunge in share prices seemed to spell a crisis of confidence. (股價暴跌似乎說明了信心危機。)

criteria

You have to meet our criterias to qualify for membership. (✗)
You have to meet our criteria to qualify for membership. (✔)
(你必須符合我們的標準才能取得會員資格。)

criteria (評定的標準) 是 criterion 的複數形, 不能再加"s"。meet/satisfy/fulfil the criteria (符合標準) 為固定用法。

critic

The book is a critic of the government's foreign policies. (✗)
The book is a critique of the government's foreign policies. (✔)
(這是針對政府外交政策的一本批判書。)

a critic 是一位『批評家』, 如: Dr. Watson is a famous literary critic. (華臣博士是一位知名的文學批評家。) a critique 是一本『批判』的書或一篇『批評』的文章或演講。另外, criticism 是指『批評』的言論或行為, 如: The politician has attracted a lot of criticism. (這名政治人物引來不少批評。)

crop

The brand-new model will be our company's biggest cash crop. (✗)
The brand-new model will be our company's biggest cash cow. (✔)
(這個全新的機種將會是本公司最大的一棵搖錢樹。)

a cash crop 是指一種『種來賣錢的』農作物。a subsistence crop 是指一種『種來自己食用的』農作物, 如: Most of the vegetables we grow are not subsistence crops but cash crops. (大部分我們種的蔬菜並非自己食用而是要賣錢的。) a cash cow 是指很賺錢的『產品』或『事業』。

cross

To be on the safe side, you'll have to cross out the check. (✗)
To be on the safe side, you'll

C

C

have to cross the check. (✔)
(為了安全起見，你必須在支票角落畫兩條斜線。)

cross out sth 是『刪除』錯誤的文字或數據, 如: I have crossed out these two words. (我已經把這兩個字刪掉了。) cross a check 是在一張支票的 (左上角) 畫上兩條斜線以策安全。

A mule is a cross of a horse and a donkey. (✗)
A mule is a cross between a horse and a donkey. (✔)
(騾是馬和驢雜交的混和種。)

a cross between A and B 是指 A 種和 B 種動/植物之間的混合種, 為固定用法。

crossroads

The accident took place at a crossroad. (✗)
The accident took place at a crossroads. (✔)
(這起事故發生在一個十字路口。)

a crossroads (十字路口) 恆用複數, 因為是兩條路交會形成。 at a crossroads 也經常作比喻的用法, 表某人處於人生或事業的一個『轉折點』, 如: My father is at a crossroads in his career. (我老爸現在正處於一個事業的轉折點。)

crude

It seems to be a crudely home-made bomb. (✗)
It seems to be a crude home-made bomb. (✔)
(那似乎是一顆土製炸彈。)

crude 是形容詞, 意為『粗製濫造的』或『未經提煉/加工的』, 如 crude oil 就是『原油』。crudely 是副詞, 用法如: The garage was crudely built. (這個車庫蓋得很粗糙。)

crush

She has a crush about John. (✗)
She has a crush on John. (✔)
(她迷戀約翰。)

have a crush on sb 意為『迷戀某人』, 是固定用法。另外, 也可以說 She is crazy/mad about John.

cry

I really need a shoulder to cry for. (✗)
I really need a shoulder to cry on. (✔)
(我真的需要找個人哭訴一番。)

cry for sb/sth 是哭哭啼啼或大聲吵著要某人或某物, 如: The little girl is crying for her mother/the toy. (這個小女孩哭著要找媽媽/拿玩具。) cry on sb's shoulder 或 need a shoulder to cry on 表 (要) 找人哭訴一番, 為固定用法。另外, be crying out for sth 表『非常需要某物』的意思, 如: The building is crying out for a facelift. (這棟大樓亟需整修門面。)

crybaby

Don't be such a crying baby. (✗)
Don't be such a crybaby. (✔)
(不要這麼愛哭好不好。)

a crying baby 是指一名正在哭的嬰兒。a crybaby 是指一個愛哭的小孩 (偶指大人), 就是俗稱的『愛哭鬼』。

C

culprit

More and more children are getting overweight, and fast food seems to be the main criminal. (✗)

More and more children are getting overweight, and fast food seems to be the main culprit. (✓)

(愈來愈多孩子變胖，速食似乎就是罪魁禍首。)

a criminal 專指一個已有犯罪事實的人。a culprit 兼指一個違法犯過的人或造成某種禍害之原因。

cultural

My boss is a cultural man. (✗)

My boss is a cultured man. (✓)

(我的老闆是個文化人。)

cultural 和 cultured 都是形容詞。但 cultural 是指『與文化有關的』, 通常用來形容事物, 如 cultural activities/exchanges/differences/background/heritage 就是指文化活動/交流/差異/背景/傳承。而 cultured 有兩個意思, 指人時意為『有文化教養的』, 指東西時意為『人工培養的』如 a cultured pearl 就是人工培養的珍珠。不過『文化振撼』該説 culture shock。

Cupid

She has vowed never to play the Cupid again. (✗)

She has vowed never to play Cupid again. (✓)

(她發誓再也不當紅娘了。)

Cuipd 本指希臘神話中的愛神『邱比特』, 所以 play Cupid 是為一對男女牽線, 即扮演『月老』或『紅娘』的角色, 為固定用法。

cure

There is no cure of diabetes, but its symptoms can be managed. (✗)

There is no cure for diabetes, but its symptoms can be managed. (✓)

(糖尿病無法治癒但病情可以控制。)

a cure for sth 意為針對某種疾病的『治療之方』, 也可引申為針對某種問題的『解決之道』, 如: There is no easy cure for the country's overpopulation. (該國的人口過剩問題不容易解決。)

curiosity

A few teenagers try smoking from curiosity. (✗)

A few teenagers try smoking out of curiosity. (✓)

(一些青少年因為好奇嘗試抽煙。)

out of curiosity 意為『由於好奇』, 是固定用法。

current

Her present boyfriend is a cop. (✗)

Her current boyfriend is a cop. (✓)

(他目前的男友是一名警察。)

present 和 current 都可指『目前的』, 而且有時用法是相通的, 如: The present/current situation is hard to handle. (目前的情況很難應付。) 不過指『較易變動』的關係或情況時, 通常用 current 這個字來形容, 如 current boyfriend/girlfriend (目前的男/女

友) 和 current prices (時價)。這個用法主要是引申自 current (水流) 的本意，因為水流是『不穩定的』。

C

custom

The old man has a custom of clearing his throat before he speaks. (✗)
The old man has a habit of clearing his throat before he speaks. (✔)
(這個老人習慣在說話前先清一下嗓門。)

custom 通常是指一個地方的『風俗習慣』，如 local/traditional customs (當地/傳統習俗)。個人的『生活習慣』需用 habit。

I'm afraid you'll have to pay custom duties. (✗)
I'm afraid you'll have to pay customs duties. (✔)
(恐怕你得繳交關稅。)

作為『海關』解時限用複數形的 customs, 如: The passengers are waiting to clear customs. (旅客正在等候通關檢查。)

customer

As a lawyer, she often advises customers on legal matters. (✗)
As a lawyer, she often advises clients on legal matters. (✔)
(作為一個律師，她時常接受客戶的法律諮詢。)

customer 是指到商店或百貨公司購物的『顧客』。client 是指向專業人士如醫師、律師等諮詢或求取服務的『客戶』。

cut

That's the third time you've cut classes this week. (✗)
That's the third time you've cut class this week. (✔)
(這已經是你這星期第三次翹課了。)

『曠/翹課』的正確說法是 cut class/school, 不需加任何冠詞或用複數形。

I cut down the picture from a fashion magazine. (✗)
I cut out the picture from a fashion magazine. (✔)
(我從一本時裝雜誌剪下這張圖片。)

cut down (on sth) 是減少 (某物的) 數量或長度, 如: My dad used to be a chain smoker, but he has cut down (on smoking). (我老爸曾是煙不離手的人, 不過他已減量了。) cut out sth 是將某物 (從另一物) 剪下。其它相關用語如 cut in (插嘴); cut off (切斷電/煤氣供應); cut up (切碎)。

Your performance is a lot above his. (✗)
Your performance is a cut above his. (✔)
Your performance is a lot better than his. (✔)
(你的表現比他好得太多了。)

be a cut above sb/sth = be a lot better than sb/sth 意為『比某人/物好得太多』, 是固定說法。

D d

D

damage

Alcoholism will cause liver damages eventually. (✗)
Alcoholism will cause liver damage eventually. (✔)
(酗酒最後會造成肝臟受損。)

damage 作為名詞意為『損害』時是不可數名詞。brain/liver/nerve damage 是指腦部/肝臟/神經受損，為固定用法。至於複數形的 damages 是指法院裁定某人 (因傷害罪或毀損罪) 須付給他人的賠償金，如: He sued the company and won $5,000 in damages. (他告那家公司後得到五千美元的賠償金。)

The house did serious damage in the fire. (✗)
The house suffered serious damage in the fire. (✔)
(這棟房子在大火中遭到嚴重的損失。)

do/cause damage (to...) 是對某物造成傷害或損失 The typhoon has done severe damage to our apartment building. (這個颱風已對我們的公寓大樓造成嚴重破壞。) suffer damage 是指某物本身遭到傷害或損失。

damaged

The motorcyclist was very lucky and was only slightly damaged. (✗)
The motorcyclist was very lucky and was only slightly hurt. (✔)
(這名機車騎士真走運，只是受到輕傷而已。)

damaged 這個形容詞不能針對人，只能針對某物或某人的部位/器官，如: The island's ecology is badly damaged because of excessive hunting. (因為濫捕濫殺之故，整座島的生態嚴重遭到破壞。) Her brain was damaged owing to lack of oxygen. (她因缺氧造成腦部受損。) 指人受傷需用 be hurt/injured (指意外所傷) 或 be wounded (指武器所傷)。

It could be very damaged to your reputation. (✗)
It could be very damaging to your reputation. (✔)
(這可能會對你的名譽造成相當的損害。)

damaged 是『受損的』。damaging 是『對某物造成損害的』。兩者都是形容詞但指涉不同。

damp

The summer in Taiwan is very hot and damp. (✗)
The summer in Taiwan is very hot and humid. (✔)
(台灣的夏天既炎熱又潮溼。)

damp 是『略為潮溼的』，經常和 cold 連用，如: I remember it was a cold, damp day. (我記得那是一個又冷又溼的日子。) humid 是『溼度高的』，經常和 hot 連用。

dance

What sort of music do you like to dance with? (✗)
What sort of music do you like to dance to? (✔)
(你喜歡跳什麼舞曲？)

dance with sb 是『跟某人跳舞』的意思，如: I would like to dance with that pretty girl. (我想跟那位漂亮美眉跳舞。) dance to sth 是『跟著音樂起舞』，如: They are dancing to a waltz. (他們正跟著一曲華爾茲起舞。) 至於 They are dancing a waltz.

是說『他們正在跳一支華爾茲舞』，強調是『舞步』，並不一定要有『音樂』。

danger

You'll be dangerous if you don't follow the instructions. (✗)

You'll be in danger if you don't follow the instructions. (✔)

(如果不遵照指示，你就會有危險。)

dangerous 是指人或物『本身具危險性的』，如: Skydiving is a highly dangerous sport, but many people are dying to do it. (高空跳傘是極具危險性的運動，可是不少人趨之若鶩。) in danger 是『身陷險境』之意。

dare

My daughter dares not talk back to me. (✗)

My daughter dare not talk back to me. (✔)

My daughter doesn't dare (to) talk back to me. (✔)

(我女兒不敢跟我頂嘴。)

dare 這個字有『助動詞』和『本動詞』兩種用法。作為助動詞時用法一如其它的助詞像 will/can/may 等 (不可加 s 於後)。作為本動詞則有 dares/dared 和 doesn't/didn't dare 的用法，後接不定詞或省略"to"的不定詞。另外值得注意的是 dare 通常用於否定句或疑問句，如: We hardly dared (to) hope that the mountaineer would survive. (我們簡直不敢奢望這名登山客會活下來。)

How dare you to treat her like this? (✗)

How dare you treat her like this? (✔)

(你竟敢這樣對待她？)

How dare you/he/she + 原形動詞……? 表說話者對某人的所作所為極為震驚或不滿。這個 dare 是『助動詞』，所以要接原形動詞。類似的助動詞用法如: How can you treat me like this? (你怎能這樣對我呢?)

Someone must have dared my son rob the bank. (✗)

Someone must have dared my son to rob the bank. (✔)

(一定有人慫恿我兒子去搶銀行。)

dare sb + 不定詞是『慫恿』某人去做危險或不法的事情，為固定用法。

dark

The room grew dark while we were having dinner. (✗)

The room went dark while we were having dinner. (✔)

(我們正在享用晚餐時突然停電一片漆黑。)

get/grow dark 指的是白天快要結束時『天色逐漸轉暗』，如: It's getting dark. We'd better go home now. (天色漸漸暗了，我們最好現在就回家了。) go dark 是指室內或屋裡突然停電變成一片漆黑。

I was kept in the darkness about the layoff plan. (✗)

I was kept in the dark about the layoff plan. (✔)

(關於公司的裁員計劃我被蒙在鼓裡。)

keep sb in the dark (about sth) 是『不把某事告訴某人』之意，為固定用法。另外，before/after dark，即『天黑之前/後』，也是固定片語，如: Avoid the park after dark. (天黑後避免到那公園。)

D

dart

Let's play dart, John. (✗)

Let's play darts, John. (✔)

(約翰，我們來玩射飛鏢的遊戲。)

dart 作為可數名詞時是『飛鏢』, 如 a dart/two darts 就是指一支/兩支飛鏢。作為『遊戲』時恆用 darts, 但 darts 作為主詞時限接單數動詞, 如: Darts is often played in English pubs. (射飛鏢的遊戲常見於英國的酒館。)

data

You can store more datas on a DVD. (✗)

You can store more data on a DVD. (✔)

(你可以在DVD碟片上儲存更多的資料。)

data (資料) 本是 datum 的複數形, 所以不能再加 "s"。不過這個字作主詞時可接單數或複數動詞, 如: The data is/are being processed. (這些資料正在被處理中。)

date

Please fill in your name, sex, and birthday on the form. (✗)

Please fill in your name, sex, and date of birth on the form. (✔)

(請在這張表格上填入你的姓名、性別和出生年月日。)

birthday 是指某人的『生日』, 強調的是每年的這個『日子』。專指某人『出生年月日』的這個『數據』需用 date of birth 或 birth date。

We agreed to hold another meeting on a future date. (✗)

We agreed to hold another meeting at a future date. (✔)

(我們同意再找一天來開會。)

at an earlier/a later/a future date (在較早/較晚/未來的日期) 為固定用法。on a date 差不多僅見於 go (out) on a date (約會) 這個片語, 如: Cathy and I are going on a date tonight. (凱西和我今晚有約會。)

Up to date, we've not received any replies. (✗)

To date, we've not received any replies. (✔)

Up to now, we've not received any replies. (✔)

(到目前為止我方尚未接獲任何回覆。)

up to date 或 up-to-date (置於名詞之前) 是極為『先進』或『能跟上時代』的意思, 如: All our equipment is up to date. (我們所有的設備都是極為先進的。) Do you have a more up-to-date edition? (你們有更新的版本嗎?) 至於 to date = so far = up to now 是『迄今』之意, 常搭配現在完成式使用。

dawn

The team decided to set out on dawn. (✗)

The team decided to set out at dawn. (✔)

(這隊人馬決定天一亮就出發。)

dawn = daybreak 是指『天亮』的那一瞬間。凡表一瞬間都用 at, 如: at sunrise/sunset/noon/midnight 等。

It finally dawned to me that I had been taken in. (✗)

It finally dawned on me that I had been taken in. (✔)

(我終於恍然大悟我受騙了。)

D

dawn on sb 是某人 (對某事)『恍然大悟』之意,為固定用法。類似的用法是 occur to sb, 如: It occurred to me that she might be falling in love. (我突然想到她也許正陷入熱戀中。)

day

I've been busy all the day. I'm beat. (✗)

I've been busy all day. I'm beat. (✔)

(我一整天忙個不停。我累斃了。)

『一整天』的固定說法是 all day (long)。

On his day, my grandfather could drink anyone under the table. (✗)

In his day, my grandfather could drink anyone under the table. (✔)

(在他年輕時，我爺爺的酒量比任何人都好。)

in sb's day = when sb was young, 意為『在某人年輕時』, 是固定用法。

By the day I work at a bank and by the night I moonlight as a taxi driver. (✗)

By day I work at a bank and by night I moonlight as a taxi driver. (✔)

(白天我在一家銀行上班，晚上我兼差當計程車司機。)

by day/night = during the day/night, 就是『在白天/晚上之時』。by the day 是『按日』計酬, 如: All the workers here are paid by the day. (這裡的工人都是按日計酬。)

His health is improving day after day. (✗)

His health is improving day by day. (✔)

(他的健康狀況逐日在改善中。)

day after day 是『日復一日』的意思, 通常用來表達『厭煩』或『不悅』的狀況, 如: I'm fed up with this tedious repetition day after day. (我受不了這種無聊的日復一日重複的工作。) day by day = gradually 是『逐漸/日』之意。

Many people go abroad for sightseeing in these days. (✗)

Many people go abroad for sightseeing these days. (✔)

(現今有很多人出國觀光旅遊。)

英文並沒有 in these days 的說法。these days = nowadays = today 表『目前』或『現今』之意。不過提到過去的某一段 (特定的) 時光則要說 in those days, 如: We lived from hand to mouth in those days. (那個時候我們過著僅能餬口的日子。)

dead

The street shoot-out left eight people for dead. (✗)

The street shoot-out left eight people dead. (✔)

(街頭的槍戰造成八個人死亡。)

leave sb for dead 是『棄某人於不顧而任其死亡』, 其主詞恆為『人』, 如: Jeff beat his wife up and left her for dead. (傑夫痛毆老婆之後就棄之於不顧任其死亡。) leave sb dead 是『造成某人死亡』, 主詞通常為事件。

When I graduated from college, my grandfather was dead long. (✗)

When I graduated from college, my grandfather was long dead. (✔)
(我大學畢業時爺爺已過世很久。)

long dead = dead for a long time 表『過世很久』, 為固定用法。

deadly

D

After the workout, I was deadly tired. (✗)
After the workout, I was dead tired. (✔)
(做完健身運動後我累死了。)

deadly 通常為形容詞, 是『致命的』之意, 如: SARS is a potentially deadly disease. (SARS 是一種極可能致命的疾病。) 至於 dead這個字除可當形容詞表『死亡的』外, 還可作副詞用。這個副詞的 dead = very/completely, 如: dead sure/drunk/right 就是『非常肯定/醉/正確』之意。另外, deadly 也有副詞的用法, 相當於 extremely 這個字, 表『極為……』之意, 常搭配 serious/dull/boring 連用, 如: It was a deadly dull lecture. (那是一場極為沉悶的講演。)

deaf

Her left ear is deaf. (✗)
She is deaf in the left ear. (✔)
(她的左耳聾了。)

說某人『耳聾』的英文恆用某人(不能用耳朵)作主詞。『瞎眼』的說法亦然。你不能說 His right eye is blind.需說 He is blind in the right eye. (他的右眼瞎了。) 至於『全聾/瞎』的狀況需用 be totally deaf/blind來表達。如果程度沒這麼嚴重可代之以 be partially deaf/blind。

deal

A large deal of money has been spent on market research. (✗)
A great deal of money has been spent on market research. (✔)
(已經砸了不少銀子來做市場調查。)

a great/good deal of + 不可數的名詞。a large/great number of + 可數的複數名詞。如: A large number of paintings have been sold. (已經賣出很多幅畫了。)

My father deals with secondhand books. (✗)
My father deals in secondhand books. (✔)
(我老爸做二手書的買賣。)

deal with是(1)應付某人/物(2)有關……(主題), 如: Your boss is a tough man to deal with. (你的老闆是個很難應付的人。) The book deals with the philosophy of Hegel. (這本書探討黑格爾的哲學。) deal in = buy and sell 是『做某物的買賣』之意。

death

Those refugees would starve to deaths if the government did not lend a hand. (✗)
Those refugees would starve to death if the government did not lend a hand. (✔)
(如果政府不伸出援手, 那些難民就會餓死。)

作為『死亡』的概念或狀態時, death 是不可數名詞。但若作為『死亡人數』時, 就有複數形的 deaths 之用法, 如: The flood caused more than twenty deaths. (水患造成二十多個人死亡。) bleed/starve/freeze to death (流血/挨餓/受凍至死) 為固定用法。

There seem to be more and more deaths of cancer. (✗)
There seem to be more and more deaths from cancer. (✓)
(似乎有越來越多的人死於癌症。)

deaths from + 疾病/意外是固定用法。

debate

The governor's speech has been a subject of many debates. (✗)
The governor's speech has been a subject of much debate. (✓)
(這位州長的演講引發了不少爭論。)

debate 作為辯論或爭論的『內容』時, 通常是不可數名詞。a subject of much/some debate, 即『引發不少/一些爭論的議題』, 是固定用法。但作為辯論的『場次』時, debate 是可數名詞, 如: There have been three debates between the two candidates. (這兩位候選人已經進行三場辯論了。)

debt

If you continue to lead such a life of luxury, you'll get into a debt. (✗)
If you continue to lead such a life of luxury, you'll get into debt. (✓)
(如果你繼續過這種奢侈的生活，你將會負債。)

debt 作為『負債的狀況』解時為不可數名詞。fall/get/go/run into debt 即『陷入負債』, 是固定用法。作為『負債的筆數』解時 debt 為可數名詞, 如: The actress found herself saddled with a huge debt. (這個女演員不知不覺已背負一筆巨債。)

deceive

The politician tried to deceive the public to think that he was honest. (✗)
The politician tried to deceive the public into thinking that he was honest. (✓)
(那名政客試圖欺騙大眾好讓人們以為他是誠實的。)

deceive sb into + Ving 為固定用法。

As you know, appearances can deceive. (✗)
As you know, appearances can be deceiving. (✓)
(你是知道的，外表會騙人。)

appearances/looks can be deceiving 為固定用法。

decided

We have won a decided battle. (✗)
We have won a decisive battle. (✓)
(我們已贏得一場具有決定性的戰役。)

decided = clear and definite, 即『明顯/確的』之意, 如: In terms of personality, there is a decided difference between the two brothers. (就個性而言, 這兩兄弟有很明顯的差異。) decisive 是『具有決定性的』之意。

decline

The moral declining in present-day society is our main concern. (✗)
The moral decline in present-day society is our main concern. (✓)

D

(我們憂心的主要是現今社會的道德淪喪。)

declining = getting worse 是『每況愈下』的意思, 作為形容詞使用, 如: My mother's health has been declining. (我老媽的健康狀況大不如前。) economic/moral decline 是指『經濟下滑/道德淪喪』, 為固定用法。

deep

D

Before he got married, Paul had been in deep debt. (✗)
Before he got married, Paul had been deep in debt. (✓)
(婚前保羅早已經負債累累。)

deep in debt 是『負債累累』的慣用語。但『處境困難』需說 in deep trouble/water。

People stood three deeps at the roadside watching the parade. (✗)
People stood three deep at the roadside watching the parade. (✓)
People stood in three lines/rows at the roadside watching the parade. (✓)
(路旁站著三排的人在觀看遊行。)

two/three/four deep (不加 s) 是指人或物成兩/三/四排, 為固定用法。

I felt deeply that a plot was being hatched against me. (✗)
Deep down, I felt that a plot was being hatched against me. (✓)
(我隱隱約約感到有人在策劃不利於我的陰謀。)

deeply 是『深深地』或『深刻地』之意。如: breathe/sigh deeply 即深深地呼吸/嘆口氣。又如: I was deeply impressed by his sincerity. (他的誠懇令我留下深刻的印象。) deep down 作為副詞片語表 (1) 隱隱約約地 (指感覺或認知) (2) 事實上 (雖然表面看不出來) 如: Deep down, Peter is a very conservative person. (彼德骨子裡其實是一個相當保守的人。)

defeat

They had lost three battles, but they just wouldn't admit defeats. (✗)
They had lost three battles, but they just wouldn't admit defeat. (✓)
(他們已經打了三場敗仗，可是他們就是不認輸。)

defeat 作為『挫敗』或『(被) 打敗』時, 通常作不可數名詞。admit/accept/concede defeat (認輸) 為固定用法。但若指挫敗或被打敗的『次數』, defeat 則為可數名詞, 如: After five consecutive defeats, the team's morale was at an all-time low. (五連敗之後，該隊的士氣空前的低落。)

I don't like your defeated attitude. (✗)
I don't like your defeatist attitude. (✓)
(我不欣賞你這種唱衰自己的態度。)

defeated 是『被打敗的』之意, 如: A man can be destroyed, but he cannot be defeated. (一個人可以被毀滅, 但是絕不可以被打敗。按: 此句出自海明威的名著《老人與海》) defeatist 可兼作名詞和形容詞, 意為『失敗主義者 (的)』。

defect

Despite some physical defectations, Byron was a literary giant. (✗)
Despite some physical defects, Byron was a literary

giant. (✔)
(雖然有些生理缺陷，拜倫仍不失為文學界的一個巨擘。)

defectation 是作為動詞的 defect (叛離/逃) 之名詞形式, 如: Discontent will lead to further defectations from the party. (不滿的情緒將造成該黨黨員的更進一步出走。) 至於 defect 作為名詞時, 意為『缺陷』。

defense

He was on the defense all the time although I did not criticize him. (✗)
He was on the defensive all the time although I did not criticize him. (✔)
(雖然我並沒有批評他，可是他卻一直忙著為自己辯解。)

英文並沒有 on the defense 的說法。defense 本身是『防禦/衛』之意, 如: The best defense is offense. (攻擊乃最佳之防禦。) the defense 是指 (法庭的) 被告律師, 如: The defense will call three witnesses at the next court. (被告律師將在下一次開庭時傳喚三名證人。) on the defensive 是『為自己辯解』之意。

deficiency

Scurvy is a disease caused by a deficit of vitamin C. (✗)
Scurvy is a disease caused by a deficiency of vitamin C. (✔)
(壞血症是一種由缺乏維他命 C 引起的疾病。)

deficit 意為『赤字』, 專指財務方面的不足或虧空。如 a budget/financial/trade deficit 就是一個預算/財務/貿易赤字。deficiency 指的是一般的不足或匱乏。

definition

An advisor is, according to definition, a person that gives advice. (✗)
An advisor is, by definition, a person that gives advice. (✔)
(『顧問』一詞按照定義就是給人建言的人。)

by definition 是『按照定義』的固定說法。according to definition 雖然『可懂』但不符『慣用』原則。

These photos lack definitions. (✗)
These photos lack definition. (✔)
(這些照片清晰度不夠。)

definition 作為『定義』時是可數名詞, 如: There are many definitions of the word "romanticism." (『浪漫主義』這個詞有很多定義。) 但作為『清晰度』解時, definition 是不可數名詞。

degree

My boyfriend has a master degree in economics. (✗)
My boyfriend has a master's degree in economics. (✔)
(我男友擁有經濟學碩士的學位。)

a bachelor's/master's/doctor's degree in (不能用 of) + 學科表某一門學科的學士/碩士/博士學位。其中 a doctor's degree 亦可說成 a doctoral degree 或 a Ph.D.。

I am studying a doctor's degree in law. (✗)
I am doing a doctor's degree in law. (✔)
(目前我正在攻讀法學博士學位。)

do a degree in + 學科是攻讀某一門學科的學位，是固定用法。

delighted

I am delightful to see you again. (✗)
I am delighted to see you again. (✔)
(再度見到你我很高興。)

delightful 是『令人高興/愉快的』之意，如: I must admit it is a delightful evening. (我必須承認今晚真是個愉快的夜晚。) delighted 是『本身感到高興/愉快的』。

demand

The job makes great physical demand on anyone taking it. (✗)
The job makes great physical demands on anyone taking it. (✔)
(這個工作極需從事者付出體力。)

demand 作『需求 (量)』解時為不可數名詞，如: Demand for organic food seems to be growing. (對於有機食品的需求似乎在成長中。) 至於需要付出心智或體力的情況則恆用複數形的 demands。

Digital cameras are much on demand these days. (✗)
Digital cameras are much in demand these days. (✔)
(現今數位相機很搶手。)

on demand 是『來取即付』或『有需求就給』之意，如: Free copies are now available on demand. (免費贈本來索即給。) in demand 是指人或物很『熱門』或『搶手』，如: The political commentator is now much in demand. (這名政論家現在紅的很。)

demanding

A teaching job can be both physically and intellectually demanded. (✗)
A teaching job can be both physically and intellectually demanding. (✔)
(教學的工作挺累人的，有時真令人身心交瘁。)

demanded 是『被要/需求的』之意，如: He is never afraid to show courage where it is demanded. (在需要發揮勇氣時他總是從不退縮。) demanding 是『吃力不討好』之意。be physically/intellectually/emotionally demanding 是固定用法。

democracy

More than two thousand years ago, Athens was a democracy state. (✗)
More than two thousand years ago, Athens was a democratic state/democracy. (✔)
(兩千多年前雅典就是一個民主城邦。)

democracy 是名詞，兼有可/不可數的用法。其形容詞是 democratic。作為不可數名詞，democracy 是『民主政治 (制度)』，如: What are the ideals of democracy? (民主政治的理想是什麼?) 作為可數名詞時，democracy 是『民主國家』，如: Many Western democracies favor the idea. (許多西方民主國家支持這個構想。)

denounce

The election was denounced a farce. (✗)
The election was denounced as a farce. (✔)
(這個選舉被斥為鬧劇一場。)

denounce sb/sth as sth 是公然抨擊某人/物為……, 是固定用法。

departure

Let's take this editorial as a departure point for our discussion. (✗)

Let's take this editorial as a point of departure for our discussion. (✓)

(咱們就拿這篇社論來作為討論的一個起始點。)

departure 是 depart 這個動詞的名詞形式, 意為『離開』。a point of departure 本是一段旅程的『起始點』, 引申為一個討論的『起始點』。另外, departure 也有『偏離』之意, 如: It would be a radical departure from the original plan. (這將與原先的計劃相去甚遠。)

depend

The stock index will soar tomorrow, depending on it. (✗)

The stock index will soar tomorrow, depend on it. (✓)

(股票指數明天會大漲, 這絕對錯不了。)

depend on it (恆用祈使句形式, 用於句首或句末, 以逗點與主要子句隔開) 表說話者對於自己的說/看法極具信心。至於 depending on sth (亦可置於句首或句末, 以逗點與主要子句隔開) 意為『視……而定』, 如: The stock index varies, depending on price fluctuations. (股票指數變動不居, 視價格升降而定。) depending on sth = according to sth。

dependence

The woman needs medical treatment for her drug dependent. (✗)

The woman needs medical treatment for her drug dependence. (✓)

(這名女子吸食毒品成癮, 需要藥物治療。)

dependence 是名詞, 意為『依/仰賴』。所以 drug/alcohol dependence 就是仰賴藥物(毒品)/酒精『成癮』。dependent 一般作為形容詞意為『依靠的』, 但作為名詞時是『家眷』之意, 如: The person in question is a young male without any dependents. (我們提到這個人是一名年輕又沒有任何家眷的男子。)

deplete

The election has severely deleted the party's funds. (✗)

The election has severely depleted the party's funds. (✓)

(這個選舉使該黨的競選基金嚴重失血。)

delete 是指在校對時將部分字句『刪除』, 如: The editor deleted the third paragraph from my article. (編輯人員把我這篇文章的第三段刪除掉。) deplete 大是『大量地減少』或『使枯竭』之意。

depression

She suffered from a depression after her husband died. (✗)

She suffered from depression after her husband died. (✓)

(老公去世後她就患有憂鬱症了。)

depression 作為『沮喪』或『憂鬱』解時是不可數名詞, 不過可以用 a fit of depression 來表達一陣/時的沮喪, 如: An unemployed man committed suicide during a fit of depression. (有位失業男子一時想不開自殺了。) 不過, 作為『蕭條』或『不景氣』解時, depression 兼有可/不可數的用法, 如: The country is sliding into an economic depression. (該國正進入經濟不景氣。)

derive

D

Many English words are deriving from Latin. (✗)

Many English words derive/ are derived from Latin. (✔)

(許多英文字源自拉丁文。)

表『源於某物』時限用 derive from sth 或 be derived from sth, 不能用進行式。

descend

The young man claims to be descending from Confucius. (✗)

The young man claims to be descended from Confucius. (✔)

(這名年輕人聲稱是孔子的後代。)

descend 的本義是『下降』。引申之後 descend/be descended from 表『自……傳下』。descending 通常作形容詞用, 表『向下的』或『遞減的』, 如: These points are listed in descending order of importance. (這幾點是按照重要性遞減的順序列出。)

I wouldn't descend to use that kind of language, right? (✗)

I wouldn't descend to using that kind of language, right? (✔)

(我該不會下三濫到講出那種話，對吧？)

descend to (介系詞) + 名詞/Ving, 意為『卑鄙到……之地步』, 如: Other people may lie about their ages to make friends, but don't descend to their level. (別人或許為了交朋友而謊報年齡, 但是你千萬不要向他們看齊。)

description

The murderer was cruel and violent beyond our description. (✗)

The murderer was cruel and violent beyond description. (✔)

(這名凶手的殘暴非筆墨所能形容。)

(be) beyond description 或 defy/beggar description 都可用來說明某種情況過於極端無法描述, 唯其間不能置入 your/my/his 這些字眼。

The theater was crowded with people of all description. (✗)

The theater was crowded with people of every description/ all descriptions. (✔)

(戲院裡擠滿了各式各樣的人。)

of every/any/some description 是固定用法, 表『每一/任一/某一種類』之意。of all descriptions 是指『所有種類』之意。這些用法的 description 相當於 type/kind/sort。

deserted

The sea is dotted with a few deserted islands. (✗)

The sea is dotted with a few desert islands. (✔)

(這片海域有一些荒島羅列其中。)

deserted 是形容詞, 表『遭人遺棄, 任其荒廢的』之意, 如 a deserted house/farm 就是指一棟廢棄屋/一個荒蕪的農莊。desert island

(荒島)是指一直沒有人煙的『原始海島』。

deserved

These criminals are deserved of their punishment. (✗)

These criminals are deserving of their punishment. (✓)

(這幾名罪犯都罪有應得。)

deserved和deserving都是形容詞,而且兩者都有『應得的』之意。不過deserved因為是過去分詞所以強調『被動』,如: These criminals have received their deserved punishment. (這幾名罪犯都已伏法,罪有應得。) be deserving of sth 是指某人應得某物,為固定用法。其中的 deserving 強調的是『主動』。

design

The book is specially designed as reference. (✗)

The book is specially designed for reference. (✓)

(這本書是專為讀者參考用而編寫的。)

be designed as sth 是指『(被) 打算/安排作為某物』, 如: The book is designed as a reference book. (這本書是打算作為參考書來使用的。) be designed for + 目的/用途是『為某種目的/用途而安排』。

desirable

I took the medicine regularly, but it did not have the desirable effect. (✗)

I took the medicine regularly, but it did not have the desired effect. (✓)

(我曾按時服用這種藥,可是並沒有預期的效果。)

desirable是『值得要的』或『可取的』之意, 如: It is a highy desirable job. (這是一份令人非常想要的工作。) the desired effect 是『被預期的效果』, 為固定用法。

despite

Despite the flight is fully booked, he still entertains hopes of getting a seat. (✗)

Although the flight is fully booked, he still entertains hopes of getting a seat. (✓)

(雖然該班次的機位被訂一空,對於取得機位他仍抱持希望。)

although/though 是連接詞, 可以引導 (副詞) 子句。despite是介系詞, 不能引導子句, 只能接名詞或 Ving。因此, 該錯誤句可另改寫如下: (1) Despite the fact that the flight is fully booked, he still entertains hopes of getting a seat. (2) Depsite the flight being fully booked, he still entertains hopes of getting a seat.

destined

The cargo ship is destined to Bangkok. (✗)

The cargo ship is destined for Bangkok. (✓)

(這一艘貨輪開往曼谷。)

be destined for + 地方是『開/駛往某地』之意。這個片語相當於 be bound for。be destined to + V 表『注定要做某事』之意, 如: We seem to be destined to make a lot of money. (我們好像注定要賺大錢似的。) 另外, be destined for sth 也有『注定要……』之意, 如: Joseph, Jacob's son, was destined for greatness. (雅各的兒子約瑟夫注定會有一番偉大的事業。)

D

destroy

The truck was only slightly damaged, but the car was completly destroyed. (✗)

The truck was only slightly damaged, but the car was completely wrecked. (✓)

The truck was only slightly damaged, but the car was totaled. (✓)

(那輛卡車只是輕微受損，可是這部汽車可就全毀了。)

destroy sth 表『將某摧毀至蕩然無存』，如: The town was destroyed by an earthquake. (這個小鎮被一個地震毀滅了。) 指車輛『全毀』應該說: The car is completely wrecked/totaled. 或 The car is a write-off. (英式用法)。

detached

We need to invite a detachable political observer. (✗)

We need to invite a detached political observer. (✓)

(我們需要請一位超然的政治觀察家。)

detachable 表『可分離/拆下的』，如: I'd like to buy a coat that has a detachable hood. (我想要買一件有可拆式兜帽的外套。) detached 是指立場『超然的』。

detail

The middle-aged man described what he had witnessed in details. (✗)

The middle-aged man described what he had witnessed in detail. (✓)

(那名中年男子將自己目睹的一切詳加描述。)

detail 作為『細節』時通常是不可數名詞。in detail 意為『詳細/盡地』，是固定用法。複數形的 details 等於 information, 即『訊息』之意, 如: Further details are available from the Net. (更進一步的訊息可從網路取得)。

For more detail information, please refer to the brochure. (✗)

For more detailed information, please refer to the brochure. (✓)

For more/further details, please refer to the brochure. (✓)

(如欲知道更多訊息, 請參閱這本手冊。)

detailed 是形容詞, 意為『詳細/盡的』, 如 detailed account/analysis/description/information 就是『詳細的說明/分析/描述/資訊』。details = information。

detect

Some cancers can be cured if found early. (✗)

Some cancers can be cured if detected early. (✓)

(某幾種癌症如果發現得早就可治癒。)

find 通常指不經意的『發現』，但癌症並非一般人能夠輕易發現。這需要醫師 (院) 的『專業』及『設備』, 難度較高。這種難度較高的『發現』需用 detect。

detective

The criminal case is being investigated by a detector. (✗)

The criminal case is being investigated by a detective. (✓)

(這個刑事案件正由一名偵探調查中。)

detector 指的是『偵測器』，如 a lie detector 就是『測謊器』; a gas detector 即為『瓦斯偵測器』。detective 指的是『偵探(人員)』, 如一名『私家偵探』的說法為 a private detective。

determined

According to the psychologist, most of our behavior is socially determining. (✗)

According to the psychologist, most of our behavior is socially determined. (✔)

(根據這位心理學家的說法，我們大部分的行為受到社會的決定。)

determining 是『決定性的』, 如: I think price is the determining factor. (我認為價格是決定性的因素。) determined 是『被決定的』。be biologically/culturally/genetically/historically/socially determined 就是『被生理/文化/社會/歷史/社會決定的』。另外 determined 亦可表『態度堅決的』, 如: Pilate found the people determined against Jesus. (比拉多發現眾人堅決反對耶穌。按: 比拉多係羅馬派駐 Judea 之總督。他下令將耶穌處死。)

developed

The developing world should provide more aid to poor countries. (✗)

The developed world should provide more aid to poor countries. (✔)

(已開發國家應該對貧窮落後的國家提供更多的援助。)

developing 是形容詞, 表『開發中的』。the developing world = developing countries, 指的是經濟剛要起步, 猶在貧窮掙扎的『落後國家』。如: Hunger and disease are very common in developing countries. (飢餓和疾病在開發中國家頗為常見。) the developed world = developed countries, 指的是經濟繁榮、工業發達的『先進國家』。

devotee

Mr. Miller is a devoter of jazz. (✗)

Mr. Miller is a devotee of jazz. (✔)

(米勒先生是一個爵士樂迷。)

英文並沒有 devoter 這個字。devotee 是指某物的『熱愛者』或某種宗教 (或其人物) 的『追隨者』。另外, fan 這個字也可指熱衷電影、音樂或運動(明星)的『迷』, 但不適用於宗教 (或其人物)。

diagnose

Molly was in her early twenties when she was diagnosed with diabetic. (✗)

Molly was in her early twenties when she was diagnosed as diabetic. (✔)

(莫莉被診斷患有糖尿病時才二十出頭。)

diagnose 這個字的用法有二: (1) be diagnosed with + 疾病 (名詞), 如: She was diagnosed with diabetes. (2) be diagnosed as + 疾病 (形容詞), 如: She was diagnosed as having diabetes/diabetic.

die

Never say death. (✗)

Never say die. (✔)

(千萬不要氣餒。)

Never say die.是固定用法。

The dice is cast. (✗)

The die is cast. (✔)

(勢在必行，不能挽回。)

dice是die (骰子) 的複數形式。一般玩『擲骰子』的遊戲都用若干個骰子, 所以要說throw/roll the dice。但是 The die is cast. 是一句固定的諺語 (按: 該句出自 Caesar 的名言)。

D

dieting

To stay slim and keep fit, you should change your dieting habits. (✗)

To stay slim and keep fit, you should change your dietary/ eating habits. (✔)

(為了身材纖細並保持健康，你們應該改變飲食習慣。)

dieting = going on a diet, 主要是作名詞用, 意為『節食』, 如: This article is about dieting. (這篇文章討論有關節食的問題。)『飲食習慣』的說法是 dietary/eating habits。

difference

There is no way we'll ever settle our difference. (✗)

There is no way we'll ever settle our differences. (✔)

(我們之間的岐見無法消弭。)

difference 作為『差異/不同』時兼有可/不可數名詞的用法, 如: It makes little difference whether he'll come. But if you are here, that will certainly make a difference. (他來與否無關緊要。不過你要是能來, 情況則大不相同。作為『岐見』解時恆用複數形的 differences。resolve/ settle your differences 為固定用法。)

difficulty

He had difficulties making himself understood. (✗)

He had difficulty making himself understood. (✔)

(他覺得很難把自己的意思說清楚。)

作為抽象的『困難/境』解時, difficulty 是不可數名詞, 如 get/run into difficulty 就是『陷入困境』之意。不過, 作為造成困難/擾的『障礙』解時, 則通常使用複數形的 difficulties, 如: learning/reading difficulties 即為『學習/閱讀方面的障礙』。

direction

Has the wind changed the direction? (✗)

Has the wind changed direction? (✔)

(風向改變了嗎?)

作為『方向』解時 direction 兼有可/不可數名詞的用法。然而表『改變方向』的固定說法是 change direction 而非 change a/ the direction。

I lost my way and had to ask for direction. (✗)

I lost my way and had to ask for directions. (✔)

(我迷路了，因此必須找人問路。)

表『問路 (詢問方向)』和『說明 (書)』時, 恆用複數形的 directions, 如: Please read the directions before use. (使用前請參閱說明書。)

disappointed

Last month's sales figures were very disappointed. (✗)

Last month's sales figures were very disappointing. (✔)
(上個月的銷售額真令人失望。)

disappointed 表『本身感到失望的』, 如: I was very disappointed at the result of the election. (我對選舉的結果非常失望的。) disappointing 是『令人失望的』。

disaster

The county was declared a disastrous area after the earthquake. (✗)
The county was declared a disaster area after the earthquake. (✔)
(地震過後該縣被宣佈為災區。)

disastrous 是形容詞, 意為『帶來災難的』, 如: Reckless driving would probably have disastrous consequences. (開車莽撞很可能會造成極為嚴重的後果。)『災區』的固定說法是 disaster area。

discipline

The teacher was unable to maintain disciplines in her class. (✗)
The teacher was unable to maintain discipline in her class. (✔)
(老師沒有辦法維持她班上的紀律。)

作為『紀律』解時, discipline 是不可數名詞。作為『訓練 (方式)』時兼有可/不可數之用法, 如: Yoga is a good discipline for learning to relax. (對於學習放鬆自己而言, 瑜珈不失為一種好的訓練。) 作為『學科』時 discipline 是可數名詞, 如: I'm interested in such traditional disciplines as history, literature, and philosophy. (我對歷史、文學和哲學這些傳統學科很有興趣。)

disclosure

A series of discoveries made by the media finally forced him to step down. (?)
A series of disclosures made by the media finally forced him to step down. (✔)
(媒體一再爆料終於迫使他下台。)

discovery 通常表達某種新事物/科技的『發現』, 如: Dr. Fleming's discovery of penicillian was a significant accomplishment. (佛萊明發現了盤尼西林是一項重大的成就。) 但是, disclosure 表『揭發祕密/隱私』。作為揭發的『行為』而言, disclosure 是不可數名詞, 如: They believe disclosure of other people's private lives is immoral. (他們認為揭發別人隱私的作法是不道德的。) 作為被揭發的『祕密』而言, disclosure 是可數名詞。

discount

I'll give you 15% discount. (✗)
I'll give you a 15% discount. (✔)
(我會給您八五折的優惠價。)

discount (折扣) 是可數名詞, 所以在使用這個字時必須以 a discount 或 discounts 出現。如: The shop is selling everything off at a special discount. (這家商店正在清倉大減價。) 又如: Airfare discounts are available during the off-season. (在淡季機票有折扣。)

discourage

The nasty weather discouraged people to go out. (✗)
The nasty weather

discouraged people from going out. (✔)
(惡劣的天候使人們打消外出的念頭。)

discourage sb from doing sth, 意為『使某人打消做某事的念頭』,是固定用法。但是 encourage sb + 不定詞, 如: We should encourage her to face reality. (我們應該鼓勵她面對現實。)

D

discreet

Nancy is very discrete in giving her opinions. (✗)
Nancy is very discreet in giving her opinions. (✔)
(南西發表意見時非常謹慎。)

discreet 和 discrete 兩字發音相同, 極易誤用。前者意為『分開的』相當於 separate 這個字, 如: The organization is made up of discrete units. (這個機構由幾個分別的單位組成。), 後者表『謹言慎行的』。

discriminate

As far as promotion is concerned, women are often discriminated. (✗)
As far as promotion is concerned, women are often discriminated against. (✔)
(就昇遷而言，婦女常遭岐視。)

discriminate against sb 表『岐視某人』之意, 為固定用法。

discuss

They are holding a meeting to discuss about the downsizing of their company. (✗)
They are holding a meeting to discuss the downsizing of their company. (✔)
(他們正在開會討論公司的瘦身計劃。)

『討論某事』應說 discuss sth 或 talk about sth。

disgrace

You've brought a disgrace on your family. (✗)
You've brought disgrace on your family. (✔)
(你已為家人帶來恥辱。)

作為『抽象名詞』時, disgrace 為不可數名詞。bring disgrace/dishonor on sb/sth 是固定用法。作為『普通名詞』時, disgrace 是可數名詞, 意指『帶來恥辱』的人/事物, 如: He is a disgrace to the teaching profession. (他是教育界的一個恥辱。)

disguise

Some soldiers disguised themselves to be civilians. (✗)
Some soldiers disguised themselves as civilians. (✔)
(有些士兵喬裝成平民。)

disguise oneself as sb/sth 或 be disguised as sb/sth 都表『喬裝成某人/物』。前者是動作, 後者表狀態。

The taxi driver turned out to be a police officer with disguise. (✗)
The taxi driver turned out to be a police officer in disguise. (✔)
(這名計程車司機結果是一名警員假扮的。)

in disguise 意為『假扮的』是固定用法。另外, a blessing in disguise 相當於『塞翁失馬焉知非福』的說法。

dish

The restaurant offers a three-dish lunch for $6.50. (✗)
The restaurant offers a three-course lunch for $6.50. (✓)
(這家餐廳提供一款三道菜的午餐，價格六點五美元。)

dish 除了指『盤碟』外亦可表『菜餚』, 如: My favorite dish is scrambled eggs. (我最喜歡的菜餚是炒蛋。) course 是指依序而上的一道菜, 如: The first course is a vegetarian dish. (第一道上的是素菜。)

Who's going to do the dish? (✗)
Who's going to do the dishes? (✓)
(誰來洗碗盤呢？)

do/wash the dishes (恆用複數) 是『洗碗盤』之意。

dislike

I dislike to be kept waiting. (✗)
I dislike being kept waiting. (✓)
I don't like being/to be kept waiting. (✓)
(我不喜歡等人家。)

like 可接『不定詞』或『動名詞』, 但 dislike 只能接『動名詞』。

disorder

Everything is a disorder. (✗)
Everything is in disorder. (✓)
(樣樣事物都雜亂無章。)

disorder 作『雜亂無章』解時是不可數名詞。作『疾病』或『身心障礙』時是可數名詞, 如: Anorexia is an eating disorder. (厭食症是一種飲食障礙。)

dispose

A rummage sale is a good way to handle unwanted goods. (✗)
A rummage sale is a good way to dispose of unwanted goods. (✓)
(舊物大拍賣是處理無用物品之好方法。)

handle sth 主要是處理問題或事件。dispose of sth = get rid of sth 是將某物『處理掉』, 即『丟棄』之意, 如: Medical waste should be disposed of carefully. (醫療廢棄物應該謹慎處理。)

distance

I can see a light flickering at a distance. (✗)
I can see a light flickering in the distance. (✓)
(我可以看到在遠處有一點燈光閃爍不定。)

at/from a distance 通常是指說話者 (刻意) 與某人/物保持一段相當距離, 如: I followed his car at/from a distance. (我尾隨著他的車, 保持一段距離。) in the distance 是指『在遠處』, 即距離你很遠的地方。

Keep that guy from a distance. (✗)
Keep that guy at a distance. (✓)
Keep your distance from that guy. (✓)
(跟那個傢伙保持距離。)

keep sb at a distance = keep one's distance from sb 意為『跟某人保持距離』, 是固定用法。

D

D

distinguish

The twins look so alike that I cannot distinguish from them. (✗)
The twins look so alike that I cannot distinguish between them. (✓)
The twins look so alike that I cannot distinguish one from the other. (✓)
(這一對雙胞胎如此相像，我無法分辨。)

distinguish between A and B = distinguish A from B 意為『分辨 AB 二者』。

distinguished

Mr. Wolf is a distinguishing general. (✗)
Mr. Wolf is a distinguished general. (✓)
(伍爾夫先生是一名傑出的將軍。)

distinguishing 和 distinguished 都是形容詞。然而前者只限於形容事物, 意為『與眾不同的』, 如: The distinguishing mark of the movie is its extensive use of montages. (這部電影與眾不同處在於廣泛使用蒙太奇的手法。) distinguished 意為『傑出的』, 兼指人和事物。

distort

Newspapers often contort facts. (✗)
Newspapers often distort facts. (✓)
(報紙經常會扭曲事實。)

contort 專指『扭曲』臉部或身體的其它部位, 如: His face was contorted with pain. (他的臉部表情因痛苦而扭曲。) distort 可兼指『扭曲』事實和表情等。

district

I drove around the business region, hoping to find a parking space. (✗)
I drove around the business district, hoping to find a parking space. (✓)
(我環繞著商業區開車，希望能找到停車位。)

region 通常指的是 (1) 一大片沒有分界的地區, 如 a border/coastal/desert/jungle region 就是一個邊境/沿岸/沙漠/叢林地區 (2) 身體或器官的部位, 如 the abdominal region 就是腹部位置。district 主要指的是『行政』或『特別規劃』的地區, 如: a voting district 是一個『選(舉)區』; a red-light district 是一個『風化區』。沒有把握用哪一個字時, 可用 area 這個籠統的字。

divided

Where is the divided line between opinion and fact? (✗)
Where is the dividing line between opinion and fact? (✓)
(意見和事實的分界線在哪？)

divided 意為『分裂/岐的』, 如: The committee is divided over the issue. (對於這個議題該委員會看法分岐。) the dividing line 是『分界線』的正確說法。

dividend

Good eating habits will pay dividend in the future. (✗)
Good eating habits will pay dividends in the future. (✓)
(良好的飲食習會在將來帶來好處。)

dividend 意為『股息』或『紅利』是可數名詞, 如: The company is expected to

declare a 10% dividend at the end of the year. (預期該公司於年底將宣佈百分之十的股息。) pay dividends (恆用複數) 引申為『帶來好處』之意。

divorce

I've heard that they are getting divorce. (✗)

I've heard that they are getting a divorce. (✔)

I've heard that they are getting divorced. (✔)

(我已聽說他們快離婚了。)

divorce 可作名詞和動詞。作名詞時兼有可/不可數用法。get a divorce 是可數的用法。不可數的用法如: Both of her marriages ended in divorce. (她的兩次婚姻皆以離婚收場。) divorced 是形容詞,『離婚』也可說 get divorced。

document

The filmmaker is making a document about life in a mangrove swamp. (✗)

The filmmaker is making a documentary about life in a mangrove swamp. (✔)

(這名導演正在製作一部有關紅樹林生態的記錄片。)

document 是『公文』或『相關文件』之意, 如: My assistant is arranging legal documents. (我的助理正在整理法律文件。) 至於 documentary 是指實地拍攝的真實『記錄片』。

doing

Do you know about their latest doing? (✗)

Do you know about their latest doings? (✔)

(你知道他們最近的所作所為嗎?)

指抽象的『作為』時, doing是不可數名詞, 如: It's all your doing! (這一切都是你做的, 該怪你!) 又如: It'll take some doing, I'm afraid. (恐怕這件事需費點工夫。) 指所做的『事情』時, 恆用複數形的 doings。

There's no doubt that it's a doing deal. (✗)

There's no doubt that it's a done deal. (✔)

(這件事已成定案不容置疑。)

done = finished = completed 作為形容詞, 表『已經完成』之意, 如: Are you done with the newspaper? (你報紙看完了嗎?) a done deal 表事情『已經定案, 不容改變』, 為固定用法。

doubt

When you are doubting, feel free to call me. (✗)

When you are in doubt, feel free to call me. (✔)

(有疑問時隨時打電話給我。)

『你有疑問時』的正確說法是 when/if (you are) in doubt。doubting 的用法僅見於 a doubting Thomas, 專指一個『狐疑不信』的人。

doubtless

You must admit it is a doubtless fact. (✗)

You must admit it is an undoubted fact. (✔)

(你必須承認這是一個毫無疑問的事實。)

The truth of the story is doubtless. (✗)

D

The truth of the story is beyond doubt. (✔)
(這個故事/說法的真實性是無庸置疑的。)

doubtless = without (a) doubt, 現今只作『副詞』用, 不作『形容詞』, 如: He will doubtless stage a comeback. (毫無疑問他將東山再起。) 形容詞的說法需用 undoubted 或 beyond doubt。

D

downstairs

I ran to downstairs to answer the telephone. (✗)
I ran downstairs to answer the telephone.
(我跑下樓去接電話。)

downstairs 和 upstairs 都是副詞, 所以 go/walk/run/be downstairs 或 upstairs 皆不可接任何介系詞, 如: The bathroom is upstairs. (洗手間在樓上。)

downtown

We live in downtown. (✗)
We live downtown. (✔)
(我們住在市中心。)

downtown 作副詞時不與介系詞連用, 如 go/live downtown。

drama

Her speciality is Elizabethan dramas. (✗)
Her speciality is Elizabethan drama. (✔)
(她的專長是伊利莎白時代的戲劇。)

drama 作為戲劇的『研究主題』時為不可數名詞。但作為電視或收音機的『劇本』時為可數名詞, 如: There will be a historical drama on TV tonight. (今晚電視有一齣歷史劇演出。)

draw

The little boy is painting a picture with chalk. (✗)
The little boy is drawing a picture with chalk. (✔)
(這個小男孩正在用粉筆畫圖。)

paint sth 是指用水彩或其它顏料來畫圖, 如: He enjoys painting in oils. (他喜歡作油畫。) draw sth 是指用鉛/鋼/粉/蠟/筆等來畫圖。

dream

I dreamed of you last night. (✗)
I dreamed about you last night. (✔)
(我昨晚夢見你。)

指『夢見某人/物』時, 用 dream about sb/sth 或 dream that..., 如: I dreamed about walking in a forest. (我夢見在一處森林中走路。) 指某人『夢寐以求』某事物時, 用 dream of/about sth, 如: My sister dreamed of becoming a famous lawyer. (我老妹夢想成為一位名律師。)

I've just met the girl of my dream. (✗)
I've just met the girl of my dreams. (✔)
(我剛遇見我的夢中情人。)

the boy/girl/car/dress of one's dreams (恆用複數), 是某人夢寐以求的人或事物。

dress

It took me only a few seconds to dress the suit. (✗)
It took me only a few seconds

to put on the suit. (✔)
(穿上那套西裝只花我幾秒鐘而已。)

穿上衣服的『動作』用 put on sth; 穿著衣服的『狀態』用 wear/have on sth。dress 作及物動詞時需以人 (主要是小孩或老/病人) 為受詞, 如: It won't take long to dress a baby. (幫嬰兒穿衣服不需花很多時間。)

dressed

There will be a dressed rehearsal tonight. (✗)
There will be a dress rehearsal tonight. (✔)
(今晚將有一場彩排。)

a dress rehearsal 即正式粉墨登場的『彩排』, 是固定用法。dressed 是形容詞, 表『穿著特別的』, 如: She was dressed to kill. (她穿得很性感。) 又如: He is all dressed up. (他穿得很正式。) 再如: They are neatly dressed. (他們穿得很整齊。)

After I took a shower, I began to dress myself. (✗)
After I took a shower, I began to get dressed. (✔)
(在我淋浴過後便開始著裝。)

指自己『穿上衣服』需說 get dressed。dress oneself 已不符現代習慣用法, 宜避免。

drink

They sat in a pavilion, drinking to the beauty of the landscape. (✗)
They sat in a pavilion, drinking in the beauty of the landscape. (✔)
(他們坐在一個涼亭裡欣賞大地風景之美。)

drink to sth/sb 是舉杯祝福某人健康/成功/幸福之意, 如: Let's drink to Cathy's happiness. (咱們舉杯祝凱西幸福美滿。) drink in sth 是『欣賞』風景或音樂之意。

drive

I wish I knew what you drove at. (✗)
I wish I knew what you were driving at. (✔)
(我真希望知道你在暗示些什麼。)

be driving at (恆用進行式) 表『暗示』之意。

The hotel is only a 15-minute driving from the airport. (✗)
The hotel is only a 15-minute drive from the airport. (✔)
(飯店離機場只需開車十五分鐘。)

driving 作為名詞時不可數, 指的是開車的『行為』, 如: Drunk driving is very dangerous. (酒醉駕車非常危險。) a drive 是一趟開車的『旅程』, 是可數的用法, 如: Let's go for a drive. (咱們去開車兜風吧。)

driver

His driver license has been revoked because of a hit-and-run accident. (✗)
His driver's/driving license has been revoked because of a hit-and-run accident. (✔)
(因為開車撞人後落跑，他的駕照已被吊銷。)

driver 是名詞, 意為『駕駛人』, 不能充當形容詞。『駕照』的正確說法為 a driver's license (美式用法) 或 a driving license (英式用法)。

D

drizzle

It's not raining hard, only dribbling. (✗)

It's not raining hard, only drizzling. (✓)

(雨並沒有下得很大，只是毛毛雨而已。)

dribble 指『流口水』, 如: The baby is dribbling. (嬰兒在流口水。) drizzle 是『(下)毛毛雨』, 兼有名詞和動詞的用法。

drop

A mountaineer dropped to his death this morning. (✗)

A mountaineer fell to his death this morning. (✓)

(今天早上有一名登山客摔死了。)

drop 表『掉落/下』時, 主要是用來說明『物』而非『人』, 如: The apples are beginning to drop from the tree. (蘋果一顆顆從樹上掉下來。) 失足的『掉落/跌倒』恆用 fall 這個字。另外, drop dead 表『猝死』而非『摔死』, 如: The famous actor dropped dead at the age of 31. (這位名演員於三十一歲時猝死。)

I'll pick you up and drop you out at the MRT station. (✗)

I'll pick you up and drop you (off) at the MRT station. (✓)

(我會開車去接你，然後在捷運站讓你下車。)

drop out (of sth) 是『退出(比賽/學業)』之意, 如: Tom sprained his knee and had to drop out. (湯姆膝蓋扭傷因而必須退出比賽。) drop sb (off) 是『讓某人在某地方下車』之意。

Use the eye drop three times a day. (✗)

Use the eye drops three times a day. (✓)

(眼藥水一天使用三次。)

作為名詞時 drop 可指水/雨滴等, 如 a rain/sweat/tear drop 就是一點『雨/汗/淚滴』。但作為『點用藥水』解時, 恆用複數形的 drops, 如 ear/eye/nose drops, 即是『耳/眼/鼻用藥水』。

drown

The boy fell overboard and was nearly drown. (✗)

The boy fell overboard and (was) nearly drowned. (✓)

The boy fell overboard and was drowning. (✓)

(這個男孩掉落船外，差點溺斃。)

drown 為原形動詞, 其過去式及過去分詞均為 drowned。這個字本身有及物和不及物的用法。drowing 也是形容詞, 表『快要溺斃的』。

drunk

That drunk man is talking nonsense again. (✗)

That drunk is talking nonsense again. (✓)

That drunken man is talking nonsense again. (✓)

(那名醉漢又在胡言亂語了。)

drunk 作為形容詞時通常充當補語用, 如 be/get drunk。擺在名詞之前直接修飾時要用 drunken, 不能用 drunk (極少數的例外如 drunk driving/driver)。另外, drunk 也可當名詞用, 意為『酒醉者』。

My husband has a drunk problem. (✗)
My husband has a drinking/drink problem. (✓)
(我老公有酗酒的問題。)

有酗酒的問題的英文說法是 a drinking problem (美式用法) 或 a drink problem (英式用法)。

dub

It is a French film translated into English. (✗)
It is a French film dubbed into English. (✓)
(這是一部配成英語發音的法語片。)

translate sth into sth 是『將某種語文譯成別種語文』, 如: The Bible has been translated into more than 100 languages. (聖經已被譯成一百多種語言。) be dubbed into sth 專指 (影片) 被配成以某種語言發音。

due

Your request will be dealt with in appropriate course. (✗)
Your request will be dealt with in due course. (✓)
(你的要求會在適當的時機處理。)

in due course = at the right/appropriate time, 即『在適當的時機』, 是固定用法。

dull

She felt so dull that she began to call friend after friend. (✗)
She felt so bored that she began to call friend after friend. (✓)
(她覺得非常無聊所以就開始一個接一個地打電話給朋友。)

dull 作『無聊/乏味的』解時, 主要是修飾事物, 如 a dull book/film/lecture。用來形容人時, dull (= slow to learn/understand) 意為『遲鈍的』, 如: As a teacher, she is devoted to her students, bright and dull alike. (作為老師, 她對學生可謂悉心付出, 不論優劣。)

durable

The product's main selling point is durable. (✗)
The product's main selling point is durability. (✓)
(這個產品的主要賣點是耐用。)

durable 是形容詞, 表『耐用的』。如: Plastic is a durable material. (塑膠是一種耐用的材質。) durability 是名詞, 表『耐用性』。我們可以說某種產品是『耐用的』, 但不能說其賣點是『耐用的』。換言之, 我們應該說某產品的賣點是『耐用性』。

duty

What time do you get off duty? (✗)
What time do you go off duty? (✓)
(你幾點下班?)

go on/off duty 意為『上/下班』, 主要適用於有『勤務』的軍警或護理人員。一般人員的上下班應該用 get to/off work, 如: I get to work at 8:00 a.m. and get off (work) at 5:30 p.m.. (我早上八點鐘上班, 下午五點半下班。)

duty-free

What do you usually do in your duty-free hours? (✗)

What do you usually do in your off-duty hours? (✔)

(你下班後通常做些什麼？)

---

duty-free 是『免稅的』，如: I bought two cartons of of cigarettes at a duty-free shop. (我在一家免稅店買了兩條煙。) off-duty hours 是『下班後的時間』。

D

Ee

each

Almost each house on the street is for sale. (✗)
Almost every house on the street is for sale. (✓)
(這條街上幾乎每一棟房子都要出售。)
Each of the members is not satisfied. (✗)
None of the members is/are satisfied. (✓)
(每一個會員都不滿意。)

英文並沒有 almost/nearly each 的說法，應該說 almost/nearly every。另外，each (of)...也不能和"not"連用，應該說 none (of)...或 neither (of)...。

We hope that you two will apologize to each others. (✗)
We hope that you two will apologize to each other. (✓)
(我們希望你們兩人彼此道歉。)

each other (彼此) 並沒有複數形。

ear

The man has the President's ears. (✗)
The man has the President's ear. (✓)
(總統對此人言聽計從。)

have sb's ear 或 have the ear of sb (恆用單數) 是指『博得某人的信任並使其言聽計從』，為固定用法。

As the political situation remains unstable, we'll have to play it by ears. (✗)
As the political situation remains unstable, we'll have to play it by ear. (✓)
(由於政情不穩，我們非得隨機應變不可。)

play sth by ear (恆用單數) 本指『不看樂譜即興演奏某種樂器』，亦可引申為『隨機應變』。

As soon as I mentioned her boyfriend, Amy was all ear. (✗)
As soon as I mentioned her boyfriend, Amy was all ears. (✓)
(我一提到她男友，阿美就很注意聽。)

be all ears/eyes 表『非常注意聽/看』，恆用複數。

earn

He earned a lot of money betting on horses. (✗)
He won a lot of money betting on horses. (✓)
(他賭馬賺了不少錢。)

earn money 定指雙手辛苦『掙來』的錢或投資事業『賺來』的錢。win money 是指投機或賭博『贏來』的錢。

earnings

I spent all my earning on that woman. (✗)
I spent all my earnings on that woman. (✓)
(我把所賺來的錢全都花在那女人身上。)

earnings (恆用複數) 指的是某人『所賺的錢』。恆用複數的類例還有 winnings/tidings/surroundings, 即『贏來的錢/消息/環境』。

earth

What on the earth are you talking

about? (✗)
What on earth are you talking about? (✔)
What in the world are you talking about? (✔)
(你究竟在說些什麼啊？)

on the earth (在世上) 是古典的用法, 現已罕用。目前流行的用法是 on earth (= in the world), 如: The Nile is the longest river on earth. (尼羅河是世界上最長的河流。) What/How/When/Why/Who on earth...? 是『強調』的用法, 表『究竟……?』。

earthy

I don't like his earthly humor. (✗)
I don't like his earthy humor. (✔)
(我不喜歡他那種粗鄙的幽默。)

earthly (塵世的) 是相對於 heavenly (天國的) 之形容詞, 如 earthly pleasures 即是『塵世的歡樂』。earthy 是『粗鄙的』或『喜開黃腔的』之意, 如 earthy language 就是『粗鄙/不堪入耳的語言』。

easily

These gadgets can be used easily. (✗)
These gadgets are easy to use. (✔)
(這些精巧的小玩意兒很容易使用。)

sth can be used easily 文法沒有錯, 但不合慣用。sth + be easy to use/make/read 才合乎慣用。

Some people are easy to get bored. (✗)
Some people get bored easily. (✔)
(有些人就是很容易感到無聊。)

get angry/bored/excited/nervous easily 表『很容易就感到生氣/無聊/興奮/緊張』, 是固定用法。至於用"easy"來表達『某人/物很容易 (被)……』的句型是 S + be easy to V (限及物)。如: Some people are easy to fool. (有些人很容易受騙。)

economic

It seems that our economical growth is slowing down. (✗)
It seems that our economic growth is slowing down. (✔)
(我們的經濟成長似乎緩慢下來了。)

economical 是『節約的』或『省錢的』, 如: My mother is always economical when it comes to buying clothes. (說到買衣服, 老媽總是捨不得花錢。) economic 是『經濟 (方面) 的』, 如: economic growth/policy/reform/system/theory 是指『經濟的成長/政策/改革/制度/理論』。

I think we'll buy economical class. (✗)
I think we'll buy economy class. (✔)
(我想我們會買經濟艙的座位。)

economy class 作為名詞時是指『經濟艙的座位』是固定用法。類例有 economy size/pack, 指的是大量購買價格便宜很多的『經濟包 (裝)』。另外, economy class 亦可當『副詞』使用, 如 fly/travel economy class 就是『搭乘經濟艙』之意。

education

They hope their children will receive good education. (✗)
They hope their children will receive a good education. (✔)
(他們希望孩子都能接受良好的教育。)

作為教育的『實施』而言, education 是不可數名詞, 如: It takes education to consolidate democracy. (落實民主政治需要依靠教育。) 但作為『某一階段』的教育, education 是可數名詞, 如 a college/university education。

effect

Any change in lifestyle will have effect on your health. (✗)

Any change in lifestyle will have an effect on your health. (✔)

(任何生活方式的改變將會對你的健康有影響。)

effect 作名詞意為『影響』時兼有可/不可數用法, 如: have an/some/little/no effect on sth 即表對某物有一種/某些/幾無/全無影響, 是固定用法。

The new law will take an effect as of July 1. (✗)

The new law will take effect as of July 1. (✔)

(這一條新法令從七月一日生效。)

take/come into effect 指法令等 (正式) 生效, 為固定用法。

The plot itself leaves a lot to be desired, but the special effect is amazing. (✗)

The plot itself leaves a lot to be desired, but the special effects are amazing. (✔)

(劇情本身乏善可陳，但是特殊聲光效果則咄咄逼人。)

作音響/燈光『特殊效果』解時, 恆用複數形的 effects。

effective

The new drug proves highly efficient. (✗)

The new drug proves highly effective. (✔)

(這種新藥證實非常有效。)

efficient 是『有效率的』, 專指某人/物工作成果極佳, 不會造成時間或金錢等之浪費, 如: She is an efficient secretary. (她是一名很有效率的祕書。) The diesel engine is very efficient. (這種柴油引擎非常有效率。) effective 是『有效果的』。

Aspirin is very effective to relieve headaches. (✗)

Aspirin is very effective in relieving headaches. (✔)

(阿司匹靈對緩和頭痛非常有效。)

be effective in doing sth 為固定用法。

effort

Writing a book requires a lot of physical and mental efforts. (✗)

Writing a book requires a lot of physical and mental effort. (✔)

(寫一本書極需付出心力和體力。)

effort 作『心/體力』解時是不可數名詞。但作為克服困難的『努力』時, effort 是『可數名詞』, 如: Efforts have been made to stop the spread of bird flu. (為了阻止禽流感的蔓延已經進行了多方的努力。)

egg

The NASA now has eggs on its face. (✗)

The NASA now has egg on its

face. (✔)
(美國太空總署這回臉上掛不住了。)

egg 作為『物質名詞 (即食材/物)』時為不可數名詞, 如: I usually have bacon and egg for breakfast. (我早餐通常吃培根蛋。) have/get egg on sb's face 本指某人被砸雞蛋因而臉上掛滿了雞蛋, 引申為『極為尷尬/難堪』之意。但若指一顆顆的雞蛋, egg 是可數名詞, 如: Don't put all your eggs in one basket. (不要孤注一擲/宜分散風險。)

either

"You won't compromise. Me, too." (✗)
"You won't compromise. Me, either." (✔)
(『你不妥協，我也是。』)

too 限用於對『肯定句』的附和, 如: I'm an amateur photographer and he is, too. (我是一個業餘的攝影師, 他也是。) 對於『否定句』的附和, 其簡略形式是 Me, either. (美式用法) 或 Me, neither. (英式用法)。

The latest opinion poll suggests that the election result could be either way. (✗)
The latest opinion poll suggests that the election result could go either way. (✔)
(最新的民意調查顯示選舉的結果兩種可能性都存在。)

could go either way 表『兩種可能性都存在』, 是固定用法。

electric

The electrical razor would make an excellent present for your father's birthday. (✗)
The electric razor would make an excellent present for your father's birthday. (✔)
(這個電鬍刀將是作為你父親生日的絕佳禮物。)
My son majors in electric engineering. (✗)
My son majors in electrical engineering. (✔)
(我兒子主修電機工程。)

electric 是『用/發/帶電的』, 如 an electric guitar (一把電吉他); an electric generator (一部發電機); an electric wire (一根電線)。electrical 表『與電力/學有關的』。

All the railroads are now electric. (✗)
All the railroads are now electrified. (✔)
(目前所有的鐵道都電氣化了。)

electrify 有兩個意思: (1) 使通電/電氣化, 如: Stay clear of the fence. It is electrified. (遠離那圍牆。它有通電。) (2) 使人極為興奮, 如: The new discovery has electrified archaeologists worldwide. (這項新發現使全球的考古學者都異常興奮。)

electronic

The electronic industry was booming during that time. (✗)
The electronics industry was booming during that time. (✔)
(在那段期間電子工業正蓬勃發展。)

electronic 是形容詞, 意為『電子的』, 即使用『電子零組件的』, 如 an electronic calculator/dictionary 就是一台電子計算機/字典。electronics 是名詞, 意為『電子學』, 如: John is an electronics engineer. (約翰是一名電子工程師。)

E

element

I had to brave elements to make it to the rendezvous. (✗)

I had to brave the elements to make it to the rendezvous. (✓)

(我必須冒著風雨趕到約定地點。)

element 是可數名詞，通常作『要素』或化學中的『元素』解，如: Integrity is an important element of Peter's success. (正直廉潔是彼德成功的一大要素。) the elements 是指『惡劣的天候』，為固定用法。

E

elevated

Beware of the dangers of elevating blood pressure. (✗)

Beware of the dangers of elevated blood pressure. (✓)

(要提防血壓升高的種種危險。)

elevating 和 elevated 都是形容詞，前者表『激發人心向上的』，如: Hearing his speech will be an elevating experience. (聆聽他的演講將是一個激發人心向上的經驗。) elevated 也是形容詞，表『升高的』(指溫度、血壓等) 或『高尚的』(指思想)。

elite

Your brother is an intellectual elite. (✗)

Your brother is a member of the intellectual elite. (✓)

(你的老哥可是知識界的精英之一。)

elite 是『精英分子』的集合名詞，代表一群人，如: The struggle for power within the political elite is very common. (政治精英之間的角力頗為常見。)『精英 (分子) 之一』應說 a member of the economic/intellectual/political/social elite。

elsewhere

Car prices in the U.K. are higher than any other place in Europe. (✗)

Car prices in the U.K. are higher than elsewhere in Europe. (✓)

(英國汽車價格要比歐洲其它地方來的高。)

英文的比較句型須遵守『對稱原則』。any other place 既不能與 car prices 對稱 (因前者是地方，後者是價格)，也無法與 in the U.K.相當 (因前者是名詞，後者作副詞)。唯有用 elsewhere (副詞) 或 in any other place 才能與 in the U.K.形成比較。

emergency

We've witnessed the company's emergency from bankruptcy. (✗)

We've witnessed the company's emergence from bankruptcy. (✓)

(我們目睹了這家公司擺脱破產，重新站起來。)

emergency 是『緊急狀況』，如: Dial this number in an emergency. (有緊急狀況時撥這個電話號碼。) emergence from sth 是『擺脱某種困境，重新走出來』之意。

The plane had to make an emergent landing. (✗)

The plane had to make an emergency landing. (✓)

(這架飛機必須作緊急迫降。)

emergent (= emerging) 是形容詞，意為『新興的』，如 an emergent nation/industry 就是一個『新興的國家/產業』。至於需要『緊急處理』或『應付緊急』的狀況一律用 emergency 來修飾, 如 emergency surgery/aid/meeting 即是『緊急手術/救援/會議』。

emphasize

We emphasize on the quality, not the quantity, of our products. (✗)

We emphasize the quality, not the quantity, of our products. (✓)

(我們強調的是產品的品質而非數量。)

emphasize 是及物動詞, 其後不需加"on", 但其名詞形式的 emphasis 則常與"on"連用, 如 place/put/lay emphasis on sth 就是『強調某物』之意。

employ

Troops have been employed in that area. (✗)

Troops have been deployed in that area. (✓)

(軍隊已經在那個地區布署完畢。)

employ 是『雇用』之意, 如: Michael is employed as a security guard. (麥可被雇用當安全警衛。) deploy 是『布署』軍隊/武器等。

enable

Technology has made us able to lead a more comfortable life. (✗)

Technology has enabled us to lead a more comfortable life. (✓)

(科技已使我們能過更為舒適的生活。)

enable sb to do sth = (1) make sb able to do sth, 意為『使某人有能力做某事』如: These tools will enable you to work more eficicently. (這些工具將可使你能夠工作得更有效率。) (2) make it possible for sb to do sth, 意為『使某人有可能做某事』。能否過一個更為舒適的生活無關『能力』。

enclose

A factory robot is simply a box with an arm enclosed. (✗)

A factory robot is simply a box with an arm attached. (✓)

(工廠用的機器人不過是一個裝上一根手臂的箱子。)

表『附上 (文件等)』時, attach 和 enclose 可以互通, 如: I attach/enclose a completed application form. (隨函附上本人已填寫完畢申請表格一份。) 表『裝/接上 (某物)』, 用 attach 這個字。

encroach

The police have encroached our rights there. (✗)

The police have encroached on our rights there. (✓)

(在那方面警方已經侵犯我們的人權。)

encroach on/upon sth 意指『侵犯/蝕』某物, 為固定用法, 如: The sea is constantly encroaching on the land. (大海不斷地侵蝕陸地。)

end

At the end, we decided to lay off a few more workers. (✗)

In the end, we decided to lay off a few more workers. (✓)

(最後，我們決定要多資遣幾名工人。)

in the end = finally = eventually, 主要是用來表達『最後之結果』。at the end需接of sth, 不能單獨使用, 表『在某件事情結束時』, 如: At the end of the meeting, everyone walked away displeased. (會議結束時大家不歡而散。)

At the end of that week, we had sold over 5000 copies. (✗)
By the end of that week, we had sold over 5000 copies. (✓)
(那個星期結束前我們已賣了五千多冊書。)

at the end of sth 是某事情/活動結束的『那一瞬間』。技術上不可能在那瞬間賣出五千多冊。by the end of sth 表從一開始到結束之前的『那段時間』。五千多冊書在那段間陸陸續續賣出, 這才合理。

The couple ended in divorce. (✗)
The couple ended up getting divorced. (✓)
(這一對夫妻最後以離婚收場。)

end in sth 恆以『事物』為主詞, 如: Their marriage ended in divorce. (他們的婚姻以離婚做收。) 而 end up doing sth 通常以『某人』為主詞, 如: Most dieters end up putting weight back on. (大部分的減肥者最後又胖回來了。)

ending

The novel has a happy end. (✗)
The novel has a happy ending. (✓)
(這部小說有個快樂的結局。)

小說、故事、電影的『結局』限用ending, 如 have a happy/perfect/surprise ending 就是有一個『快樂/完美/令人想像不到的結局』。end是指『結束』, 如: The movie is coming to an end. (這場電影快結束了。)

endure

I cannot endure the idea of having to wait two hours. (✗)
I cannot bear the idea of having to wait two hours. (✓)
(想到必須等兩個鐘頭我就無法忍受。)

endure sth 指的是『長期忍受某種痛苦(甚至毫無怨言)』, 如: It seems that the woman has endured domestic violence for quite a long time. (這名婦女似乎忍受家庭暴力很久了。) 至於要表達『無法接受某種情況』應說 cannot bear/stand sth。

energy

Scientists are trying to find more energies that are environmentally friendly. (✗)
Scientists are trying to find more energy sources that are environmentally friendly. (✓)
(科學家們正在努力尋找更多對環境無害的能源。)

各種形式的『能』, 如 electrical/nuclear/solar energy (電/核/太陽能) 均不可數。但指其『來源』或『資源』時是可數名詞, 如 energy sources/resources。另外, 指某個人的心力、體力時常用複數形的energies, 如: She devotes all her energies to teaching. (她盡心盡力為教學奉獻。)

engaged

Joy is engaged with Franky, isn't she? (✗)
Joy is engaged to Franky, isn't she? (✓)
(喬伊和法蘭基訂婚了，是不是？)

be engaged to sb 表『與某人訂婚』, 是固定用法。engage with sb/sth 表試著『去管管某人/事』, 如: As a career woman, she has no time and no energy to engage with her children. (作為一名職業婦女, 她沒有時間也沒有體力去管管她的孩子。) 另外, engage in sth 表『忙於 (從事) 某活動』之意。

Sorry, the line is engaging. (✗)
Sorry, the line is engaged. (✔)
Sorry, the line is busy. (✔)
(抱歉,忙線中。)

指『電話線忙碌打不進去』需用 engaged (英式用法) 或 busy (美式用法)。engaging 是『迷人的』之意, 如 an engaging smile/manner, 即指『迷人的微笑/風度』。

English

Emily is an American, but her husband is an English. (✗)
Emily is an American, but her husband is an Englishman. (✔)
Emily is American but her husband is English. (✔)
(艾蜜莉是美國人但她老公是英國人。)

English 作名詞時指的是『英文』, 且為不可數名詞。作形容詞時是『英國籍的』。『英國人』的說法是 an Englishman/Englishwoman。

enough

You are enough old to know better. (✗)
You are old enough to know better. (✔)
(你的年紀夠大,應該懂事了。)

作為『形容詞』時 enough 通常置於名詞之前, 如: I think I have enough money to live on. (我想我有足夠的錢過活。) 作為『副詞』時 enough 限置於被修飾的字之後, 如: You did not work hard enough. (在工作上你努力不夠。)

enter

The bullet entered into his brain, and he died. (✗)
The bullet entered his brain, and he died. (✔)
(子彈穿入他的腦部,接著他就死了。)

enter sth = go into sth 表『進/穿入』之意。enter into sth 意為『開始從事某活動』或『捲入某種情況』, 如: The government has entered into a genuine dialogue with the rebel forces. (該政府已經開始與叛軍展開實質的對話。) Leaders of the two parties are entering into ideological conflicts. (兩黨的黨魁正捲入一場意識型態的衝突。)

enterprise

Bill Gates is full of enterprises. (✗)
Bill Gates is full of enterprise. (✔)
(比爾蓋茲是個充滿企圖心的人。)

作『企業』解時, enterprise 是可數名詞, 如: It is a state/private enterprise. (這是一家國/民營企業。) 作為『企圖心』或『新思維』解時, enterprise 是不可數名詞。

entirely

The movie will be shown again entirely. (✗)
The movie will be shown again in its entirety. (✔)
(這部影片將完全不剪再放映一次。)

E

entirely (完全地) 主要的用法是結合否定副詞 "not" 或直接修飾某一形容詞, 如: I'm not entirely satified with their offers. (對於他們答應給的條件我不完全滿意。) 或如: We speak entirely different dialects. (我們講完全不同的方言。) in its/their entirety 意為『完整無缺地』。

entry

How did the burglar gain an entry? (✗)

How did the burglar gain entry? (✔)

(小偷是怎麼進來的？)

作為『進入』解時, entry 是不可數名詞, 如: They were denied entry into the country. (他們未能獲准進入該國。) 作為『條目』解時, entry 是可數名詞, 如: The dictionary has over 80000 entries. (這部字典收集了八萬多個條目。)

equal

The two countries are roughly equal of size. (✗)

The two countries are roughly equal in size. (✔)

The two contries are roughly of equal size. (✔)

(這兩個國家的面積大小差不多相當。)

be equal in size/length/height/quality = be of equal size/length/height/quality 指在『大小/長度/高度/品質』方面相等。

I'm sure your son is equal for the challenge. (✗)

I'm sure your son is equal to the challenge. (✔)

(我確信你兒子能夠應付這項挑戰。)

be equal to sth 是指某人的能力足以勝任/應付某事, 是固定用法。

In terms of intelligence, she is every bit his equality. (✗)

In terms of intelligence, she is every bit his equal. (✔)

(就智力而言她處處與他相當。)

equal 作為名詞時是指與某人實力或地位『相當的人』, 如: He treats all the employees as his equals. (他對待所有員工一律跟他平等。) equality 是『平等』的抽象名詞, 不可數。如 a campaign for racial equality 就是『主張種族平等的一項運動』。

Everybody is born equally. (✗)

Everybody is born equal. (✔)

(每個人都生而平等。)

就生物學的角度而言, 人不可能生下來大小、尺寸、重量甚至聰明才智都一樣。因此不能說 Everybody is born equally.就政治的理想或哲學的理論而言, 可以說 Everybody is born equal.因為這是指『地位』的平等。

equipment

We need to upgrade our office equipments. (✗)

We need to upgrade our office equipment. (✔)

(我們的辦公室設備需要升級了。)

A time clock is an important equipment we'll have to buy. (✗)

A time clock is an important piece of equipment we'll have to buy. (✔)

(打卡鐘是我們必須買的一件重要設備。)

equipment 是不可數名詞, 所以沒有 an equipment 或 equipments 的說法。如果一

定要數，需用 a piece/two pieces of equipment。

equivalent

Nodding your head is equal to saying yes. (✗)

Nodding your head is equivalent to saying yes. (✔)

(你點頭就等於說『是』。)

作為形容詞時 equal 和 equivalent 在『數量』、『大小』或『價值』方面有共通之處，如: A mile is equal/equivalent to 1760 yards. (一英里等於 1760 碼。) 但在『意義相等』方面需用 be equivalent to sth, 如: His silence is equivalent to admitting defeat. (他的沉默等於是承認挫敗。)

There is no English equal for this Chinese word. (✗)

There is no English equivalent for this Chinese word. (✔)

(這個中國字沒有相等的英文字。)

作為名詞時，equal 表實力相當的『對手』或『匹敵』。equivalent 可表『等義語』或『等值/量物』，如: You've lost the equivalent of 100 dollars by giving up the opportunity. (放棄這個機會你等於是損失了一百元。)

erase

She could not sweep her miserable childhood from her mind. (✗)

She could not erase her miserable childhood from her mind. (✔)

(她一直無法將童年的悲慘自心中掃除。)

sweep sth 表『打掃』地方之意，如: I want you to sweep the floor. (我要你去掃地。)

erase sth from sb's mind/memory 意為『將(尤指不愉快的)經歷/驗從心中或記憶中掃除』，是固定用法。

erupt

The Peloponnesian War erupted in 431 B.C. (✗)

The Peloponnesian War broke out in 431 B.C. (✔)

(伯羅奔尼撒戰爭於公元前四三一年爆發。)

erupt 通常指火山的『爆發』，如: An active volcano can erupt anytime. (活火山可能隨時會爆發。) 戰爭的『爆發』需用 break out 這個片語。

escape

Divorce is a reality that he cannot escape. (✗)

Divorce is a reality that he cannot escape from. (✔)

(離婚一直是他無法逃避的現實。)

escape from + (痛苦/危險的) 地方/遭遇，是固定用法，如: The war prisoner has tried to escape from the enemy's camp several times. (這名戰俘試圖逃離敵營已經好幾次了。) 另外，escape 也有及物動詞的用法，如: escape arrest/criticism/punishment, 即『沒有被逮捕/批評/處罰』。

especially

I'm not specially interested in politics. (✗)

I'm not especially interested in polities. (✔)

(我對政治並不特別感興趣。)

E

not especially = not particularly = not very 皆用來表『程度上』並不特別如何如何。至於 specially 大都用來表達『以特別的方式』或『為特定的目的』，如 The cheongsam is specially designed for your wedding. (這件旗袍是特別為你的婚禮設計的。)

Especially toddlers need a lot more attention. (✗)

Toddlers especially need a lot more attention. (✔)

(尤其是剛學會走路的小孩更需要多加照顧。)

especially 不可置於句首修飾主詞，限置於主詞之後。

essential

The book deals with the essential of Web page design. (✗)

The book deals with the essentials of Web page design. (✔)

(這本書講的是網頁設計的基礎知識。)

作為形容詞時，essential 表『基本的』或『精粹的』，如: The essential difference between us is that I never take life seriously. (我們兩人的基本差異在於我從不把人生看得太嚴肅。) 或如: Essential oils are extensively used in aromatherapy. (精油被廣泛使用於芳香療法中。) 作為『基礎知識』解時，恆用複數形的 essentials。

estimate

I can give you only a rough estimation of the cost. (✗)

I can give you only a rough estimate of the cost. (✔)

(至於需花費多少，我只能給你一個粗估。)

estimate 可兼作動詞及名詞，都是表『估計/算』之意。a rough estimate (粗略的估計) 是固定用法。至於 estimation 通常用來表達『意見』或『判斷』，如: In my estimation (= opinion), he is one too many for you. (依我看來，你根本不是他的對手。)

An estimate 20,000 people joined the demonstration. (✗)

An estimated 20,000 people joined the demonstration. (✔)

(估計有兩萬人參加了這個示威遊行。)

estimated 是形容詞，意為『被估算的』。an estimated + 數字是固定用法。

evaluate

Several investment proposals are being estimated by us. (✗)

Several investment proposals are being evaluated by us. (✔)

(目前有幾個投資案我們正評估當中。)

estimate 主要是以『數字』為主的估算，如: The total cost was estimated at $1,000,000. (總成本估計是一百萬美元。) 強調『價值』、『品質』或『可行性』等方面的評估，需用 evaluate/assess。

eventually

I'm glad to receive their reply eventually. (✗)

I'm glad to receive their reply at (long) last. (✔)

(我很高興終於接到他們的回音。)

eventually 這個副詞調的是『最後之結果』，如: If you do not team up, you will eventually lose. (你們如果不合作，最後的

E

結果就是慘敗。) at (long) last 通常是用在『期盼/等待很久』的事情上。這個『終於』有令人鬆一口氣的感覺，即我們平常說『最後總算如何如何』之意。

everyday

I tune in to the program everyday. (✗)
I tune in to the program every day. (✔)
(我每天收聽/看這個節目。)

everyday 是形容詞，意為『每日/日常的』，如: For many Americans watching TV is a part of everyday life. (對許多美國人而言，看電視是他們日常生活的一部分。) every day 是副詞片語。

everyone

Everyone of you will have to bring a small gift next time. (✗)
Every one of you will have to bring a small gift next time. (✔)
(你們每個人下次都要帶一份小禮物來。)

everyone (= everybody) 指『每一個人』，只能單獨使用不能接 of 引導的修飾語，如: You cannot please everyone. (你無法討好每一個人。) every one 可接 of 引導的修飾語，兼指人和物，如: I've read every one of her novels. (我讀過她的每一部小說。)

every time

Everytime Tony goes to a pub, he gets roaring drunk. (✗)
Every time Tony goes to a pub, he gets roaring drunk. (✔)
(東尼每次上酒館都喝得爛醉。)

everytime 並無此字。正確的說法是 every time。

everywhere

I like this small town. Every place is so quiet. (✗)
I like this small town. Everywhere is so quiet. (✔)
(我喜歡這個小鎮，到處都那麼安靜。)

every place 強調的是『所有的地方』，與 this small town (一個地方) 格格不入。everywhere 作為代名詞時是指某個(小)地方的『到處』。

evidence

There may not be enough evidences against him. (✗)
There may not be enough evidence against him. (✔)
(也許並沒有不利於他的足夠證據。)

evidence 為不可數名詞，沒有複數形。不過，我們可以說 a shred/piece of evidence，即『一點/項證據』。

She was summoned to appear in court to make evidence. (✗)
She was summoned to appear in court to give evidence. (✔)
(她被傳喚出庭作證。)

(被傳喚) 在法庭『作證』的正確說法是 give evidence。

exact

I can't remember the right date. (✗)
I can't remember the exact date. (✔)
(我記不得那個確切的日期。)

『確切的日期』應說 the exact/precise date。

example

You are supposed to make an example to your little brother. (✗)

You are supposed to set an example to your little brother. (✔)

(你應該為你的弟弟立下好榜樣。)

『為某人立下好榜樣』的正確說法是 set an example/a good example to sb。而 make an example of sb 是『懲罰某人以儆效尤』, 如: The teacher made an example of the student who cheated. (老師懲罰那名作弊的學生以儆效尤。)

except

Mom eats everything besides sashimi. (✗)

Mom eats everything except sashimi. (✔)

(除了生魚片以外，老媽什麼都吃。)

besides = in addition to 是包含進來的『除外』。except = not including 是不包含進來的『除外』。

exception

Most people enjoy being praised. I'm not an exception. (✗)

Most people enjoy being praised. I'm no exception. (✔)

(大多數人喜歡被人讚美。我不也例外。)

be no exception 是固定用法。

I never lent my car to anyone, but I'll take an exception for you. (✗)

I never lent my car to anyone, but I'll make an exception for you. (✔)

(我從不把車子借人，不過我可以為你破例一次。)

make an exception (for sb) 即『(為某人)破例』, 是固定用法。take exception to sth 表『對某事很反感』, 如: We all take exception to her snobbery. (我們對她的勢利眼都很反感。)

exchange

What is the rate of exchanges between the dollar and the euro? (✗)

What is the rate of exchange between the dollar and the euro? (✔)

(美元和歐元之間的兌換率如何？)

作『兌換 (外弊)』解時, exchange 為不可數名詞, 如: The country seems to have accumulated a lot of foreign exchange. (該國似乎累積了不少外匯。) 作為『交換/易/流』解時, exchange 通常是可數名詞, 如: They are conducting an exchange of war prisoners. (他們正在進行一次交換戰俘的行動。) 又如: Is it a fair exchange? (這筆交易公平嗎?) 再如: Because of the Net, cultural exchanges between nations are more common. (因為有網路, 國與國之間的文化交流日益頻繁。)

Fred was dripping wet, so he went home to exchange clothes. (✗)

Fred was dripping wet, so he went home to change clothes. (✔)

(弗瑞德全身都淋溼了，因此回家換衣服。)

『換衣服』的正確說法是 change (而非

exchange) clothes。exchange sth (for sth) 是『以物易物』或『退換』之意, 如: I'd like to exchange the pink dress for a yellow one. (我想把這件粉紅色洋裝拿去換一件黃顏色的。)

excluding

These prices are excluding sales tax. (✗)

These prices are exclusive of sales tax. (✔)

(這些價格均不含營業稅。)

excluding + n. (= n. + excluded) 表『不包含某物』是附帶説明的介系詞用法, 如: It will cost around 500 dollars, excluding shipping. (不含運費的話, 約需花費五百元。)

excuse

Excuse me. I didn't mean it. (✗)

I'm sorry. I didn't mean it. (✔)

(抱歉，我方才不是故意的。)

Excuse me 通常用於下列場合: (1) 當你要打斷別人説話時 (2) 當你打噴嚏或咳嗽時 (3) 當你要經過某人時 (4) 當你想跟一個陌生人講話時。因為做錯事或説錯話而向人道歉時, 你應該説 I'm sorry.才是。

exercise

The doctor urged me to get more exercises to stay healthy. (✗)

The doctor urged me to get more exercise to stay healthy. (✔)

(醫生一直勸我多運動以保持健康。)

指如走路、跑步或游泳的『體能運動時』, exercise 為不可數名詞。作為『練習』或『操練』時, exercise 是可數名詞, 如 They're doing gymnastic/military exercises. (他們正在做體操/軍事演練。)

Basketball is a popular exercise in the U.S. (✗)

Basketball is a popular sport in the U.S. (✔)

(籃球在美國是一種廣受歡迎的運動。)

exercise 是指體能方面的運動, 不可數。sport 是指有競賽活動的運動項目, 可數。

exhausted

This is by no means an exhausted list. (✗)

This is by no means an exhaustive list. (✔)

(這張表所列的絕非詳盡。)

exhausted 是形容詞, 表 (1) (人物) 疲憊不堪的, 如: He is both physically and mentally exhausted. (他心力交瘁。) (2) (物資) 耗用完的, 如: Our money supplies will soon be exhausted. (我們的財源很快就會耗盡。) exhaustive 是形容詞, 表『完全的』或『詳盡的』。

exhibit

Please don't touch the exhibitions. (✗)

Please don't touch the exhibits. (✔)

(展覽物品請勿觸碰。)

exhibition 是『展覽會』之意, 如: She will hold an exhibition of her paintings. (她將舉辦一次個人畫展。) exhibit 可當動詞或名詞用。當動詞時意為『展示/出』, 如: The latest fashions are exhibited in the

E

show window. (最新的時裝展示在櫥窗裡。) 作為名詞時, exhibit 兼有『展覽品』和『展覽會』(美式用法) 之意。

expectation

The four-star hotel did not live up to her expectation. (✗)

The four-star hotel did not live up to her expectations. (✔)

(這家四星級的飯店並沒有符合她的期望。)

come up to/live up to/meet sb's expectations (恆用複數) 表某人/物符合某人的期望。

The average life expectation in our country has been raised. (✗)

The average life expectancy in our country has been raised. (✔)

(我們國人的平均壽命已經提高了。)

life expectancy 意為某人/物的『壽命預期值』, 是固定用法。

expense

I'll publish the book at my (own) expenses. (✗)

I'll publish the book at my (own) expense. (✔)

(我要自掏腰包來出版這本書。)

at sb's expense (恆用單數) 表: (1) 自費 (2) 讓某人出糗, 如: They were making jokes at my expense. (他們說說笑笑就是要讓我出糗。)

You may rest assured that the company will pay all your expense. (✗)

You may rest assured that the company will pay all your expenses. (✔)

(你大可放心，公司會支付你一切費用。)

『差旅費』或其它可以報帳的『費用』一律用複數形的 expenses, 如: Let me pay the bill. I can put it on expenses. (讓我來付好了, 我可以報帳。)

experience

My sister has some experiences in graphic design. (✗)

My sister has some experience in graphic design. (✔)

(我老姊在圖案設計方面有些經驗。)

experience 若指知識/技巧方面的『經驗』是不可數名詞。若指特殊的『經歷 (即遭遇)』時則為可數名詞, 如: I had a strange experience the other day. (前幾天我有過一次不尋常的遭遇。)

experiment

The students are making an experiment. (✗)

The students are doing an experiment. (✔)

(學生們正在做實驗。)

『做實驗』的正確說法是 do/carry out/conduct/perform an/the experiment。

Some people believe it is worng to experiment with animals.(✗)

Some people believe it is wrong to experiment on animals. (✔)

(有些人認為用動物做實驗是不對的。)

experiment on + 人/動物 (即實驗的直接對

象)。experiment with + 物質 (即實驗所用的材料), 如: The doctor is experimenting with a new drug. (這名醫師正在實驗一種新藥。)

expertise

It takes a medical expertise to fight the serious epidemic. (✗)

It takes medical expertise to fight the serious epidemic. (✓)

(對抗這種嚴重的疫情需要醫學的專業知識。)

expertise (專業知識/技術) 是不可數名詞。

expire

Check the expire date on the bottle. (✗)

Check the expiration date on the bottle. (✓)

(查看一下瓶子上面的使用期限。)

expire 是動詞, 意為『期滿』或『過期』, 如: My passport expired two months ago. (我的護照兩個月前就過期了。) 『使用期限』的正確說法是 expiration date (美式用法) 或 expiry date (英式用法)。

explain

There seems to be a crisis of confidence in our company. It's time the boss tried to explain everybody's doubts. (✗)

There seems to be a crisis of confidence in our company. It's time the boss tried to explain away everybody's doubts. (✓)

(我們公司似乎已產生了信心危機。該是老闆出來澄清釋疑的時候了。)

explain sth 是針對某事/物作解釋或說明, 如: Please explain the meaning of the word to me. (請你跟我解釋這個字的意思。) explain away sth 是作解釋以消除誤解/疑慮等。

explosion

Police have found explosions hidden in the garage. (✗)

Police have found explosives hidden in the garage. (✓)

(警方已找到被藏在車庫裡的爆裂物。)

explosion 是爆炸 (事件), 不可能被藏在某地方。explosive 是『爆裂物』, 兼有可/不可數的用法。

export

Illegal immigrants risk being exported. (✗)

Illegal immigrants risk being deported. (✓)

(非法的移民皆冒著被驅逐出境之危險。)

export/import 專指貨物的『出口/進口』。將人物『驅逐出境』限用 deport。

exposure

Both candidates have got a lot of exposures in the media recently. (✗)

Both candidates have got a lot of exposure in the media recently. (✓)

(兩位候選人最近在媒體頻頻曝光。)

exposure 表『暴露』在某種危險之前/下時兼有可/不數的用法, 如: Avoid (a) long exposure to the sun. (避免暴露在太陽底下

E

過久。) 表在各種媒體的『曝光』, exposure 恆為不可數的名詞。

express

The package must be sent by expression. (✗)
The package must be sent by express. (✓)
(這個包裹必須寄快遞。)

基本上 express 有下列三種用法: (1) 作動詞意為『表達』, 如: I don't know how to express myself. (我不知道如何表達我的意思。) expression 是其名詞形式。(2) 作名詞意為『快車 (可數)』或『快遞 (不可數)』, 如: I took an express to London. (我搭一班快車到倫敦。) (3) 作形容詞意為『快速的』, 如 an express train/bus 就是『快速』火車/巴士。

E

extinct

It is an extinguished volcano. (✗)
It is an extinct volcano. (✓)
(這是一座死火山。)

extinguished 是指『用人為/工的方式』加以熄/撲滅, 如: The blaze was finally extinguished by the firemen. (這場大火終於被消防隊員熄滅了。) 已經熄滅的火山 (即死火山) 的正確說法是 an extinct volcano。

extreme

The senator never uses words that smell of racial or sexual discrimination. It is political correctness carried to extreme. (✗)
The senator never uses words that smell of racial or sexual discrimination. It is political correctness carried to extremes. (✓)
(這名參議員從不使用帶有種族或性別歧視的用語。這可以說是政治潔癖的極端形式。)

carry/take sth to extremes, 即將某事物帶至極端之境。另外 go to extremes 則表『走極端』, 皆恆用複數。

Bungee jumping is an extemist sport. (✗)
Bungee jumping is an extreme sport. (✓)
(高空彈跳是一種挑戰極限的運動。)

extremist 可作名詞或形容詞, 意為『政治立場極端的 (人)』, 如: My cousin is a right-wing extremist. (我表哥是一個極右派人士。)『挑戰極限』的運動應該說 an extreme sport。

F f

fabric

Ethnic conflicts pose a great threat to the fabrics of society. (✗)

Ethnic conflicts pose a great threat to the fabric of society. (✓)

(族群的衝突對整個社會的結構構成一大威脅。)

fabric 作為『布料』時兼有可/不可數的用法, 如: air-tight/durable/synthetic fabrics 即是指『不透氣的/耐用的/合成的布料』。作為『結構』解時, fabric 是不可數名詞。

face

Never show face around here again. (✗)

Never show your face around here again. (✓)

(你今後不要在這附近露臉了。)

show sb's face 指某人『露臉/出現』, 是固定用法。另外 lose/save face, 即『失去/挽回面子』也是固定用法, 如: I don't want to risk losing face by doing so. (我可不願冒著丟臉的危險去做這種事情。)

They remained optimistic on the face of defeat. (✗)

They remained optimistic in the face of defeat. (✓)

(雖然挫敗他們還是保持樂觀。)

in the face of sth = in spite of sth 表『雖然/儘管』。on the face of sth 意為『從表面上來看』, 如: On the face of it, the document seems genuine. (從表面上來看, 這份文件似乎是真的。)

Can you face to lose your son? (✗)

Can you face losing your son? (✓)

(你能面對失子之痛嗎?)

face doing sth 表『面臨/對某種不愉快的經驗』, 常用於否定句或疑問句。

facility

Each room has a private facility. (✗)

Each room has private facilities. (✓)

(每個房間都有私人的衛浴設備。)

一般的設備常用複數形的 facilities。特指『衛浴設備』時恆用複數形。至於單數的形式指的是『才能』, 如: She has a facility for languages. (她有語言方面的才能。)

fact

People must all grow old and die. That's a way of life. (✗)

People must all grow old and die. That's a fact of life. (✓)

(人人都會老死,這是一個無法逃避的事實。)

a way of life 是『一種生活方式』, 如: They have a different way of life from ours. (他們有不同於我們的生活方式。) a fact of life 是一個無法逃避/必須面對的『事實』。

Parents should be encouraged to prepare their older children for the fact of life. (✗)

Parents should be encouraged to prepare their older children for the facts of life. (✓)

(應該鼓勵為人父母者要為較大的子女灌輸有關性方面的知識。)

the facts of life 指的是『性知識』, 恆用複數。另一 (較幽默的) 說法是 the birds and the bees.。

Is this a fact or fiction? (✗)
Is this fact or fiction? (✔)
(這件事情究竟是事實抑或虛構？)

fact (事實) 兼有可/不可數的用法, 但 fact or fiction (事實或虛構) 為固定說法, 皆不可數。

factory

All the wheat will be sent to a flour factory. (✗)
All the wheat will be sent to a flour mill. (✔)
(所有的小麥將被送往一家麵粉工廠。)

factory 通常指的是生產成衣/傢具/玩具/運動器材等的工廠。mill 指的是麵粉/造紙廠。plant 指的是核電/兵工/化學/製藥廠。works 指的是生產水泥/磚塊/鋼筋等建材的工廠。

faculty

Both students and faculties oppose these measures. (✗)
Both students and faculty oppose these measures. (✔)
(全體學生和教職員都反對這些措施。)

作為『全體教職員』解時, faculty 是集合名詞, 不可數。作為身心方面的『能力』解時, faculty 是可數名詞且常用複數形, 如: The old man has not lost his mental faculties. (這個老人並未喪失心智能力。)

fail

I passed math but failed in English. (✗)
I passed math but failed English. (✔)
(我數學考及格但英文沒過。)

fail + 學科 (不搭配 in) 表某學科『不及格』。fail in sth 是指在某方面『失敗』, 如: Her father failed in business. (她父親經商失敗。)

failed

She made a failing attempt to escape. (✗)
She made a failed attempt to escape. (✔)
(她企圖逃走但失敗。)

作為形容詞時 failed 意謂『失敗的』, 如: Mr. White is a failed father. (懷特先生是一個失敗的父親。) failing 意為『衰退/體弱的』Her father retired because of his failing eyesight. (她父親因視力衰退而退休。)

failure

I'll be there on time without failure. (✗)
I'll be there on time without fail. (✔)
(我會準時到場絕不失誤。)
Nobody is perfect: everyone has some failures. (✗)
Nobody is perfect: everyone has some failings. (✔)
(人都不完美，大家都有點缺陷。)

作為名詞時 failing 是可數名詞, 意為『缺陷/點』。failure 兼有可/不可數的用法, 意為 (1)『失敗 (者)』, 如: As an actor, he is a failure. = He is a failed actor. (作為演員, 他是一個失敗者。) (2)『器官衰竭』, 如: She died from kidney failure. (她死於腎臟衰竭。)

F

fair

I hope all of you will play fairly. (✗)
I hope all of you will play fair. (✓)
(我希望你們大家要公平競爭。)

play fair 意為『公平競爭/比賽』, 是固定用法, 其中的 fair 是副詞。另一個固定的用法是 fair and square, 意為『誠實無欺地』, 如: Make sure every deal is made fair and square. (每筆交易務必要誠實無欺。) 其它情形可用 fairly 來表『公平地』, 如: You're not treating them fairly. (你並沒有公平對待他們。) 另外, fairly 亦可『相當地』, 如: You speak Japanese fairly well. (你日文講得相當好。)

F

faith

We've lost faiths in the government's promises. (✗)
We've lost faith in the government's promises. (✓)
(我們對政府所作的種種承諾已失信心。)

作『信心』解時 faith 是不可數名詞, 如: have/lose faith in sb/sth 就是『對某人/事有/沒有信心』。作『宗教信仰』解時, faith 兼有可/不可數用法, 如: People of different faiths will be invited. (屆時將邀請一些不同宗教信仰的人士。)

fall

Hopefully, there will be a fall of oil prices. (✗)
Hopefully, there will be a fall in oil prices. (✓)
(希望油價能夠下降。)

a fall in + (數量、價格等) 名詞, 如: There has been a fall in demand recently. (最近需求量在下降。) a fall of + (雨雪、樹葉等) 具體名詞, 如: There was a fall of snow last night. (昨晚有下雪。)

Luke had a heavy fall and broke his leg. (✗)
Luke had a bad fall and broke his leg. (✓)
(路可重重地跌了一跤, 腿斷了。)

a heavy fall 是用來說明下雨/雪, 如: It is expected that there will be a heavy fall of rain this afternoon. (預期今天下午將有一場豪雨。)『重重地跌了一跤』應該說 a bad/hard fall。

At that time we were swimming under the fall. (✗)
At that time we were swimming under the falls. (✓)
(當時我們正在一個瀑布下面游泳。)

the falls 或 a/the waterfall 是『瀑布』的正確說法。

false

Buying a secondhand car can sometimes be a fake economy. (✗)
Buying a secondhand car can sometimes be a false economy. (✓)
(買二手車有時反而更不划算。)

fake 和 false 意為『假造的』時有共通之處, 如 a fake/false passport 就是一本『假護照』。但 a false economy (意指本想省錢反而花更多錢之舉) 是固定用法。另一固定用法是 a false alarm, 即『虛驚一場』。

fame

That book has helped him make

international fame. (✗)
That book has helped him achieve international fame. (✓)
(那本書幫助他在國際上聲名大噪。)

『成/出名』的說法是achieve/gain/rise to/win fame。另外, shoot to fame 強調的是『很快就成名』。

family

Nowadays single-parent family is increasingly common. (✗)
Nowadays single-parent families are increasingly common. (✓)
(現今單親家庭愈來愈常見了。)

作『家庭』解時 family 是可數名詞, 如: Supporting a family of five on one salary is not easy. (單靠一份薪水來維持一家五口的生活可不容易。) 作『家/親人』解時, family 是集合名詞, 通常採單數形, 如: They spent a week visiting family in Tokyo. (他們花了一個星期到東京探親。)

famous

The famous drug lord has been arrested. (✗)
The notorious drug lord has been arrested. (✓)
(那個惡名昭彰的藥頭已經被捕。)

famous 指的是『好的方面有名』。反之 notorious指的是『惡名昭彰』或『聲名狼藉』。

fantasy

It is entirely normal for people to have sexual fantasy sometimes. (✗)
It is entirely normal for people to have sexual fantasies sometimes. (✓)
(人們偶有性幻想純屬正常。)

fantasy 作為『幻想的行為』時常用複數, 如: have erotic/romantic/sexual fantasies 表『有色情方面的/浪漫愛情的/性方面的幻想』。作為『幻境』時fantasy是不可數名詞, 如: It seems that Don Quixote cannot distinguish between reality and fantasy. (唐吉柯德似乎無法分辨實境與幻境。)

Her sick mother always lives in a fantastic world. (✗)
Her sick mother always lives in a fantasy world. (✓)
(她生病的母親一直生活在一個幻想的世界。)

a fantastic world 是一個『極為美妙的世界』如: The Disneyland is fantastic world for small children. (迪斯奈樂園對小朋友而言是一個美妙的世界。)。a fantasy world 才是一個『幻想的世界』之正確說法。

far

Los Angeles is far from New York. (✗)
Los Angeles is a long way from New York. (✓)
(洛杉磯離紐約很遠。)

表『距離』時 far 主要用於『疑問句』或『否定句』, 如: How far is it to the airport? (到機場有多遠?) 或如: It is not far from here. (離這兒不遠。) 於『肯定句』中需用 a long way, 如: It's a long way from here. (離這兒很遠。) 不過, 值得注意的是, too/so/as far 和 far away 可以用於『肯定句』, 如: Why not take a taxi? It's too far to walk. (為何不搭計程車呢? 這段路走起來太遠了。)

F

fashion

Women's fashion keeps changing all the time. (✗)
Women's fashions keep changing all the time. (✓)
(女人的時裝一直在改變。)

作『流行』解時fashion是不可數名詞, 如: Miniskirts are in/out of fashion. (迷你裙正在/不再流行。) 作『時裝』解時fashion是可數名詞且常用複數。

fat

You'll grow fat if you keep eating like this. (✗)
You'll get fat if you keep eating like this. (✓)
(照你這樣吃下去你會變胖的。)

變胖/更胖的習慣說法是 get fat 和 grow fatter。不過因為英美人士不太喜歡聽到 fat 這個字, 還是少用為妙。替代的禮貌性說法有: (1) overweight (稍嫌重些) (2) plump (豐滿) (3) chubby (胖嘟嘟, 指嬰兒) (4) put on weight (體重增加) (5) have a weight problem (有體重方面的問題)。另外, obese (過胖) 主要是醫學用語。

fault

You missed the flight, and it's all my mistake. (✗)
You missed the flight, and it's all my fault. (✓)
(你沒趕上班機，這一切都是我的錯。)

mistake 是指某人言行方面的『錯/失誤』, 如: You've made the same mistake again. (你又犯了同樣的錯誤。) fault 強調的是『過錯的責任』。error 兼有 mistake 和 fault 的用法, 是較正式的用語。另外, blunder 是『重大錯誤/疏失』, 如: The patient died because of a medical blunder. (那名病人死於重大醫療疏失。)

The fire must have been caused by an electrical mistake. (✗)
The fire must have been caused by an electrical fault. (✓)
(這個火災一定是電路故障所造成。)

mistake 大都指『人為的錯誤』。『機件的故障』需用 fault。另外 fault 亦可指某人性格上的『缺陷』, 如: Despite her faults, Mary is a good mother. (儘管性格上有些缺陷, 瑪麗是位好母親。)

favor

Tatoos found a favor with local youngsters several years ago. (✗)
Tatoos found favor with local youngsters several years ago. (✓)
(數年前本地的青少年開始喜歡刺青。)

作『幫忙/助』解時, favor 是可數名詞, 如: You owe me a favor. (這個忙你非幫我不可, 你欠我的。) 但作為『(被) 喜愛/支持』解時, favor 為不可數名詞, 如 find/gain/win favor (with sb) 就是受到 (某人的) 喜愛/支持。而 lose favor (with sb) 即不再被 (某人) 喜愛/支持, 如: Technology stocks have lost favor with most investors. (科技股已經不受多數投資人垂青了。)

favorite

My little daughter has a lot of toys, but these Barbie dolls are her favorite. (✗)
My little daughter has a lot of toys, but these Barbie dolls are her favorites. (✓)

F

(我小女兒有不少玩具，但是這些芭比娃娃才是她的最愛。)

favorite 兼有名詞和形容詞的用法。作為名詞時, favorite 是可數名詞, 意為『最喜歡的人或事物』, 如: Teachers ought not to play favorites. (老師不應有偏袒之舉。) = Teachers ought not to show favoritism. 作為形容詞時 favorite 意為『最喜歡的』美式用法可結合 most/least 連用, 但英式用法則否, 如: Milan Kundera is my (most) favorite author. (米蘭・康德拉是我最喜歡的作家。)

feature

The movie features Marlon Brando to be the Godfather. (✗)
The movie features Marlon Brando as the Godfather. (✓)
(這部電影主打馬龍白蘭度飾演教父一角。)

作為動詞時 feature sb/sth 表『以某人/物為主軸』, 如: The November issue features the rise and fall of the Roman Empire. (十一月份的雜誌以羅馬帝國興亡錄為主軸。) feature sb as sth 專指『影劇主打某人飾演某一角色』, 是固定用法。

feed

Japanese people feed on rice as a staple. (✗)
Japanese people live on rice as a staple. (✓)
(日本人依賴米飯為主食。)

feed on sth 主要是指動物『賴某種食物為生』, 如: Carnivores do not feed on grass. (肉食動物不吃草。) 指人『賴某種食物為生』需用 live on sth。

I'm fed with this boring job. (✗)
I'm fed up with this boring job. (✓)
(我無法忍受這種無聊的工作了。)

be fed up with sth 表『厭倦於某事/物』, 是固定用法。feed sb with sth 表『提供資訊/情報給某人』, 如: Someone keeps feeding the media with her private life. (有人一直將她的私生活爆料給媒體。)

feedback

We need more feedbacks from our consumers to keep business going. (✗)
We need more feedback from our consumers to keep business going. (✓)
(為了使營運不輟我們需要知道更多消費者的反應。)

feedback 是不可數名詞, 意為『反饋/應』, 指的是學生/讀者/消費者等的反應。

feel

I like the feeling of the fabric. (✗)
I like the feel of the fabric. (✓)
(我喜歡這塊布料摸起來的感覺。)

feeling 指的是 (1) 喜樂哀怒的『情緒』, 如: I had mixed feelings about meeting my first love again. (對於再度遇見我的初戀情人, 我的感覺真是五味雜陳。) (2) 某人的『看法』或『意見』, 如: My feeling is that we should offer more after-sales service. (我的看法是我們公司應該提供更多的售後服務。) (3) 某人身體內的『感覺』, 如: He suddenly had a feeling of nausea. (他突然有一種噁心想吐的感覺。) 指東西『摸起來的感覺』限用 the feel of sth。

F

feeling

Jill didn't want to hurt your feeling. (✗)
Jill didn't want to hurt your feelings. (✓)
(吉兒不想惹你不高興。)
My grandpa lost all the feelings in his right arm after he had a stroke. (✗)
My grandpa lost all the feeling in his right arm after he had a stroke. (✓)
(我爺爺中風後右手臂就完全失去了知覺。)

feeling 作為『情緒』時是可數名詞。hurt sb's feelings (恆用複數) 是固定用法。作為『知覺』時, feeling 是不可數名詞。

F

festivity

The wedding festivity included a cocktail party and an open-air concert. (✗)
The wedding festivities included a cocktail party and an open-air concert. (✓)
(這個結婚喜慶活動包含了一個雞尾酒會和一個露天音樂會。)

作為『歡樂氣氛』時 festivity 是不可數名詞, 如: There is an air of festivity in the banqueting hall. (宴會廳裡洋溢著一股歡樂氣氛。) 作為『慶祝活動』時, 恆用複數形的 festivities。

fetch

Every time I throw a stick in the air, my dog brings it. (✗)
Every time I throw a stick in the air, my dog fetches it. (✓)
(每次我把一根棍子丟向半空中，我的狗就會把它撿回來。)

bring sth 表『將某物帶來 (説話者地方)』。fetch sth = go and bring sth, 即『去把某物帶過來』。

The painting is expected to sell between two and three million dollars. (✗)
The painting is expected to fetch between two and three million dollars. (✓)
(這一幅畫預計可賣在兩三百萬元之間。)

fetch (a sum of money) 特別指某物在 (拍賣會) 賣出的價錢, 是固定説法。

fever

The island nation was in the grip of an election fever. (✗)
The island nation was in the grip of election fever. (✓)
(整個島國陷入選舉的狂熱中。)

fever 作『發燒』解時, 兼有可/不可數的用法, 如: Aspirin can reduce fever. (阿司匹靈可退燒。) 或如: The child is running a fever. (這個孩子正在發燒。) 但作『狂熱』解時 fever 是不可數名詞, 如: carnival/election/soccer fever 就是指嘉年華會/選舉/足球的狂熱。

fiber

Dried fruit like raisins is rich in fibers. (✗)
Dried fruit like raisins is rich in fiber. (✓)
(像葡萄乾這種乾燥水果有很豐富的纖維素。)

表『纖維素』時, fiber 是不可數名詞。表

『衣料 (纖維)』時, fiber 兼有可/不可數的用法, 如: I prefer to wear natural fibers. (我比較喜歡穿天然材質的衣料。)

fight

The boy is fighting against his older brother again. (✗)

The boy is fighting (with) his older brother again. (✔)

(這個男孩又再跟他哥哥打架了。)

fight against sb/sth 通常是指必須『長期對抗』的狀況, 如『貧窮/疾病/壓迫等』, 如: All his life he has been fighting against poverty. (他的一生都在跟貧窮搏鬥)。一般的『打架』用 fight (with) sb 即可。

He had to fight with three other candidates for the position. (✗)

He had to fight three other candidates for the position. (✔)

(他必須跟另外三個人選角逐這個職位。)

fight sb for sth 表『與某人角逐/競爭某物』, 是固定用法。

figure

Next year's sales figure will definitely exceed this year's. (✗)

Next year's sales figures will definitely exceed this year's. (✔)

(明年的銷售額一定會超越今年。)

figure 作『數字/據』解時常用複數形式, 如: sales/trade/employment figures, 即『銷售/貿易/失業數字』, 是固定用法。另外, figure 還有兩個重要的意思: (1) 人物, 如: She is a key/leading figure in the literary circles. (她在文壇算是一位重要/執牛耳的人物。) (2) 身材, 如: No sugar, please. I have to watch my figure. (請不要放糖。我必須注意身材。)

fill

Make yourself at home and eat your full. (✗)

Make yourself at home and eat your fill. (✔)

(不要拘束, 儘情地吃。)

full 是形容詞, 意為『滿滿的』, 不能置於 your/my/his 之後。不過我們可以換個方式說, 如: I usually eat until I'm full. (我通常吃到吃不下為止。) fill 作為名詞時意為『滿量』, 如: Drink/Weep your fill. (儘情地喝/哭吧。)

final

The fireworks will be the grand final of the celebrations. (✗)

The fireworks will be the grand finale of the celebrations. (✔)

(施放煙火將為這一系列的慶祝活動畫下完美句點。)

作為名詞的 final 有兩個意思: (1) 期末考, 如: I'm busy preparing for the finals. (我正忙著準備期末各科考試。) (2) 決賽, 如: I do hope we can make it all the way to the final. (我真希望我們可以一路打到最後一場決賽。) finale 專指音樂會或其它表演活動的『終場』。

finance

Is the company's finance sound? (✗)

Are the company's finances sound? (✔)

(這家公司的財務健全嗎？)

作『財政』或『理財』解時, finance 是不可數名詞, 如: She is an expert in finance. (她是理財高手。) 不過, 作『資金/財務狀況』解時, 恆用複數形的 finances。

find

The rare curio is a real finding. (✗)

The rare curio is a real find. (✓)

(這件珍奇的古董真是得來不易。)

findings (恆用複數) 主要是指官方的『調查結果』, 如: They'll publish their findings soon. (他們即將公佈他們的調查結果。) a real/big/great find 是指『得來不易的人或物』。

fine

There is only a slender line between thrift and miserliness. (✗)

There is only a fine/thin line between thrift and miserliness. (✓)

(節儉與吝嗇只有一線之隔。)

表『細薄的』一般可用 thin 或 fine, 如: After we came back home from vacation, everything was covered with a fine/thin layer of dust. (我們度假回來之後, 家裡的一切東西都蒙上一層薄薄的灰塵。) 至於 slender 通常用來形容某人身材『細瘦好看』, 如: Though in her forties, she still has a slender figure. (雖然年過四十，她仍有苗條的身材)。

Let him off with fine. (✗)

Let him off with a fine. (✓)

(讓他罰款了事。)

作名詞時 fine 表『罰款』, 是可數名詞, 如: I'm afraid you'll have to pay heavy fines. (恐怕你得繳幾筆很重的罰金。)

Illegal parking must be fined. (✗)

Illegal parking is subject to a fine. (✓)

(非法停車必須科以罰金。)

fine 作為動詞時, 對象是『某人』而非『某事』如: Ted was fined for speeding. (泰德因超速而被罰款。) be subject to sth 是『(必須) 受某物所規範』。

fingerprint

The suspect will have to undergo DNA fingerprints.(✗)

The suspect will have to undergo DNA fingerprinting. (✓)

(對於這名嫌犯將進行 DNA 比對。)

fingerprint 是『指紋』, 為可數名詞, 如: The murderer's fingerprints are all over the knife. (這把刀子上面滿是凶手的指紋。) fingerprinting 是指採取某人的指紋以作比對。DNA fingerprinting 是引申的用法。另外還有兩個說法是 DNA profiling/testing, 都指警方對某人所作的 DNA 比對。不過 DNA testing 可兼指為證實有無血緣關係所作的 DNA 測試。

finish

I won't buy your story. It is a lie from starting to finishing. (✗)

I won't buy your story. It is a lie from start to finish. (✓)

(我不會相信你的說法，從頭至尾都是謊話。)

finish 可作名詞用, 意為『結束』。from start to finish 為固定用法。

F

The essay lacks the finish touches. (✗)
The essay lacks the finishing touches. (✓)
(這篇文章就差最後之潤色。)

the finishing touch/touches 指的是作品等『最後的潤色/飾』工作, 為固定用法。

first

At first, I'd like all of you to take a look at this chart. (✗)
First of all, I'd like all of you to take a look at this chart. (✓)
(首先，我要大家看一下這張圖表。)

at first 表『起初』, 常用來暗示後來的變化, 如: At first I didn't like him, but we became good friends later. (起初我並不喜歡他, 可是後來我們成了好友。) 至於 first/firstly/first of all 則專用於介紹一系列事項的第一項。

If you didn't like her, why did you date her first of all? (✗)
If you didn't like her, why did you date her in the first place? (✓)
(如果你不喜歡她，為何一開始就約她出來呢？)

用來列舉理由事項時, first of all 和 in the first place 有共通之處, 如: There are several reasons we should not keep any pets. First of all/In the first place, we do not have enough room. (我們不應該養任何寵物有幾項理由。首先, 我們沒有足夠的空間。) 但指事情的『一開始』應該用 in the first place。

You must have started early because you came here first. (✗)
You must have started early because you were the first to come here. (✓)
(因為你第一個到，你一定很早就出發。)

do sth first 是『先做某事 (再做其它的)』之意, 如: I'll go to the bank first. (我先去銀行。) 至於『第一個做某事』的正確說法是 the first to do sth。

fit

Dark colors fit her best. (✗)
Dark colors suit her best. (✓)
(深色的系列最適合她。)

fit sb 是指『衣物大小適合某人 (尺寸)』, 如: This dress fits you like a glove. (這件洋裝簡直是為妳量身訂做的。) suit sb 是指『衣物適合某人的造型/身分』, 使其穿戴起來更為出色或得體。

It is a new workplace, but I'm sure I can fit pretty soon. (✗)
It is a new workplace, but I'm sure I can fit in pretty soon. (✓)
(這是一個新的工作地方，不過我相信我很快就能融入。)

fit in (with sb/sth) 意為『適應/融入 (某團體或工作)』, 如: Can you fit in with your new colleagues? (你能適應你的新同事嗎?)

fitness

You may try it on in the fitness room. (✗)
You may try it on in the fitting room. (✓)
(你可以在試衣間試穿一下。)

fitness 通常指的是『健身』, 如: a fitness center 就是一個『健身/減肥中心』。『試衣間』的正確說法是 a/the fitting/dressing room。

F

flat

All his jokes fell flatly. (✗)

All his jokes fell flat. (✔)

(他講的笑話都沒有收到預期之效果。)

flatly是『以一種堅定的態度』或『斷然』之意, 如: She flatly refused their bribes. (她斷然拒絕他們的賄賂。) fall flat 是指笑話/故事/演出等『沒有收到預期之效果』, 為固定用法。

flavor

Our herbal teas contain no artificial flavors. (✗)

Our herbal teas contain no artificial flavorings. (✔)

(我們的花果茶系列絕不添加人工香料。)

flavor 指的是食物或飲料特有的『味道』, 如: The drink has a strong ginger flavor. (這種飲料有一股濃郁的薑味。) flavoring 指的是『香料添加物』。

flesh

I was overjoyed to see the President in the flash. (✗)

I was overjoyed to see the President in the flesh. (✔)

(見到總統本人令我樂不可支。)

英文並沒有 in the flash 這個說法, 不過倒是有 in a flash 表『在一瞬間/很快地』, 如: It will be done in a flash. (這件工作將很快做完。) in the flesh = in person, 意為『本人』, 是固定用法。

Brave as the hero is, he is only blood and flesh. (✗)

Brave as the hero is, he is only flesh and blood. (✔)

(這名英雄雖然勇敢，也不過是血肉之軀罷了。)

flesh and blood 是固定用法順序不能更動, 除了表『血肉之軀 (即平凡人)』之外, 亦可表『骨肉/親人』, 如: Your daughter is your flesh and blood. How can you treat her like that ? (你的女兒是你的骨肉。你怎能如此待她?)

floor

When Dad came in, we were sitting on the ground watching TV. (✗)

When Dad came in, we were sitting on the floor watching TV. (✔)

(當老爸進門時，我們正坐在地板上看電視。)

ground 是室外的地面, floor 是室內的地板。

flu

The child came down with a flu last week. (✗)

The child came down with (the) flu last week. (✔)

(這個孩子上個星期罹患了流感。)

『流感』的說法為 flu 或 the flu, 是不可數名詞。

following

The desk can be assembled as following. (✗)

The desk can be assembled as follows. (✔)

(這張桌子可以組合方式如下。)

『如下』的說法是 as follows 或 in the

following way。

The political leader has a lot of followings. (✗)
The political leader has a lot of followers. (✔)
The political leader has a large following. (✔)
(這名政治領袖有很多追隨者。)

following 是集合名詞, 指的就是一群『追隨者』。

food

I don't like Japanese foods. (✗)
I don't like Japanese food. (✔)
(我不喜歡日本料理。)

food 的一般用法是不可數名詞。不過, 指特殊的食物時可用複數形, 如 baby/health foods 即是『嬰兒/健康食品』。

Your advice has given us food of thought. (✗)
Your advice has given us food for thought. (✔)
(你的勸告值得令我們深思。)

food for thought 意為『令人深思的事物』, 是固定用法。

fool

I was fool to believe her. (✗)
I was a fool to believe her. (✔)
I was fool enough to believe her. (✔)
(我真傻居然相信她。)

fool 意為『傻瓜/笨蛋』, 是可數名詞。be fool enough to do sth (不加冠詞) 表『笨到居然做出某事』是固定用法。

forbidden

Forbidding fruit is always more attractive. (✗)
Forbidden fruit is always more attractive. (✔)
(被禁止的事物總是具誘惑力。)

forbidden fruit 本指『禁果』, 是上帝禁止亞當和夏娃採食的『知識之果』, 後引申為被禁止的事物, 乃固定用法。

force

We must not ignore Japan's economic force. (✗)
We must not ignore Japan's economic power. (✔)
(我們絕不能忽視日本的經濟力量。)

作為『力量』時 force 通常指個人的『氣力』或大自然的『力量』或『武力』如: The army took over the region by force. (這支軍隊以武力接管了該地區)。power 指的是『影響力』。

forget

Oh, no, I must have forgotten my keys in the car. (✗)
Oh, no, I must have left my keys in the car. (✔)
(糟了，我一定是把鑰匙留在車上。)

forget sth 可表『忘了拿/帶某物』, 但不與地方副詞 (片語) 連用, 如: I've forgotten my umbrella! (我忘了拿傘!)。提到地方時要用 leave, 如: She left her purse at home. (她把錢包留在家裡, 沒帶出來。)

F

formality

We had to go through a lot of formality then. (✗)

We had to go through a lot of formalities then. (✓)

(當時我們必須辦理一大堆手續。)

作為『手續』解時，幾乎都用複數形的 formalities。作為『形式』解時多用單數形，如: The interview is just a formality. (這個面試只不過是一種形式而已。)

forthcoming

The Presidential election is forthcoming. (✗)

The Presidential election is at hand. (✓)

(總統大選快到了。)

作為形容詞表『即將到來/發生』時，forthcoming 限置於名詞之前，如: Here is a list of forthcoming books. (這裡有一張即將到來書籍的書單。) 置於 be 動詞之後要用 at hand/around the corner。另外，oncoming 表車輛等『迎面而來的』，如: She crashed into an oncoming car. (她的車撞上一部迎面而來的汽車。) incoming 表『(正要) 進來的』，如: We tape all incoming calls. (所有打進來的電話我們都有錄音。)

Joshua is a very forthcoming person when you need any information. (✗)

Joshua is very forthcoming when you need any information. (✓)

(當你需要任何資訊時，賈許很樂於助人。)

作為『樂於助人的』解時，forthcoming 不可直接置於名詞之前，只能接在 be 動詞之後作『補語』。接在名詞之前可以用 helpful，如: She is a very helpful colleague. (她是一個非常樂於助人的同事。)

fortune

Many people here believe jade will bring a good fortune. (✗)

Many people here believe jade will bring good fortune. (✓)

(此地很多人相信玉會帶來好運。)

fortune 作為『命運/運氣』解時是不可數名詞，如: Fortune seems to be smiling on you this time. (你這次似乎得到命運之神的眷顧。) 作為『財富』解時，fortune 是可數名詞但通常用單數形式，如: The pearl necklace must have cost you a small fortune. (這一串珍珠項鍊一定花你不少銀子吧。)

foundation

The new discovery has shaken the foundation of traditional beliefs. (✗)

The new discovery has shaken the foundations of traditional beliefs. (✓)

(這一項新發現已經動搖了傳統看法之根基。)

foundation 作為『創立/建』解時是不可數名詞，如: The foundation of the military academy began in 1900. (這所軍事學府的創建始於一九〇〇年。) 表『根基/本』時，恆用複數形的 foundations，如: shake/rock the foundations of sth 意為『動搖某物的根基』，是固定用法。

frame

When it comes to buying sunglasses, I prefer a plastic frame. (✗)

When it comes to buying sunglasses, I prefer plastic

frames. (✔)
(說到買太陽眼鏡，我喜歡塑膠框架的。)

作為門/窗/圖畫等的具體『框架』時, frame 是可數名詞, 兼有單/複數用法, 如: The window has a frame made of aluminum. (這個窗戶的框架是鋁製的。) 指眼鏡的『框架』時恆用複數形的 frames。

Progress must be made within the existing frame of democracy.(✗)
Progress must be made within the existing framework of democracy. (✔)
(必須在現有的民主架構上追求進步。)

抽象的『框架/架構』, 用 framework, 如 social/political framework 即是『社會/政治的架構』。另外, framework 亦有具體的『架/結構』之意, 主要用來說明建築物或交通工具, 如: This building has a metal framework. (這棟大樓採金屬結構。)

free

Please make free to contact us at any time. (✗)
Please feel free to contact us at any time. (✔)
(任何時候都可以跟我們連繫，不要客氣。)

feel free to do sth (= don't hesitate to do sth) 是口語的用法, 用在請某人做某事時『不要客氣/猶豫』。make free with sth 是『擅自取用某人之物』的意思, 如: He used to make free with his girlfriend's money. (他過去時常擅自取用女友的錢。)

freezing

It's frozen cold outside! (✗)
It's freezing cold outside! (✔)
(外頭冷得令人受不了。)

frozen 是『結冰/冷凍的』, 如: frozen food 就是『冷凍食品』。『冷得令人受不了』的說法是 freezing/biting cold。

front

I prefer to sit in front of the car. (✗)
I prefer to sit in the front of the car. (✔)
(我比較喜歡坐在車子的前座。)

in front of sth 是在某物之前 (可以面向它) 的位置, 如: Her husband sat in front of the television all day. (她老公整天坐在電視機前。) at/in the front of sth 是『在一個範圍內的前面』, 如: I sit at the front of the class. (我在班上坐最前面的位置。)

fruit

You should eat plenty of fresh fruits and vegetables. (✗)
You should eat plenty of fresh fruit and vegetables. (✔)
(你應該多吃些新鮮的果蔬。)

fruit 作為『水果』籠統的指稱時是不可數名詞, 如: She has a piece of fruit at every meal. (她每餐都吃一個水果。) 指『水果種類』時 fruit 為可數名詞, 如: Do they sell tropical fruits like bananas and pineapples? (他們有賣香蕉、鳳梨這類熱帶水果嗎?)

I'm sure your efforts will bear fruits. (✗)
I'm sure your efforts will bear fruit. (✔)
(我相信你的努力一定會開花結果。)

bear fruit 是指某事/物有良好的結果, 為固定用法。另外 the fruits of sth (恆用複數) 也是固定的用法, 如: It's time to enjoy the fruits of victory. (該是享受勝利成果的時

F

候了。)

full

The theater is full of capacity. (✗)

The theater is full to capacity. (✔)

(這家戲院座無虛席。)

be full of sth/sb 意為充滿某物/人, 如: The playground is full of kids. (遊戲場上滿是小朋友。) be full to capacity 指的是『塞/爆滿』, 是固定用法。

All the flights to Athens have been booked in full. (✗)

All the flights to Athens have been fully booked. (✔)

(飛往雅典的所有班次都已被訂一空。)

be fully booked 是指機位或餐廳等『被訂一空』, 為固定用法。in full 是『全額/如數』之意, 如: Your deposit will be refunded in full. (你的押金將如數退還。)

fun

The field trip is not very fun. (✗)

The field trip is not much fun. (✔)

(這趟實地考察旅行並不好玩。)

這個 fun 是名詞, 不能用 very 修飾, 需用 much 或 a lot of 修飾。作為形容詞時 fun 限置於名詞之前修飾, 如: a fun person/city (一個有趣的人/好玩的城市)。

funny

It was a great party and everybody had a funny time. (✗)

It was a great party and everybody had fun/a good time. (✔)

(這個派對很棒，大家都玩得很開心。)

funny 是形容詞, 意為『好笑的』或『奇怪的』, 如: He told a funny story. (他講了一則很好笑的故事。) 或如: The soup tastes funny. (這道湯味道挺怪的。)『玩得很開心』應該說 have fun/a good time。

fur

These kittens don't have many furs yet. (✗)

These kittens don't have much fur yet. (✔)

(這幾隻小貓毛還沒長齊。)

作為動物身上的『毛皮』解時, fur 是不可數名詞。但作為『毛皮大衣』解時, 則為可數名詞, 如: She is wearing an expensive fur. (她身穿一件昂貴的皮草。)

further

Family Mart plans a farther 50 stores in Taipei. (✗)

Family Mart plans a further 50 stores in Taipei. (✔)

(全家便利商店計劃在台北地區另外再開五十家。)

作為『更遠』解時, farther 與 further 可以通用, 如: Now we are living farther/further away from the city center. (我們現在居住在更遠離市中心的地方。) 但作為『更進一步』或『另/額外的』解時, 限用 further, 如: The patient's health may worsen still further. (這名病人的健康情況可能會更進一步惡化。)

future

To put all your money in the future market would be too risky. (✗)

To put all your money in the futures market would be too risky. (✓)

(你要是把所有的錢投進期貨市場，這未免太冒險了吧。)

指『期貨』時限用複數形的 futures。另外, 表『在將來』, 限用 future, 如: I hope I can become a billionaire in the future. (我希望我將來能夠成為一個億萬富翁。) 表『從今以後』, 可用 in (the) future, 如: In future, ask before you borrow my books. (從今以後要跟我借書, 請你先打招呼一下。)

F

A Quick Note

Gg

gain

I've got a lot of weight these two months. (✗)

I've gained a lot of weight these two months. (✔)

(這兩個月以來我胖了不少。)

gain/put on weight 意為『長胖』, 是固定用法。

That politician is only seeking personal gains. (✗)

That politician is only seeking personal gain. (✔)

(那名政客只是在尋求個人利益而已。)

作為名詞表『利益(尤指金錢)』時, gain 通常作不可數名詞, 如: material/personal/financial gain 即是指『物質/個人/財務方面的利益』。不過, ill-gotten gains (恆用複數) 意為『不義之財』。

G

game

The 2008 Olympic Game will be held in Beijing. (✗)

The 2008 Olympic Games will be held in Beijing. (✔)

(二〇〇八年奧運將於北京舉行。)

作為『遊戲/競賽』解時, game 是可數名詞, 如: You are playing a losing game. (你玩的是穩輸不贏的遊戲。) 但指大型的國際競賽則恆用複數形的 games。

Public figures like politicians are fair games. (✗)

Public figures like politicians are fair game. (✔)

(搞政治的公眾人物是容易被大家攻擊的對象。)

作為『獵物』解時, game 是不可數的 (集合) 名詞, 如: They hunt lions, tigers and other game. (他們獵捕獅子、老虎和其他獵物。) fair game 本指大家認為『可以捕殺的獵物』, 引申為『可以批評、攻擊的人物』。

gang

Her only son ends up being an armed gang. (✗)

Her only son ends up being an armed gangster. (✔)

(她的獨生子竟然成為一個持刀槍的歹徒。)

gang 指的是一群『歹徒/古惑仔』, 如: The night club was vandalized by a gang of youths. (這一家夜總會遭一群古惑仔砸店。) gangster 是 gang 的個別分子。

gather

We haven't seen each other for years. Let's find some time to gather together. (✗)

We haven't seen each other for years. Let's find some time to get together. (✔)

(我們都已經好幾年沒見面，找個時間聚一聚吧。)

gather together 是 (把) 現場的人/物『集合起來』, 如: Let's gather together for a photo. (我們來合拍一張照片吧。) 失聯或許久未見面的人『相聚』應該用 get together。

They live by collecting edible mushrooms and snails. (✗)

They live by gathering edible mushrooms and snails. (✔)

(他們靠採集可食的菇類和蝸牛為生。)

表『收集資訊/證據』時, 可說 collect/gather information (or evidence)。但作為一種興趣或嗜好的『收集』, 限用 collect, 如: I enjoy collecting stamps/teddy bears. (我喜歡收集郵票/泰迪熊。) 但『採集某物』為生限用 gather 這個字。

gathering

She's responsible for an intelligence gathering. (✗)

She's responsible for intelligence gathering. (✔)

(她負責收集情報。)

作『收集』的行為解時, gathering 為不可數名詞。作『聚會』解時, gathering 是可數名詞, 如: It is a social gathering. (這是一場社交聚會。)

gear

The police are all wearing riot gears. (✗)

The police are all wearing riot gear. (✔)

(所有的警察全著鎮暴裝。)

作『齒輪/排檔』解時, gear 兼有可/不可數名詞的用法, 如『開車換檔』的說法是 change gears (美式用法) 或 change gear (英式用法)。但作特殊的『服裝/設備』解時, gear 恆用單數, 如: camping/hunting/hiking/fishing gear 就是指『露營/打獵/健行/釣魚的裝備』。

gene

Some doctors believe that longevity is in the gene. (✗)

Some doctors believe that longevity is in the genes. (✔)

(有些醫師認為長壽的祕訣在基因。)

be in the genes 表『透過基因遺傳下去』是固定用法。

The condition is caused by a gene defect. (✗)

The condition is caused by a genetic defect. (✔)

(這類情況是某一種基因缺陷所造成。)

gene 是名詞, 罕與其它名詞連用。比較常見的例外是 gene therapy, 即『基因療法』。其它的情形都用 genetic 來形容名詞, 如: genetic engineering/fingerprinting/screening (基因工程/比對/篩檢)。

genuine

The restaurant serves genuine Chinese food. (✗)

The restaurant serves authentic Chinese food. (✔)

(這家餐廳供應道地的中國料理。)

作『真正的』解時, genuine 與 authentic 可以互通, 如: It is a(n) authentic/genuine painting. (這一幅畫是真跡。) 但表『道地/傳統的』時宜用 authentic。

given

Giving that he is young and inexperienced, you shouldn't be too hard on him. (✗)

Given that he is young and inexperienced, you shouldn't be too hard on him. (✔)

(要是考慮到他既年輕又無經驗，你就不應該對他過於嚴苛。)

given (that)... = considering that...表『要

是考慮到……』。

glue

Tommy is glued on the TV whenever cartoons are on. (✗)

Tommy is glued to the TV whenever cartoons are on. (✔)

(卡通片一播放湯米就盯著電視不放。)

glue 本為『膠水』, 作動詞時表用膠水來『黏住』某物。引申後, be glued to sth 指某人盯著某物一直看, 為固定用法。

go

I'd like the letter to send by express. (✗)

I'd like the letter to go/be sent by express. (✔)

(我希望以快遞寄送這封信。)

go = be sent 表『被寄送』。

They don't like eating out for lunch. (✗)

They don't like going out for lunch. (✔)

They don't like eating out at lunchtime. (✔)

(他們不喜歡出外吃午餐。)

go out for breakfast/lunch/a meal 是固定用法。

It takes me about twenty minutes to go to work. (✗)

It takes me about twenty minutes to get to work. (✔)

(去上班地點約需花我二十分鐘。)

go to work 表『開始出發去上班』, 這指一個時間上的『點』, 如: When do you usually go to work? (你通常幾點出門去上班?) get to work 表『到達上班地點 (或其過程)』, 兼指一個時間上的『點』和『段』, 如: She always gets to work at 8:30. (她總是在八點半到班。)

For here or going?. (✗)

For here or to go? (✔)

(內用還是外帶 ?)

For here or to go?是速食餐廳店員經常用來詢問顧客『內用還是外帶 ?』的制式説法。有關 go 的其它用法, 如: (1) Her fever just won't go. (她的高燒就是不退。) (2) His eyesight is going. (他的視力愈來愈差了。) (3) Those good old days are all gone. (從前那些美好的日子已經消逝了。)

goggles

It's better for you to wear a pair of glasses when swimming. (✗)

It's better for you to wear a pair of goggles when swimming. (✔)

(游泳時你最好戴上泳鏡。)

glasses 指的是一般 (閱讀) 的眼鏡。goggles 指的是用來保護眼睛的『泳鏡/防風鏡/護目鏡』等。

gossip

She heard a lot of gossips about me. (✗)

She heard a lot of gossip about me. (✔)

(她聽到有人講我一堆閒言閒語。)

作『閒話』解時, gossip 是不可數名詞。作『一段閒話的進行』解時, 恆用 a gossip, 如: They're having a gossip. (他們正在閒扯。) 作『喜歡講人閒話的人』解時,

G

gossip 是可數名詞, 如: She is an old gossip. (她是一名長舌婦。)

grab

Do we have time to get a bite before the movie? (✗)

Do we have time to grab/have a bite before the movie? (✔)

(看電影前我們有時間吃點東西嗎？)

get a bite 是指釣魚時『魚來咬餌』, 如: I sat for hours and never got a bite. (我坐了好幾個鐘頭, 魚兒都不來咬。) grab/have a bite 指的是『隨便吃點東西』。

grace

I'll give you three days' delay to pay the rent. (✗)

I'll give you three days' grace to pay the rent. (✔)

(我可以給你寬限三天付租金。)

表『寬限期』應該用 grace 才正確。

grade

Mike got a B grade in math. (✗)

Mike got a grade B in math. (✔)

(麥克的數學成績是 B 級。)

get a grade A/B/C 是固定用法。

Her younger brother is a sixth grade. (✗)

Her younger brother is a sixth grader. (✔)

Her younger brother is in the sixth grade. (✔)

(她的弟弟讀六年級。)

grade 是『年級』, grader 是『年級生』。

graft

The politician is accused of grafts. (✗)

The politician is accused of graft. (✔)

(這名政客被指控貪污受賄。)

作『貪污受賄』解時, graft 為不可數名詞。但作『接枝』或皮膚/骨骼的『移植』時, graft 是可數名詞, 如: The burns victim needs to have several skin grafts. (這名被火燒傷的病患需要做幾處的皮膚移植手術。) 注意: 整個器官的『移植』應該用 transplant。

grain

The breakfast is made from mixed grains. (✗)

The breakfast is made from mixed grain. (✔)

(這一份早餐是五穀雜糧做的。)

作『穀物/糧食』解時, grain 為不可數名詞。作『顆粒』解時, grain 是可數名詞, 如: There are grains of sugar on the table. (桌上有一些砂糖顆粒。)

grasp

These questions are all beyond my grasping. (✗)

These questions are all beyond my grasp/understanding. (✔)

(這些問題都超出我的理解範圍。)

beyond/out of sb's grasp 表『超出某人理解

的範圍』，為固定用法。grasping是形容詞，是『貪財的』之意，如: He is both grasping and lecherous. (他既貪財又好色。)

green

When Bill saw my new car, he turned red with envy. (✗)
When Bill saw my new car, he turned green with envy. (✔)
(當比爾看到我的新車時，他顯得非常嫉妒。)

be/turn green with envy 表某人『顯得非常嫉妒』。be/turn red with anger/embarrassment 表某人『生氣/尷尬到臉都紅了』。皆為固定用法。

grilled

I enjoy eating grilled duck a lot. (✗)
I enjoy eating roast duck a lot. (✔)
(我非常喜歡吃烤鴨。)

grilled food 指的是放在烤架上的『燒烤食品』，如: grilled shrimp/steak (烤蝦/牛排)。grilled duck 好像沒有這種『吃法』。至於放在烤箱/爐裡烤的東西，需用 roast 這個字。

grind

A single accident happens, and traffic will go to a halt. (✗)
A single accident happens, and traffic will grind to a halt. (✔)
(只要有單一事故發生，交通就為之停擺。)

grind 本來是『將某物磨成粉末』，是及物動詞的用法。表機器/車輛緩慢又不順暢的『運轉』時, grind 是不及物動詞, 如: grind to a halt 意為車輛等『慢慢地停頓下來』，是固定用法。

grip

At that time we were still in the grips of poverty. (✗)
At that time we were still in the grip of poverty. (✔)
(那個時候我們仍為貧窮所困。)

be in the grip of sth 表『受制/困於某物』，是固定用法。另外, come to grips (恆用複數) with sth 表『積極處理某事』，如: It's time our government should come to grips with the economy. (該是政府積極處理經濟問題的時候了。)

grope

The accused hesitated, seeming to grope words. (✗)
The accused hesitated, seeming to grope for words. (✔)
(被告猶豫了一下，似乎不曉得該說什麼才好。)

fumble/grope for words 竟為『摸索如何講話或回答』，是不及物的用法。至於及物的用法見於 grope one's way, 如: I had to grope my way in the dark. (我只好在黑暗中摸路前進。)

ground

He lost his balance and fell on the ground. (✗)
He lost his balance and fell to the ground. (✔)
(他失去平衡跌倒在地。)

純粹講『位置』或作較『靜態』的描述用 on the ground, 如: That little boy lay on the ground crying. (那個小男孩躺在地上哭。) 作『動態』的描述用 to the ground。

The hospital is small, but its ground is very large. (✗)

The hospital is small, but its grounds are very large. (✔)

(這所醫院很小，可是園區卻很大。)

指學校、醫院、飯店的周遭園區, 恆用複數形的 grounds。

On what ground am I fired? (✗)

On what grounds am I fired? (✔)

(基於什麼理由要解雇我？)

作『理由』解時, 恆用複數形的 grounds, 如: My father had to retire on (the) grounds of poor health. (我老爸因健康欠佳必須退休。)

grounded

These accusations are not grounded. (✗)

These accusations are groundless/unfounded. (✔)

(這些指控沒有根據。)

作為『有根據的』解時, 需用 be grounded in/on sth, 如: Her argument is grounded in fact. (她的論點有事實根據。) 表飛機『被迫停留地面』或人員『被禁足』時, 可以直接使用 be grounded, 如: The jetliner was grounded because of a thunderstorm. (因為雷雨關係, 這架噴射客機暫緩起飛。)或如: The child is grounded again. (這孩子又被禁足了。)

grow

As you know, money does not grow in trees. (✗)

As you know, money does not grow on trees. (✔)

(你是知道的，金錢得來不易。)

sth does not grow on trees 是指『某物得來不易, 應該珍惜』, 為固定用法。另外, sth grows on sb 是指『某人逐漸喜歡某物』, 如: Classical music began to grow on me after a long while. (過了好久一陣子之後, 我才開始喜歡古典音樂。) 此句的另一說法是: I grew to like classical music after a long while。

guarantee

The cellphone is still under a guarantee. (✗)

The cellphone is still under guarantee. (✔)

(這支手機仍在保固期限。)

be under guarantee (在保固期內) 是固定用法。另一個相關用法是 come with/carry a guarantee, 如: Do your products carry a guarantee? (你們的產品都有保固嗎?)

guard

If we drop our guards, we will eventually lose the game. (✗)

If we drop our guard, we will eventually lose the game. (✔)

(如果我們輕敵的話，最後會輸掉這場比賽。)

作『警覺/戒心』解時, guard 是不可數名詞。drop/lower/let down sb's guard 就是『放鬆警戒』之意。作『衛兵/看守人員』解時, guard 是可數名詞, The two prison guards are reasonably friendly. (這兩名監獄的管理員還算相當友善。)

guess

We can only guess the murderer's real motives. (✗)

G

We can only guess at the murderer's real motives. (✔)
(對於這名凶手的真正動機，我們只能猜測而已。)

guess sth 是『猜中/對』某事物, 如: I think I've guessed the answer. (我想我已經猜對答案了。) guess at sth 只是『猜測』而已。

To tell you the truth, I got the correct answer by guess. (✗)
To tell you the truth, I got the correct answer by guessing/guesswork. (✔)
(跟你說真的，我的正確答案是猜中的。)

作為『名詞』時 guess 是可數名詞, 如: make/take a guess 就是『做猜測的行為』。guesswork (= guessing) 是不可數名詞。

G

guide

Children often need parents' guide in money matters. (✗)
Children often need parents' guidance in money matters. (✔)
(在金錢方面孩子經常需要父母的指導。)

作『名詞』時, guide 通常指的是旅行時的『導遊』或旅遊的『指南 (書)』。其它方面的『指導』需用 guidance。

Before going abroad, I'd like to buy a tour guide. (✗)
Before going abroad, I'd like to buy a travel guide. (✔)
(出國前我想買一本旅遊指南。)

a tour guide 是一名『導遊』, 如: There is a tour guide on every bus. (每部遊覽車上都有一名導遊。) a travel guide 是一本『旅遊指南/手冊』。

guilty

The man was judged guilty and sentenced to life imprisonment. (✗)
The man was found guilty and sentenced to life imprisonment. (✔)
(這名男子被裁定有罪並判終身監禁。)

find sb (not) guilty 意為 (法庭) 判某人有(無) 罪, 是固定用法。

I felt guilty of causing you so much trouble. (✗)
I felt guilty about causing you so much trouble. (✔)
(為你造成這麼多困擾，我覺得很不好意思。)

be guilty of sth 是『犯了某種罪行』之意, 如: He was guilty of libel. (他犯了誹謗罪。) feel guilty about sth 是對自己的言行『感到抱歉/不好意思』。

gut

It takes a lot of gut to accept a challenge like this. (✗)
It takes a lot of guts to accept a challenge like this. (✔)
(要接受這樣的挑戰是需要很大的勇氣。)

gut 作為『胃、腸等內臟』解時是可數名詞, 可視情況需要用單/複數, 如: I felt like someone had just hit me in the gut. (我覺得好像有人剛在我的胃部揍了一拳。) 指『勇氣/膽識』時恆用複數的 guts。

Hh

habit

The girl has a custom of biting her nails. (✗)
The girl has a habit of biting her nails. (✓)
(這個女孩有咬指甲的習慣。)

custom 是某地的『風俗習慣』, 如: It is a Western custom to give presents at Christmas. (在耶誕節送禮物是西方人的習俗。) habit 是指個人的『生活習慣』。

The habit of smoking is hard to alter. (✗)
The habit of smoking is hard to break/kick. (✓)
(抽菸的習慣很難改。)

alter 是『改變以使之不同』的意思, 如: She altered her appearance with surgery. (她藉手術來改變自己的容貌。) 戒除某種習慣的正確說法是 break/kick/quit a habit。

H

hair

She has a fine hair and big eyes. (✗)
She has fine hair and big eyes. (✓)
(她一頭秀髮並有一對大眼睛。)
I started to lose my hairs when I turned 30. (✗)
I started to lose my hair when I turned 30. (✓)
(我三十歲後就開始掉頭髮了。)

『整體』而言, hair 是不可數名詞。『個別』來說, hair 是可數名詞, 如: You're starting to get a few gray hairs. (你開始有幾根白髮了。) 複數的用法另見於 split hairs (吹毛求疵) 這個片語, 如: Why split hairs over such trivia? (為何要對這種瑣事吹毛求疵呢?)

I used to divide my hair in the middle. (✗)
I used to part my hair in the middle. (✓)
(過去我習慣於頭髮中分。)

part one's hair in the middle/on the side 指某人『將頭髮中/旁分』, 是固定用法。

half

We are going to stay in Cairo for three and half days. (✗)
We are going to stay in Cairo for three and a half days. (✓)
(我們將在開羅待三天半的時間。)

one/two/three and a half 是固定的用法。

He's only read the half of the novel. (✗)
He's only read half of the novel. (✓)
He's only read the first half of the novel. (✓)
(這本小說他目前只讀到一半。)

the half of sth 在英文中幾乎不用。正確的說法是: (1) half of sth (2) the first/second/other half of sth。

My mother cut the cake in halves. (✗)
My mother cut the cake in half. (✓)
(媽媽把那塊蛋糕切成兩半。)

break/cut/divide/tear sth in half 意為『把某物折/切/分/撕成兩半』, 是固定用法。halves 的用法見於 go halves (兩人平均分攤費用), 如: Let's go halves/fifty-fifty on a pizza. (我們平均分攤一個披撒吧。)

halt

The referee brought a halt to the game because of the rain. (✗)

The referee called a halt to the game because of the rain. (✔)

(因為下雨裁判對比賽喊停。)

bring sth to a halt 意為『使某活動停頓/擺』, 如: The power failure brought our work to a halt. (停電使我們的工作停擺。) call a halt to sth 是正式對某動件喊停 (即結束某動作之意)。

hand

The future of our citizens should not be at the hands of a few politicians. (✗)

The future of our citizens should not be in the hands of a few politicians. (✔)

(我們國人的未來不能交到幾名政客的手中。)

at the hands of sb 是指 (痛苦、挫敗或死亡) 由某人造成, 如: They suffered their first defeat at the hands of the home team. (地主隊使他們遭到第一場挫敗。) in the hands of sb = handled or controlled by sb, 即『由某人操控』之意。

handle

They have been trained to handle with difficult customers. (✗)

They have been trained to deal with/handle difficult customers. (✔)

(針對應付難纏的顧客他們已有訓練。)

handle sb = deal with sb 意為『應付某人』。結合 with 的用法見於下例: All chemicals must be handled with care. (一切化學物必須謹慎處理。) 當注意的是這裡的 with care = carefully。

hands-free

It's a hands-off phone. (✗)

It's a hands-free phone. (✔)

(這是免持聽筒的電話。)

hands-off 是『不加干涉的』, 如: He favors a hands-off style of management. (他偏好無為而治的管理模式。) hands-free 是指電器設備等『免用手的』。

hang

"Get lost!" Mary shouted, and hung up to me. (✗)

"Get lost!" Mary shouted, and hung up on me. (✔)

(瑪麗大喊一聲『你很煩唉！』然後就掛我的電話。)

hang up 是『掛電話』。hang up on sb 是『掛某人的電話』, 為固定用法。

harassment

The pretty girl has been subject to several sexual harassments. (✗)

The pretty girl has been subject to sexual harassment several times. (✔)

(這位美女已經被性騷擾好幾次了。)

harassment (騷擾) 是不可數名詞。

hard

Don't be too hard to him. He's green. (✗)

Don't be too hard on him. He's green. (✔)

(不要苛責他。他還沒什麼經驗。)

be hard on sb 就是『苛責某人』之意, 為固定用法。另外, be hard on sth 表『對某物不利』之意, 如: Jogging is hard on the knees. (慢跑對膝蓋不利。)

My grandpa is hard at hearing. (✗)

My grandpa is hard of hearing. (✔)

(我爺爺有點重聽。)

be hard of hearing 意為『重聽』, 是固定用法。be hard at it/work 是『努力工作』之意。

hardware

Military hardwares alone cannot ensure victory. (✗)

Military hardware alone cannot ensure victory. (✔)

(只靠軍事硬體不能確保勝利。)

hardware/software (硬體/軟體) 均為不可數名詞。

head

They run a ranch with 300 heads of dairy cattle. (✗)

They run a ranch with 300 head of dairy cattle. (✔)

(他們經營一個牧場，擁有 300 頭乳牛。)

計算牲口『頭數』時恆用 head。丟銅板決定勝負時恆用 heads/tails, 如: I'll toss a coin. Heads or tails? (我來丟銅板。正面或反面?) 另外, 表植物的『棵數』時, head 有單/複數之分, 如: a head/two heads of lettuce (一棵/兩棵萵苣)。

heading

It looks like the company is heading to bankruptcy. (✗)

It looks like the company is heading for bankruptcy. (✔)

(看來這家公司好像快要破產了。)

be heading/headed for + 地方表『前往某地』。be heading/headed for sth 表『某事快要發生』。另外, 作名詞的 heading 表書頁/章節的『標題』。

headline

The scandal hit the headline again. (✗)

The scandal hit the headlines again. (✔)

(這件醜聞又上了頭條。)

a/the headline 是指一則新聞的『大標題』, 如: The headline reads, "Two Senators Assassinated." (大標題寫著:『兩名參議員遇刺』) the headlines 指的是最重要的消息或『頭條新聞』。make/hit/grab the headlines (成為頭條) 是固定用法。

head-on

It was a head-to-head crash. (✗)

It was a head-on crash. (✔)

(那是兩部車頭撞在一起。)

head-to-head 專指『面對面的比賽或對峙』, 如: The two teams will go head-to-head tomorrow. (這兩支球隊明天就要面對面比賽。) a head-on crash/collision 指『兩部車頭撞在一起』, 是固定用法。

H

heal

The cut will take about two weeks to cure. (✗)

The cut will take about two weeks to heal. (✔)

(這個傷口約需兩個星期即可痊癒。)

指『痊癒』時, cure 針對『疾病』, heal 針對『受傷』。

health

Food with too much salt in it is bad for health. (✗)

Food with too much salt in it is bad for your health. (✔)

(太鹹的食物對你的健康不好。)

be good/bad for sb's health 表『對某人的健康有好處/害處』, 是固定用法。

I'd like to go to a healthy spa this afternoon. (✗)

I'd like to go to a health spa this afternoon. (✔)

(今天下午我想去一家健康水療中心。)

healthy 是形容詞, 意為 (某人)『健康的』或 (食物、生活方式等)『有益健康的』, 如: She gave birth to a healthy baby yesterday. (她昨天產下一名健康的寶寶。) 而 a healthy diet/lifestyle 就是指『健康的飲食/生活方式』。health 是名詞, 與另一名詞結合時通常作『與健康有關的』解, 如: a health club/center/spa/service, 即是指健康俱樂部/中心/水療中心/服務中心。

hearing

The old man has a good hearing, considering his age. (✗)

The old man has good hearing, considering his age. (✔)

(要是考慮到他的年齡, 這老人的聽覺算很不錯了。)

作為『聽覺/力』解時, hearing 是不可數名詞。作為『聽證會』解時, hearing 是可數名詞, 如: A hearing has been scheduled for April 16. (已於四月十六日安排了一場聽證會。)

heat

The billy goat seems to be in heat. (✗)

The billy goat seems to be in rut. (✔)

(這山羊哥似乎在發情。)

雄性動物的『發情』用 in rut。雌性動物的『發情』用 in heat, 如: The nanny goat is in heat. (這隻母羊在發情。) 注意: 英式的用法是 on heat。

heated

Members of the two parties are engaged in a hot debate. (✗)

Members of the two parties are engaged in a heated debate. (✔)

(兩黨人士正展開一場激烈的辯論。)

hot 通常用來形容『議題』, 如: a hot issue/topic 就是指一個『炙手可熱的』議/話題。heated 通常用來說明『激烈的』過程, 如: a heated argument/debate/discussion, 即是一場『激烈的』爭/辯/討論。

heavy

You must know that it is a heavy crime. (✗)
You must know that it is a serious crime. (✔)
(你必須知道這是一件重罪。)

『一件重罪』的說法是 a grave/serious crime。『重感冒』的說法是 a bad/heavy/serious cold。

heel

The thief was running away, with an angry crowd at his heel. (✗)
The thief was running away, with an angry crowd at his heels. (✔)
(小偷在逃跑，有一群憤怒的人緊追在後。)

heel是『腳/鞋跟』之意，常用複數。at sb's heels 或 (close/hard/hot) on sb's heels 都是『緊跟在後』之意。

H

height

The aircraft began to lower height. (✗)
The aircraft began to lose height. (✔)
(飛機開始降低高度。)

指飛機的『向上攀升』或『向下降/墜落』，英文的說法是 gain/lose height。

help

Can you help me finding my glasses? (✗)
Can you help me (to) find my glasses? (✔)
(你能幫我找眼鏡嗎？)

help sb (to) do sth 意為『幫忙某人做某事』，是固定用法。

I know I'm being too nervous, but I can't help. (✗)
I know I'm being too nervous, but I can't help it. (✔)
(我知道我實在是太緊張了，可是我也沒辦法。)

cannot help (doing) sth/it 表『沒有辦法避免某種動作/狀況』，是固定用法。

You've been real help to me. (✗)
You've been a real help to me. (✔)
(你一向是我的好幫手。)

help 作『名詞』時，表『幫助』時是不可數名詞，表『助/幫手』時是可數名詞。

here

The weather in here is very sultry. (✗)
The weather here is very sultry. (✔)
(這裡的天氣很悶熱。)

in here 只能用於一個 (有範圍的) 空間裡，如: This is my office. You can stay in here for a while. (這是我個人的辦公室。你可以在裡面待一會兒。)

hidden

There are hiding cameras everywhere, so be on your guard! (✗)
There are hidden cameras everywhere, so be on your guard! (✔)

(到處都有隱藏式的攝影機，所以你還是小心為妙！)

hidden是『被隱藏的』或『不為人知的』, 如: Her hidden talents as a dancer have recently been discovered. (她跳舞方面不為人知的才藝最近被發掘出來了。) hiding是『(供) 隱藏的』, 如: It is a good hiding place. (這是一個很好的隱藏地點。) 另外, give sb a good hiding 是『痛毆/修理某人』之意。

high

The price of oil reached a new height last week. (✗)

The price of oil reached a new high last week. (✓)

(石油的價格上週創下新高。)

指『價格』或『指數』的高點一律用high, 如: a new/all-time/record high 即是指『新高或歷史新高點』。height是『高度』, 如: She's about the same height as you. (她大約跟你一般高度。)

historic

I enjoy reading historic novels. (✗)

I enjoy reading historical novels. (✓)

(我喜歡閱讀歷史小說。)

historic是『歷史上有名的』或『會在歷史留下記錄的』之意, 如: There are many ancient historic sites in Rome. (羅馬有不少歷史古跡。) historical 是『根據歷史的』或『曾於歷史存在的』, 如: Is Odysseus a historical figure or fictitious character? (木馬屠城記的奥迪修斯是歷史人物抑或虛構的角色?) 另外,『歷史書籍/博物館』的說法是 history books/museums。

hit

Turning around, I hit a goblet and it broke into pieces. (✗)

Turning around, I knocked over a goblet and it broke into pieces. (✓)

(轉身時我撞倒一個高腳杯，然後杯子就碎了。)

hit 作『撞擊』解時, 其行為通常來自車輛或某人 (故意或非故意) 的動作, 如: A pedestrian was hit by a speeding car this morning. (有一名行人今早被一部超速的汽車給撞了。) 或如: The boy slipped and hit his head on the wall. (那個男孩滑了一跤, 頭撞到牆上。)『不小心撞倒/打翻』某物需用 knock over sth。

They hit me on the stomach. (✗)

They hit me in the stomach. (✓)

(他們打我的肚子。)

hit sb on the arm/back/shoulder, 但 hit sb in the face/eye/stomach。比較『硬』的部位用 on, 比較『軟』的部位用 in。

The movie was a heat at the box office. (✗)

The movie was a hit at the box office. (✓)

(這部電影的票房極佳。)

作為『非常成功或很熱門的人物』解時, hit 是可數名詞, 如: The comedian is now a hit with people of all ages. (這名諧星現深受各個年齡層的人士喜愛。) heat 意為『炎熱』, 是不可數名詞。另外, hit 亦可表『暗殺』, 如: The media tycoon was gunned down by a hit man. (這位媒體大亨被職業殺手槍殺了。) a hit man/squad 指的是一名職業殺手/一個暗殺小組。

H

hobby

Beaseball is the national hobby in the U.S. (✗)

Baseball is the national pastime in the U.S. (✔)

(棒球運動是美國全國性的消遣。)

hobby 和 pastime 意義很接近。前者表『嗜好』,通常指益智或陶冶性情的(個人)業餘活動,如: My favorite hobby is cooking. (我最喜歡的嗜好是烹飪。) 後者表藉以打發時間的『消遣』。

hold

A bellboy came over and held my suitacase. (✗)

A bellboy came over and took hold of my suitcase. (✔)

(有一名服務生過來幫我拿手提箱。)

hold sth 表『已拿著某物』, 如: He held a stick in his hand. (他手裡拿著一根棍子。) take/get hold of sth 是『開始拿某物』。

The lieutenant was held a prisoner for three months. (✗)

The lieutenant was held prisoner for three months. (✔)

(這名中尉被俘長達三個月之久。)

hold sb captive/hostage/prisoner (均不加冠詞) 意為抓住某人當俘虜/人質/囚犯, 是固定用法。

holder

Who is the current world 400m record keeper? (✗)

Who is the current world 400m record holder? (✔)

(當今世界 400 米記錄保持人是誰?)

holder是『保持人』或『持有人』之意, 如: ticket/passport holders就是指『持票者/持護照者』。keeper 是『管理員』, 如: a park/lighthouse keeper即是『公園/燈塔管理員』, 而 a goalkeeper 則是『足球守門員』。

holding

My dad has 45% holding in the company. (✗)

My dad has a 45% holding in the company. (✔)

(我老爸在這家公司持股佔 45 %)

holding 意為『持股』或『持有之土地』時是可數名詞。

hole

My socks have a few holes on them. (✗)

My socks have a few holes in them. (✔)

(我的襪子有幾處破洞。)

a hole/two holes in sth 為固定用法, 如: Look, here is a hole in the ozone layer. (你看, 此處臭氧層有一個破洞。) 或如: There is an obvious hole in the law covering drunk driving. (適用於酒醉駕車的這條法令顯然有漏洞。)

home

Shall we stay here or go to their home? (✗)

Shall we stay here or go to their house? (✔)

(我們要待在這裡呢還是去他們家?)

H

指自己的家時用 go/stay at/leave home。指別人的家時說 go to/stay at/leave sb's house。

honestly

Honestly, Jill is really not my type. (✗)

To be honest (with you), Jill is really not my type. (✔)

To tell (you) the truth, Jill is really not my type. (✔)

(不瞞你說，吉兒真的不是我喜歡的典型。)

honestly (可置於句首或句末) 主要用來強調說話者希望聽話人相信自己所言為真, 如: It was not my fault, honestly. (老實說, 這並非我的錯。) 但告訴別人你的判斷或真正感受時, 須用 to be honest (with you) 或 to tell (you) the truth。像 Jill is really not my type.這個句子無關『是非真假』只是個人的判斷或感受, 不宜用 honestly 來強調。

hope

Do I have to go there again? I don't hope so. (✗)

Do I have to go there again? I hope not. (✔)

(我須要再去那兒一趟嗎？希望不必。)

英文並沒有 I don't hope so.的說法, 只有 I hope so.或 I hope not.這兩種說法。

I hope you would get well soon. (✗)

I hope you will get well soon. (✔)

(希望你會很快康復。)

hope 表『希望某事/物能發生或成真』, 其後的子句不宜接含有『假設語氣』的 would。

I hope against hoping that the girl will show up. (✗)

I hope against hope that the girl will show up. (✔)

(我一再希望這個女孩會出現。)

hope against hope (that)...表『明知其不可能但一再希望』某事發生, 為固定用法。

hopeful

Hopeful, we'll get our money back. (✗)

Hopefully, we'll get our money back. (✔)

(希望我們能把錢要回來。)

hopeful 是形容詞, 表對某事抱很大的希望, 如: Everyone in our company is hopeful about the future. (公司裡的每個人對將來都很樂觀。) hopefully 是副詞, 常置於句首強調希望成真。

hopeless

They all felt hopeless because they had worked hard and failed. (✗)

They all felt disappointed because they had worked hard and failed. (✔)

(大家都覺得很洩氣因為已經很努力但失敗了。)

hopeless 表『無望的』, 通常用來形容某種『情況』而非『人』, 如: The outlook for the unemployed seems hopeless. (失業者的前景似乎不被看好。) 形容『人』的失望/氣餒需用 disappointed/discouraged/disheartened。不過, hopeless 還是可以用來形容『人』, 表 (1) 差勁的, 如: My wife is a hopeless cook. (我老婆菜做得很差。) (2) 極端的類型, 如: Peter is a hopeless romantic. (彼德是一個極端浪漫的人。)

horizon

To travel widely can help broaden your horizon. (✗)

To travel widely can help broaden your horizons. (✓)

(到處旅遊可以增廣你的見聞。)

指『地平線』時用 the horizon, 如: We could see the setting sun on the horizon. (我們可以看到地平線上的落日。) 指『見聞/知識』的界限用 sb's horizons (恆用複數)。

horror

It is a horrible movie. (?)

It is a horror movie. (✓)

(這是一部恐怖片。)

a horrible movie 是指一部『很爛』的電影。a horror movie 是一部『恐怖片』。

host

Beijing will play the host to the next Olympic Games. (✗)

Beijing will play host to the next Olympic Games. (✓)

(北京將主辦下一屆奧運。)

作為名詞時, host 是 (接待來賓的) 主人。play/be host to sth 是『主辦某活動』之意, 為固定用法。當動詞時, host sth 是『主辦/持』某活動/節目, 如: Beijing will host the next Olympic Games.或如: Mr. White is currently hosting a talk show. (懷特先生目前在主持一個脫口秀節目。)

hostility

They display a hostility toward foreigners. (✗)

They display hostility toward foreigners. (✓)

(他們對外國人表現敵意。)

作『敵意』解時 hostility 是不可數名詞。作『戰爭』解時恆用複數形的 hostilities, 如: The people have been rather uneasy since the outbreak of hostilities. (自從開戰以來, 人民一直顯得很不安。)

hot

The bath water is scorching hot. (✗)

The bath water is scalding hot. (✓)

(洗澡水燙得很。)

scorching hot 是指溫度高到可以把東西燒焦, 通常用來指天氣, 如: It is scorching hot today. (今天天氣熱死了。) 用來形容『液體』不宜。描述『液體』很燙應該說 boiling/scalding/steaming hot。

The news about his stepping down is hot of the press. (✗)

The news about his stepping down is hot off the press. (✓)

(他下台的消息剛被披露。)

be hot off the press 是指消息『剛被披露』, 為固定用法。

housebroken

Is your pet housebreaking? (✗)

Is your pet housebroken? (✓)

(你家的寵物有訓練不隨地大小便了嗎？)

housebreaking 是名詞, 意為『闖入民宅行竊』, 如: The man was charged with housebreaking. (這個人被控以闖入民宅罪名。) housebroken = house-trained (英式用法), 是形容詞, 專指貓狗等寵物『有訓練, 不隨地大小便』。

household

More land has to be found for new household. (✗)

More land has to be found for new housing. (✔)

(必須多找一些土地來加蓋新房子。)

housing (= houses or buildings) 本身是集合名詞, 不可數。household 表: (1) 家庭, 是可數名詞, 如: It is a five-person household. (這是一個五人的家庭。) (2) 家庭/用的, 是形容詞, 如: Jordan is a household name. (喬丹是家喻戶曉的人物。)

housekeeper

Most Chinese women are housekeepers. (?)

Most Chinese women are housewives. (✔)

(大多數的中國婦女當家庭主婦。)

housekeeper 是受僱於人的『管家』。housewife 是『家庭主婦』。

how

How does her new boyfriend look like? (✗)

What does her new boyfriend look like? (✔)

(她的新男友長得怎麼樣?)

請人描述某人/物的長相或狀態時, 需用 What...like? 不能說 How...like? 如: What does the soup taste like? (這道湯的味道如何?) 或如: What does it feel like to be elected? (選上的感覺如何?)

How do you think of the job offer? (✗)

What do you think of the job offer? (✔)

(這樣的工作條件你覺得如何?)

詢問別人意見時說 What do you think of...? 不可用 How 來引導。

human

It must have been caused by human's error, not mechanical failure. (✗)

It must have been caused by human error, not mechanical failure. (✔)

(這一定是人為疏失所造成的，不是機件故障。)

human 通常作形容詞用, 直接修飾名詞, 如 human behavior/life/society, 即是指人類的行為/生活/社會。

The announcement demands human treatment of POWs. (✗)

The announcement demands humane treatment of POWs. (✔)

(這項聲明要求善待戰俘。)

human 是『人類/為的』而 humane 是『仁慈/人道的』, 可兼指對人類或動物的行為, 如: They are advised to use a more humane method of killing animals. (有人建議他們在宰殺動物時要盡量減少牠們的痛苦。) 至於 humanitarian (人道主義的) 這個字僅限於用在關懷 (弱勢/痛苦的) 人類, 如: humanitarian aid/assistance/relief 都是指『人道的救援/濟』。

hurry

Why's the hurry? (✗)

What's the hurry? (✔)

Why the hurry? (✔)

H

(有什麼好趕的？)

What's the hurry? = There is no hurry.用來表說話者認為『不需要這麼趕/急』做某事。其中的 hurry 也可以用 rush 代替。

hyphenated

They are foreign Americans. (✗)

They are hyphenated Americans. (✓)

(他們是外裔美國人。)

hyphenate sth 本指用 hyphen (短線) 連接兩個英文單字, 如: all-out (全面的)。因為外裔美國人像 Chinese-Americans 或 Spanish-Americans 都是用 hyphen 連接形成, 所以才有 hyphenated Americans 的說法。

H

I i

ice

Two icy coffees, please. (✗)
Two ice(d) coffees, please. (✔)
(來兩杯冰咖啡。)

『冰咖啡』的正確說法是 ice(d) coffee。icy 通常用來形容天候或人的表情/態度, 如: The weather is icy cold today. (今天真是天寒地凍。) 或如: She gave me an icy look. (她冷冰冰地望我一眼。)

It was a great party, and the mayor's presence was just the ice on the cake. (✗)
It was a great party, and the mayor's presence was just the icing on the cake. (✔)
(這個派對很成功，而市長到場不過是錦上添花罷了。)

the icing on the cake 本指蛋糕上面裝飾用的糖霜, 引申為『錦上添花』是固定用法。

ideal

A few young people are ideal just about everything. (✗)
A few young people are idealistic just about everything. (✔)
(有些年輕人幾乎對每樣事物都抱著理想主義。)

作為『形容詞』時 ideal = perfect, 表『理想/完美的』, 如: It is an ideal place for bird watching. (這個地方是賞鳥的最佳去處。) idealistic 是『抱理想主義的』。另一個字 idealized 是『被理想化的』, 如: Some fictional characters are often idealized. (小說人物常被理想化。)

idol

She's got a chance to star opposite her former icon. (✗)
She's got a chance to star opposite her former idol. (✔)
(她獲得機會與她從前的偶像演對手戲。)

表『偶像』時, icon 是代表某一種主張/精神/流行等的風雲人物, 如: She has become a fashion icon. (她已成為一位代表時尚的偶像人物。) idol 特指個人崇拜的『偶像人物』。

ill

These volunteers are being trained to take care of ill people. (✗)
These volunteers are being trained to take care of sick people. (✔)
(這批志工正在接受訓練以照顧病患。)

作『生病的』解時, ill 通常不置於名詞之前直接修飾人物。這種情況要用 sick。不過 ill 之前若有副詞則可直接修飾名詞, 如: critically/mentally/terminally ill patients, 即是『危急的/精神/末期的』病患。

illicit

She is having an illegal relationship with a married man. (✗)
She is having an illicit relationship with a married man. (✔)
(她目前跟一位已婚的男人有一段不倫的關係。)

表『非法的』時, illicit 和 illegal 是同義字, 如: He seemed to be involved in illicit/illegal ivory trading. (他似乎捲入非法的象牙交易。) 表『不見容於社會的』或『不倫

I

的』關係應該用 illicit。

illusion

The UFO must have been an optical delusion. (✗)

The UFO must have been an optical illusion. (✓)

(該不明飛行物一定是視覺的幻象。)

表『錯誤的想法』時 delusion = illusion, 如: Many people have the delusion/illusion that money is the best guarantee of a happy life. (很多人都有這種錯誤的想法, 以為金錢是快樂人生的最佳保證。) 表『假象/幻覺』時要用 illusion, 如: A mirage is only an illusion. (海市蜃樓不過是一種幻覺而已。) 另外, delusion 可表『妄想症』, 如: He suffers from delusions of grandeur. (他患有自大妄想症。)

image

The ruling party is working hard to raise its image. (✗)

The ruling party is working hard to improve its image. (✓)

(執政黨正努力在提昇自己的形象。)

『提昇形象』的正確說法是 improve/promote sb's image, 『破壞形象』的說法是 damage sb's image。

imaginative

You have to be imaginary enough to be a good novelist. (✗)

You have to be imaginative enough to be a good novelist. (✓)

(你必須要有豐富的想像力才能當個出色的小說家。)

imaginary 是『純想像/虛構的』, 如: A unicorn is an imaginary animal. (獨角獸是一種虛構的動物。) imaginative 是『想像力豐富的』。另有 imaginable 表『可以想像/出的』, 如: They have medicines for every imaginable illness. (任何說得出口的疾病他們都有藥可治。)

imitate

She worries that Tom will imitate his father and become a gambler. (✗)

She worries that Tom will copy his father and become a gambler. (✓)

(她擔心湯姆會模仿他老爸成為賭徒。)

imitate sb 指『模仿某人的說話或動作』, 其目的經常是為了取笑某人或讓人覺得好笑, 如: The comedian is imitating a politician. (這名諧星正在模仿一位政治人物。)『仿效性』的模仿需用 copy。

imitation

We learn many things by imitations. (✗)

We learn many things by imitation. (✓)

(我們藉著模仿學習很多事物。)

指『模仿』的行為時 imitation 通常是不可數的用法。by imitation 是固定用法。作『模仿物』解時, imitation 是可數名詞, 如: It is a pale imitation of the original. (這個仿作與原作相去甚遠。) 另外, imitation 亦可置於名詞之前表『仿造/人工的』, 如: imitation leather/pearl 即為『仿造皮革/人工珍珠』。

immediate

Mr. Adams is my direct superior. (✗)
Mr. Adams is my immediate superior. (✔)
(亞當斯先生是我的頂頭上司。)

表『直接/最接近的』關係用 immediate, 不用 direct, 如: She told only her immediate family. (她只告訴最接近的親人。)

immigrate

More and more people are planning to immigrate because of growing political unrest here. (✗)
More and more people are planning to emigrate because of growing political unrest here. (✔)
(因為此地政局動盪不安加劇，越來越多的人打算移民到國外。)

immigrate 是『移入』, emigrate 是『移出』。

immune

Diplomats are immune to prosecution. (✗)
Diplomats are immune from prosecution. (✔)
(外交人員可豁免起訴。)

be immune to sth 通常是指『對某種疾病免疫』, 如: The child is immune to polio as a result of vaccination. (因為施打過疫苗, 這個孩子對小兒麻痺免疫。) be immune from sth 是指『對某種權責豁免』。另外『外交豁免權』的說法是 diplomatic immunity。

impact

The brain drain will surely cause an impact on that country. (✗)
The brain drain will surely make an impact on that country. (✔)
(人才外流的現象一定會對該國造成衝擊。)

『造成衝擊』的正確說法是 have/make an impact (on sth)。

impatient

She was impatient to wait for him. (✗)
She ran out of patience waiting for him. (✔)
(她等他等得不耐煩了。)

be impatient to do sth = can't wait to do sth 表『迫不及待想做某事』, 如: The students are impatient to know the results of the exam. (學生們急著想知道考試的結果。)『失去耐性』或『不耐煩』的說法是 lose/run out of patience 或 get/become impatient。

impending

A disaster is impending. (✗)
A disaster is imminent. (✔)
(一場災難快要發生了。)

impending 與 imminent 都可以用來說明某種 (不愉快的) 事情快要發生。不過, impending 僅能置於名詞之前修飾, 如: They are not aware of the impending danger. (他們並不知道危險快要降臨。) 而 imminent 可置於 be 動詞之後亦可置於名詞之前。

I

implication

The anchorwoman denied any implications in the extramarital affair. (✗)

The anchorwoman denied any implication in the extramarital affair. (✓)

(這位女主播否認捲入婚外情。)

作為『涉及/捲入』解時, implication 是不可數名詞。作為『暗示/聯想』解時, 多用複數形的 implications, 如: We have to take into account the sexual implications of the movie. (我們必須考慮這部電影裡的性暗示。)

impossible

He is impossible to come. (✗)

He is unlikely to come. (✓)

It is impossible for him to come. (✓)

(他是不可能會來的。)

表『不可能』時 impossible 針對的是事物而非人, 所以一般不能使用 sb is impossible to..., 需用 sb is unlikely to...或 it is impossible for sb to...的句型。不過表『不可理喻』時, impossible 可針對人物來形容, 如: She is impossible at times. (她有時會令人受不了。)

impression

George has decided to change his impression by giving up drinking. (✗)

George has decided to change his image by giving up drinking. (✓)

(喬治已決定戒酒來改變形象。)

impression 意為『印象』, 專指你對某人/物的 (短暫) 感覺或看法, 如: My first impression of her family was very positive. (我對她家人的第一次印象十分良好。) image 是指你留在某人心中的『形象』。

improve

We hope to improve last year's turnover. (✗)

We hope to improve on last year's turnover.

(我們希望今年有比去年更好的業績。)

improve sth 是針對『目前的狀況』作改善, 如: Try to improve your quality of life. (試著改善你的生活品質。) improve on/upon sth 是針對『以前的狀況』作改善。

imprudent

It would be impudent to invest all your money in the stock market. (✗)

It would be imprudent to invest all your money in the stock market. (✓)

(把你所有的錢投資在股市是不智的。)

impudent 和 imprudent 字形相像, 的確很容易搞混。impudent 意為『無恥/禮的』, 如: He is an impudent child. (他是一個粗野的孩子。) imprudent = unwise, 是『不智的』之意。

incarnate

They all shun me as if I were incarnate evil. (✗)

They all shun me as if I were evil incarnate. (✓)

I

They all shun me as if I were the incarnation of evil. (✔)
(他們都對我避之唯恐不及，好像我是邪惡的化身似的。)

be beauty/evil/greed/wisdom incarnate = be the incarnation of beauty/evil/greed/wisdom 表某人『是美麗/邪惡/貪婪/智慧的化身』，是固定用法。

incentive

Bonus offers will give employees an impulse to work harder. (✗)
Bonus offers will give employees an incentive to work harder. (✔)
(分紅將可刺激員工更加努力工作。)

impulse 是『一時的衝動』，如: Mary felt a sudden impulse to eat ice cream. (瑪麗突然有股想吃冰淇淋的衝動。) incentive 是『某種鼓勵或刺激』。

incidence

The police are determined to reduce the incident of burglary around here. (✗)
The police are determined to reduce the incidence of burglary around here. (✔)
(警方決心要讓附近的竊盜案件數減少下來。)

incident 是指某一『事件』，incidence 是指犯罪或疾病發生的『件數』。

incident

A military spokesman said that the soldier's defection was a single incident. (✗)
A military spokesman said that the soldier's defection was an isolated incident. (✔)
(一位軍事發言人說該士兵的叛逃純屬單一的事件。)

a single incident 是『僅僅一個事件』，而非兩個或三個。an isolated incident 是與其它事情無關的『單一事件』。

inclined

You may take a dip in the pool if you are inclined so. (✗)
You may take a dip in the pool if you are so inclined. (✔)
(有興緻的話，你可以下池游泳。)

if you are/feel so inclined 表『如果你想這麼做的話』，是固定用法。

include

The Divine Comedy by Dante includes three parts. (✗)
***The Divine Comedy* by Dante consists of three parts. (✔)**
(但丁的《神曲》包含有三部分。)

include sth 是『包含某物作為一部分』之意，如: The price includes a 10% service charge. (這個價格包含了 10%的服務費在內。) 全部的『包含或組合』需用 consist of/comprise/be composed of/be made up of sth。

Her bag includes a hodgepodge of everything. (✗)
Her bag contains a hodgepodge of everything. (✔)
(她的包包裡有一堆亂七八糟的東西。)

include 是『包含』，contain 指容器或袋子裡『內含』。

I

increase

We've been trying to increase the level of our performances. (✗)

We've been trying to raise the level of our performances. (✓)

(我們一直在設法提昇表演的水平。)

Their professional standards have increased. (✗)

Their professional standards have risen. (✓)

(他們的專業水準已經提昇了。)

increase (sth) 專門用在『數或量』的增加。指 level/standard 的提昇需用 raise 或 rise。

An increase of working hours may become necessary if we receive a larger order. (✗)

An increase in working hours may become necessary if we receive a larger order. (✓)

(如果接到更大的訂單，增加工作時數恐有必要。)

(an/the) increase in sth 表『某物的增加』，是固定用法。

incumbent

Her incumbent boyfriend is a baseball player. (✗)

Her current boyfriend is a baseball player. (✓)

(她現任的男友是一位棒球選手。)

incumbent 專指『現任的』公職人員, 如: Who is the incumbent mayor? (現任市長是誰?) current 是『目前的』或『現今的』，如『時事』的英文就是 current news。

independent

I hope I can be economically independent from my family by the time I'm twenty. (✗)

I hope I can be economically independent of my family by the time I'm twenty. (✓)

(我希望二十歲以前就能在經濟上不再依靠家庭。)

be independent of sb 意為『不再依靠某人』是固定用法。

indication

Her face gave no indicator of being annoyed. (✗)

Her face gave no indication of being annoyed. (✓)

(她的臉上並沒有露出不悅的跡象。)

indicator 是『指示物』或『指標』, 如: Purchasing power is an important economic indicator. (購買力是一項重要的經濟指標。) indication 是『指出』或『跡象』之意。另外, index 是『指數』, 如: the consumer price index 就是『消費者物價指數』。

indigestion

Beef usually causes me indigestion. (✗)

Beef usually gives me indigestion. (✓)

(牛肉通常讓我引起消化不良。)

give sb indigestion 意為『使某人消化不良』，是固定用法。

I

indoor

Plants grown indoor need special care. (✗)

Plants grown indoors need special care. (✓)

(種在室內的植物需要特別照顧。)

indoor/outdoor 是形容詞, 意為『室內/外的』, 如: They have an indoor swimming pool. (他們有一座室內游泳池。) indoors/outdoors 是副詞, 意為『在室內/外』。

industrial

Many countries in the world are still not industrial. (✗)

Many countries in the world are still not industrialized. (✓)

(世界上仍有很多尚未工業化的國家。)

industrial 意為『工業的』或『與工業有關的』, 僅能置於名詞之前修飾, 不可置於 be 動詞作補語, 如: industrial country/development/alcohol 就是指『工業國家/發展/酒精』。而 industrialized 是『(被)工業化』之意, 可置於名詞之前或 be 動詞之後。另外一個易混淆的形容詞是 industrious, 意為『勤勉的』。

industry

Industries as a whole have become more and more environmentally friendly in recent years. (✗)

Industry as a whole has become more and more environmentally friendly in recent years. (✓)

(近幾年來整體的工業越來越注意環保了。)

作為整體的『工業』而言, industry 是不可數名詞。作為個別的『工業』而言, 是可數名詞, 如: a textile/nuclear/chemical/pharmaceutical industry 即是一個紡織/核子/化學/製藥工業。

infected

Don't drink the water. It may be infectious. (✗)

Don't drink the water. It may be infected. (✓)

(不要喝那兒的水，可能含有細菌。)

infectious 是指『有傳染性的』常用來形容某種疾病或帶原的人畜。如: Tuberculosis is a highly infectious disease. (肺結核是一種高傳染性的疾病。) infected 指人畜時是『被感染的』, 指食物或水時是『帶有細菌的』。

influence

Antibiotics have almost no influence on the virus. (✗)

Antibiotics have almost no effect on the virus. (✓)

(抗生素對於這種病毒幾乎沒有任何影響。)

influence 表『影響』, 強調的是對某人或某物『後續發展』的影響, 如: Parents' behavior has a strong influence on children's character development. (父母的行為對兒童人格的成長有相當的影響。) effect 作『影響』解時, 強調的是對某人或某物的『改變』, 如: Eating right will have a good effect on your health. (謹慎飲食將會對你的健康產生很好的影響。)

inform

It seems that one of our neighbors has informed the police of us. (✗)

I

It seems that one of our neighbors has informed on/against us. (✔)
(似乎是我們的某鄰居去告我們的密。)

inform sb of/about sth 即『提供資訊給某人』, 介系詞 of/about 之後恆接事物。Please inform us of any change in your prices. (價格有任何變動, 煩請告知我方。) 向警方或其它主管單位『告密』的說法是 inform on/against sb。

information

Do tell us if you need more informations. (✗)
Do tell us if you need more information. (✔)
(如果您需要更多的資訊, 務必告訴我們。)

information (資訊) 為不可數名詞, 恆用單數。如要計算, 需說 a piece/two pieces of information, 即『一/兩件訊息』。

Can you give me any further information of the music camp? (✗)
Can you give me any further information about the music camp? (✔)
(可否提供有關該音樂營更進一步的資訊給我呢?)

information about/on sth 是固定用法。

ingenius

I must admit your idea is a genius one. (✗)
I must admit your idea is an ingenius one. (✔)
(我必須承認你提出一個聰明的點子。)

genius 是名詞, 意為『天才』, 如: Leibnitz was a genius in mathematics. (萊布尼茲是一位數天才。) ingenius 是形容詞, 意為『聰明/靈巧的』。

inhibit

Shyness inhabits her from speaking aloud. (✗)
Shyness inhibits her from speaking aloud. (✔)
(害羞使她不敢大聲點說話。)

inhabit 表『居住/生活在』某地, 是及物動詞, 如: A variety of insects inhabit the cave. (這個山洞有各式各樣的昆蟲生存著。) inhibit = prevent, 是『阻止/妨礙』之意。

injure

Working so hard may injure your health. (✗)
Working so hard may damage your health. (✔)
(你如此賣力工作恐會傷及健康。)

injure 表『傷到』時常用被動形式且以某人或身體部位為主, 如: He/His back was badly injured. (他/他的背部嚴重受傷。) 『傷及某人的健康』的正確英文說法是 damage sb's health。不過, injure 也有引申的用法, 如: injure sb's reputation/pride, 即是『傷到』某人的名譽/自尊。

Five soldiers were mortally injured in the fighting. (✗)
Five soldiers were mortally wounded in the fighting. (✔)
(有五名士兵在戰鬥中受重傷, 生命垂危。)

be injured是指『在意外中受傷』, 如: A car racer was injured in the accident. (有一名賽車選手在意外中受傷。) be wounded 是指『在戰爭或打鬥中』被兵/武器所傷。

injury

It doesn't matter—a flesh injury only. (✗)
It doesn't matter a flesh wound only. (✓)
(這不礙事，不過是皮肉之傷而已。)

『皮肉之傷』的正確說法是 a flesh wound (非 injury)。

To add an insult to an injury, she kept speaking ill of her in-laws. (✗)
To add insult to injury, she kept speaking ill of her in-laws. (✓)
(使關係雪上加霜的是，她一直講夫家的壞話。)

to add insult to injury 是『使情況更加惡化』, 為固定用法。

inquiring

The child is very inquiring. (✗)
The child is very inquisitive. (✓)
(這孩子老愛問東問西的。)

inquiring 和 inquisitive 皆為形容詞, 均可表『喜歡探究的』。不過前者限置於名詞之前直接修飾, 不能置於 be 動詞之後。如: It takes an inquiring mind to build up knowledge. (要做學問需有喜歡探究的精神。) 而 inquisitive 則可置於名詞之前或 be 動詞之後, 且經常帶有『貶義』。

inside

Luke's sweater is on inside. (✗)
Luke's sweater is on inside out. (✓)
(路可的毛衣穿反了。)

inside out 是副詞片語, 表 (裡面的部分)『翻轉過來』, 如: My umbrella blew inside out. (我的雨傘被大風吹翻過來了。) 或如: You are wearing your socks inside out again. (你的襪子又穿反了。)

The company is accused of inside trading. (✗)
The company is accused of insider trading. (✓)
(這家公司被指控涉內線交易。)

inside 是『裡邊』或『內部』, 如: an inside track 就是 (跑道的) 內圈。an inside job 是『內賊所為。』而 insider 是『知道內幕的人』, 所以『內線交易』的說法為 insider trading/dealing。

insomnia

I used to be an insomnia. (✗)
I used to be an insomniac. (✓)
(我曾是一名失眠患者。)

insomnia 是『失眠 (症)』, 為不可數名詞, 如: Lots of people suffer from insomnia nowadays. (今天不少人患有失眠。) insomniac 是『失眠 (症) 患者』, 為可數名詞。

installment

I think I'll pay for the car in a monthly installment. (✗)
I think I'll pay for the car in monthly installments. (✓)
(我想我會按月分期付款買這部車子。)

an/the installment 是指每一期應付的款, 如: When is the next installment due? (下一期款什麼時候該繳?) in/by (...) installments (恆用複數) 是指『分期付款』購買某物, 如: They let me buy the computer in 12 installments. (他們讓我分十二期買這部電腦。)

I

instant

Don't bother. I never like immediate coffee. (✗)
Don't bother. I never like instant coffee. (✓)
(別麻煩了。我一向不喜歡即溶咖啡。)

在一般事物的『立即性』上, immediate和instant 可以互通, 如: We demand instant/immediate solutions. (我方要求立即解決。) 在『立即』可以食用的食品上, 一律用 instant 來形容, 如: instant coffee/noodles (即溶咖啡/速食麵)。

instinct

For a matter like this, you'd better follow your instinct. (✗)
For a matter like this, you'd better follow your instincts. (✓)
(像這類事情，你最好憑直覺去做。)

instinct 意為『本能/直覺』, 兼有可/不可數用法。follow/trust sb's instincts 表『依照/信賴某人的直覺』行事, 是 (美語) 固定用法。另外, instinct tells/warns sb (that)... (恆用單數), 如: Instinct tells me that his sincerity is all put on. (本能告訴我他的誠懇都是裝出來的。)

institute

It is a charitable institute. (✗)
It is a charitable institution. (✓)
(這是一個慈善機構。)

institute 和 institution 都可作『機構』解, 不過前者偏指教育或科學等研究機構, 如: an institute for medical research 即是一個醫學研究機構。其它有關『政治/社會/財務』的機構多用 institution 這個字。另外, 指『制度』時限用 insitution, 如: the institution of monarchy 就是『君主政治』制度。

instruction

Read the instruction carefully before you assemble it. (✗)
Read the instructions carefully before you assemble it. (✓)
(組裝前請先詳閱說明書。)

作為『教育/導』解時, instruction 是不可數名詞, 如: All high school students should receive some instruction on CPR. (所有中學生都應研習一點心肺復甦術。) 作為『指示/令』或『說明書』時, 恆用複數的 instructions。

intact

Only a few buildings have survived the earthquake intactly. (✗)
Only a few buildings have survived the earthquake intact. (✓)
(只有幾棟大樓逃過地震一劫仍完好如初。)

remain/survive (sth) intact 表 (度過難關或逃過一劫後) 仍完好如初, 是固定用法。此處的 intact 作主詞補語。

intake

Reduce your intakes of salt and fat to prevent high blood pressure. (✗)
Reduce your intake of salt and fat to prevent high blood pressure. (✓)
(要減少鹽分、脂肪的攝取量以預防高血壓。)

作為食物的『攝取量』時, intake 是不可數名詞。作為『吸取』空氣的動作時, intake 是可數名詞, 如: a sharp intake of breath 即是『猛吸一口空氣』。

I

intellectual

Is there any intellectual life in outer space? (✗)

Is there any intelligent life in outer space? (✓)

(外太空有任何高等生物存在嗎？)

His intelligent ability was questioned for the first time. (✗)

His intellectual ability was questioned for the first time. (✓)

(他的知識能力第一次遭到質疑。)

intellectual 表『與知識 (追求) 有關的』; intelligent 表『能思考並運用知識的』。因此, intellectual life 是指某人的『知性活動』, 而 intelligent life/beings 則是指『高等生物』。另外, intellectual ability/capacity (=intelligence) 則是指某人的『知識能力』或『智力』。

intelligence

He may belong to some intelligent organization. (✗)

He may belong to some intelligence organization. (✓)

(他也許隸屬某情報機構。)

intelligence 有兩個意思: (1) 智力, 如: an intelligence test 就是一次『智力測驗』(2) 情報, 如: an intelligence agency/organization 就是一個『情報單位/機構』。

intelligible

The article is written in such plain language that it is intelligent even to the layman. (✗)

The article is written in such plain language that it is intelligible even to the layman. (✓)

(這篇論文是用一種連門外漢都看得懂的淺易文字寫的。)

intelligible 表『容易看/聽得懂的』。

intention

I have no intention to spend the weekend there. (✗)

I have no intention of spending the weekend there. (✓)

(我並不打算在那兒度過週末。)

表『意圖/打算』做/不做某事的句型有: (1) intend to do sth (2) have no/every intention of doing sth (3) with the/no intention of doing sth。

interactivity

More interactivities between teacher and student should be encouraged. (✗)

More interactivity between teacher and student should be encouraged. (✓)

(應該多鼓勵老師和學生之間的互動。)

interactivity (互動) 是不可數名詞。另一個表『互動』的字是 interaction, 兼有可/不可數的用法, 如: Watch their classroom interaction(s)! (注意看他們上課時的互動!)

interested

I'm interested to run a coffee shop. (✗)

I'm interested in running a coffee shop. (✓)

(我對經營咖啡店有興趣。)

be interested in (doing) sth 表『對 (做) 某事有興趣』, 是固定用法。不過, 表『很想

I

知道某人的看法或訊息』時，可用 be interested to hear/know/read/learn, 如: I'd be interested to hear your opinion. (我很想聽聽你的意見。)

interfere

You don't have the right to interfere her affairs. (✗)

You don't have the right to interfere in her affairs. (✔)

(你無權干涉她的事情。)

interfere 是不及物動詞, 不能直接接受詞。interfere in sth 是『干涉/預』某事之意。interfere with sth 是『妨礙』某事之意, 如: You may take a part-time job if it doesn't interfere with your schoolwork. (如果不妨礙課業的話, 你可找份兼職的工作做。)

interior

My brother specializes in internal design. (✗)

My brother specializes in interior design. (✔)

(我的哥哥專門做室內設計。)

『室內設計 (師)』的固定說法是 interior design/designer。至於 internal 表『內部/服的』則見於 internal affairs (內政), internal bleeding (內出血), internal medicine (內服藥), internal struggle (內心的掙扎)。

internet

You can use Internet to shop online. (✗)

You can use the Internet to shop online. (✔)

(你可以使用網路進行線上購物。)

指『(網際) 網路』時恆用 the Internet。至於不加"the"的用法通常於固定的片語, 如: internet cafes (網咖) 或 internet services (網路服務)。

intolerable

It is absolutely intolerant! (✗)

It is absolutely intolerable! (✔)

(是可忍，孰不可忍！)

be intolerant (of sb/sth) 表某人對 (某人/物) 無法忍受, 如: I'm intolerant of narcissism/vegetarianism. (我對自戀狂/素食主義無法忍受。) 而 intolerable 是『令人無法忍受的。』

intrude

I hope we are not intruding your privacy. (✗)

I hope we are not intruding on your privacy. (✔)

I hope we are not invading your privacy. (✔)

(希望我們沒有侵犯你的隱私。)

intrude (侵入/犯) 是不及物動詞, 不可直接接受詞, 須結合 on/upon/into 形成片語, 再接受詞。或者也可單獨使用, 如: Am I intruding? (我有侵犯你了嗎?) invade (侵入/犯) 是及物動詞。

invest

We should invest more money on real estate. (✗)

We should invest more money in real estate. (✔)

(我們應該多投資點錢在房地產上。)

invest (money/time) in sth 指在某方面投入『資金/時間』, 是固定用法。

invitation

They traveled to Shanghai by the invitation of the mayor. (✗)
They traveled to Shanghai at the invitation of the mayor. (✔)
(他們受市長之邀到上海旅遊。)

at sb's invitation 或 at the invitation of sb 表『受某人之邀』, 是固定用法。另外 by invitation (only)表『僅限受邀人士 (參加)』, 如: The dinner party is by invitation only. (該餐會僅限受邀人士參加。)

invite

I'll invite them to a drink in a few days. (✗)
I'll invite them for a drink in a few days. (✔)
(再過幾天我會邀他們去喝兩杯。)

invite sb for a drink/meal 但 invite sb to a party/wedding/meeting。

involve

My present job needs a lot of administration. (✗)
My present job involves a lot of administration. (✔)
(我目前的工作需要做不少行政工作。)

need sth 表『對某物有需求』, 如: We need your endorsement for this product. (這個產品我們需要你來代言。) involve sth = include sth as a necessary part, 即『包含某事/物為其中必要部分』。

issue

You'll only blur the issue by saying that. (✗)
You'll only confuse the issue by saying that. (✔)
(你那樣說只會模糊問題的焦點。)

blur sth 通常是指『(使) 眼睛或照片等模糊』, 如: Tears blurred my eyes when I finished reading the story. (我讀完這個故事時, 淚水已經使我的眼睛模糊了。) 『模糊 (問題的) 焦點』的正確英文說法是 cloud/confuse/fudge the issue。

itchy

They were itchy for a dip in the water. (✗)
They were itching for a dip in the water. (✔)
(他們巴不得趕快跳下水去玩一玩。)

be itching for/to do sth 表『迫不及待想做某事』為固定用法。相當於『不覺技癢』這個說法。itchy 是形容詞, 表『發癢的』, 如: I felt itchy all over. (我感到全身發癢。) 另有引申的用法, 如: The man has itchy feet. (這個男士想出外旅遊/跳槽。) 又如: Keep your eye on that boy. He has itchy fingers. (盯著那個男孩。他會順手牽羊。)

item

The shot put is her best item. (✗)
The shot put is her best event. (✔)
(擲鉛球是她最拿手的項目。)

運動比賽的項目是 event。item 指的是一組物品或議事討論的項目, 如: Sorry, this item is not for sale. (抱歉, 這項東西不賣。) 或如: Let's go on to discuss the last item of the agenda. (咱們接下去討論本議程的最後一項。)

I

J j

J

jail

He spent three years in the jail. (?)
He spent three years in jail. (✔)
(他曾坐牢三年。)

指『牢獄』的地方時 jail 是可數名詞, 如: The Rev. William Smith went to a jail to preach. (威廉・史密斯牧師前往一所監獄傳道。) 指『坐牢/囚禁』的狀況時, jail 是不可數名詞, 如 (be) in/out of jail 即是『坐牢/出獄』, 而 break (out of) jail 是『越獄』之意。

jam

We were stuck in traffic jam for an hour. (✗)
We were stuck in a traffic jam for an hour. (✔)
(我們卡在車陣當中一個小時。)

指『交通壅塞』時, jam 是可數名詞。作為『果醬』解時, jam 兼有可/不可數的用法, 如: I want some strawberry jam. (我想要一點草莓果醬)。

The switchboard was crowded with complaints only several minutes later. (✗)
The switchboard was jammed with complaints only several minutes later. (✔)
(才幾分鐘過後，抱怨的電話便不絕於耳。)

crowded 表『人滿為患的』; jammed 表交通/電訊方面『壅塞的』。

jargon

This article is full of legal jargons. (✗)
This article is full of legal jargon/terms. (✔)
This article is full of legalese. (✔)
(這篇文章滿是法律學術語。)

jargon (術語/行話) 是不可數名詞, 如: legal/medical/computer jargon 就是指『法律/醫學/電腦術語』。term 是可數名詞。

jewel

The thief stole a lot of jewel. (✗)
The thief stole a lot of jewels. (✔)
(竊賊偷走很多珠寶。)

jewel 指的是一顆顆的『寶石』, 是可數名詞。jewelry 是指鑲有寶石的『首飾』或其它珠寶的集合名詞, 不可數, 如: She has spent a small fortune on jewelry. (在首飾、珠寶上她所費不貲。)

job

Tony has been out of job since the factory closed down. (✗)
Tony has been out of a job since the factory closed down. (✔)
(自從工廠關閉後東尼就一直沒工作。)

job 是『工作』的可數名詞, work 不可數。因此『沒有工作或失業』的說法是 be out of work/a job。

I'm willing to receive any job, even a part-time one. (✗)
I'm willing to accept/take any job, even a part-time one. (✔)
(我願意接受任何工作，甚至兼職的也行。)

提供一個工作 (機會) 是 offer a job, 接受一個工作是 accept/take a job。receive sth 通

J

常表『接到/獲』信件或邀請等。

What is your job? (✗)
What do you do (for a living)? (✔)
(你從事哪種行業？)

What is your job?固然文法無誤，但這個說法很『突兀』，不合英語習慣。詢問某人的職業應該說: What do you do (for a living)?

join

My son wants to join in the army. (✗)
My son wants to join the army. (✔)
(我兒子想加入陸軍的行列。)

『加入』某團體/機構的正確說法是 join sth，如: join a club/company，即成為某一俱樂部/公司的一員。join in (doing) sth 表『也加入某活動』，如: More people will join in the hunger strike. (將有更多人再加入此次絕食抗議的活動。)

You go on ahead, and I'll join with you later. (✗)
You go on ahead, and I'll join you later. (✔)
(你繼續往前走，我待會兒跟你會合。)

純粹表『跟某人會合』用join sb即可。join with sb (in dong sth) 表『與某人共同做某事』，如: I'm sure everybody joins with me in wishing you a pleasant journey. (我相信大家都願意跟我一起來祝你旅途愉快。)

joint

The two presidents are going to make a joined statement. (✗)
The two presidents are going to make a joint statement. (✔)
(兩位總統將發表一項共同聲明。)

表『聯合/共同的』一律用joint來形容名詞，如: It is our joint effort. (這是我們的共同努力。) 另外，a joint venture 是一個『共同投資事業』。joined 不能作形容詞使用。

joke

Everyone likes Jeff because he can play jokes. (✗)
Everyone likes Jeff because he can make jokes. (✔)
(每一個人都喜歡傑夫，因為他很會搞笑。)

play a joke/jokes (on sb)是 (對某人)『惡作劇』，如: If you play a joke on her, she may get irritated. (如果你對她惡作劇，她可能會生氣。) make/crack/tell a joke (或 jokes) 是『搞笑』或『說笑話』。

Are you joking me? (✗)
Are you joking? (✔)
Are you kidding (me)? (✔)
(你在開我玩笑嗎？)

joke 作動詞時是不及物的用法，kid 則兼有及/不及物的用法。不過，joke 可搭配若干介系詞使用，如: Ted enjoys joking with his colleagues. (泰德喜歡跟同事說笑。) 或如: She kept joking about my hairstyle. (她一直取笑我的髮型。)

journey

I took a journey to Amsterdam last month. (✗)
I made a journey to Amsterdam last month. (✔)
(上個月我往阿姆斯特丹做了一趟旅行。)

make/undertake/go on a journey to a

place 或 take/make/go on a trip to a place 均表『到某地去旅行』。

joy

It is joy to see you are friends again. (✗)
It is a joy to see you are friends again. (✔)
(看到你們言歸於好真是令人高興。)

作為『喜悅的感覺』時, joy 是不可數名詞, 如: We all jumped for joy on hearing the good news. (一聽到這好消息, 我們都雀躍不已。) 作為『令人喜悅的事物』時, joy 是可數名詞, 如: Come and discover the joys of snorkeling! (來發掘浮潛的種種樂趣吧!)

jump

The price of gold jumped up overnight. (✗)
The price of gold jumped overnight. (✔)
(黃金的價格一夕之間突然飆高。)

指價格或數量的突然增加, 用 jump 即可。jump up 是『向上跳』之意, 如: The cat jumped up onto the table. (那隻貓跳到桌上。)

juncture

At this junction, it's hard to predict the company's future. (✗)
At this juncture, it's hard to predict the company's future. (✔)
(在這個時間點上，還很難預測該公司的未來。)

junction 是道路或河川的『會合處』。juncture 是一個 (重要的)『時間點』。at this juncture 差不多等於 at present, 即『目前』之意。

junk

The park is full of junk. (✗)
The park is full of litter. (✔)
(公園裡滿是人們丟棄的垃圾。)

junk 通常是指存放在家中 (櫥櫃、車庫、地下室等) 不用的廢棄物, 如: You should dispose of all the junk in your garage. (你應該把車庫裡的所有廢棄物處理掉。) litter 指的是棄置在公共場所的『垃圾』。

justice

I don't think your criticism gives him justice. (✗)
I don't think your criticism does him justice. (✔)
(我認為你對他的批評不公。)

do justice to sb/sth 是『公平對待』某人/物之意, 如: The photo does not do justice to you. (你本人比照片漂亮/好看。)

K k

K

keen

Some women have a clear eye for bargains. (✗)
Some women have a keen eye for bargains. (✔)
(有些婦女對於揀便宜貨很犀利。)

clear 表『清澈的』, 如: She has a pair of big, clear eyes. (她有一對清澈的大眼睛。) keen 是指在感覺/判斷上『銳利的』。另外, be keen on sth/sb (主為英式用法) 表『對某物/人極有興趣』, 如: My dad is keen on fishing. (我老爸對釣魚極為熱衷。)

keep

Keep to right until I tell you to make a turn. (✗)
Keep right until I tell you to make a turn. (✔)
(靠右行駛直到我叫你轉彎為止。)

keep right/left/straight on 表『靠右/靠左/直直』行駛, 指的是『方向』。keep to a path/road 表『順著一條路』而行, 指的是『道路』, 如: Keep to the road until the end and then turn left. (順著這條路走到底, 然後再向左轉。)

It is hoped that the younger generation will keep on this tradition. (✗)
It is hoped that the younger generation will keep up this tradition. (✔)
(希望年輕的一代會繼續保持這傳統。)

keep (on) doing sth 表『繼續做某事』之意, 如: The reporters kept (on) asking him question after question. (記者們問題一個接一個地向他問不停。) Keep up sth 指的是『繼續保持某事物, 使之不中斷』, 主要以 tradition, custom, friendship 等為受詞。

You should get a job and earn your keeping. (✗)
You should get a job and earn your keep/living. (✔)
(你應該找份工作以維持生計。)

作名詞時 keep 意為『生計』。earn your keep = earn your living, 即『賺錢以維持你的生計』。keeping 有兩個意思: (1) 保管, 如: I'll leave the documents in your keeping. (我會把這些文件交與你保管)。 (2) 協調/配合, 如: In keeping with the occasion, we all wore black. (我們都穿黑色衣服以配合這個場面。)

key

Is there a key for these grammar exercises? (✗)
Is there a key to these grammar exercises? (✔)
(這些文法練習有附解答嗎?)

a/the key to sth 表作為某物的『鑰匙/關鍵/解答』, 是固定用法。

kick

The hoodlum kicked me at the stomach. (✗)
The hoodlum kicked me in the stomach. (✔)
(那個不良少年踢了我肚子一下。)

kick sb in the face/head/stomach, 即『踢某人的臉/頭/肚子』, 是固定用法。另外, aim a kick at sth 表 (準備)『朝某物踢過去』, 如: She aimed a kick at his leg

K

but missed. (她朝他的腿踢過去但沒踢著。)

They meant no harm. They just did it for a kick. (✗)

They meant no harm. They just did it for kicks. (✔)

(他們沒有惡意，只是為了好玩而已。)

for kicks = for fun 表『為了好玩』, 是固定用法。

I usually get the kick out of their banter. (✗)

I usually get a kick out of their banter. (✔)

(他們之間的嬉笑怒罵時常讓我感到興奮又開心。)

get a kick out of/from sth 是『從某事/物得到一種興奮的快感』。這個用法的 kick 也可換成 thrill。get the kick = be fired (被解僱), 是現已『罕用』的說法。

kill

She's made a kill in the stock market. (✗)

She's made a killing in the stock market. (✔)

(她進出股市頗有斬獲/獲利。)

make a killing = made a lot of money quickly, 即『在短期內賺大錢』。make a kill 是指猛獸/禽『獵殺了一隻 (弱小的) 動物』, 如: The lion must have made a kill because its fur has bloodstains on it. (這隻獅子一定獵殺過動物, 因為牠的毛皮血跡斑斑。)

Linda is dressed for the kill tonight. (✗)

Linda is dressed to kill tonight. (✔)

(琳達今晚打扮得真是嬌艷動人。)

be dressed to kill 表某人『穿得很吸引人』, 令人為之神魂顛倒, 是固定說法。另外, move/close/go in for the kill 是指某人/物 (逼近), 準備攻擊或打敗某人/物, 如: The shark is now closing in for the kill. (這一隻鯊魚現正逼近, 準備大開殺戒。)

kind

The hostess did not serve the best tea. She gave us something of the kind. (✗)

The hostess did not serve the best tea. She gave us something of a kind. (✔)

(女主人並沒有泡出最好的茶來請客。她給我們喝比較差的茶。)

sth of the/that kind 表『類似 (提過的) 某物之東西』, 如: My boss drives a fancy sports car, and I just want something of the kind. (我的老闆開了一輛很炫的跑車, 我也正想要擁有那樣的車子。) sth of a kind 是『較差/劣等的某物』。

David and his cousin are one of a kind. No wonder, they get along. (✗)

David and his cousin are two of a kind. No wonder, they get along. (✔)

(大衛和他的表弟真是物以類聚。難怪他們相處得來。)

one of a kind 是指某人/物『自成一族』或『很另類』, 與眾不同的意思, 如: My grandfather is one of a kind. He is eighty and still thinking of going back to school! (我的爺爺很另類, 都已經八十歲了, 還想回學校唸書!) two/three of a kind 是指『兩/三人性情喜好相同』, 物以

類聚之意。

K

knack

Once you get the knacks of using the joystick, you'll enjoy the game. (✗)

Once you get the knack of using the joystick, you'll enjoy the game. (✓)

(你一旦懂得如何使用操縱桿的竅門，你就會喜歡上這種遊戲。)

a/the knack (恆用單數) of doing sth 表『做某事的竅門/訣竅』。

knee

Tommy, come and sit on my knees. (✗)

Tommy, come and sit on my knee. (✓)

(湯米，來坐在我的大腿上。)

on sb's knee = on sb's lap 表『在某人(坐下時)的大腿上』。至於 on your knees是指『跪下來』的姿勢, 如: They were all on their knees praying. (他們都跪下來祈禱。) 另有引申用法, 如: The economy is still on its knees. (經濟仍然疲弱。)

knee-deep

After it had rained for three days, the mud was almost knee-high. (✗)

After it had rained for three days, the mud was almost knee-deep. (✓)

(下了三天雨之後，路上的泥巴都幾乎到膝蓋了。)

knee-high主要用來形容草或其它植物, 襪子或靴子『高及膝蓋』。如: The hedge was still only knee-high last year. (去年這樹籬還只有膝蓋這般高。) knee-deep 專用於形容水、下雪或泥巴『深及膝蓋』。另外, knee-length 則用來描述衣服、褲、裙等『長及膝蓋』, 如: She is wearing a knee-length skirt. (她穿著一件長及膝蓋的裙子。)

knock

I stood up to answer questions, my knees shaking. (✗)

I stood up to answer questions, my knees knocking. (✓)

(我站起來回答問題時，膝蓋不停地抖動。)

sb's knees are knocking (together) 表某人處於一種害怕或緊張的情況, 是固定用法。

That big man could knock anyone unconsciously with one punch. (✗)

That big man could knock anyone unconscious with one punch. (✓)

(那名大漢可以用一拳把任何人擊昏。)

knock sb unconscious/cold/senseless 表『將某人打成不省人事』, 是固定用法。

knotty

The new management faces some knotted problems. (✗)

The new management faces some knotty problems. (✓)

(新的經營團隊面臨一些棘手的問題。)

knotted 和 knotty 都是 knot (繩結/枝節) 的形容詞。前者表『打結的』, 如: a

K

knotted rope/handkerchief就是一條打結的繩子/手帕。後者表『棘手的』。

know

I walked to the balcony to know what was happening. (✗)

I walked to the balcony to find out what was happening. (✔)

(我走到陽台想知道到底發生什麼事。)

know sth 表對某事/物『已知』或『確知』的情況，如: He knows how serious the situation is. (他知道情況的嚴重性。) 表『想/探知』時應該用 find out。

When it comes to camping, my dad knows better. (✗)

When it comes to camping, my dad knows best. (✔)

(說到露營，聽我老爸準沒錯。)

sb knows best 表『某人對某方面的知識、經驗最豐富，聽他/她的絕對錯不了』。sb knows better 表『某人 (因知道的更多) 對某事深不以為然』，如: Everyone believes it was an innocent mistake, but I know better. (大家都以為這是一件無心之過，但我深不以為然。)

know-how

What we need is not the equipment but the know-hows. (✗)

What we need is not the equipment but the know-how. (✔)

(我們目前所需要的不是設備而是專業技術。)

know-how (專業技術) 是不可數名詞。

I'm afraid they do not have the know-how of handling the problem. (✗)

I'm afraid they do not have the know-how to handle the problem. (✔)

(恐怕他們沒有處理這個問題的技術。)

have the (necessary/technical) know-how + to V 為固定用法。

knowledge

To learn more knowledge, you have to read extensively. (✗)

To acquire more knowledge, you have to read extensively. (✔)

(為了獲取更多的知識，你必須廣泛地閱讀。)

儘管中文可說『學習』或『得到』知識，英文卻不能說 learn/get knowledge。正確的說法是: acquire/gain knowledge。learn something/a lot 是固定用法，如: You can learn a lot through reading. (你可以從閱讀當中學到很多知識。)

They got married without my knowing. (✗)

They got married without my knowledge. (✔)

(他們結婚時我並不知情。)

without sb's knowledge 或 without the knowledge of sb 表『沒有讓某人知道/情』，是固定用法。

knowledgeable

K

The programs on the Discovery Channel are very knowledgeable. (✗)

The programs on the Discovery Channel are very informative. (✓)

(『探索頻道』的節目都很有知識性。)

knowledgeable 是指某人 (在某方面)『很有知識』, 如: She is very knowledgeable about classical Chinese literature. (她對中國古典文學的知識十分淵博。) 至於 informative 專門用來形容報章、書籍或電視節目等『很有知識性』。

L

L

label

The bottle should be labeled with "Poison." (✗)

The bottle should be labeled "Poison." (✔)

(這瓶子上面應標示『毒藥』字樣。)

label sth with sth 表『以 (籠統的) 某名稱來標示』, 如: The test tube is labeled with his name. (這根試管有標示他的名字。) label sth sth 表『以(具體的) 名稱來表示』, 如: The test tube is labeled"Huntington." (這根試管標有『杭亭頓』的名字。)

labor

A few countries in SE Asia are a source of cheap labors. (✗)

A few countries in SE Asia are a source of cheap labor. (✔)

(若干東南亞國家是廉價勞工的來源。)

指『勞力/工』時 labor 為不可數名詞, 如: It'll take a lot of manual labor. (這個東西頗費手工。)

For me, writing the book is labor of love. (✗)

For me, writing the book is a labor of love. (✔)

(寫這本書對我而言是一件心甘情願的工作。)

a labor of love 是固定用法, 指某人『歡喜做, 甘願受』的工作。此用法引申自 labor 的另一意義: 分娩/生產。表『分娩/生產』時 labor 兼有可數 (恆用單數) 及不可數的用法, 如: She is in labor. (她正在生小孩。) 或如: The woman had a difficult labor. (這位女士生產困難。)

lack

As a politician, he seems to lack in political acumen. (✗)

As a politician, he seems to lack political acumen. (✔)

As a politician, he seems to be lacking in political acumen. (✔)

(作為一個政治人物，他似乎欠缺政治靈敏度。)

作為動詞時 lack 是及物的用法, 其後不可接介系詞。作為名詞時, lack 之後常接 of, 如: There is no lack of volunteers. (不缺志工。) 另外有一個用法是 be lacking in sth 表『缺乏某物』。

lane

It is a four-line highway. (✗)

It is a four-lane highway. (✔)

(這條公路是四線道。)

在道路上所分的『線道』應該說 lane 而非 line, 如: the inside/middle/outside lane 就是『外/中/內線道』, 而 the fast/slow lane 是指『快/慢車道』。另外, 『變換車道』的說法是 change lanes, 如: You changed lanes without giving a signal! (你變換車道時沒打信號燈!)

language

The principal has never used such a strong language. (✗)

The principal has never used such strong language. (✔)

(校長從來沒有措辭如此強硬過。)

作為某國家/地區的『語言』時, language 是可數名詞, 如: Latin is now a dead language. (拉丁文現是一種不再被用的語言。)作為『用語/措辭』時, language是不可數名詞, 如: literary/poetic language 即為『文學/詩的用語』。

lap

When he was watching TV, his little daughter came and sat on his thighs. (✗)

When he was watching TV, his little daughter came and sat on his lap/knee. (✔)

(他看電視時小女兒就過來坐在他大腿上。)

thigh (大腿) 限用於指身體部位時。表『坐在某人的大腿上』應該說 sit on sb's lap/knee。此為固定用法。

She fell down on the last circle of the race. (✗)

She fell down on the last lap of the race. (✔)

(在跑最後一圈時她跌倒了。)

circle 是指一般的圓圈, 如: Draw a circle or put an ✕ on it. (畫個圈或打個✕在上面。) 賽跑/車的『圈 (數)』應該用 lap。

lapse

A lapse into concentration would cost you the game. (✗)

A lapse of concentration would cost you the game. (✔)

(注意力稍或不濟就會讓你輸掉這場比賽。)

a lapse into sth 如同 lapse (v.) into sth 皆表『陷入』某種不好或不尋常的狀況, 如: The accident must have been caused by his lapse into sleep. (這起意外一定是他陷入睡眠狀態所造成。) a lapse of sth 表在某方面『有些閃失/失誤』。

large

It was in large a matter of poor management. (✗)

It was largely a matter of poor management. (✔)

It was in large part/measure a matter of poor management. (✔)

(這主要是經營不善的問題。)

largely = mainly = in large part/measure 意為『主要 (地)』。另外, be at large 表『逍遙法外』, 如: The murderer is still at large. (這名凶手仍逍遙法外。)

last

In the last years, many people have gone on a diet. (✗)

In recent years, many people have gone on a diet. (✔)

Over the last few years, many people have gone on a diet. (✔)

(近幾年來很多人在進行節食。)

in recent years/months/weeks 或 over the last few years/months/weeks 為固定用法。

This product is the last work in fashion. (✗)

This product is the last word in fashion. (✔)

(這種產品是目前最為流行的。)

the last word in sth 是某方面的極品或最為先進之物, 為固定用法。

The last but not least, I'd like to thank all the backstage staff. (✗)

Last but not least, I'd like to thank all the backstage staff. (✔)

(最後但也同樣重要的一點是我要感謝全體幕後工作人員。)

last but not least 是列舉事項時強調『最後但也同樣重要』的一點。

L

late

You are late for 30 minutes. (✗)
You are 30 minutes late. (✔)
(你遲到三十分鐘。)

be late for sth (不接時間) 表『做某事遲到』, 如: He was late for school/work this morning. (他今天早上上學/班遲到。) 表『遲到多久』應該用 be + 一段時間 + late。

I often had to work until late night. (✗)
I often had to work until late at night. (✔)
(以前我時常必須工作至深夜。)

late night 為名詞而且是可數用法, 如: He has had too many late nights recently. (他最近熬夜太多了。) late-night 是形容詞, 如: What about a late-night movie? (去看午夜場電影如何?) late at night 是副詞片語。

lately

Lately she told me something about her past. (✗)
Recently she told me something about her past. (✔)
(最近她跟我說一些有關她自己的過去。)

lately (最近) 限與現在完成式搭配。recently (最近) 可搭配現在完成式或過去簡單式使用。

latest

The latest election was full of muckraking. (✗)
The last election was full of muckraking. (✔)
(上一次選舉充滿了互揭瘡疤的現象。)

latest 意為『最新近的』, 主要用來形容最近『研發/設計/出版』的某物, 如: Have you read Milan Kundera's latest novel? (你讀過米蘭・康德拉的最新小說嗎？) last 表『上一個』。

latter

Politicians are generally branded as either conservatives or radicals. She belongs to the later group. (✗)
Politicians are generally branded as either conservatives or radicals. She belongs to the latter group. (✔)
(政治人物一般被歸納為保守派或激進派。她屬後者。)

later 表『時間上較晚』, 如: We can settle on the price at a later date. (我們往後再找個時間來敲定價格。) latter 表『順序上較後』。the latter 就是指『後者』。

laugh

Mr. Yamamoto burst into laugh when he heard the joke. (✗)
Mr. Yamamoto burst into laughter when he heard the joke. (✔)
(山木先生聽到那則笑話就笑了。)

laugh 作名詞是可數用法, 如: We all had a good laugh. (我們都笑得極為開心。) laughter 是不可數名詞。burst into laughter 為『突然笑了出來』, 是固定用法。

launch

The opposition parties will all launch their candidates for the presidency. (✗)

The opposition parties will all put up their candidates for the presidency. (✔)

(所有的反對黨都會推出候選人來角逐總統的寶座。)

launch sth 可表: (1) 發射, 如: launch a satellite (發射人造衛星) (2) 發動, 如: launch an attack/assault/offensive (發動一次攻擊) (3) 推出 (限商品), 如: The company will launch a new version of its software soon. (這家公司不久就要推出一款新的軟體。)『推出候選人』的說法是 put up a candidate/candidates。

launder

It is a new law designed to prevent money washing. (✗)

It is a new law designed to prevent money laundering. (✔)

(這是一條設計出來防止洗錢的新法令。)

launder money 或 money laundering 是『洗錢』的正確說法, 意指『將非法得來的錢透過合法的管道 (如存入銀行等) 後再加以動用』。

laundry

You go shopping without me because I'll have to do a laundry. (✗)

You go shopping without me because I'll have to do the laundry. (✔)

(你自己去購物好了，因為我有一堆衣服要洗。)

作為『待/已洗的衣服』解時, laundry 是不可數名詞。do the laundry (洗衣服) 是固定用法。作為『洗衣店』解時, laundry 是可數名詞, 如: Send the tuxedo to a laundry. (將這件小禮服送洗衣店洗吧。)

law

The legislature is an insitution that has the power to make law. (✗)

The legislature is an institution that has the power to make laws. (✔)

(立法機關是擁有權力制定法律的機構。)

作為『法律的整個體系』解時, (the) law 是不可數名詞, 如: We are all equal before the law. (法律之前人人平等。) 作為『個別的法令』或其它『規則』解時, law 是可數名詞, 如: draft a new law 即是『起草一條新法令』。

lay

They lay down their weapons and surrendered. (✗)

They laid down their weapons and surrendered. (✔)

(他們棄械投降。)

lie down (躺下) 的過去式為 lay down, 是不及物的用法, 如: Lie down and relax. (躺下來放鬆一下嘛。) 作『放下』解時, lay down 的過去式是 laid down, 是及物的用法。

layoff

If the economy keeps on worsening, there will be more layouts. (✗)
If the economy keeps on worsening, there will be more layoffs. (✔)
(如果經濟持續惡化，將會有更多的解雇效應發生。)

layout 是指房子或建築物的『格局』或書籍雜誌等的『版面編排』, 如: All the apartments have the same layout. (所有的公寓格局相同。) layoff 是指『(短暫的) 解雇』。

lazybones

Come on, lazybone, it's time to get up! (✗)
Come on, lazybones, it's time to get up! (✔)
(快點，懶鬼，該起床了。)

lazybones 單、複數同形, 是口語中用來稱呼『懶人』的說法。

lead

He plays the lead role in the labor movement. (✗)
He plays a leading role in the labor movement. (✔)
(在這次勞工運動中他扮演一重要角色。)

play the lead (role)專指某人在戲中 (電影或電視) 扮演男主角或女主角, 如: She'll play the lead (role) in the opera. (她將在這齣歌劇扮演女主角。) play a leading role 專指某人在活動中扮演一重要角色, 是『比喻』的用法。

Henry's joke went over like a leaded ballon. (✗)
Henry's joke went over like a lead ballon. (✔)
(亨利的笑話根本不好笑。)

a lead ballon 是指用『鉛』做成的氣球, 根本就飛不起來, 用來比喻某事徹底失敗。leaded 是形容詞, 意為『含鉛的』, 如 leaded gas 即是『含鉛汽油』。另外『無鉛汽油』是 lead-free gas。

leaf

The maple trees are already in leaves. (✗)
The maple trees are already in leaf. (✔)
(楓樹的葉子都已經長齊了。)

be in leaf (恆用單數) 是指樹葉 (重新) 長齊。come into leaf (恆用單數) 是指樹葉開始生長, 如: The tree is just coming into leaf. (這棵樹剛開始長葉子。) 其它情況使用複數形的 leaves 居多, 如: I had to sweep up the dead leaves that morning. (當天早上我必須清掃枯葉。)

leak

A water pipe took a leak because of the earthquake. (✗)
A water pipe sprang a leak because of the earthquake. (✔)
(因為地震一條水管突告破裂。)

水管或其它容器『突然破裂、漏水』的說法是 spring a leak。take a leak = take a

piss是『小便』之意,是較粗魯的說法。比較可以接受的說法是 go for/have/take a pee。

lean

Most people in China lean on Buddhism in religious beliefs. (✗)
Most people in China lean toward Buddhism in religious beliefs. (✔)
(大部份中國人在宗教信仰上傾向於相信佛教。)

lean on sb/sth是『依靠或倚靠某人/物』之意, 如: We all need someone to lean on in times of trouble. (遇到麻煩時我們都須依靠別人的幫忙。) lean toward sth是『傾向於支持/相信……』之意。

leaning

My father has a conservative political leaning. (✗)
My father has conservative political leanings. (✔)
My father has a leaning toward political conservatism. (✔)
(我老爸在政治立上傾向於保守主義。)

表『傾向於某種主義/思想』的英文句型有二: (1) (have) political/religious/feminist/socialist leanings (恆用複數) (2) (have) a leaning toward sth (多用單數)。

learn

How did you learn our new product? (✗)
How did you learn about our new product? (✔)
(你怎麼會知道我們的新產品？)

learn sth 是『學習某物』, 以語言/學科為主。learn about/of sth 是『得知/獲悉』某物。另外, learn (that)...亦可表『得知/獲悉』某種狀況, 如: I was surprised to learn that she had resigned. (得知她已辭職的消息我感到很驚訝。)

learned

The voluntary work isn't much fun, but it is a real learned experience. (✗)
The voluntary work isn't much fun, but it is a real learning experience. (✔)
(這種志工的工作並不怎麼有趣，不過確是很寶貴的學習經驗。)

learned 是形容詞。指人時是『有學問的』, 如: a learned man。指刊物時是『學術性的』, 如: a learned journal 即是一本『學術期刊』。a learning experience 是一種『寶貴的學習經驗』為固定用法。

leave

You won't get homesick until you leave home. (✗)
You won't get homesick until you are away from home. (✔)
(人總是在遠離家鄉時才會想家。)

leave home 的真正含意是『離開父母, 搬到外面獨立生活』, 如: I left home when I was only 17. (我才十七歲時就搬到外面獨立生活了。) be away from home 是『(暫時) 離開家』。

If I'm out, leave a message with me. (✗)
If I'm out, leave a message for

L

me. (✔)
(如果我不在，留個信息給我。)

leave a message/note with sb 是『留信息/字條給某人代為轉交』, 如: If I'm out, leave a message with my secretary. (如果我不在那兒，留個信息由我秘書轉交。)

Leave all the housework for me. I can manage. (✗)
Leave all the housework to me. I can manage. (✔)
(家事全留給我做好了。我可以搞定。)

leave sth for sb 是『將信息或食物留給某人』, 如: Leave some cake for us. (留點蛋糕給我們吧。) leave sth to sb 是『將某事留給某人做』。

She is now on a maternity leave. (✗)
She is now on maternity leave. (✔)
(她目前正在休產假。)

作名詞時 leave 意為『休假』或『准許』, 均為不可數用法。如: sick leave 是『病假』, maternity/paternity leave 是『產/陪產假』。

leeway

I think I'll give my children more leeways to make their own decisions. (✗)
I think I'll give my children more leeway to make their own decisions. (✔)
(我想我會給我的子女更多的空間去做決定。)

leeway 意為『自由的空間』, 是不可數名詞。

left-hand

Left-hand people were once thought of as freaks. (✗)
Left-handed people were once thought of as freaks. (✔)
(左撇子在從前曾被認為怪胎。)

left-hand 為形容詞, 指『在左手方的』, 如: The trash can is on the left-hand side. (垃圾桶就在左手邊。) left-handed 是『慣用左手的』。a left-handed person 也可說成 a left-hander/southpaw。另外, left-handed 也可作副詞用, 如: My son writes left-handed. (我兒子用左手寫字。)

leftover

They use leftover to feed stray dogs. (✗)
They use leftovers to feed stray dogs. (✔)
(他們用剩菜剩飯來餵流浪狗。)

leftover 是形容詞, 表『剩餘/下的』, 如: Leftover chicken makes a wonderful salad. (剩下來的雞肉可以做一道不錯的沙拉。)至於講『剩菜/飯』時恆用複數形的 leftovers。

legal

Prince Charles is the legal heir to the British throne. (✗)
Prince Charles is the legitimate heir to the British throne. (✔)
(查理斯王子是英國王位的合法繼承人。)

legal 與 legitimate 都可表『合法的』, 不過 legal 這個字另偏向『與法律有關的』, 如: legal action/limit/system 即指『法律的行動/限制/制度』。指『合法的婚姻/繼承』時, 限用 legitimate 這個字。

legend

A legend has it that the king was the devil incarnate. (✗)

Legend has it that the king was the devil incarnate. (✓)

(傳說這位國王是惡魔的化身。)

作為『傳說/奇故事』解時, legend 兼有可/不可數用法。不過 Legend has it that... (傳說……) 是固定用法。另外, 作為『傳奇人物』解時, legend 是可數名詞, 如: He is a Wall Street legend (他是華爾街的一位傳奇人物。)

legislation

Your son can be sentenced to three years in prison under the existing legislations. (✗)

Your son can be sentenced to three years in prison under the existing legislation. (✓)

(按現行的法令你的兒子可能被判三年。)

legislation 意為『立法 (程序)』或『法律/令』均為不可數用法。

leisure

The package tour caters to the leisure classes. (✗)

The package tour caters to the leisured classes. (✓)

(這趟包辦旅遊是以有閒階級為主打對象。)

leisure 與名詞的搭配見於 leisure time/activities/facilities/industry 即『休閒時間/活動/設備/事業』。the leisured classes 是『有錢有閒階級』的固定說法。

lens

Where are my contact lens? (✗)

Where are my contact lenses? (✓)

(我的隱形眼鏡哪裡去了?)

lens 是『透鏡』的單數形式, 其複數形為 lenses。

less

I think I'll vote for him because he is the less of two evils. (✗)

I think I'll vote for him because he is the lesser of two evils. (✓)

(我想我會把票投給他，因為兩害相權取其輕。)

less 表『較少』或『較不』, 如: You should eat less and exercise more. (你應該少吃多運動。) the lesser of two evils 或 the lesser evil 是指『兩個很濫的選擇中稍好的一個』, 為固定用法。

lethargic

The cold pills may make you feel lazy. (✗)

The cold pills may make you feel lethargic/listless. (✓)

(這種感冒藥可能會使你感到懶洋洋的。)

lazy 是『懶惰的』, 即偷懶不想做事之意。lethargic/listless 是『懶洋洋的』, 即沒精打采之意。

letup

There is still no letdown in the rain. (✗)

There is still no letup in the rain. (✔)
(雨勢仍舊沒有緩和的跡象。)

letdown 是指一件『令人失望的事』, 如: Your performance was a real letdown. (你的表現真令人失望。) letup 是『停止/減緩』之意。

L

liberty

I took the liberties of borrowing your bike while you were away. (✗)
I took the liberty of borrowing your bike while you were away. (✔)
(我很冒昧於你外出時借用了你的腳踏車。)

take the liberty of doing sth 是『很冒昧地做了某事』, 為固定用法。另外, take liberties with sth 是『竄改』某物, 如: The filmmaker took liberties with the original text of *The Iliad*. (該導演竄改了幾處《木馬屠城記》的原文。)

license

All these goods are sold under a license. (✗)
All these goods are sold under license. (✔)
(所有這些貨物的販售都是經過授權的。)

作為『執照』時 license 是可數名詞, 如: Do you have a driver's license? (你有駕駛執照嗎?) 作為『許可 (授權)』時, license 為不可數名詞。

Don't worry. He is a license physician. (✗)
Don't worry. He is a licensed physician. (✔)
(不用擔心。他是一名有照醫師。)

licensed 是形容詞, 意為『持/領有證照的』, 用來形容人或物, 如: a licensed gun 就是指『領有證照的槍枝』。

lie

The decision lies in our manager. (✗)
The decision lies with our manager. (✔)
(決定權在於我們的經理。)

lie in sth 表『在於某物』, 如: Our main interest lies in developing new software. (我們的興趣主要在於開發新的軟體。) lie with sb 表『在於某人』, 如: The blame seemed to lie with the police. (過失似乎在於警方。)

life

The island abounds in bird lives. (✗)
The island abounds in bird life. (✔)
(這個島上鳥類繁多。)

表『生物』時, life 為集合名詞, 不可數, 如: There is a wide variety of insect life in this area. (這一帶的昆蟲種類極多。) 指『生命』或『生活』時 life 兼有可/不可數用法, 如: A blood donation can save a life. (捐血一袋救人一命。)

He didn't expect to get a life for such a crime. (✗)
He didn't expect to get life for such a crime. (✔)
(他沒想到這種罪會判無期徒刑。)

指『無期徒刑/終身監禁』時的 life = life imprisonment, 為不可數名詞。get a life 是口語的用法, 用來『提醒某人找些有趣/意義的事做』, 如: Stop your idle talk and get a life! (不要再閒扯了, 趕快找些有意義事做吧!)

lift

Whenever I need Tom's help, he never lends a finger. (✗)
Whenever I need Tom's help, he never lifts a finger. (✔)
Whenever I need Tom's help, he never lends a hand. (✔)
(每當我需要湯姆幫忙時，他從不伸出援手。)

『伸出援手』的說法是 lend a hand 或 lift/raise a finger。

If you want to go into town, I can give you a raise. (✗)
If you want to go into town, I can give you a lift/ride. (✔)
(如果你想進城，我可以讓你搭個便車。)

give sb a raise 是給某人『加薪』, 如: My boss promised to give me a raise. (老闆允諾要給我加薪。)『讓某人搭便車』的說法是 give sb a lift/ride。

light

The clouds parted, and a light fell on the roof. (✗)
The clouds parted, and a ray of light fell on the roof. (✔)
(雲朵散開來，然後一道光線就投射在屋頂上。)

指『光線』或『明亮』時, light 為不可數名詞。『一道光線』的正確說法是 a beam/flash/ray/shaft of light。

Do you have light? (✗)
Do you have a light? (✔)
(借個火吧。)

指點菸的『用火』時, 如火柴或打火機, 恆用單數的 a light。指『交通號誌燈』時須視情況用單數或複數, 如: I nearly ran a red light. (我差一點就闖了紅燈。) 或如: Turn left at the next lights. (在下一個紅綠燈左轉。)

My dad is a shallow sleeper. (✗)
My dad is a light sleeper. (✔)
(我老爸是個淺眠者。)

shallow 是指『水淺』或某人言行舉止『膚淺』。『睡眠很淺的人』的說法是 a light sleeper。反之, 『睡得很沉的人』是 a heavy sleeper。

Some people prefer to travel lightly. (✗)
Some people prefer to travel light. (✔)
(有些人喜歡輕便旅行。)

不帶很多行李的『輕便旅行』之固定說法是 travel light。至於 travel lightly 如果硬要解釋, 則是指『淺嘗即止』的旅行方式。

lighting

Some cases of myopia are the result of poor lightings. (✗)
Some cases of myopia are the result of poor lighting. (✔)
(有些近視的病例是照明不足之結果。)

lighting 意為『照明 (設備)』, 是不可數名詞。

lightning

A car sped away at lightening speed. (✗)
A car sped away at lightning speed. (✗)
(一部汽車以閃電般的速度疾馳而去。)

L

『閃電』的英文是 lightning, 是不可數名詞。所以『一道閃電』不可說成 a lightning, 應該說 a flash of lightning。至於 lightening 是由動詞 lighten 變化而來。lighten 有二義: (1) 使/變輕鬆, 如: My mood was gradually lightening. (我的心情逐漸輕鬆起來。) (2) 放光明, 如: The sky is lightening in the east. (東邊的天空開始在放光明了。)

like

Do you like me to show you around? (✗)

Would you like me to show you around? (✓)

(你要我帶你四處參觀嗎？)

Do you like...? 純粹在問『你是否喜歡某人/物?』, 如: Do you like ice cream? (你喜歡冰淇淋嗎?) Would you like...? 則含有『邀請/請客』之意, 如: Would you like some ice cream? (你想不想吃點冰淇淋?)。

How do you like about Venice? (✗)

What do you like about Venice? (✓)

(你喜歡威尼斯的哪一點？)

like sth about sb/sth 表『喜歡某人/物的某一點 (特色)』, 如: What/The thing I like about John is his generosity. (我喜歡約翰的一點就是他的慷慨。) How do you like sth? 表『詢問對方對某事/物的看法』, 如: How do you like Venice? (你對威尼斯的看法如何?)

I know absolutely nothing about his like and dislike. (✗)

I know absolutely nothing about his likes and dislikes. (✓)

(我對他的好惡一概不知。)

sb's likes and dislikes (恆用複數) 表某人的『好惡』, 是固定用法。

Mr. Thompson was a real angel. We'll never see his likes again. (✗)

Mr. Thompson was a real angel. We'll never see his like again. (✓)

(湯普生先生真是個大好人。我們再也見不到像他這種人。)

sb's/sth's like (恆用單數) 是指『像某人/物 (一樣好) 的人或事物』, 如: The movie is fabulous! Have you ever seen its like? (這一部電影太棒了!你有看過這麼棒的嗎?) 另外, the like(s) of sb/sth 專指『某一特殊種類的人/物(尤指說話者討厭的)』, 如: I don't want you to associate with the likes of him. (我不希望你跟像他這種人打交道。)

limit

Don't exceed the speed limitation. (✗)

Don't exceed the speed limit. (✓)

(不要超過速限。)

作為名詞時, limit 指的是數量、時空或法律方面的『限制』, 如: age/speed/time/legal limit 即是年齡/速度/時間/法律的『限制』。複數的 limits 可指某人的『能耐』, 如: I know my limits. (我知道自己的能耐。) 至於 limitation 的主要用法有二: (1) 強調限制性的行為, 如: strategic arms limitation talks 指的是過去 (美俄) 舉行的『限制戰略武器談判』(2) 侷限性/缺陷 (常用複數), 如: He has his limitations as an actor. (作為演員, 他有他的侷限性。)

line

Most of our medical staff now work on the line. (✗)

Most of our medical staff now work on line. (✔)
(我們院方大多數的醫療人員都已在線上作業。)

on the line = on the phone 是指某人『正在(等人) 講電話』, 如: We have a customer on the line from Hongkong. (有一名香港的客戶現在電話線上。) on line 指的是『與電腦網路連線』。

listen

Everyone was listening to the signal to start. (✗)
Everyone was listening for the signal to start. (✔)
(每個人都在聽候出發的信號。)

listen to sth 是『聆聽音樂或某人講話』, 強調的是『一段時間』, 如: He was listening to music all day. (他一整天都在聽音樂。) listen for sth 是『聽候某個信號的發出』, 強調的是『瞬間』。另外, listen in on sb/sth 是『偷聽』之意, 如: Someone is listening in on us. (有人在偷聽我們說話。)

literate

All the employees are required to be computer literary. (✗)
All the employees are required to be computer literate. (✔)
(公司要求所有的員工都要會用電腦。)

literary 是『文學的』, 如: Mr. Evans is a famous literary critic. (伊凡斯先生是一位知名的文學批評家。) 至於 literate 本義為『識字的』, 後引申為『具有某方面知識的』, 如: She is musically literate. (她懂音樂。)

litter

The park and the lake are full of litters. (✗)
The park and the lake are full of litter. (✔)
(公園和湖裡滿是垃圾。)

litter 作為路人或遊客隨手丟棄的『垃圾』解時, 為不可數名詞。作為『一窩』小豬/狗/貓時, 為可數名詞。如: a litter of kittens 就是指『一窩小貓』。另外, 喜歡在公共場所亂丟垃圾的人, 英文稱之為 a litterbug。

live

Despite his unhealthy lifestyle, my grandfather lived to 92. (✗)
Despite his unhealthy lifestyle, my grandfather lived to be 92. (✔)
Despite his unhealthy lifestyle, my grandfather lived to the age of 92. (✔)
(雖然生活方式不健康，我的爺爺還是活到九十二。)

『活到多少歲數』的說法是 live to be + 數字或 live to the age of + 數字。

The game will be broadcast lively this evening. (✗)
The game will be broadcast live this evening. (✔)
(這場比賽今晚將現場轉播。)

live 作為形容/副詞時均表『現場的』, 如: a live broadcast 或 be broadcast live 都是『現場轉播』的意思。至於 lively 恆為形容詞, 表『活躍/熱烈的』, 如: The issue provoked a lively debate. (這個議題引發一場熱烈的辯論。)

L

living

The old woman makes a life as a medium. (✗)

The old woman makes a living as a medium. (✓)

(這名老婦人當靈媒謀生。)

『謀生』的一般說法是 make/earn a living。至於『勉強混口飯吃』的說法是 scratch/scrape out a living, 如: He managed to scratch a living by working as a lifeguard. (他當救生員總算可以勉強混口飯吃。)。

Life standards have improved over the past two decades. (✗)

Living standards have improved over the past two decades. (✓)

(過去二十年來生活水準已獲改善。)

與『生活/存』或『活生生』有關的名詞多搭配 living, 如: living conditions/standards 就是『生活條件/水準』; a living hell/death 即是一個『人間地獄/行屍走肉般的生活』。與『終身』或『生命』有關的名詞多搭配 life, 如: life imprisonment/partner 就是『終身監禁/伴侶』, 而 life form/sciences 即為『生命形式/科學』。

locate

The firefighters hurried to the scene and tried to locate the fire. (✗)

The firefighters hurried to the scene and tried to localize the fire. (✓)

(消防隊員趕到現場並設法使火勢不再擴大。)

作為『找出……之位置』解時, locate 和 localize 是同義字, 如: Several engineers are trying to localize/locate the flaw. (有幾位工程師正設法找出出問題的地方。) 但 localize sth 另有一個意思是『使……局部化』, 即控制使不致於擴大之意。

lone

A two-month-old baby was the lonely survivor of the car accident. (✗)

A two-month-old baby was the lone/sole survivor of the car accident. (✓)

(這起車禍的唯一倖存者是一名兩個月大的嬰兒。)

lonely 是『寂寞的』之意, 如: He is a lonely old man. (他是一個寂寞的老人。) lone = sole = only 是『單獨/唯一』之意。

long

It will take long to get the feel of the machine. (✗)

It will take a long time to get the feel of the machine. (✓)

(要懂這部機器的竅門需要花一段長時間。)

take long 僅限用於否定句或疑問句, 如: It won't take long to get there. (到那兒不需很久。) 肯定句須用 take a long time。

How long will you come back? (✗)

How soon will you come back? (✓)

(你多久會回來?)

how long 表『多久』時, 問的是停留某地或做某事的一段時間, 如: How long are you going to stay here? (你準備在這裡待多久?) how soon 問的是『還要多久』。

As long as you get to know him, you'll like him. (✗)

Once/As soon as you get to know him, you'll like him. (✔)

(你只要認識他，你就會喜歡他。)

as/so long as = on condition that (只要……) 是表『以某情況為條件』, 如: As long as it doesn't rain, we can go out to play. (只要不下雨, 我們就可以出去玩。) once/as soon as 這個『只要』是『一旦』的意思。

long-term

We are going to make a long-standing investment. (✗)

We are going to make a long-term investment. (✔)

(我們準備做一項長期投資。)

表『長期的』時, long-standing 強調的是『持續至目前已經很久的』, 如: As you know, he is a long-standing member of the club. (如你所知, 他是該俱樂部的長期會員。) long-term 強調的是『持續至未來很久的』。

look

Sophie got her good look from her mother. (✗)

Sophie got her good looks from her mother. (✔)

(蘇菲的美貌得自母親。)

表『容貌/姿色』時恆用複數的 looks, 如: She began to lose her looks at the age of 40. (四十歲時她開始喪失姿色。) 作『表/神情』解時, 用單數的 look, 如: He had a tired look on his face. (他一臉疲憊的表情。)

looker

A handful of lookers gathered at the scene of the accident. (✗)

A handful of watchers gathered at the scene of the accident. (✗)

A handful of onlookers gathered at the scene of the accident. (✔)

(有幾個圍觀的群眾聚集在事故的現場。)

looker 在現代英文的用法表『容貌姣好的人』, 尤指女性, 如: My aunt was quite a looker when young. (我姑媽年輕時是個大美女。) watcher 表『觀賞者』, 如: bird/whale watchers 就是指『賞鳥/鯨人士』。至於『旁觀者』應該用 onlooker/looker-on/spectator。

lose

We have missed the crucial time by doing nothing. (✗)

We have lost the crucial time by doing nothing. (✔)

(什麼事也沒做，我們已錯過關鍵時機。)

miss sth 表『錯過上課/機會/班車』等。如: Her illness caused her to miss a lot of lessons. (生病使她錯過了很多課。)『錯過/喪失』時機需用 lose 這個字。

lost

The key is lost from its usual place. (✗)

The key is missing from its usual place. (✔)

(鑰匙從平常放的地方不見了。)

『從原來的地方不見』, 用 missing。lost 表『被遺失在某個地方』, 如: The key is

lost somewhere in the house. (不知道鑰匙被遺失在屋子裡什麼地方。)

lot(s)

L

The war ended a lot of years ago. (✗)
The war ended many years ago. (✔)
(這場戰爭很多年前就結束了。)

a lot of (= lots of) 可接複數名詞或不可數名詞。接複數名詞時 a lot of 相當於 many, 接不可數名詞時則相當於 much。如: I have a lot of friends/time. (我有很多朋友/時間。) 但 a lot/lots of 不接 days/weeks/months/years。習慣用法是 many days/weeks/months/years。

love

We went to Sydney last month and loved it very much. (✗)
We went to Sydney last month and loved it. (✔)
(我們上個月到雪梨便愛上了它。)

作『動詞』時 love 的用法如下: (1) love sb (very much) 表『(非常)愛某人』(2) love sth (不接 very much), 表非常喜歡某物, 因為 love sth = like sth very much。

Romeo is Juliet's first lover. (✗)
Romeo is Juliet's first love. (✔)
(羅蜜歐是茱麗葉的初戀對象。)

lover 意為『情人/侶』, 其複數的用法 (兼指男女時) 較為中性, 如: I saw a pair of young lovers sitting on the bench. (我看到一對年輕的情侶坐在長椅上。) 單數的用法往往含負面的意思, 即已婚人士外遇的對象, 如: He killed his wife's lover. (他殺死老婆的情夫。)『初戀的對象』是 first love, 為固定用法。

low

The helicopter seemed to be flying very lowly. (✗)
The helicopter seemed to be flying very low. (✔)
(那一架直昇機似乎飛得很低。)

low 可作形容詞或副詞用。至於 lowly 只作形容詞用, 表身分/地位『卑微的』, 且僅限於文學用語, 如: a man of lowly birth 就是一個『出身卑微的人』。

The euro fell to new low against the dollar last Friday. (✗)
The euro fell to a new low against the dollar last Friday. (✔)
(上週五歐元兌美元跌至一個新低點。)

作名詞時, low 是可數名詞, 意為『低點』, 如: an all-time low 或 a record low 就是指一個『有史以來』或『創記錄』的新低點。

luck

Many people believe it's a bad luck to walk under a ladder. (✗)
Many people believe it's bad luck to walk under a ladder. (✔)
(不少人認為從梯子底下走過會帶來霉運。)

luck 意為『運氣』是不可數名詞。若要可數, 須加單位, 如: a bit/piece/stroke of luck 指的就是『一點/個 (好) 運氣』。Winning the lottery was quite a stroke of luck. (贏得樂透彩真是好運氣。)

You have been lucky enough tonight. Don't pull your luck! (✗)
You have been lucky enough tonight. Don't push your luck! (✔)
(你今晚運氣夠好了，見好就收吧！)

push your luck 表『想冒險將自己的好運推至極限』, 是固定用法。

As luck should have it, they failed again. (✗)
As luck would have it, they failed again. (✓)
(很不幸的是，他們又失敗了。)

as luck would have it 是固定用法, 可依前後文意釋為『很幸運 (地)』或『很不幸 (地)』, 如: As luck would have it, the soldier came home safe and sound. (很幸運地, 這個士兵安然無恙返抵家門。)

luxury

We cannot afford such luxury things. (✗)
We cannot afford such luxury goods. (✓)
We cannot afford such luxuries. (✓)
(我們負擔不起像這樣的奢侈品。)

luxury 作為不可數名詞時意為『奢侈 (行為)』, 如: The young couple used to live in luxury. (這一對年輕的夫妻曾經生活奢侈。) 作可數名詞時, luxury 是『奢侈品』。作形容詞時, luxury 是『奢侈昂貴的』, 如: luxury goods/items 是『奢侈品』的另一種說法。沒有 luxury things 的說法。

L

A Quick Note

Mm

M

machine

All the eggs are sorted by machinery. (✗)

All the eggs are sorted by machine. (✔)

(所有的雞蛋都經過機器分類。)

machine 雖為可數名詞, 但 by machine 是固定用法。machinery (= machines) 是『機器』的集合名詞, 不可數, 用法如: A lot of new machinery has been installed. (很多新機器已被裝置完畢。)

mad

They had to work like madness to meet the deadline. (✗)

They had to work like mad to meet the deadline. (✔)

(他們必須拚命地工作以便如期完工。)

like mad = like crazy 表『拚命地』或『極快地』, 是固定用法。

magic

The medicine works like magics. (✗)

The medicine works like magic. (✔)

(這種藥功效神奇。)

作為名詞時, magic 為不可數用法。

David did some magical tricks to amuse us. (✗)

David did some magic tricks to amuse us. (✔)

(大衛變了幾道魔術來取悅我們。)

magic tricks 是『魔術』的英文習慣說法。至於 magical 除了表『神奇的』, 如: The crystal ball has some magical power. (這顆水晶球具有某種神奇的力量。) 亦可表『美妙的』或『浪漫的』, 如: We spent a magical evening at the beach. (我們在海灘上共度一個美妙的夜晚。)

mail

The player has received a lot of fan mails. (✗)

The player has received a lot of fan mail. (✔)

(這名球員接獲不少球迷寄來的郵件。)

作為名詞時, mail (郵件) 為不可數名詞。junk mail 是『垃圾郵件』。

major

The major opinion is that foreign labor should be decreased. (✗)

The majority opinion is that foreign labor should be decreased. (✔)

(大多數的意見是外勞應該減少。)

major 是『主要的』之意, 但意見並沒有主要/次要之分。the majority opinion/view 是『大多數 (人) 的意見』。

make

What brand is your cellphone? (✗)

What make is your cellphone? (✔)

(你的手機是什麼廠牌?)

brand 是一般產品的廠牌如: We have all leading brands of perfume in stock. (所有主要廠牌的香水我們都有現貨。)。車輛或機器的廠牌一律用 make, 如: It is a very popular make of computer. (這是一個很受歡迎的電腦廠牌。)。

makeup

She did not wear any cosmetics. (✗)
She did not wear any makeup. (✔)
(她脂粉不施。)

cosmetics (恆用複數) 指的是像乳液、口紅、粉餅等『化妝品』的總稱, 強調的是這類瓶瓶、罐罐的產品。makeup (不可數) 強調的是塗抹在臉上的脂粉或彩妝。

making

You have the making of a first-rate lawyer. (✗)
You have the makings of a first-rate lawyer. (✔)
(你具備有一流律師的條件。)

表『造就』或『造成』時, 用單數形的 making, 如: Two years of army life was the making of him. (兩年的軍旅生活造就了他。) 又如: All the trouble was of your own making. (所有的麻煩都是你自己惹出來的。) have the makings of sth 表『具備成為某物之條件』, 恆用複數的 makings。

manner

Mind your table manner. (✗)
Mind your table manners. (✔)
(注意你的餐桌禮儀。)

表行事的『方式』或『態度』時, 恆用單數的 manner, 如: See that everything is done in the correct manner. (每件事務必要以正確的方式來做。) 表『禮貌/儀』時, 恆用複數形的 manners。

The supermarket has all manners of vegetables for sale. (✗)
The supermarket has all manner of vegetables for sale. (✔)
(超市有各式各樣的蔬菜出售。)

all manner of sth 表『各式各樣的某物』, 恆用單數形的 manner。這個用法相當於 all kinds/sorts/types of sth。

maneuver

A large-scale military maneuver will be carried out next month. (✗)
Large-scale military maneuvers will be carried out next month. (✔)
(下個月將進行大規模的軍事演習。)

表『軍事演習』時, 恆用複數的 maneuvers。表『策略』或『手腕』時, maneuver 兼有單/複數的用法, 如: It was a maneuver designed to divert public attention from the real issue. (這種手法就是為了轉移民眾對於真正問題的注意力。)

manic

His sister has suffered from maniac depression for years. (✗)
His sister has suffered from manic depression for years. (✔)
(他的妹妹患有躁鬱症已有好幾年了。)

maniac 是名詞, 意為『瘋子』或『狂熱分子』, 如: Her father is a religious maniac. (她父親是一名宗教狂熱分子。) manic 是形容詞, 表『躁狂的』。manic depression 是『躁鬱症』的固定說法。

map

They never taught us how to look at a map at school. (✗)

They never taught us how to read a map at school. (✔)
(在學校他們從來沒有教我們如何看地圖。)

『看地圖』的正確說法是 read a map。

mark

I suggest you buy only toys that carry a brand. (✗)
I suggest you buy only toys that carry a mark. (✔)
(我建議你只買有廠商標記的玩具。)

brand是『廠牌』, mark是『廠商標記』。carry a mark 是固定用法。

Your guess was way of the mark. (✗)
Your guess was way off the mark. (✔)
Your guess was wide of the mark. (✔)
(你猜得太離譜了。)

way off the mark = wide of the mark, 均表『差得太遠』或『錯得離譜』。

market

Many people are now on the market for this kind of product. (✗)
Many people are now in the market for this kind of product. (✔)
(目前很多人都想買這種產品。)

on the market是指產品『上市』, 如: Their new products are not yet on the market. (他們的新產品尚未上市。) be in the market for sth 是『想買某物』之意。

A few friends of mine are playing stocks. (✗)
A few friends of mine are playing the market. (✔)
(我有幾個朋友在玩股票。)

『玩股票』的正確說法是 play the (stock) market。至於『買賣股票』的說法是 buy and sell stocks/shares。

You should contact the company's market manager. (✗)
You should contact the company's marketing manager. (✔)
(你應該跟該公司的行銷經理接觸。)

market 是『市場』之意, 而 marketing 則為『行銷』。marketing manager 是『行銷經理』, 為固定說法。

marriage

We are related by a marriage. (✗)
We are related by marriage. (✔)
(我們是姻親。)

marriage 兼有可/不可數的用法。可數的用法如: Many marriages end in divorce. (許多的婚姻以離婚收場。) 不過 by marriage (以婚姻關係) 是固定用法。其它的慣用法如: My parents do not approve of sex before marriage. (我父母不贊成婚前性行為。)

married

My older sister was married with a dentist five years ago. (✗)
My older sister was married to a dentist five years ago. (✔)
(我老姊五年前跟一個牙醫師結婚。)

be/get married to sb 表『與某人結婚』, 是固定用法。另外, be married to sth 表『專心投入/從事某事』, 如: She's married to her job. (她專心投入自己的工作。)

martial

The government may declare marshal law islandwide. (✗)
The government may declare martial law islandwide. (✔)
(政府可能宣布全島實施戒嚴法。)

marshal 是某些國家的『陸軍或空軍元帥』或美國某些地區的警政/消防最高首長。martial 是形容詞, 意為『戰爭/鬥的』。因此 martial law 就是『戒嚴法』, martial arts 就是像柔道或空手道的『武術』。

massage

I was doing a full-body massage then. (✗)
I was having a full-body massage then. (✔)
(當時我正在做全身按摩。)

have a massage 表某人接受按摩師或其他人的按摩動作。give sb a massage 表幫某人做按摩。

master

The mother tape is missing. (✗)
The master tape is missing. (✔)
(那捲母帶不見了。)

表『可以用來複製』的母帶/碟, 用 master 來形容, 如: a master disk/tape。

The man is suspected of being the master behind the assassination. (✗)
The man is suspected of being the mastermind behind the assassination. (✔)
(這個男子被懷疑是這起暗殺事件背後的主謀。)

the mastermind of/behind sth 表某人是某(不法) 行為背後之主謀。

match

The yellow tie does not match with your shirt. (✗)
The yellow tie does not match/go with your shirt. (✔)
(這條黃色的領帶和你的襯衫不相配。)

match sth = go with sth 表『與某物相配』之意。

material

He's collecting materials for a novel. (✗)
He's collecting material for a novel. (✔)
(他正在為一本小說收集題材。)

作『布料』或『建築材料』解時, material 兼有可/不可數的用法, 如: These materials are soft and comfortable to wear. (這些布料穿起來柔軟舒適。) 又如: Brick is still used as a main building material in this country. (磚在這個國家仍舊被用為一種主要的建材。) 作為小說、電影的『題材』時, material 是不可數名詞。

maternal

From now on you have to wear maternal clothes. (✗)
From now on you have to wear maternity clothes. (✔)
(從現在開始你必須穿孕婦裝了。)

maternal 表『(已)為人母的』或『母系的』

M

如: Her maternal instincts are quite strong. (她的母性本能十分強烈。) 又如: He is my maternal uncle. (他是我的母舅。) maternity 是『孕婦的』, 如: She's now on maternity leave. (她現正在休產假。)

matter

I think it's a problem of opinion. (✗)
I think it's a matter of opinion. (✔)
(我想這是個人看法的問題。)

problem 指的是造成困擾, 亟待解決的『問題』, 如: a problem of unemployment 就是一個『失業問題』。matter 指的是需要考慮或抉擇的事情/問題, 如: It's a matter of personal taste/choice. (這是一個個人品味/喜好的問題。) 另外, a matter of + 一段時間強調『在短短的一段時間裡』, 如: The ambulance arrived in a matter of a few minutes. (救護車在短短的幾分鐘裡就趕到了。)

mean

If you go alone, it will mean to risk your life. (✗)
If you go alone, it will mean risking your life. (✔)
(如果你單獨前往，這將意謂著你要冒生命之危險。)

mean + 不定詞 表『意圖……』, 如: He meant to give you a surprise. (他意圖給你一個驚喜。) mean + Ving 表『意謂 (某種結果)』。

George and Mary were born for to each other. (✗)
George and Mary were meant for each other. (✔)
(喬治和瑪麗真是天生一對。)

be meant/made for each other 指兩人很適合在一起, 是『天生一對』的固定說法。

means

She's determined to get what she wants by all means. (✗)
She's determined to get what she wants by any means. (✔)
(她決定要用一切手段來得到她想要的。)

by all means = of course (當然) 用來表達『同意』別人的要求或建議。指『用任何手段』時, 需說 by any/ whatever means。除了表『手段』之外, means 亦可表個人的『財力』, 如: Try to live within your means. (要量入為出。) 反之, live beyond your means 就是『入不敷出』。

measure

A salesclerk took my measures and showed me a pair of pajamas in my size. (✗)
A salesclerk took my measurements and showed me a pair of pajamas in my size. (✔)
(一名店員量了我的尺寸，然後拿出符合我身材的一套睡衣給我看。)

take (adj.) measures 是『採取 (某種) 措施』之意, 如: The government really should take drastic measures to bring down unemployment. (政府應該採取強烈措施來降低失業率。) take sb's measurements 表『量某人的尺寸』。

mechanic

The flight has been cancelled due to mechanic failure. (✗)

The flight has been cancelled due to mechanical failure. (✔)
(由於機械故障，這個班機取消了。)

mechanic 是名詞, 意為修理汽車或機械的『技 師/ 士』, 如: Bruce is an airplane mechanic. (布魯斯是一名飛機機械技士。) mechanical 是形容詞, 意為『機械的』。

media

The role of media is to form public opinion. (✗)
The role of the media is to form public opinion. (✔)
(媒體的角色就是要形成輿論。)

指電視、收音機、報紙的『媒體』時, 恆用 the media, 如: Both political parties accused the media of bias. (兩個政黨都指控媒體報導不公。) 但 media attention/coverage/interest 其前通常不如"the", 如: The event received wide media coverage. (這個事件獲得媒體廣泛的報導。)

Television is a very influential media. (✗)
Television is a very influential medium. (✔)
(電視是一個非常有影響力的媒體。)

medium 是『媒體』的單數形式, media 為其複數形式。

medicine

I forgot to eat my medicine. (✗)
I forgot to take my medicine. (✔)
(我忘了吃藥。)

『吃藥』或『喝藥』, 英文不能說 eat/drink medicine, 須說 take (your) medicine。

I think I'll study traditional Chinese medicines. (✗)
I think I'll study traditional Chinese medicine. (✔)
(我想我會學習傳統中醫。)

作『藥物』解時 medicine 兼有可/不可數的用法, 如: Good medicine tastes bitter. (良藥苦口。) 或如: We have a variety of cough medicines. (我們有各式各樣的咳嗽藥。) 但作『醫學』或『療法』解時, medicine 恆不可數。

medium

My husband is a man of medium intelligence. (✗)
My husband is a man of average intelligence. (✔)
(我老公是一個智力中等的人。)

指『尺寸大小』或『烹調程度』中等的, 用 medium, 如: He's of medium height. (他不高不矮。) 或如: I'd like my steak medium. (我的牛排要五分熟的。) 指中等的『智力』或『技巧』要用 average。

member

Turkey is not yet a formal member of the EU. (✗)
Turkey is not yet a full member of the EU. (✔)
(土耳其尚未成為歐盟的正式會員。)

『正式會員』的英文是 a full member。formal的中文意思雖有『正式的』之意, 但其強調的是『官方』或『公開』的內涵, 如: The government has promised to launch a formal investigation. (政府已答應展開正式的調查。)

Show your member card when you enter. (✗)

M

Show your membership card when you enter. (✔)
(進入時請出示會員卡。)

『會員卡』的英文說法是 membership card。

memo

I will keep the coin as a memo of making a trip here. (✗)
I will keep the coin as a memento of making a trip here. (✔)
(我會留下這枚硬幣以作為到此一遊的紀念物。)

memo 是 memorandum 的縮寫, 意為『備忘錄』, 如: She sent me a memo remiding me of the briefing. (她送來一則備忘錄, 提醒我關於簡報之事。) memento 是某人特別留下來提醒自己某事/物之紀念品。另外, souvenir 則是指從旅遊地點買回來送親友的紀念品。

memoir

Hillary Rodham Clinton has just published her memoir. (✗)
Hillary Rodham Clinton has just published her memoirs. (✔)
(希拉蕊剛出版她的回憶錄。)

表公眾人物(自已寫)的『回憶錄』時, 恆用複數的 memoirs。單數的 memoir 是別人為你寫的一篇『傳記』。

memory

They are having a party in memory of their 25th wedding anniversary. (✗)
They are having a party in celebration of their 25th wedding anniversary. (✔)
(他們為紀念結婚二十五周年而舉行一個派對。)

in memory of sb 只能用於『紀念亡故的人』, 如: A statue will be erected in memory of the hero. (將立一座銅像來紀念這名英雄。) 另外, in honor of sb/sth 則兼有『紀念某人』和『慶祝某事』之意, 如: St. Petersburg was renamed Leningrad in honor of Lenin. (為了紀念列寧, 聖彼德堡被改名為列寧格勒。) 或如: Robert Frost recited one of his poems in honor of the occasion. (詩人羅伯・佛洛斯特朗誦自己寫的一首詩來慶祝這個重要場合。)。

mere

Tom's mere a child. (✗)
Tom's a mere child. (✔)
Tom's merely a child. (✔)
(湯姆不過是個孩子。)

a mere + n. = merely a (n) + n.表『只是一個……』。

mess

Don't make mess of the kitchen. (✗)
Don't make a mess of the kitchen. (✔)
(不要把廚房弄得髒兮兮的。)

make a mess of sth, 是固定用法, 表『把某個地方弄髒』或『把某事搞砸』, 如: He felt he had made a mess of his marriage. (他覺得他已經把婚姻搞砸了。)

message

I'm sorry. Mr. White is out right now. Can I leave a message? (✗)

I'm sorry. Mr. White is out right now. Can I take/you leave a message? (✔)
(抱歉，懷特先生目前外出，能留言嗎？)

Can I leave a message? (我能留言嗎?) Can I take a message? = Can you leave a message? (你能留言嗎?) 另外, a text message是手機的『簡訊』, 如: I have just received a text message from my partner. (我剛接獲一則來自合夥人的簡訊。)

metal

They deal in such precious metal as gold and silver. (✗)
They deal in such precious metals as gold and silver. (✔)
(他們做金、銀等貴金屬的買賣。)

作為『金屬』的總稱時, metal 為不可數名詞, 如: The gate is made of metal. (大門是金屬做的。) 指個別的『金屬』時, metal為可數名詞。另外, heavy metal (不可數) 是指一種極為刺耳的『搖滾樂』, 如: Heavy metal really gets on my nerves. (重金屬的搖滾樂真的會令我心神不寧。)

middle

My wife woke me up at the middle of the night. (✗)
My wife woke me up in the middle of the night. (✔)
(我老婆在半夜時把我叫醒。)

in the middle of the night 泛指在『深夜』的任何一個時間。at midnight 特指『午夜』十二點時。

Her boyfriend is of middle height and wears a pair of glasses. (✗)
Her boyfriend is of medium height and wears a pair of glasses. (✔)
(她的男友中等身材並戴一副眼鏡。)

指『中等的』高度或體重時, 限用 medium而非 middle。middle 表『中間的』, 通常用來形容地方或時間, 如: The bankbook is in the middle drawer. (銀行的存摺在中間的抽屜)。

migrate

We are planning to migrate to New Zealand after we retire. (✗)
We are planning to emigrate to New Zealand after we retire. (✔)
(我們計劃退休後移民至紐西蘭。)

migrate 一般是指野生動物季節性的遷移, 或表某人為找工作而遷移至某地/國。既然人都退休了, 用 migrate 不恰當。『移民』要用 emigrate (移出) 或 immigrate (移入)。

mind

He seldom gets angry. He must have a lot in his mind. (✗)
He seldom gets angry. He must have a lot on his mind. (✔)
(他平常很少動怒。他一定有不少煩心的事。)

in sb's mind 表『在某人心裡 (想著)』, 如: I wonder what's going on in your mind. (我很想知道你心裡在想些什麼。) on sb's mind 是『(有事) 令某人憂慮、心煩』。

My brain is a complete blank. (✗)
My mind is a complete blank. (✔)
(我的腦筋一片空白。)

brain 指的是『腦』這個器官。blank 是『空白的』或『空無一物』。因此, brain 搭配 blank 豈不得了『無腦症』? mind 是

M

思考、想像、推理的一個內心世界，是 brain 這個器官的『發用處』。

minor

The university does not discriminate against minor students. (✗)
The university does not discriminate against minority students. (✔)
(這所大學不會岐視少數族群的學生。)

minor 意為『較小的』或『次要的』，如：She played a minor role in the play. (她在這齣戲中扮演一個小角色。) minority 是『少數』，相對於『多數』的 majority。

minus

Before I make the final decision, I have to weigh up the plus and minus. (✗)
Before I make the final decision, I have to weigh up the pluses and minuses. (✔)
(在我做最後決定之前，我必須先權衡利弊的問題。)

作為名詞時，minus = disadvantage，指的是『弊病』或『缺點』，是可數名詞，如：Being a public figure is sometimes a minus, too. (當個公眾人物有時候也是一項缺點。) pluses and minuses (恆用複數)，指的是事物的『利弊得失』。

Bill got a minus B on his essay. (✗)
Bill got a B minus on his essay. (✔)
(比爾寫的文章得到乙下。)

A/B/C/D minus 或 plus 為評定成績/等級的固定說法。

minute

Wait for a minute, and I'll be right with you. (✗)
Wait a minute, and I'll be right with you. (✔)
(稍候一下，我馬上過來陪你。)

wait a minute = just a minute 是固定說法。使用情況有二：(1) 用來告訴別人稍候。(2) 用來告訴別人不要驟下結論，如：Wait a minute, that can't be right. (等一等，那不可能是對的)

We need someone to take the minute. (✗)
We need someone to take the minutes. (✔)
(我們需要有人來做會議記錄。)

take the minutes (恆用複數) 表『做會議記錄』是固定說法。

miracle

T'ai Chi has worked a miracle for me. (✗)
T'ai Chi has worked miracles for me. (✔)
(打太極拳已經對我產生奇蹟式的功效。)

a miracle 通常是指一件極為幸運又不可思議之事，如：It's a miracle that you are back safe and sound. (你能安然無恙回來真是一件奇蹟。) work/perform miracles (恆用複數) 表『產生奇蹟式的功效或結果』，是固定用法。

mire

The ruling party is sinking into the mud of a power struggle. (✗)
Thr ruling party is sinking

into the mire of a power struggle. (✔)
(執政黨正陷入權力鬥爭的泥淖。)

mud 表『泥巴』, 如: His shoes are covered in mud. (他的鞋子沾滿了泥巴。) mire 本義為一片『泥淖』, 引申為『難以自拔的困境』the mire of sth 是其引申。

mirror

Daisy looked at the mirror and was satisfied with the way she dressed. (✗)
Daisy looked (at herself) in the mirror and was satisfied with the way she dressed. (✔)
(黛西照了鏡子，對自己的穿著很滿意。)

look at a mirror 只是看著一面鏡子, 未必有『照』的動作。『照鏡子』的英文說法是 look (at oneself) in a mirror。

misgiving

Some scholars have expressed deep misgiving about the policy. (✗)
Some scholars have expressed deep misgivings about the policy. (✔)
(部分學者對該項政策深表疑慮。)

misgiving 是名詞, 表『疑慮不安』, 通常以 express deep/grave/serious misgivings (about)...的型式出現。

mislead

People are often misguided into believing those TV commercials. (✗)
People are often misled into believing those TV commercials. (✔)
(民眾經常被誤導因而相信那些電視廣告。)

misguided 現今只用作形容詞, 不作被動使用。misguided = wrong, 如: He is still clinging to his misguided belief. (他仍然堅持自己的錯誤想法。) be misled into doing sth 表『被誤導去做某事』, 是固定用法。另外, misleading 是形容詞, 表『誤導(人)的』, 如: Statistics, as we know, can be very misleading. (我們都知道, 統計數字相當容易誤導人。)

mist

We drove through the thin fog carefully. (✗)
We drove through the thin mist carefully. (✔)
(我們在薄霧中小心行駛著。)

fog 是『濃霧』, 經常用 dense, heavy 或 thick 來形容, 如: All the aircraft were grounded because of dense fog. (因為濃霧所有的飛機都停飛。) mist 是『薄霧』。

mixed

Danny had mixing emotions about getting a divorce. (✗)
Danny had mixed emotions about getting a divorce. (✔)
(丹尼離婚時百感交集。)

mixed feelings/emotions 為『百感交集』的固定說法。另外, a mixed blessing 是『利弊互見』或『毀譽參半』之意。至於 mixing 的用法大概僅見於 a mixing bowl (調理碗) 一詞。

M

M

mobility

A car would give you a greater mobility. (✗)
A car would give you greater mobility. (✓)
(擁有一部汽車可以讓你行動更為自如。)

mobility 意為『行動(能力)』,是不可數名詞。另外, the mobility impaired 是指『行動不便的人們』, 如: There is a special passageway for the mobility impaired. (有一條專為行動不便人士準備的通道。)

moist

The cave is dark and moist. (✗)
The cave is dark and damp. (✓)
(這個山洞既黑暗又潮溼。)

moist 是『溼潤的』,用於正面評價的情況, 如: Her hair is shiny and moist. (她的頭髮亮麗又溼潤。) damp 通常是『溼冷的』之意,用於較為負面的情況。

moment

At the moment, the monster made a grab at the knight. (✗)
At that moment, the monster made a grab at the knight. (✓)
(就在那個時候,怪物向那名騎士抓過去。)

at the moment = now = at the present time 是『目前』之意, 如: At the moment he is out of work. (目前他失業中。) at that moment 限用於對過去事件或故事的敘述。另外, in a moment = soon, 意為『很快』或『不久』之意, 如: I'll be back in a moment. (我很快就回來。) 再者, for a moment 表『片刻之久』, 如: He lapsed into thought for a moment. (他陷入沉思片刻之久。)

monopoly

The rich don't have a patent on being happy. (✗)
The rich don't have a monopoly on being happy. (✓)
(快樂並非有錢人的專利。)

patent 是指政府發給廠商的『專利(證)』, 允許其在一段時間內『單獨』製造/販售某產品。monopoly 本義為『專賣』,引申為『獨佔』或『壟斷』之意。

moral

I'll give him my spiritual support. (✗)
I'll give him my moral support. (✓)
(我會給他精神/道義上的支持。)

spiritual 意為『精神/心靈的』, 是相對於 physical (肉體的) 的境界。但英文並無 spiritual support 的說法。至於 moral support 本來是『道德上的認可並鼓勵』, 引申為『精神/道義上的支持』。

Does she have any moral? (✗)
Does she have any morals? (✓)
(她還有任何道德觀念嗎?)

moral 可以作名詞用。指『道德觀念/原則』時, 恆用複數的 morals (= morality)。而單數的 moral 指的是小說、戲劇等內含之『教訓』, 如: The moral of the story is that all is vanity. (這個故事的教訓是一切都是虛榮。)

mortality

For decades there has been a decline in infant mortalities. (✗)
For decades there has been a decline in infant mortality. (✓)

(這幾十年來，嬰兒死亡率一直有下降的趨勢。)

mortality 表『死亡率』, 恆為不可數名詞。mortality = mortality rate。

mother

To tell you the truth, Japan is my father country. (✗)

To tell you the truth, Japan is my mother country. (✔)

(事實上，日本是我的祖國。)

英文裡並沒有 father country 這個說法。『祖國』的英文是 mother country 或 fatherland 或 motherland。

What's your mother language? (✗)

What's your mother tongue? (✔)

What's your native language/tongue? (✔)

(你的母語是什麼？)

『母語』的英文説法是 mother tongue 或 native language/tongue。

motive

The motif behind the murder remains obscure. (✗)

The motive/motivation behind the murder remains obscure. (✔)

(這樁謀殺案背後的動機仍舊是撲朔迷離。)

motif是文學或藝術的主題, 如: Revenge is a recurrent motif in Greek mythology. (復仇是希臘神話中一直出現的主題。)『動機』的英文是 motive 或 motivation。

Most of the students here lack motive. (✗)

Most of the students here lack motivation. (✔)

(這裡的大多數學生缺乏主動精神。)

表『動機』時 motive = motivation。但 motivation 另有一義, 即『主動精神』或『自動自發的精神』。

motor

The pump is powered by an electric engine. (✗)

The pump is powered by an electric motor. (✔)

(這個幫浦是由電動馬達啟動的。)

engine (引擎) 指的是使用汽油等讓汽車、輪船或飛機啟動的機件, 如: There was something wrong with my car. I could not get the engine started. (我的車子有毛病。我就是無法啟動引擎。) 而 motor 指的是將電力轉換成動力的機組。

move

Moving is no picnic. (？)

Moving house/home is no picnic. (✔)

(搬家的事可不輕鬆。)

『搬家』一般英文的說法是 move house/home (接 home 主英式用法)。move 這個動詞本身, 雖説也可表『搬家』之意, 但使用時多搭配介系詞(片語)以使意義明確, 如: We kept moving from place to place because of my dad's job. (因為老爸職業的關係, 我們以往老是在搬家。)

movement

The police are monitoring the suspect's movement. (✗)

The police are monitoring the suspect's movements. (✔)
(警方正在密切注意該嫌犯的活動。)

指某人四處『活動』時，恆用複數形的 movements。指政治或社會『運動』時，兼有單複數的用法，如：a political/social movement。

M

murder

He was charged with attempting murder. (✗)
He was charged with attempted murder. (✔)
(他被控告殺人未遂。)

attempted murder 是『殺人未遂』的固定說法。

muscle

George limped out of the game after pulling muscle. (✗)
George limped out of the game after pulling a muscle. (✔)
(肌肉拉傷後，喬治一跛一跛地離開比賽場地。)

pull/strain a muscle 是『肌肉拉傷』的固定說法。指『體力』時，muscle 是不可數名詞，如：The work takes a lot of muscle. (這件工作非常需要體力。)

music

The radio was playing a music. (✗)
The radio was playing a piece of music. (✔)
(收音正播著一曲音樂。)

music 是不可數名詞。『一曲音樂』的說法是 a piece of music。

I went to a music concert yesterday evening. (✗)
I went to a concert yesterday evening. (✔)
(昨晚我去聽了一場音樂會。)

concert 就是『音樂/演奏會』，不能再用 music 修飾，除非特別指明某種類型的音樂會，如：It is supposed to be a classical music concert. (這應是一場古典音樂的演奏會。) 同理，『一組樂團』也不能說成 a music band，需說 a band。

musical

The phantom of the Opera is a music. (✗)
***The phantom of the Opera* is a musical. (✔)**
(《歌劇魅影》是一齣音樂劇。)

musical 兼有名詞和形容詞的用法：作名詞時，表『音樂劇/片』，作形容詞時，表『與音樂有關的』或『擅長音樂的』，如：musical theory 就是『樂理』，a musical family 即為一個『懂音樂的家庭』。

must

Warm clothes are a need in the mountains. (✗)
Warm clothes are a must/must-have in the mountains. (✔)
(保暖的衣服在山區是必備之物。)

a need 指的是一種『需求性』，如：We feel there is a need to recruit more staff. (我們認為有必要多招一些員工。) a must 指的是必須擁有的一種東西或必須做的一件事情。a must 可依實際狀況說成 a must-have/must-see/must-read 等。

myself

Myself will take care of that noisy customer. (✗)
I myself will take care of that noisy customer. (✔)
(我親自來應付那位聒譟的客人好了。)

myself 是『反身代名詞』, 不可直接當主詞使用, 需用 I myself...。另外, 有一個貫用法值得一提的是 not be/feel oneself, 表『某人覺得(身心) 不對勁』, 如: Sorry, I'm not myself today. (對不起, 我今天好像不太對勁。)

mystery

The entire case is full of mysteries. (✗)
The entire case is full of mystery. (✔)
(整個事件充滿了詭異。)

指『神祕事件』或一件不可解之『謎』時, mystery 是可數名詞, 如: The murderer's motives remain a mystery. (這名凶手的動機仍舊是個謎。) 指『神祕』或『詭異 (氣氛)』時, mystery 是不可數名詞。另外, 指『深奧難懂』或『鮮為人知』的事物時, 恆用複數形的 mysteries, 如: The unsolved mysteries of the Egyptian pyramids will have a timeless appeal. (埃及金字塔諸多不解之謎, 其吸引力將歷久不衰。)

M

A Quick Note

Nn

nag

Don't be so nagging! (✗)
Don't be such a nag! (✓)
(不要這麼嘮叨，好不好？)

nagging 意為『嘮叨/煩人的』, 限置於名詞之前作形容詞, 如: He could not stand his nagging wife. (他無法忍受他嘮叨的老婆。) nag 本身可當名詞和動詞。當動詞時意為『嘮叨/煩人』, 當名詞時是指『嘮叨/煩人的人』。

N

naked

Millions of stars are invisible to the naked eyes. (✗)
Millions of stars are invisible to the naked eye. (✓)
(數以百萬計的星星是肉眼看不見的。)

the naked eye 是『肉眼』固定的說法, 恆用單數。

name

The magician went in the name of Martin Faustus. (✗)
The magician went by the name of Martin Faustus. (✓)
(這位魔術師以馬丁・浮士德之名行走江湖。)

in the name of sth 是指『以某事物之名義』, 如: The meeting is called in the name of peace. (這個會議是以和平之名召開的。) 而 (go) by the name of sth 是指『用某個假名或藝名』之意, 主詞是人。主詞是物時則需用 under the name of sth, 如: All her novels were written under the name of George Eliot. (她所有的小說都是用喬治・艾略特的筆名寫的。)

He is president in the name only. (✗)
He is president in name only. (✓)
(他只是名義上的總統。)

sth in name only/alone 為固定用法, 表『有名無實的』某地位或頭銜。相反的情況是 in all/everything but name, 即『有實無名的』, 如: She is his wife in all but name. (其實她就是他的老婆, 只差名分而已。)

nap

I think I'll sleep a nap this afternoon. (✗)
I think I'll take/have a nap this afternoon. (✓)
(今天下午我想睡個午覺。)

nap 兼有名詞及動詞的用法, 皆指『小睡片刻』之意。take/have a nap 是固定用法。另外, be caught napping 是指『某人一時大意/失神』, 如: The host team were caught napping and Beckham scored another goal. (地主隊一時大意, 又讓貝克漢進了一球。)

national

It is a national industry. (✗)
It is a nationalized industry. (✓)
(這是一家國營企業。)

national 是『國家的』, 如: a national park/holiday 就是『國家公園』及『國定假日』。強調『國營的』企業/公司需用 nationalized。

There has been a national search for a missing foreigner. (✗)
There has been a nationwide search for a missing foreigner. (✓)

(已經針對一名失蹤的外籍人士展開全國性的搜尋。)

nationwide 兼有形容詞和副詞的用法, 皆表『遍及全國的』, 如: a nationwide protest/strike 就是指『全國性的抗議/罷工』。或如: We have 168 sales outlets nationwide. (遍及全國我們有 168 處銷售通路。)

native

Pandas are native in China. (✗)
Pandas are native to China. (✔)
(貓熊的原產地是中國。)

be native/indigenous to + 地名表動/植物的『原產地』。

Spoken English should be taught by natives. (✗)
Spoken English should be taught by native speakers. (✔)
(口說的英語課程應由以英語為母語的人士來講授。)

作名詞時 native 是指『土生土長在某地的人』或未開發地區的『土著』。native speaker 專指以某種語言為母語的人士。

natural

My hair is natural curly. (✗)
My hair is naturally curly. (✔)
My hair has a natural curl. (✔)
(我的頭髮是自然捲。)

natural 是形容詞, 可以修飾名詞 curl。curly 是形容詞, 應該用副詞 naturally 修飾。

nature

The committee is only temporary by nature. (✗)
The committee is only temporary in nature. (✔)
(這個委員會只是暫時性質。)

by nature 指的是某人/物『天生具有某種特質』, 如: He is by nature a very sensitive person. (他天生就是一個極為敏感的人。) in nature 表 (1) 在自然界 (2) 在 (事物的) 性質上。

nauseous

Every time I take a bus, I feel nauseating. (✗)
Every time I take a bus, I feel nauseous. (✔)
(每次搭乘巴士我就想吐。)

nauseating 專指東西或食物『令人作嘔的』, 如: The smell of rotting fish is nauseating. (魚發臭的味道令人作嘔。) 而 nauseous 是指人『想吐的』。

near

Their wedding day is drawing nearly. (✗)
Their wedding day is drawing near. (✔)
(他們結婚的日子快到了。)

draw near 是指某一件事情舉行的時間『拉近』了, 為固定用法。nearly 是『幾乎』之意, 如: The work took me nearly an entire week to complete. (這件工作幾乎花我一整個星期才完成。)

N

N

need

I'll work overtime if a need be. (✗)

I'll work overtime if need be. (✔)

I'll work overtime if there is a need. (✔)

(如果有必要的話，我會加班。)

作為名詞時, need 兼有可/不可數的用法。但 if need be 是固定說法。if need be = if there is a need (for sth) = if it is necessary。

neglect

The sergeant was court-martialed for neglecting of duty. (✗)

The sergeant was court-martialed for neglect of duty. (✔)

(這名士官因為怠忽職守被軍法審判。)

neglect 可作名詞 (不可數) 或動詞使用。neglect of duty 為『怠忽職守』的固定用法。

neighbor

Neighbor watch is also a good way to prevent crime. (✗)

Neighborhood watch is also a good way to prevent crime. (✔)

(鄰居守望相助也是預防犯罪的一種好方法。)

英文沒有 neighbor watch 的說法。『鄰居守望相助』的固定說法是 neighborhood watch。

neighborly

The fair attracted thousands of people from the neighborly towns. (✗)

The fair attracted thousands of people from the neighboring towns. (✔)

(這個市集吸引了數千名來自鄰近城鎮的人士。)

neighborly 表『(像鄰居般) 和睦的』, 如: We should strengthen our neighborly relations. (我們應該加強敦親睦鄰。) 而 neighboring 表『鄰/附近的』。

nerve

It takes a lot of nerves to report a colleague for sexual harassment. (✗)

It takes a lot of nerve to report a colleague for sexual harassment. (✔)

(舉發同事性騷擾需要相當的勇氣。)

nerve 作為『神經』解時是可數名詞, 如: A pinched nerve will cause you a lot of pain. (壓迫到一根神經就會使你感到相當疼痛。) 表『勇氣』時, nerve (= courage) 為不可數名詞。另外, 表緊張/煩躁的『情緒』時, 恆用複數的 nerves, 如: The child's crying was really getting on my nerves. (這個小孩的哭泣聲真叫我心煩。)

net

You might find some useful information in the net. (✗)

You might find some useful information on the Net/net. (✔)

(你可以在網路裡找到一些有用的資料。)

in the net 是指『在 (捕魚或鳥獸的) 網子裡』, 如: A wild duck was caught in the net. (有一隻野鴨被捕在網。) on the Net/net (主英) 表『在網路上』。

netspeak

A lot of netspeech is being used widely. (✗)

A lot of netspeak is being used widely. (✔)

(很多網路的用語正被廣泛地使用。)

netspeak是『網路用語』之意, 為不可數名詞。netspeech 查無此字, 是誤用。

new

Most of our customers are the newly rich. (✗)

Most of our customers are the new rich. (✔)

(我們大部分的客戶都是一些新貴。)

the new rich 是指新近突然變富有的人, 即所謂的『新貴』, 為固定用法。newly 一般接過去分詞, She is the newly elected mayor. (她是新當選的市長。) 另外, newly arrived/appointed 就是『剛抵達/新任命的』。

news

I was shocked by these news. (✗)

I was shocked by this news. (✔)

(這個消息令我很震驚。)

news是不可數名詞, 不能接在these之後。要講『一/兩則消息』需說 a piece/two pieces of news。

newspaper

The bunch of flowers is wrapped in a newspaper. (✗)

The bunch of flowers is wrapped in newspaper. (✔)

(這一束花是用報紙包裹住。)

指『一/兩份』報紙時, newspaper 為可數名詞, 如: Kevin sat in the corner reading a newspaper. (凱文坐在角落裡看報紙。) 但是指報紙的『紙張』時, newspaper為不可數名詞, 如: Old newspaper can be recycled. (舊報紙是可以回收的。)

N

nice

I remember it was a nice and warm day. (✗)

I remember it was a nice warm day. (✔)

(我記得那是極為暖和的一天。)

nice and + adj. = very + adj.表『非常/極為……』, 如: It is nice and cool in the woods. (在這片森林中極為涼爽。) 但是這個語法用來修飾名詞時, 須去掉 and, 如: It is a nice cool day, isn't it? (今天真是涼爽, 是不是?)

night

Nocturnal animals are active only in the night. (✗)

Nocturnal animals are active only at night. (✔)

(夜行的動物只有在晚上才活躍。)

in the night 專指『在夜裡的某一特定時候』, 如: A burglar sneaked into their house in the night. (有一名小偷在夜裡潛入他們的家。) at night 指的是『在 (整個) 夜晚』。

You can call me any time, day and night. (✗)
You can call me any time, day or night. (✔)
(你可以在白天或夜晚隨時打電話給我。)

day and night = night and day = all the time 表『日以繼夜不停地』, 如: I had to work day and night to support a family of five. (我必須日以繼夜的工作以維持一家五口的生活。) day or night = night or day 表『在白天或夜晚 (隨時)』之意。

N

nobody

No body was there to greet us. (✗)
Nobody was there to greet us. (✔)
(沒有人出來跟我們打招呼。)

『沒有人』應該說 nobody 或 no one。no body = not a dead body 意為『沒有一具屍體』, 如: There was no body found. (沒有找到任何屍體。)

none

None of my parents got a college education. (✗)
Neither of my parents got a college education. (✔)
(我的雙親都沒有受過大學教育。)

none 對不可數名詞表『沒有』, 如: It's none of your business. (這沒有你的事。) 對 (三者或以上的) 可數名詞表『無一』, 如: None of my friends agreed to my proposal. (我的朋友都不贊成我的提議。) neither 針對兩者表『無一』。

nonsense

Look, someone is talking nonsenses. (✗)
Look, someone is talking nonsense. (✔)
(注意，有人在胡說八道了。)

nonsense 為不可數名詞, 指的是『荒唐的想法/意見』等。talk nonsense 是『胡說八道』的正確說法。

normal

The supply of water and electricity is now back to the normal. (✗)
The supply of water and electricity is now back to normal. (✔)
(水電的供應現已恢復正常。)

normal 可兼為名詞及形容詞。作形容詞時表『正常的』, 如: Your child is perfectly normal. (你的孩子十分正常。) 作名詞時表『正常的狀態/程度』。come back/be back/return to normal 是『恢復正常』的固定說法。

nose

The money just disappeared before my nose. (✗)
The money just disappeared under my nose. (✔)
(這筆錢就在我面前不見了。)

『在某人的面前』應該說 under sb's (very) nose 才正確。這個片語強調的是『該注意卻未注意』。另外, before sb's eyes 亦表『在某人的面前』, 但這個片語強調的是『在某人注視之下』, 如: They came to blows before everybody's eyes. (他們就在眾目睽睽之下扭打起來。)

note

You should take a note at every lecture. (✗)

You should take notes at every lecture. (✔)

(每堂課你都應該做筆記。)

在上課中或閱讀時『做筆記』的英文說法是 take/make notes (恆用複數)。take note (of sth)是『注意 (某事)』之意, 如: If the people are criticizing any policies, politicians ought to take note. (如果人民在批評任何政策時, 政治人物就該注意了。) 另外, write/leave a note 是『寫/留一則短箋/信』之意。

nothing

The cake is a cinch to make. There's nothing in it. (✗)

The cake is a cinch to make. There's nothing to it. (✔)

(做這個蛋糕很簡單。真的沒什麼。)

There is nothing in it. 是說『蛋糕裡面沒有任何東西』, 與前文不能連貫。There is nothing to it.是說『這件事很簡單, 沒什麼了不起』。

notice

The meeting is adjourned until a further notice. (✗)

The meeting is adjourned until further notice. (✔)

(這個會議目前暫停，直到另行通知為止。)

notice 表『通知 (的行為)』時是不可數名詞。until further notice (直到另行通知為止) 是固定用法。但表『佈告/啟事』時, notice 是可數名詞, 如: We've put up a notice on the door to say we're open. (我們在門口張貼佈告, 聲明本店開張。)

nowhere

A negative attitude will get nowhere. (✗)

A negative attitude will get you nowhere. (✔)

(消極的態度將使你一事無成。)

get/go nowhere 是指計劃/提議/工作等『在原地踏步, 沒有任何進展』, 如: Our investigation got nowhere. (我們的調查工作沒有任何進展。) 而 get sb nowhere 是『使某人一事無成』。

nude

There are several naked scenes in the movie. (✗)

There are several nude scenes in the movie. (✔)

(這部電影中有幾處裸露的場面。)

naked 意為『裸露的』, 但這個字是針對人的身體或部位而言, 如: The police found the body lying half naked in the grass. (警方在草叢中發現那半裸的屍體。) nude 這個字除了有 naked 的含意外, 另有『呈現裸露場面的』之意。

number

I don't need the exact figure. Just give me a complete number. (✗)

I don't need the exact figure. Just give me a round number. (✔)

(我不想要精確的數字，只要給我一個整數就行了。)

英文的『整數』說法是 a round number, 即

N

尾數是『零』的數。, 這是因為阿拉伯數字中的 0 是『圓的』。『奇數』是 an odd number;『偶數』是 an even number。

nut

All these phone calls have been driving me nut. (✗)

All these phone calls have been driving me nuts. (✔)

(這一通通的電話都快把我給逼瘋了。)

nut 作名詞時主要表 (1) 堅果 (2) 瘋子 (3) 熱衷者, 都是可數用法。但 nuts = crazy, 是形容詞, 意為『瘋狂的』。所以 go nuts = go crazy (發瘋), drive sb nuts = drive sb crazy (把某人逼瘋)。

N

O o

oath

Witnesses are required to take an oath in a court of law. (✗)
Witnesses are required to take the oath in a court of law. (✓)
(證人在法庭上必須宣誓絕不說謊。)

take the oath 專指『在法庭上宣誓絕不說謊』。take/swear an oath 則指其它方面的『宣誓』, 如: All new American citizens must officially take an oath of allegiance. (所有美國的新公民都必須宣誓效忠國家。)

object

I am afraid you have become a subject of ridicule. (✗)
I am afraid you have become an object of ridicule. (✓)
(恐怕你已成為被糗的對象。)

指人時, subject 專門指『被實驗的對象』, 如: The subjects of the experiment are between the ages of 16 and 21. (這個實驗的對象是介於 16 歲和 21 歲之間的人。) object 指的是引起他人有興趣或其它情緒的『對象』, 如: Street people are often objects of pity. (遊民經常是被同情的對象。)

What are your career objects? (✗)
What are your career objectives? (✓)
(您的生涯規劃是什麼?)

object 和 objective 均可表『目標』, 但 object 通常指的是『某種行/活動的』目標, 如: The object of the game is to promote parent-child relations. (這個遊戲的目標是要加強親子關係。) 但特指『事業/生涯/政治/經濟』方面的目標時, 需用 objective。

O

obliged

The salesclerk is very obliged. (✗)
The salesclerk is very obliging. (✓)
(這名售貨員態度很親切。)

be/feel obliged to do sth 表『有義務做某事』, 如: I felt obliged to tide him over. (我覺得我有義務助他度過難關。) obliging 是形容詞, 表『態度親切的』。

occasion

He will certainly deal with the occasion in case of emergency. (✗)
He will certainly rise to the occasion in case of emergency. (✓)
(有緊急狀況時他一定會挺身而出。)

deal with sth 是『處理』或『應付』某問題。rise to the occasion 是『挺身而出解決問題』, 為固定的搭配用法。

It seems that we met on occasion. (✗)
It seems that we met on one occasion. (✓)
(我們似乎見過一次面。)

on occasion (= sometimes) 表『有時候』, 如: On occasion I pamper myself with some luxuries. (有時候我會縱容自己買一些奢侈品。) on one occasion = once 表『(曾經) 一次』之意。

occupy

Now women occupy about 35% of the workforce. (✗)
Now women account for about 35% of the workforce. (✓)
(目前婦女約佔總勞動人口的百分之三十五。)

occupy sth 表『佔用/據某物』, 如: The bathroom is occupied. (洗手間目前有人使用。) 或如: The island was once occupied by enemy troops. (這個島曾經被敵軍佔領。)『佔若干百分比』一律用 account for 來表達。

occur

The dinner party will occur at seven o'clock this evening. (✗)

The dinner party will take place at seven o'clock this evening. (✓)

(晚宴將於今晚七點舉行。)

occur 通常指的是『臨時發生』的情況, 如: The explosion occurred at 4:30 p.m. (這起爆炸案發生在下午四點三十分。) 事先計劃好的『活動/事件』需用 take place。

It happened to me that she might be in love with me. (✗)

It occurred to me that she might be in love with me. (✓)

(我突然想到，她也許愛上我了。)

表『發生』時 happen 差不多等於 occur, 不過, 後者是較為『正式』的說法, 如: When did the accident happen/occur? (這起意外何時發生的?)。但表『某人突然想到……』時, 限用 it occurred to sb that...這個句型。

occurrence

Flooding in this area is common occurrence. (✗)

Flooding in this area is a common occurrence. (✓)

(在這個地區水患發生頻仍。)

occurrence 意為『發生』或『發生的事件』, 兼有可/不可數的用法。不過, a rare/common/regular/everyday/annual occurrence (很少/經常/定期/每天/每年發生的事件) 是固定用法。

o'clock

You'll have to give a briefing at half past three o'clock. (✗)

You'll have to give a briefing at half past three. (✓)

(你三點半時必須做簡報。)

o'clock 限用於『整點』, 也可省略, 如: I got up at six (o'clock) this morning. (今天早上我六點鐘起床。) 搭配『分鐘』的說法一律省略 o'clock, 如: It's twenty of/to (英式用法) two. (現在時間是一點四十分。)

of

It was generous for you to donate so much money. (✗)

It was generous of you to donate so much money. (✓)

(你真慷慨捐出了這麼多錢。)

一般而言, 說明事物的形容詞接 for, 如: It is easy/difficult/convenient/necessary/possible for sb to do sth 是常用句型。說明人物的形容詞接 of, 如: It is kind/nice/generous/sweet of sb to do sth。

The child didn't give me a minute of peace. (✗)

The child didn't give me a minute's peace. (✓)

(這個孩子不給我片刻的安寧。)

說明某事時間的長度時, 一律用 a minute's/two hours'/three days' sth。

O

My younger sister is frightened by spiders. (✗)
My younger sister is frightened of spiders. (✓)
(我的小妹怕蜘蛛。)

be composed/frightened/tired of sth 意為『由某物組成/害怕某物/厭倦某物』,是固定用法。

off

The plane veered of course. (✗)
The plane veered off course. (✓)
(這架飛機偏離了航線。)

of course 表『當然』,通常用來作為『肯定』的答覆。off course 是『偏離方向/航線』之意。

I'm planning to take a week away in September. (✗)
I'm planning to take a week off in September. (✓)
(我計劃在九月休假一週。)

take a day/two weeks/three months off 表『休一天/兩週/三個月的假』,是固定用法。

offense

No offenses, but the soup you cooked tastes funny. (✗)
No offense, but the soup you cooked tastes funny. (✓)
(沒有冒犯之意,不過你的這道湯味道怪怪的。)

offense 作為『冒犯/得罪』解時是不可數名詞。作為『犯罪/不法行為』解時則為可數名詞, 如: Murder is a serious offense, not a minor one. (謀殺是重罪而非輕罪。)

Are you ready to take the offense? (✗)
Are you ready to take the offensive? (✓)
(你們準備展開攻勢了嗎?)

take offense (at sth) 表『(對某事) 動怒』, 如: There is no need to take offense at her words. (沒有必要對她說的話動怒嘛。) go on/take the offensive 是『發動攻勢』之意。

offer

Did he take an offer for your used car? (✗)
Did he make an offer for your used car? (✓)
(你那部舊車他出價錢了沒?)

take/accept an offer 表『接受某人所提出的條件/待遇』, 如: He's decided to take your offer. (他已決定接受你提的條件。) make an offer for/on sth 是『對某物出價』。

office

I have no desire to seek the public office. (✗)
I have no desire to seek public office. (✓)
(我沒有意願尋求公職。)

作為『辦公室』或『辦公機構』解時, office 是可數名詞, 如: We have a branch office in Denver. (我們在丹佛市有一個支局。) 作為『職/官位』時, office 通常作不可數用法, take office 就是『上任/就職』, 如: The President takes office two months after the election. (總統於選舉兩個月後就職。)。

O

officer

My son is an air force official. (✗)
My son is an air force officer. (✓)
(我的兒子是一名空軍軍官。)

指『軍/警官』時恆用 officer。但指政府各部門的『官員』則用 official, 如: She is a city government official. (她是市政府的官員。)

offspring

Their offsprings are all short and heavy. (✗)
Their offspring are all short and heavy. (✓)
(他們的子女個個都又矮又胖。)

offspring 指的是人或動物的『子女/後代』, 單複數同形。

oil

He prefers to paint in oil. (✗)
He prefers to paint in oils. (✓)
(他比較喜歡畫油畫。)

作『石油』解時, oil 為不可數名詞。作『烹調用油』解時, oil 兼有可/不可數的用法, 如: vegetable/fatty oil(s)就是『蔬菜/脂肪油』, 另外, an essential oil 表一種從植物萃取提鍊的『精油』。『油畫顏料』恆用複數的 oils。

on

She stayed in bed late in Sunday morning. (✗)
She stayed in bed late on Sunday morning. (✓)
(星期天早上她很晚才起床。)

in the morning 是固定說法。但指『特定一天的早晨』需用 on, 如: on Monday/Wednesday/Friday morning。afternoon 和 evening 的用法一如上述。

I read about it on the newspaper. (✗)
I read about it in the newspaper. (✓)
(我在報上讀到這則報導。)

in a newspaper/magazine 為固定用法。

You look really beautiful on the silk dress. (✗)
You look really beautiful in the silk dress. (✓)
The silk dress looks really beautiful on you. (✓)
(這件絲質的洋裝穿在妳身上真是漂亮極了。)

sb looks good/beautiful in sth = sth looks good/beautiful on sb 表『某人穿某種衣服很好看/漂亮』, 為固定用法。

once

Staff meetings take place once in a month. (✗)
Staff meetings take place once a month. (✓)
(員工大會每個月舉行一次。)

once a day/week/month/year (不可加 in) 為固定用法。但 once in a while (= sometimes) 是固定片語。

one

I as one never like the idea of buying secondhand things. (✗)

I for one never like the idea of buying secondhand things. (✔)
(我個人就不曾有過想買二手貨的念頭。)

for one 是『就說話者個人而言』。as one (=unanimously) 表『全體一致』, 如: They all stood up as one. (他們全體一致起立。) 另外, (all) in one 是指某人或某物『集某些身分/功能於一身』之意, 如: She is a poet, scholar, and musician (all) in one. (她集詩人, 學者和音樂家於一身。)

Guests were arriving in one and two. (✗)
Guests were arriving in ones and twos. (✔)
(客人稀稀疏疏地地抵達。)

in ones and twos 表『稀稀疏疏』或『零零落落』。

O

ooze

The small cut on his cheek was still gushing blood. (✗)
The small cut on his cheek was still oozing blood. (✔)
(他臉頰上的小傷口仍流著少量的血。)

gush blood 是『大量出血』, 如: The wound is gushing blood. (傷口一直大量出血。), ooze blood 是『少量又緩緩地流著血』。

open

I did not buy anything because the shop was not opened. (✗)
I did not buy anything because the shop was not open. (✔)
(因為當天商店沒營業，我什麼也沒買到。)

be opened 表『開門』, be open 表『營業』, 如: The shop was opened at 9 a.m. and stayed open until 8 p.m. (這家商店上午九點開門, 一直營業到下午八點。)

She was lying still on the bed, with her eyes widely open. (✗)
She was lying still on the bed, with her eyes wide open. (✔)
(她靜靜地躺在床上，眼睛睜得大大的。)

(be) wide open 表某物『張得很開』, 是固定用法。

open-hearted

Your husband will have to undergo open-hearted surgery. (✗)
Your husband will have to undergo open-heart surgery. (✔)
(妳的老公需要接受開心手術。)

open-hearted 表『親切友善的』, 如: They gave us an open-hearted welcome. (他們親切友善地歡迎我們。) open-heart surgery 是『開心手術』的正確說法。

operate

The doctor may have to operate your leg. (✗)
The doctor may have to operate on your leg. (✔)
(醫師可能會對你的腿進行手術。)

operate 表『手術』時是不及物動詞。operate on sb's sth 表『對某人的某部位進行手術』。表『操作』機器時, operate 是及物的用法, 如: Her job is to operate the telephone switchboard. (她的工作是操作電話的總機。)

operation

She's going to take an emergency operation. (✗)
She's going to have/undergo an emergency operation. (✔)
(她馬上需要做緊急手術。)

operation 表『手術』時是可數用法, 如: a major/minor/emergency operation 就是一個『重大/小/緊急的手術』。病患『接受手術』的正確說法是 have/undergo an operation。

opinion

According to his opinion, the new law is a good thing. (✗)
In his opinion, the new law is a good thing. (✔)
According to him, the new law is a good thing. (✔)
(照他的看法，這條新法令是美事一樁。)

習慣上,『按照某人的看法/意見』不能說 according to sb's opinion, 需說 according to sb 或 in sb's opinion。

They have a high evaluation of your work. (✗)
They have a high opinion of your work. (✔)
(他們對你的工作評價很高。)

evaluation 指的是對某事/物『評估/價』的行為, 這個『行為』本身無關高低/好壞。對某人/物『有高/低/好/壞的評價』, 正確的英文說法是 have a high/low/good/bad opinion of sb/sth。

opponent

Who do you think is your leading enemy in the election? (✗)
Who do you think is your leading opponent in the election? (✔)
(在這次選舉中你認為誰是你的頭號敵手？)

opponent 表『處於相反立場的敵/對手』, 未必有『敵意』存在其間。enemy 是『敵人』, 頗有『敵意』存在其間, 且往往欲置對方於死地。

opposite

Players from the opposite team were all tall and heavy. (✗)
Players from the opposing team were all tall and heavy. (✔)
(對方的球員個個高大健壯。)

作為形容詞時, opposite 表『相反/異的』, 如: There's a truck coming from the opposite direction. (有一部卡車從反方向過來了。) 而 the opposite sex 就是指『異性』。指『對抗』的球隊/軍隊需用 opposing 來形容。

optical

My boss enjoys collecting optic instruments. (✗)
My boss enjoys collecting optical instruments. (✔)
(我的老闆喜歡收集光學儀器。)

optic 表『與視覺有關的』, 如: the optic nerve 就是『視覺神經』。而 optical 表『與光學有關的』, 如: an optical disk/fiber 就是指『光盤/纖』。

O

oral

Your oral English leaves nothing to be desired. (✗)
Your spoken English leaves nothing to be desired. (✓)
(您的口說英語無懈可擊。)

oral 雖表『口說的』，但只能用於下列片語，如: oral skills/exams, 即『口說技巧/口試』。另外, oral 亦可表『與口腔/服有關的』，如: oral hygiene/contraceptives 就是『口腔衛生』和『口服避孕藥』。spoken/written English 是『口說/筆寫』英文之固定說法。

organ

He has agreed to be an organic donor. (✗)
He has agreed to be an organ donor. (✓)
(他已經同意當一個器官捐贈者。)

organ donation/donor/transplant 為『器官捐贈/捐贈者/移植』的固定說法。organic 一般表『有機的』之意, 如: organic vegetables 就是『有機蔬菜』。另外, organic 表『與器官有關的』之意時見於 organic diseases/degeneration, 即『器官的疾病/退化』。

original

All meat should be clearly labelled with its original country. (✗)
All meat should be clearly labelled with its country of origin. (✓)
(所有的肉類都應明確標示原產國。)

country/place of origin 表『原產國/地』，是固定用法。

originate

The theory of evolution did not originate in Darwin. (✗)
The theory of evolution did not originate with Darwin. (✓)
(進化論的原理並非肇始於達爾文。)

表『起源於某物/地』用 originate from/in sth; 表『起源於某人』由 originate with sb, 如: A lot of our medicines originate from herbs. (我們很多的藥方來自草本植物。) 或如: The idea of "star wars" originated with Ronald Reagan. (『星戰計劃』的構想源自雷根。)

otherwise

Many people believed Nick was honest, but I thought opposite. (✗)
Many people believed Nick was honest, but I thought otherwise. (✓)
(很多人相信尼克誠實，可是我不以為然。)

say/think/decide otherwise 表『有不同或相反的』說法/想法/決定, 是固定用法。

outbreak

I was really shocked by his outbreak of anger. (✗)
I was really shocked by his outburst of anger. (✓)
(我著實被他突如其來的憤怒嚇壞了。)

an outbreak of sth 指的主要是『突如其來的』戰爭/疫情/暴亂, 如: The outbreak of the plague claimed thousands of lives. (這場瘟疫的爆發奪走了數千條人命。)『突然而來的』強烈情緒反應, 需用 an outburst of sth。

outdoors

I'm a great lover of outdoors. (✗)
I'm a great lover of the outdoors. (✓)
(我極為喜歡野外。)

outdoors 是副詞, 表『在戶/野外』, 如: Their wedding party was held outdoors. (他們的婚禮派對在戶外舉行。) 而 the (great) outdoors 為名詞, 指的是『野外/鄉間』。

outlook

Exercise may improve your looks as well as your outlooks. (✗)
Exercise may improve your looks as well as your outlook. (✓)
(運動也許可以美麗你的外表和人生觀。)

outlook 表『人生觀』或『展望』均以單數的形式出現, 如: The economic outlook is still uncertain. (經濟的前景仍充滿不確定性。)

outrage

The government's decision has provoked public outrages. (✗)
The government's decision has provoked public outrage. (✓)
(政府的這項決定已引發群情激憤。)

作為『激憤/震怒』時, outrage 是不可數名詞。作為『暴行』時, outrage 是可數名詞, 如: It is an outrage against justice. (這是藐視公平正義的暴行。)

outright

He refused the job offer outrightly. (✗)
He refused the job offer outright. (✓)
(他斷然拒絕這個工作機會。)

英文中並沒有 outrightly 這個字, 是誤用。outright (斷然) 兼有形容/副詞的用法。作形容詞時 outright = flat, 如: an outright refusal = a flat refusal, 即『斷然的拒絕』。作副詞時, outright = flatly。

outside

"Aliens" are creatures coming from outside space. (✗)
"Aliens" are creatures coming from outer space. (✓)
(『異形』是來自外太空的生物。)

outer space 是『外太空』的固定說法。至於 the outside world 表『外界』, 如: After the earthquake, the small town was virtually cut off from the outside world. (地震過後, 這個小鎮簡直與外界隔絕。)

overall

On the overall, your prices are quite reasonable. (✗)
On the whole, your prices are quite reasonable. (✓)
Overall, your prices are quite reasonable. (✓)
(整體來看，你們的價格相當合理。)

overall 作為副詞時表『整體來看』, 相當於 on the whole。

O

overdue

The library books are expired. (✗)

The library books are overdue. (✓)

(這些圖書館的書過期未還。)

expire 特指『證照』過期, 需要重新申請才能使用, 如: The library card has expired. (這張借書證過期了。) overdue 專指 (1) 帳單過期未繳 (2) 圖書過期未還 (3) 嬰兒過了預產期未生。

overseas

A lot of oversea visitors will be here tomorrow. (✗)

A lot of overseas visitors will be here tomorrow. (✓)

(明天將有一大批來自海外的訪客來這裡。)

overseas 表『來自/前往海外』, 兼有形容詞和副詞的用法, 如: overseas students 就是『留學生』。或如: Quite a few manufacturers have moved overseas. (很多製造業者已經遷廠至海外。)

overwork

His heart attack was caused by overworks. (✗)

His heart attack was caused by overwork. (✓)

(他心臟病突發是工作過量造成。)

overwork 作為名詞時是不可數名詞。

overworked

They are overworking and understaffed. (✗)

They are overworked and understaffed. (✓)

(他們員工不足又必須超量工作。)

overworked 是形容詞, 表『(被情勢所迫) 非超量工作不可』。

own

You have problems on your own. (✗)

You have problems of your own. (✓)

(你有你自己的一些問題。)

n. + of your own 表『你自己的……』。on your own 表『獨力/靠自己』, 如: You have to solve problems on your own. (你必須自己去解決問題。)

O

P p

pace

We should allow students to make progress at their own paces. (✗)
We should allow students to make progress at their own pace. (✔)
(我們應該讓學生按自己的步調進步。)

表『步調/速度』時, 恆用單數形的 pace, 如: The pace of life here is slow and easy. (這裡的生活步調既輕鬆又緩慢。) 指行走的『腳步』時則常用複數的 paces, 如: I took a few paces toward the door. (我朝門口走了幾步路。) 這個 paces = steps。

package

Send the pack by airmail. (✗)
Send the package/parcel by airmail. (✔)
(將這個包裹以航空郵件寄出。)

pack 在美語的用法中, 指的『小包裝的販售東西』, 如: a pack of cigarettes, 即『一包香菸』。也可以用來指一群狼或獵狗, 如: a pack of wolves/hounds。package 或 parcel 指的是郵寄的『包裹』。

packing

We are leaving for Greece this evening, and I haven't done my packaging yet. (✗)
We are leaving for Greece this evening, and I haven't done my packing yet. (✔)
(我們今晚就要去希臘了，而我卻尚未把行李打包好。)

packaging 指的是『包裝』商品的行為或其『包裝紙/盒等』, 如: All this packaging will create a lot of garbage. (所有這些包裝紙、盒將會製造一堆垃圾。) packing 則是『打包行李』的動作。

pain

After a week's convalescence, I still feel very painful. (✗)
After a week's convalescence, I still feel a lot of pain. (✔)
(經過一個星期的休養之後，我仍舊覺得很痛。)

painful 通常是指事物『造成痛苦』, 如: a painful experience/memory 就是一個痛苦的經驗/記憶。或如: My mother suffers from stiff and painful joints. (我老媽患有關節僵硬疼痛的毛病。)『感到痛苦』的說法是 feel pain 或 be in pain。

It seems that we have to take pain to improve our company's image. (✗)
It seems that we have to take pains to improve our company's image. (✔)
(我們似乎須要努力來提昇公司的形象。)

pain 是『疼痛』之意。pains 是『努力/苦心』之意。take/go to (great) pains to do sth 就是『盡心盡力做好某事』。另外, be at pains to do sth 也是類似的用法, 如: He was at pains to point out that he had nothing to do with the Mafia. (他極力撇清他與黑手黨無關。)

paint

She paints mainly in watercolor. (✗)
She paints mainly in watercolors. (✔)
(她主要以水彩顏料作畫。)

paint in oils/watercolors 表『以油畫/水彩顏料作畫』, 恆 用複數, 是固定用法。

pair

They work in a pair when they are on patrol. (✗)

They work in pairs when they are on patrol. (✔)

(他們巡邏時兩人一組。)

a pair (of...) 是指『一對/雙/副』某人/物, 如: a pair of lovers 就是『一對情侶』, a pair of earrings 即為『一副耳環』。另外, the pair for/to sth 是指『一對/雙/副』某物其中之一個, 如: I can't find the pair for this sock. (我找不到另一隻襪子。) 至於 in pairs 是『兩人一組』, 為固定用法。

palate

Spicy food suits her palette. (✗)

Spicy food suits her palate. (✔)

(辛辣的食物適合她的胃口。)

palette 和 palate 兩個字的發音相同, 但意義大為不同。前者指的是畫畫用的『調色板』, 後者本指人口腔中的『上顎』, 引申為人們對食物的『鑑賞力』或『胃口』。

panic

The news prompted a wave of frightened selling. (✗)

The news prompted a wave of panic selling. (✔)

(這一則消息引發一波恐慌性的拋售。)

frightened主要用來說明某人『害怕』, 如: My little sister is frightened of rats. (我小妹很怕老鼠。) panic 是『恐慌』。panic buying/selling 即恐慌性的『搶購/拋售』, 是固定說法。

paper

Why not put down your ideas on the paper? (✗)

Why not put down your ideas on paper? (✔)

(為何不把你的想法寫下來呢?)

put down sth on paper 是『將構想/計劃等寫下來』, 為固定用法。表『紙張』時 paper本身不可數。要說『一張紙』需用a piece/sheet of paper。a paper 指的是一份『報紙』或『讀書報告』。另外, papers指的是『文件』, 如: Some important papers are missing from the files. (某些重要文件從檔案中不見了。)

paperwork

My job involves a lot of paperworks. (✗)

My job involves a lot of paperwork. (✔)

(我的工作需做一堆文書業務。)

paperwork 表『文書工作』或『文件』時均為不可數名詞。

par

His performance has been below a par recently. (✗)

His performance has been below par recently. (✔)

(他最近的表現一直在水準以下。)

par 表高爾夫球的『標準桿』或股票/債券的『票面價格』。below/under par = not up to par 均表『不夠水準』之意。par 是不可數名詞。唯一的例外見於 on a par (with sb/sth), 如: Her intelligence is on a par with yours. (她的智力與你的智力同等級。)

P

parking

My car was parking outside the hotel all night. (✗)
My car was parked outside the hotel all night. (✓)
(我的車子整晚停放在飯店外面。)

指『人停放車』時用主動語態, 如: I was then parking my car when I heard an explosion. (我正在停車時忽然聽到一起爆炸聲。) 指『車被停放』的狀況, 用被動語態。

It's getting more and more difficult to find a parking near the station. (✗)
It's getting more and more difficult to find parking/a parking space near the station. (✓)
(要在車站附近找到停車位越來越難。)

表『停車位』時 parking 是不可數名詞, a parking space 是可數的說法。另外,『(大型) 停車場』的說法是 a parking lot (美式) 或 a car park (英式)。

part

I think I'll take a part in the hunger strike. (✗)
I think I'll take part in the hunger strike. (✓)
(我想我會參加這個絕食抗議活動。)

『參加』某活動/比賽等一律用 take part in sth, 但使用形容詞修飾 part 時則需加 a(n) 於其前, 如: My dad took an active part in politics when young. (我老爸年輕時曾積極參加政治。)

Most part of the land in this area is barren. (✗)
Most of the land in the area is barren. (✓)
A good part of the land in this area is barren. (✓)
(這個地區大部分的土地是貧瘠的。)

英文並沒有 most part of sth 的說法。要說『大部分的』某物時, 需用 most of sth 或 a good/large part of sth。不過, for the most part 表『大體上』, 如: For the most part, the natives were kind and friendly. (大體上, 這些土著既親切又友善。)

Another reason is that he doesn't want to part with his friends. (✗)
Another reason is that he doesn't want to part from his friends. (✓)
(另外一個理由就是他不想離開他的朋友。)

part from sb 是『離開某人』之意。part with sth 是『把某物送給別人』, 如: I won't part with any of the puppies. (任何一隻小狗我都不會割愛。)

partial

The referee was clearly partial to the other team. (✗)
The referee was clearly partial toward the other team. (✓)
(這位裁判顯然偏袒另一隊。)

be partial to sb/sth 是『獨鍾/偏愛』某人/物, 如: I'm very partial to ice cream for dessert. (餐後甜點我特別偏愛冰淇淋。) be partial toward sb 則是『偏袒某人/隊』。

particular

My husband is very particular for his food. (✗)
My husband is very particular about his food. (✓)

(我的老公對吃的很講究。)

be particular (= choosy = fussy) about sth 是『對某物很挑剔/講究』之意。

Send your particular to us by e-mail. (✗)

Send your particulars to us by e-mail. (✔)

(請把你個人的詳細資料用電子郵件傳給我們。)

sb's particulars (恆用複數) 是指某人的姓名、年齡、工作、地址等等之『個人詳細資料』。

pass

She is nearly fifty, but she could pass by thirty-five. (✗)

She is nearly fifty, but she could pass for thirty-five. (✔)

(她年近五十了，不過要是說她三十五也都還過得去。)

pass by 是『經過某人/物』之意, 如: Three buses passed by, but none of them was the right one. (三輛公車過去了, 可是沒有一輛是我想搭的。) pass as/for/sth sb 表可以『充當某物/人』之意。

passing

The child was found by a past motorist. (✗)

The child was found by a passing motorist. (✔)

(這個小孩被一位開車經過的人士發現。)

past 作形容詞時表『過去/從前的』, 如: She is a past employee of the company. (她是這家公司以前的一位員工。) passing 是『經過的』, 如: A cat was run over by a passing car. (有一隻貓被開過去的車子輾過。) 另外, a passing grade/mark 是指通過考試的『成績/分數』。

path

The tornado destroyed everything on its path. (✗)

The tornado destroyed everything in its path. (✔)

(這陣龍捲風所經之處一切皆被摧毀。)

in sb's/sth's path 表『在某人/物所經之處』, 是固定用法。

Their path first crossed when they were in the army. (✗)

Their paths first crossed when they were in the army. (✔)

(他們初次邂逅是在軍中。)

sb's paths cross 是指兩個人『不期而遇』, 恆用複數形的 paths。

patron

Thank you very much for your patron. (✗)

Thank you very much for your patronage. (✔)

(衷心感謝你們的惠顧。)

patron 指的是『(藝術活動) 贊助人』或『(商店、餐廳的) 顧客』, 是可數名詞, 如: Catherine is a patron of the arts. (凱撒琳是各種藝術活動的贊助者。) patronage 表『贊助』或『惠顧』的行為, 是不可數名詞。

pause

The high price gave me a pause for thought. (✗)

The high price gave me pause for thought. (✓)

(價位過高使我考慮良久。)

give sb pause (for thought) 表『某物令某人深思, 不敢貿然進行』, 是固定用法。表『停頓』時, pause 是可數名詞, 如: After a short pause, Henry went on with the story. (停頓片刻之後, 亨利又繼續說故事。)

P

pay

I'll pay your travelling expenses. (✗)

I'll pay for your travelling expenses. (✓)

(我會幫你出旅費。)

pay for sth 表『(為某人) 出錢/付帳』, 是固定說法。pay sth 的用法見於 pay a bill/fine/tax, 即『繳帳單費用/罰金/稅金』, 如: Did you pay the gas bill? (你瓦斯費繳了沒?)

How soon will you pay the loan? (✗)

How soon will you pay off the loan? (✓)

(你多久才能還清貸款?)

pay off/repay a loan/debt 是『還清一筆貸款/債務』之意, 是固定用法。另外, sth pays off 表某事/物『成功/奏效』, 如: It seems that our strategy has paid off. (看來我們的策略奏效了。)

payment

We did not even have enough money to make down payment. (✗)

We did not even have enough money to make a down payment. (✓)

(我們甚至沒有足夠的錢來付頭期款。)

作為『該/已付的款項』時, payment 是可數名詞, a monthly payment 就是一筆『月付的款項』。作為『付款的行為』解時, payment 是不可數名詞, 如: Payment can be made by check or by credit card. (可用支票或信用卡付費。)

peak

The company was on its peak in the 1990s. (✗)

The company was at its peak in the 1990s. (✓)

(一九九〇年代是這家公司的顛峰時期。)

peak 本指『山頂/尖』。at sth's peak 或 at the peak of sth 表『處於某物的顛峰時期』, 如: He's now at the peak of his career. (他現正處於事業的顛峰時期。) 另外, at peak times 表『在尖峰時段』, 如: Avoid the freeway at peak times. (在尖峰時段避免上高速公路。)

peculiar

You won't understand. The excitement is particular to bird watchers. (✗)

You won't understand. The excitement is peculiar to bird watchers. (✔)

(你不會瞭解的。這種興奮是賞鳥人士獨享的。)

particular 表『特別/殊的』或『挑剔的』。be peculiar to sb/sth 是『某人/物所特有/獨享的』, 如: Sex discrimination is not peculiar to this culture. (性別歧視並非這個文化所特有的。)

peddle

He was accused of pedaling drugs. (✗)

He was accused of peddling drugs. (✔)

(他被控販售毒品。)

pedal 和 peddle 發音相同, 容易混淆。前者當名詞時是腳踏車的『踏板』, 作動詞時, 表『騎腳踏車』, 如: He began to pedal home as fast as he could. (他開始猛踩腳踏車趕回家。) peddle sth 是『販售某物』之意。

pending

Sales of the new drug have been stopped, depending further research. (✗)

Sales of the new drug have been stopped, pending further research. (✔)

(該新藥的販售已被停止，須候更進一步的研究。)

depending on sth = according to sth, 是『依據/按照某物』之意, 如: Prices will vary, depending on supply and demand. (價格會按供需實際情形而有變化。) pending sth 是介系詞的用法, 相當於 while waiting for sth, 表『須等候某物之意』。

percent

A high percent of our people are very superstitious. (✗)

A high percentage of our people are very superstitious. (✔)

(國人迷信的情況比率偏高。)

percent 限與明確的數據連用, 如: Women now account for 38 percent of the entire workforce. (婦女目前佔整個就業人口的百分之三十八。) percentage 用於較『籠統的』百分比說法, 如: a high/low/large/small percentage (of sth)即某物佔『高/低/大/小的比率』。

perfection

The lamb chops were cooked to a perfection. (✗)

The lamb chops were cooked to perfection/a turn. (✔)

(小羊排煎得恰到好處。)

perfection 表『完美的狀態』, 是不可數名詞。be cooked/done to perfection/a turn 是指食物烹調至『恰到好處』。

periphery

Folk medicine is now on the peripheral of medical practice. (✗)

Folk medicine is now on the

P

periphery of medical practice. (✔)
(民俗療法在醫療上已淪為末流。)

peripheral 作名詞時指的是像印表機等的電腦『周邊設備』，如: We need more peripherals to expand the use of computers. (我們需要更多的周邊設備來擴大電腦的用途。) periphery 意為『外圍』或『末梢』。on/at the periphery of sth 是指『處於較不重要/非主流的地位』。

permit

Have you got a work permission? (✗)
Have you got a work permit? (✔)
(你有工作許可證嗎？)

permission 表『許可』，是不可數名詞，如: Ask permission before you light up. (點菸前須先徵求許可。) permit 作為名詞時是『許可證』，如: a parking/residence permit 就是『停車/居留證』。

P

pernicious

Her illness was diagnosed as vicious anemia. (✗)
Her illness was diagnosed as pernicious anemia. (✔)
(她的病症被診斷為惡性貧血。)

pernicious anemia 是『惡性貧血』的固定說法。vicious circle/cycle 是『惡性循環』的說法。另外, malignant tumor 是『惡性腫瘤』的說法。

persecute

The Puritans left England to escape being prosecuted. (✗)
The Puritans left England to escape being persecuted. (✔)
(清教徒逃離英國以免遭到迫害。)

be prosecuted 是『被起訴』之意，如: Those who offer or take bribes will be prosecuted. (行賄或收賄的人通通將被起訴。) be persecuted 是『被迫害』之意。

persist

If the symptom perseveres, you must see a doctor. (✗)
If the symptom persists, you must see a doctor. (✔)
(假如該症狀持續的話，你就必須去看醫生。)

作為『堅持/持續』做某事時, persevere 和 persist 幾乎是同義字, 如: I believe he will persevere/persist in his research. (我相信他會堅持他的研究工作下去。) 但作為症狀或病痛的『持續』時, 限用 persist。另外, insist (that) + S + (should) + V 表『堅持非 (做)……不可』, 如: I insisted he have his hair cut short. (我堅持他非把頭髮剪短不可。)

person

The comedian is one of the most popular TV persons. (✗)
The comedian is one of the most popular TV personalities. (✔)
(這名諧星是最受人歡迎的電視名人之一。)

a TV person 是指一個『喜歡看電視的人』。a cat/night/fast-food person 即是一個『喜歡貓/夜生活/速食的人』。personality = celebrity, 是經常出現在電視等媒體的『名人』; 如: He is a sports personality. (他是一名運動明星。)

personnel

You will be interviewed by the personal manager. (✗)
You will be interviewed by the personnel manager. (✓)
(你將接受人事主任的面試。)

personal 是『個人的』, 如: It's a matter of personal preference. (這是個人好惡的問題。) 亦可表『涉及人身攻擊的』, 如: Let's not get personal about this. (關於這件事我們不要涉及人身攻擊。) personnel 指的是公司或機構的全體員工或人事部門。

perspective

You have to put all these problems into a perspective. (✗)
You have to put all these problems into perspective. (✓)
(你必須將所有問題納入通盤考量。)

作『觀點/看法』解時, perspective 差不多等於 viewpoint, 是可數名詞, 如: The problem needs to be looked at from a historical perspective. (這個問題需從歷史的觀點來看待。) 作『通盤考量』解時, perspective 是不可數名詞, 如: Remember to keep things in perspective. (切記將各種事情作通盤考量。)。

photogenic

Rachel looks nice on TV. She is very photogenic. (✗)
Rachel looks nice on TV. She is very telegenic. (✓)
(瑞秋上電視很好看。她很上鏡頭。)

photogenic 是指某人在照片上很好看, 即『很上相』之意。telegenic 是『很上鏡頭』之意。

pick

I pick out the language mainly by osmosis. (✗)
I pick up the language mainly by osmosis. (✓)
(我學習這種語言主要是靠耳濡目染。)

pick out (= choose)是『挑選』之意, 如: I picked out a dress for the party. (我挑了一件洋裝, 準備在派對上穿。) pick up 是非正式地『學習』。

picnic

Supporting a family of five is not a picnic. (✗)
Supporting a family of five is no picnic. (✓)
(要維持一家五口的生活可不輕鬆。)

be no picnic 意為『不容易/輕鬆』, 是固定說法。

place

In the race, she finished in the first place. (✗)
In the race, she finished first/in first place. (✓)
(她賽跑得第一名。)

名次如 first/second/third place 一般不加定冠詞 the 於其前, 如: He took third place in the long jump. (他跳遠得第三名。) in the first place 表『首先/第一』, 用於介紹一系列事物的開場, 如: In the first place, I would like to thank my parents. (首先, 我要感謝我的父母。)

P

plain

I know there are several police officers in casual clothes. (✗)

I know there are several police officers in plain clothes. (✓)

(我知道有幾名員警著便衣。)

in casual clothes 是指穿著休閒服之類的『非正式打扮』。in plain clothes 是指警察/探『穿著便衣』,以方便辦案。

plastic

I have little cash. Do they take plastics? (✗)

I have little cash. Do they take plastic? (✓)

(我沒什麼現金。他們收信用卡嗎?)

plastic 作『塑膠』解時, 兼有可/不可數的用法, 如: The use of plastics in industry is widespread. (工業界使用塑膠的情形很普遍。) 但 plastic 作塑膠貨幣 (即信用卡) 解時是不可數名詞。

plead

Both defendants admitted guilty. (✗)

Both defendants pleaded guilty. (✓)

(兩名被告都認/服罪了。)

plead guilty/not guilty 是『認/不服罪』的固定說法。不過,『認輸』須說 admit/accept/concede defeat。

plebiscite

The colony will hold a plebiscite for independence in December. (✗)

The colony will hold a plebiscite on independence in December. (✓)

(該殖民地將於十二月針對獨立問題進行全民公投。)

a plebiscite/referendum on sth 是針對某重大議題進行『全民公投』, 是固定用法。

poisoning

It is a case of food poison. (✗)

It is a case of food poisoning. (✓)

(這是一起食物中毒事件。)

poison 是『毒藥』, poisoning 則是『中毒』。alcohol/lead/mercury poisoning 即是『酒精/鉛/汞中毒』。

poll

The result of the polls has not been declared. (✗)

The result of the poll has not been declared. (✓)

(選舉的結果尚未揭曉。)

the polls 是指『投開票所』, 如: More than 12 million votes went to the polls. (超過一千兩百萬人前往投票。) the poll 是指選舉結果的『總票數』。另外, carry out/conduct a poll 是『進行一項民調』, 如: According to a poll conducted last week, most people insisted that the status quo be maintained. (根據上週所進行的一項民調, 大多數人堅持維持現狀。)

pollution

Drastic measures have been taken to reduce chemical pollutions. (✗)

P

Drastic measures have been taken to reduce chemical pollution/pollutants. (✔)
(業已採取嚴厲措施來減少化學污染。)

pollution是『污染(物)』,為不可數名詞。pollutant 是『污染物』,為可數名詞。

portable

According to a study conducted recently, the groundwater around here is not portable. (✗)
According to a study conducted recently, the groundwater around here is not potable. (✔)
(根據最近的一項研究調查,這裡附近的地下水都不符飲用標準。)

portable 表 (機器等)『可攜式的』, 如: I'd like to buy a portable TV. (我想買一台手提式電視機。) potable = drinkable = safe to drink, 表 (水質)『可安全無虞飲用的』。

pool

If we pull our ideas, we may find a solution. (✗)
If we pool our ideas, we may find a solution. (✔)
(如果大家集思廣益,就能找出解決之道。)

pool 當名詞時除了表『水池』外, 亦可表『總賭金』。作為動詞時, pool sth 表將金錢、想法、技術等『集合在一起』以便共同運用, 如: Let's pool our money to buy lottery tickets. (咱們集資來買樂透彩。) pull sth 表『拉動/扯某物』, 如: Stop pulling my ear! (不要拉我的耳朵!) pull your ideas 無意義。

possesion

The man was arrested and charged with a possession of marijuana. (✗)
The man was arrested and charged with possession of marijuana. (✔)
(這名男子以持有大麻的罪名被逮捕。)

表『持有』時, possession 是不可數名詞。但表『持有物』時, possession 則是可數名詞, 如: His house and possessions were all destroyed in the fire. (他的房子和財物全都付之一炬了。)

pot

The government let the whole country go to a pot. (✗)
The government let the whole country go to pot. (✔)
(這個政府讓整個國家向下沉淪。)

pot 表『鍋/壺』時是可數名詞, 如: a cooking/coffee pot 就是指一個『燒鍋/咖啡壺』。go to pot 是固定片語, 表『沒落』或『向下沉淪』之意。另外, take pot luck 是『(鍋子) 有什麼就吃什麼』,即『吃便飯』之意。

power

The general has seized a power in a bloody coup. (✗)
The general has seized power in a bloody coup. (✔)
(這位將軍在一次流血政變中奪權。)

指『權力/功能/能源』時, power 是不可數名詞。但指『強國』時, power 是可數名詞, 如: China has emerged as an economic power in Asia. (中國儼然已成為亞洲的經濟大國。)

P

practicing

Few practiced doctors have time to do such medical research. (✗)
Few practicing doctors have time to do such medical research. (✔)
(很少開業的醫師有時間做這類的醫學研究。)

practiced 是『訓練有素的』, 如: Don't worry. He is a practiced surgeon. (不用擔心。他是一位訓練有素的外科醫師。) practicing 表『開業的』或『積極從事的』。

praise

The film has earned praises from both audiences and critics. (✗)
The film has earned praise from both audiences and critics. (✔)
(這部影片已經贏得觀眾與影評人一致的讚美。)

praise (讚美) 兼有動詞和名詞的用法。名詞主要作不可數的用法。但 sing sb's praises 是例外, 如: She was singing your praises this morning. (她整個早上一直在誇你。)

premature

The baby was five weeks precocious. (✗)
The baby was five weeks premature. (✔)
(這名嬰兒早產了五個星期。)

precocious 是『早熟的』, 如: Margaret is a precocious child. (瑪格莉特是個早熟的孩子。) premature 是『早產的』。

presence

He always finds himself speechless in the face of pretty girls. (✗)
He always finds himself speechless in the presence of pretty girls. (✔)
(面對漂亮女孩時, 他總是說不出話來。)

in the face of sth (不接 sb) 表『儘管面對某種困難或危險』, 相當於 in spite of sth 的說法。詳參 face 條。in the presence of sb 表『有某人在場時』。

press

Her latest book has gone to the press. (✗)
Her latest book has gone to press. (✔)
(她的新書已經付印了。)

go to press 是書、報『付印』的固定說法。至於 the press 是指『媒體』, 如: She finally plucked up the courage to face the press. (她終於鼓起勇氣來面對媒體了。) 另外, get a good/bad press 是指某事/物『頗受 (媒體) 好評/非議』, 如: The government's new policy is getting a good press. (政府的新政策頗受好評。)

pressed

We are now hard pressing for cash. (✗)
We are now hard pressed for cash. (✔)
(我們目前急需現金。)

pressing 用來說明事情/問題的『緊迫性』, 如: The brain drain is the most pressing problem facing our country. (人才外流是我們國家面臨的最迫切問題。) 至於 be (hard) pressed/hard-pressed for sth 是『急

需某物』之意。

pressure

Teenagers often start taking drugs because of peer pressures. (✗)

Teenagers often start taking drugs because of peer pressure. (✓)

(青少年通常是因為同儕壓力而開始嗑藥。)

peer pressure (同儕壓力) 是不可數的名詞用法。其它方面的『壓力』則兼有可/不可數的用法, 如: The pressures of modern life are great. (現代生活的壓力很大。) 或如: He did not put any pressure on her. (他並沒有對她施加任何壓力。)

prevail

Your courage will enable you to prevail on life's obstacles. (✗)

Your courage will enable you to prevail over life's obstacles. (✓)

(你的勇氣將可以使你克服人生的重重障礙。)

prevail on/upon sb 是『說服某人』之意, 如: We must prevail on our people to trust the government. (我們必須說服國人要相信政府。) prevail over sb/sth 表『戰勝/克服』某人/物。

prevalent

Glue-sniffing was especially prevailing among teenagers. (✗)

Glue-sniffing was especially prevalent among teenagers. (✓)

(吸膠過去在青少年族群中特別流行。)

作為形容詞的 prevailing 表『目前的』或『現行的』, 僅能置於名詞前面形容, 如: The prevailing market conditions are not favorable to small investors. (目前的市場狀況不利於小額投資人。) prevalent 是『盛行/普遍的』之意。

prey

Homeless children are easy prey to drug dealers. (✗)

Homeless children are easy prey for drug dealers. (✓)

(流浪兒容易成為毒販利用的對象。)

prey 本為『獵物』的總稱, 是不可數名詞。捕食牠 (們) 的動物就是 beast/bird of prey, 即『猛獸/禽』。其引申的用法見於 (1) fall/be prey to sth, 意為『成為某物之受害者』, 如: She is prey to nameless fears. (她深為莫名的恐懼所苦。) (2) be easy prey for sb, 意為『成為某人下手/利用之對象』。

principle

It's a matter of principal. (✗)

It's a matter of principle. (✓)

(這是一個原則問題。)

principal 作形容詞時是『主要的』之意, 如: Teaching is my principal source of income. (教書是我收入的主要來源。) 作名詞時, principal 是 (中、小學)『校長』或 (不含利息的)『本金』。principle 是『原則』, 因與 principal 發音相同, 易生混淆。

printing

We often receive a lot of printing matter on weekends. (✗)

We often receive a lot of printed matter on weekends. (✓)

P

(我們通常於週末收到一堆印刷品。)

printing 通常作名詞用, 可指 (1) 印刷 (術), 如: The invention of printing caused significant changes in society. (印刷術的發明造成社會的重大變化。) (2) 印書量, 如: a first printing of 20,000 copies, 即『第一刷兩萬本』。printed matter 是『印刷品』的正確說法, 不可數。

prison

He's currently in the prison because of insurance fraud. (✗)

He's currently in prison because of insurance fraud. (✓)

(他因詐領保險金而目前在坐牢。)

與『坐牢』有關時, prison 之前不加 the (除非指監牢)。比較: They will be sent to prison for armed robbery. (他們因武裝搶劫將被送去坐牢。) 表『監獄』時, prison 是可數名詞, 恆以 a/the prison 或 prisons 出現, 如: More troops will be sent to the prison to suppress the revolt. (軍方將調派更多的士兵至該監獄以鎮壓暴動。)

problem

Several thorny problems happened after he resigned. (✗)

Several thorny problems arose after he resigned. (✓)

(他離職後發生了幾件棘手的問題。)

問題的『產/發生』, problem 須搭配 arise 而非 happen。

product

They sell both canned goods and fresh products. (✗)

They sell both canned goods and fresh produce. (✓)

(他們同時販售罐頭食品和新鮮的果蔬。)

product 是指一般出售的『工商產品』。produce 專指『農產品』, 而 production 特指『影劇、廣播的產品』, 如: Several new productions will appear on Broadway. (有幾齣新戲將在百老匯上演。)

promise

My younger sister shows great promises as an artist. (✗)

My younger sister shows great promise as an artist. (✓)

(我妹妹展現了當藝術家的無比潛力。)

表『承諾/諾言』時, promise 是可數名詞, 如: Don't make promises that you can't keep. (不要許下你自己無法信守的諾言。) 表『潛力』時, promise (= potential) 是不可數名詞。

prompt

Thank you for your reply to my letter promptly. (✗)

Thank you for your prompt reply to my letter. (✓)

(感謝您很快地給我回信。)

reply 兼有動詞和名詞的用法, 所以在使用修飾語時應避免詞性錯亂。要之, 用副詞 (promptly) 修飾動詞 (reply), 但需用形容詞 (prompt) 修飾名詞 (reply)。

proportion

The spread of the contagious disease has reached epidemic proportion. (✗)

The spread of the contagious disease has reached epidemic

P

proportions. (✔)
(該傳染病的擴散已經達到疫情的規模了。)

表『比例』時, proportion 兼有可/不可數的用法, 如: Only a small proportion of graduates have found employment. (只有小比例的畢業生找到工作。) 但指『大小/規模』時, 恆用複數形的 proportions。

provide

As you know, I have to provide my wife and children. (✗)
As you know, I have to provide for my wife and children. (✔)
(你是知道的，我必須養老婆和孩子。)

provide sb with sth = provide sth to sb 表『提供某人某物』, 如: We provide free legal advice to old clients. (對老客戶我們提供免費法律諮詢。) provide for sb 是『提供某人生活所需的一切』。

provided

I'll lend you the money provide that you pay me back by Monday. (✗)
I'll lend you the money provided/providing that you pay me back by Monday. (✔)
(只要能在星期一前還我，我就借你錢。)

provided (that) = providing (that) = if only = on condition that, 表『只要……』, 是連接詞的用法。

public

Their company will make public at the end of the year. (✗)
Their company will go public at the end of the year. (✔)
(他們公司今年年底就要掛牌上市了。)

make sth public 是『公布』某事之意, 如: Are they going to make the results public? (他們快要公布結果了嗎?) go public 是指公司『掛牌上市』, 可以在股票市場買賣其股票了。

publication

Emily's poems were not intended for publications. (✗)
Emily's poems were not intended for publication. (✔)
(艾蜜莉的詩篇本不打算出版。)

表『出版』時 publication 是不可數名詞。作『刊物』解時, publication 為可數名詞, 如: Are you sure it is a weekly publication? (你確定這是一本週刊嗎?)

pull

She grabbed the boy's arm and pulled him into the classroom. (✗)
She grabbed the boy's arm and dragged him into the classroom. (✔)
(她用力抓住那男孩的手臂，然後強拉他進入教室。)

表一般『拉動』的行為, pull 和 drag 幾乎可以互通 (雖然 drag 較為費勁), 如: The lifeguard had to pull/drag the woman out of the water. (救生員必須把那個女人拉離開水面。) 但是表『強行將某人拉/拖到某處』, 則需用 drag 這個字。另外, pull (sth) into sth 是『將車輛停靠/放於某處』之意, 如: She pulled her car into the garage. (她將車子開進車庫停放。)。

P

punch

Don't forget to punch the card when you leave work. (✗)
Don't forget to punch the clock when you leave work. (✔)
(下班時別忘了打卡。)

punch the clock 是指上/下班時在打卡鐘上『打卡』。分開來說，上班打卡用 punch in 或 clock in (英式說法)。下班打卡用 punch out 或 clock out (英式說法)。

I'm tired of being my husband's punched bag. (✗)
I'm tired of being my husband's punching bag. (✔)
(我不想再當我老公的出氣筒了。)

punching bag 或連為一字的 punchbag (英式說法) 本指拳擊手練習用的『沙包吊袋』，亦可引申為別人的『出氣筒』。

P

pushed

We are pushing for time today. (✗)
We are pushed for time today. (✔)
(我們今天的時間很緊迫。)

be pushed/pressed for sth 表『由於急需某物而覺得緊迫』。pushing 的用法見於 be pushing 30/40/50 等，表某人的年齡『接近三十/四十/五十』等，如: I'm afraid she is pushing 50 by now. (恐怕她目前都快接近五十歲了。)

Qq

qualified

It is a qualified match that we must win. (✗)

It is a qualifying match that we must win. (✓)

(這是一場我們非贏不可的晉級賽。)

qualified 是指 (某人)『夠資格……的』, 如: a qualified teacher/doctor/accountant 就是指一名『合格的教師/醫師/會計師』。而qualifying是『取得資格的』, 即『晉級的』, 用來形容比賽。

quarrel

Are you trying to find a quarrel with me? (✗)

Are you trying to pick a quarrel with me? (✓)

(你是不是存心來找我的喳兒?)

pick a fight/quarrel (with sb) 表『(存心)要和某人打/吵架』, 是固定用法。

Q

quarter

The company's profits rose by 15% in the first season of the year. (✗)

The company's profits rose by 15% in the first quarter of the year. (✓)

(這家公司的獲利在今年的第一季上升百分之十五。)

season 是根據天氣的變化所規定的『季節』或指『球季』。但指企業/金融界的『第一/二/三/四季』時, 一律用 quarter 這個字。

quench

We ordered some soft drinks to extinguish our thirst. (✗)

We ordered some soft drinks to quench our thirst. (✓)

(我們點了幾杯冷飲來止渴。)

表『熄火』時可說 extinguish/quench a fire, 但表『止渴』時, 只能說 quench sb's thirst。另外, 『止血』的說法是 stanch (the flow of) blood; 『止痛』的說法是 relieve pain。

question

His loyalty is without question. (✗)

His loyalty is beyond question. (✓)

(他的忠誠度是不容置疑的。)

without question 表『毫無疑問地』, 作副詞片語用, 如: She is without question the best partner of yours. (她絕對是你最好的夥伴。) beyond question 表『毫無疑問的』, 是形容詞的用法。

questionnaire

All students were asked to write a questionnaire about their school. (✗)

All students were asked to complete a questionnaire about their school. (✓)

(所有的學生都被要求填寫一份關於學校的問卷。)

『填寫問卷』的正確說法是 complete/fill in/fill out a questionnaire。

They conducted a questionnaire to find out what students think about "compensated dating." (✗)

They conducted a survey to find out what students think about "compensated dating." (✔)

(他們進行一項問卷調查，以瞭解學生對『援交』的看法。)

questionnaire是『問卷』本身。從事/進行『問卷調查』應該說 carry out/conduct a survey 才正確。

quick

They disappeared without trace, quickly as a flash. (✗)

They disappeared without trace, quick as a flash. (✔)

(霎時他們消失得無影無蹤。)

(as) quick as a flash 表『快如閃電一般』是固定的慣用語。

Because we are busy all the time, we often have to eat a fast lunch. (✗)

Because we are busy all the time, we often have to eat a quick lunch. (✔)

(因為我們一直很忙，我們通常必須很快吃完午餐。)

fast 表速度上的『快』，所以速食恆說 fast food。quick 表趕時間的『快』。

quiet

They moved to the countryside for some peace and quietness. (✗)

They moved to the countryside for some peace and quiet. (✔)

(他們為追求一點寧靜而搬至鄉下。)

peace and quiet 表『寧靜』是固定搭配的用法。

A Quick Note

Rr

race

Human race seems to be at the top of the food chain. (✗)

The human race seems to be at the top of the food chain. (✓)

(人類似乎是位於食物鏈的最高階。)

表『全體人類』的一般說法有: (1) man (2) mankind (3) humanity (4) human beings (5) the human race. 另外 homo spaiens 是『人類』在生物學的說法。

radio

You might be able to contact them by the radio. (✗)

You might be able to contact them by radio. (✓)

(你或許用無線電可以和他們連絡上。)

by radio 表『以無線電』收發訊息, 是固定用法。on the radio 表『在 (收音機) 廣播中』, 如: I heard of his death on the radio. (我從收音機聽到他死亡的消息。)

rag

Oliver was in rag when I first met him. (✗)

Oliver was in rags when I first met him. (✓)

(我第一次見到他時，奧利佛可真是衣衫襤褸。)

單數的 rag 是『破布』, 為可數名詞, 如: He used an old rag to wipe the dirt off his shoes. (他用一塊破舊的布料來擦掉鞋子上的塵土。) rags (恆用複數) 是指『破衣服』。另外, rags 亦可引申為『貧窮』, 如: Because of winning the lottery, the old man went from rags to riches overnight. (因為贏了樂透, 這個老人一夕之間由貧窮變富有。)

raindrop

The annual raindrop in this region is extremely low. (✗)

The annual rainfall in this region is extremely low. (✓)

(這個地區的年降雨量極低。)

raindrop 是『雨滴』, 為可數名詞, 如: Raindrops keep falling on my head. (雨滴一直打在我的頭上。按: 這是經典名片《虎豹小霸王》主題曲之歌名。rainfall 是『降雨量』)。

raise

Raising flowers used to be one of my hobbies. (✗)

Growing flowers used to be one of my hobbies. (✓)

(種花曾經是我的嗜好之一。)

表『種植花木果蔬』或『飼養動物』時, raise sth 是以『經濟或食用』目的為主。由於『好玩或興趣』來種植花木時, 應該用 grow sth 較妥。

rank

It is expected that more people will join the rank of the unemployed at the beginning of next year. (✗)

It is expected that more people will join the ranks of the unemployed at the beginning of next year. (✓)

(預期在明年初時將有更多的人加入失業的行列。)

表『官階』時 rank 通常是不可數的名詞, 如: Her father is a police officer of senior rank. = Her father is a high-ranking police officer.

(她老爸是一名高階的警官。)表某特定機構/族群的『所有人員』時, 恆用 the ranks。

Agassi was at that time sixth in the world ranks. (✗)
Agassi was at that time sixth in the world rankings. (✔)
Agassi was at that time ranked sixth in the world. (✔)
(阿格西當時的世界排名為第六。)

指球員等的『排名』時, 不可用 rank(s)這個字, 限用 ranking(s), 如: She has improved her ranking this season from 35th to 23rd. (這一季她將自己的排名從第35提昇至第23。)另外,『排名』的說法亦可用 be ranked first/number one/second/number two, 即『排名第一/第二』等來表達。

rarity

These antique coins are valuable because of their rarities. (✗)
These antique coins are valuable because of their rarity. (✔)
(這些古幣因為稀有而值錢。)

表某物的『稀有/珍貴』時, rarity為不可數名詞。但表『稀客』或『珍品』時, rarity是可數名詞, 如: He owns a Ming vase and other rarities. (他擁有一個明朝的花瓶以及其它珍玩。)

rash

Most babies get a diaper rash at some stage. (✗)
Most babies get diaper rash at some stage. (✔)
(大多數嬰兒在某一個階段都會長尿布疹。)

身體『發疹』的一般說法是 break/come out in a rash, 如: My daughter breaks out in a rash if she eats shrimps. (我女兒吃蝦子身上就長疹子。) a heat rash 是長『痱子』。但 diaper rash 是不可數的用法。

rate

What's the coming rate for baby-sitting these days? (✗)
What's the going rate for baby-sitting these days? (✔)
(現今請褓母的一般費用為何？)

the going rate for sth 是某事/物的『一般費用』, 為固定說法。另外, the hourly/daily/weekly rate是指『每小時/日/週』需付的費用。

rating

The president's approval rate has fallen in recent months. (✗)
The president's approval rating has fallen in recent months. (✔)
(最近幾個月總統的施政滿意度下滑了。)

sb's approval/popularity rating 表某人的『施政滿意度』, 是固定說法。

The new drama series has enjoyed high rating. (✗)
The new drama series has enjoyed high ratings. (✔)
(這齣新連續劇的收視率一直很高。)

rating是可數名詞, 單、複數的意義不同。收『收視率』時恆用複數形的 ratings。所以, a ratings battle 就是電視台之間的『收視率大戰』。a high/low rating 是指『很高/低的評價』, 如: This university has

R

received a high rating. (這所大學一直獲有很高的評價。) 另外, rating 也表電影的『分級』, 如: A "G" rating means the movie is appropriate for anyone. (普級就是適合任何人看的電影。)

ration

News of food ration created panic buying. (✗)

News of food rationing created panic buying. (✔)

(食物配給的消息產生了恐慌性的購買。)

ration是指食物等的『配給額』, 兼有可/不可數的名詞用法, 如: a coal ration of five kg a month 就是『每個月五公斤煤炭的配給額』。rationing 指的是『配給制度 (的實施)』, 是不可數名詞。

raw

The documentary shows city life in the nude. (✗)

The documentary shows city life in the raw. (✔)

(這一支記錄片呈現赤裸裸的都市生活。)

in the nude (= wearing no clothes) 專沒穿衣服的『赤裸裸狀態』, 而 in the raw 兼指 (1) in the nude, 即沒穿衣服的赤裸裸狀態, 和 (2) 不掩蓋事實/真相的『赤裸裸狀態』, 此為引申用法。

ray

Why don't you go out and catch some ray? (✗)

Why don't you go out and catch some rays? (✔)

(你何不出去曬曬太陽呢?)

ray 表『光線』是可數名詞, 如: a ray of hope, 即『一線希望』, 為引申的用法。catch/bag some rays (恆用複數) 表『坐/躺著曬太陽之意』。

reach

Keep all medicines out of the reaches of children. (✗)

Keep all medicines out of the reach of children. (✔)

(把所有的藥物放在兒童拿不到的地方。)

作為 (伸手等) 可達的『範圍』時, reach 是不可數名詞, 如: Keep a flashlight within reach. (留一支手電筒在你拿得到的地方。) 複數形的 reaches 通常指『河段』, 如: the upper reaches of the Amazon, 即『亞馬遜河的上游』。

react

Iron reacts to water and air to produce rust. (✗)

Iron reacts with water and air to produce rust. (✔)

(鐵和水、空氣反應後就會生銹。)

react to sth 是指『對一般事物的反應』, 如: Oil prices reacted sharply to news of the war. (油價對戰爭的消息反應很激烈。)『化學反應』須用 react with sth。

read

He can read anyone as a book. (✗)

He can read anyone like a book. (✔)

(他可以看透任何人的心。)

read sb like a book 表『知道某人心裡在想些什麼』, 是固定用法。read sth as sth 是

R

『將某物解讀為某物』, 如: I read her silence as a refusal. (我把她的沉默解讀為拒絕。) 另外, read sth into sth 表『將某物作過多或不必要的解讀』, 如: I think you're reading too much into his casual remark. (我認為你把他那番漫不經心的話作過多的解讀。)

reading

Romantic novels seem to be her main readings. (✗)

Romantic novels seem to be her main reading. (✔)

(浪漫愛情的小說似乎是她主要的讀物。)

reading 作『閱讀(行為)』或『讀物』解時, 均為不可數名詞。但作為『朗讀』或『詮釋』解時, reading 是可數名詞, 如: She is giving a poetry reading tonight. (她今晚要朗誦詩歌。) 或如: It's a modern reading of Adam Smith. (這是對亞當．史密斯的現代詮釋。) 另外, 立法機關對於新法案的一/二/三讀, 也是用 reading 這個字, 如: The bill has received its second reading. (該法案已獲二讀。)

real

It's time for a real check here. Do we have a positive attitude toward work? (✗)

It's time for a reality check here. Do we have a positive attitude toward work? (✔)

(現在該是大家面對現實的時候了。我們對於工作的態度積極嗎？)

a reality check 是指『一番務實的檢查』, 即『面對現實』的做法。

reason

There is no way of making my younger brother see the reason. (✗)

There is no way of making my younger brother see reason. (✔)

(根本沒法讓我的老弟明白道理。)

表『理性』時, reason 是不可數名詞。see reason 就是『明理』, 為固定片語。表『理由』時, reason 是可數名詞, 如: I see no reason why you should resign. (我不認為你有辭職的理由。)

rebate

You may be entitled to a tax reclaim. (✗)

You may be entitled to a tax rebate/refund. (✔)

(你或許可以申請退稅。)

reclaim 是動詞, 表『要回』金錢或失物, 如: You may be entitled to reclaim some tax. (你或許可申請退點稅。) a tax rebate/refund 是『退稅』的名詞說法。

recall

The cars will have to be recycled because of an engine fault. (✗)

The cars will have to be recalled because of an engine fault. (✔)

(因為引擎設計不良，這一批車子將必須收回。)

be recycled 是指產品『回收』再利用之意。be recalled 是指產品『收回』不再販售。

R

receipt

A booking will be made on the receipt of a deposit. (✗)

A booking will be made on receipt of a deposit. (✓)

(一收到定金即完成訂位手續。)

作為『收據』時, receipt 是可數名詞, 如: Make sure you get receipts for anything you buy. (你買任何東西都要拿收據。) 表『收到/接獲』時, receipt 為不可數名詞。

recess

The City Council is now in recession. (✗)

The City Council is now in recess. (✓)

(市議會目前在休會中。)

in recession 是『在不景氣中』, 如: Our economy is still in recession. (我們的經濟仍處於不景氣中。) in recess 是指議會/法庭『在休會中』。

recharge

Can these batteries be refilled? (✗)

Can these batteries be recharged? (✓)

Are these batteries rechargeable? (✓)

(這些電池可再充嗎?)

refill 兼有名/動詞的用法, 都表『再加滿』之意, 如: Would you like a refill? (你要不要續杯?) recharge 是『再充電』之意, 亦有引申用法, 如: I'd like to stay home and recharge my batteries. (我想待在家裡養精蓄銳。)

recommend

The restaurant is powerfully recommended for its good food. (✗)

The restaurant is strongly recommended for its good food. (✓)

(這家餐廳的美食大受強力推薦。)

『強勢/大力』推薦某物的說法是 strongly/highly recommend sth。

The hotel has little to recommend itself. (✗)

The hotel has little to recommend it. (✓)

(這家飯店乏善可陳。)

sth has much/little to recommend it 表『某物頗有可取之處/乏善可陳』, 是固定用法。

recruit

New soldiers are sent there for basic training. (✗)

New recruits are sent there for basic training. (✓)

(新兵被送至該地接受基本訓練。)

soldier 是指已經接受過訓練的陸、海、空軍士兵。『新兵』的說法是 recruit。最為『菜鳥』的新兵是 new/fresh/raw recruit, 如: Drill sergeants have eight weeks to turn new recruits into soldiers. (教育班長有八週的時間將菜鳥訓練成士兵。)

redeeming

The only redeemable feature of the hotel is that it is cheap. (✗)

The only redeeming feature of the hotel is that it is cheap. (✓)

R

(這家飯店的唯一可取之處是價廉。)

redeemable 表 (債券/郵票等)『可贖/買回的』, 如: Stamps are redeemable for cash or goods. (郵票可換回現金或換取物品。) redeeming 表『彌補 (缺陷) 的』。a redeeming feature/quality 就是一個 (可以彌補缺陷的)『可取之處』, 相當於 a saving grace 的說法。

redundancy

Many words and phrases were deleted because of redundancies. (✗)
Many words and phrases were deleted because of redundancy. (✔)
(很多單字和詞組因為贅述而被刪除。)

表『贅述』時 redundancy 是不可數的名詞。當公司或工廠因應不景氣必須裁員, redundancy 表『資遣 (件數)』時, 是可數名詞。如: The rationalization of the company has resulted in over 200 redundancies. (該公司重整人事已造成兩百多名員工遭資遣。) redundancy 表『資遣』是英式用法, 其意義相當於 layoff。另外值得一提的是,『資遣費』的英文說法是 redundancy pay (英式用法) 和 severance pay (美式用法)。

reflect

She could see herself reflected on the water. (✗)
She could see herself reflected in the water. (✔)
(她可以看到自己的身影映在水中。)

be reflected in sth 指 (某物) 被映在某物裡。至於 reflect on sth 是『仔細考慮』某事, 如: It's necessary for you to reflect on your future. (你有必要仔細考慮你的未來。)

refuge

During the air raid, people took refuges in caves. (✗)
During the air raid, people took refuge in caves. (✔)
(空襲時人們都找山洞避難。)

refuge 表『避難』是不可數名詞。而『尋求避難 (所)』的說法是 take/seek/find refuge。

refugee

The flood refugees are being housed in temporary accommodations. (✗)
The flood victims are being housed in temporary accommodations. (✔)
(水患的難民目前被安置在臨時的收容所。)

refugee 指的是因戰爭/政治/宗教因素離開國家避禍的『難民』。而 victim 指的是飽受疾病/天災的『難民』, 如: famine/earthquake/flood victim 即是飽受『飢荒/地震/水患』的難民。

refute

The scholar has made several attempts to overthrow Darwin's theories. (✗)
The scholar has made several attempts to refute/rebut Darwin's theories. (✔)
(這名學者嘗試推翻達爾文的理論已有好幾次了。)

overthrow 是以『推翻』政府/權為主, 如: That government was overthrown in a

R

military coup. (該政府在一次軍事政變中被推翻。)『推翻/反駁』理論/思想須用 refute/rebut sth。

regard

The road was widened without regards for the safety of residents. (✗)
The road was widened without regard for the safety of residents. (✔)
(這條道路拓寬時根本沒有考慮附近居民的安全。)

表『注意/關心』或『尊敬/重視』時, regard 是不可數名詞, 如: She has little regard for her colleagues. (她並不尊重她的同事。) 但表『問候』時, 限用複數的 regards, 如: Give my regards to your parents. (代我問候一下你的父母。)

regimen

The old man has never seen any doctors because he has maintained a dietary cure for 30 years. (✗)
The old man has never seen any doctors because he has maintained a dietary regimen for 30 years. (✔)
(這個老人從來沒有看過醫生，因為他維持飲食養生已有三十年。)

a dietary cure 是針對糖尿/腎臟病患的一種『飲食 (控制) 療法』。a dietary/exercise regimen 是一種藉調整飲食/規律運動而使身體健康的『養生術』。

registration

Fall registrations will start next Monday. (✗)
Fall registration will start next Monday. (✔)
(秋季註冊於下週一開始。)

表『註冊/登記』時, registration 是不可數名詞。表『行車執照』時, registration 是可數名詞, 如: May I see your license and registration, ma'am? (小姐, 可否看一下你的駕照和行照?)

regret

My son and his wife are divorced, much to my regrets. (✗)
My son and his wife are divorced, much to my regret. (✔)
(使我頗為遺憾的是，我兒子跟他老婆離婚了。)

to sb's regret (恆用單數) 表『使某人感到遺憾』, 是固定用法。另外, give/send (sb) your regrets (恆用複數) 是委婉表示你不能參加某活動之意, 如: I'm afraid we might have to give you our regrets. (恐怕要告訴你我們無法參加了。)

regular

The security guards are all wearing blue uniforms and regular shoes. (✗)
The security guards are all wearing blue uniforms and regulation shoes. (✔)
(所有的安全警衛都穿著藍色制服和制式的鞋子。)

regular shoes 是指沒有任何特色的『一般鞋子』。regulation shoes 是照規定穿著的『制式鞋子』。

Fill it up with regulars, please. (✗)
Fill it up with regular, please. (✔)

R

(請加滿普通汽油。)

表『普通汽油』時, regular 是不可數名詞。『高級汽油』premium 也是不可數名詞。作為酒吧/餐廳的『常客』或軍隊中的『正規軍』解時, regular 是可數名詞, 如: The bartender knows all the regulars by name. (這名酒保知道每一個常客的名字。)

reimburse

All your travel expenses will be compensated for by the company. (✗)

All your travel expenses will be reimbursed by the company. (✓)

(你的一切差旅費將可獲得公司補助。)

compensate for sth 表『彌補某物之不足』, 詳參 compensate 條。reimburse sth 表針對(員工/廠商)的支出或代墊作如數的『補助或發還』。

reject

They all have a feeling that they are society's rejections. (✗)

They all have a feeling that they are society's rejects. (✓)

(他們都覺得自己是社會的棄嬰。)

rejection 是指『排斥/拒絕』的行為, 如: Be prepared for a lot of rejections before you land a job. (你要有心理準備, 在找到工作前你可能會到處碰壁。) 或如: The rejection of transplanted organs is a common occurrence. (器官移植的排斥現象經常發生。)。reject 兼有動/名詞的用法, 作名詞時表『被人排斥的對象』或『不合格的產品』。

relation

The diplomatic relation between our two countries should be strengthened. (✗)

The diplomatic relations between our two countries should be strengthened. (✓)

(我們兩國的外交關係應該要加強。)

單數的 relation 通常表兩件事物的『關聯性』, 如: There seems to be a direct relation between smoking and lung cancer. (抽菸和肺癌似乎有直接的關聯性。) 兩個(或以上)的人/族群/國家之間的『互動關係』, 一律用複數形的 relations。至於 relationship 這個字兼有 relation 上述的兩個意義, 如: (1) There is a close relationship between crime and poverty. (犯罪與貧窮之間有密切的關聯性。) (2) The special relationship between Britain and the US was best summarized by Churchill as "Blood is thicker than water." (英美之間的特殊關係曾被邱吉爾巧妙地概括為:『血濃於水。』一句話。) 另外, relation 可表『親人/戚』, 即等於 relative, 而 relationship 可表『男女關係』, 二者不能恆通。

remember

No one fell asleep, as long as I can remember. (✗)

No one fell asleep, as far as I can remember. (✓)

(就我記憶所及, 當時沒有一個人睡著。)

as far as sb can remember 表『就某人記憶所及』, 是固定慣用法。另外, for as long as sb can remember 表『非常久』之意, 如: They have lived here for as long as I can remember. (他們在此地居住很久了。)

R

repair

The broken computer needs to be mended. (✗)

The broken computer needs to be repaired/fixed. (✔)

(這台破電腦需要修理。)

在美式用法中, mend sth 主要是用來表『修理/補』衣物等, 如: These socks need to be mended. (這幾隻襪子需要修補了。) 其它需要專業技巧的『修理』用 repair/fix sth。

repeat

It's a new series, not a repetition. (✗)

It's a new series, not a repeat. (✔)

(這是新的連續劇，不是重播。)

repetition 表事情的『重複』或事件的『重演』, 如: Can we avoid a repetition of such man-made disasters? (我們能否避免這些人禍的一再重演?) 電視或收音機節目的『重播』應該說 repeat 或 rerun。

replicate

The virus clones itself a number of times in the computer. (✗)

The virus replicates itself a number of times in the computer. (✔)

(這種病毒會在電腦裡面自行複製很多次。)

clone 是利用動/植物的 DNA 在實驗室『人工』複製某物。replicate 是 (類似) 細胞分裂後的『自行複製』。

resolution

Have you made a New Year's decision? (✗)

Have you made a New Year's resolution? (✔)

(你有沒有在新年時痛下決心？)

a New Year's resolution 是固定說法, 指的是在元旦時所做的決定, 大都是『改過遷善』或『展現企圖心』之類的。

respect

Disease respects no persons. (✗)

Disease is no respecter of persons. (✔)

(罹患疾病不分男女老少。)

be no respecter of persons 是指某物『影響所有人, 不分老少、貴賤, 一律一視同仁』。是固定說法。

respectful

The woman is highly respectful for her courage. (✗)

The woman is highly respected for her courage. (✔)

(這個女士的勇氣大為受人尊敬。)

be respectful of sth 表『尊重某事/物』, 如: You should be respectful of his decisions. (你應當尊重他的決定。) respected 表『被/受尊敬的』。另外, respectable 表『高尚的』, 即值得尊敬的。

responsive

I tried to get him talking, but he wasn't very responsible. (✗)

I tried to get him talking, but

R

he wasn't very responsive. (✔)
(我試著找他談話，可是他卻沒什麼反應。)

responsible是『負責的』或『該負責的』之意，如: Mr. Black is responsible for training new staff. (布雷克先生負責訓練新進的員工。) responsive表『有反應的』。

result

Peter breaks rules, but he always gets result. (✗)
Peter breaks rules, but he always gets results. (✔)
(彼德不按排理出牌，不過他總是能完成任務。)

result表結果 (考試、選舉等) 時, 兼有單/複數的用法, 如: We are waiting for the election result(s). (我們在等候選舉的結果揭曉。) get results (恆用複數) 表『順利成功』。另外, 公司的『財務報表』也恆用複數的 results。

reunion

New Year is a time for a family reunification. (✗)
New Year is a time for a family reunion. (✔)
(新年是家人團聚的時節。)

reunification是指『(國家) 統一』, 如: The reunification of Germany took place in 1990. (德國的統一發生在一九九〇年。) reunion 指的是 (家人或朋友等的)『相/團聚』。如: a high-school reunion 就是一個『中學同學會』。

reversible

I often wear the jacket because it is returnable. (✗)
I often wear the jacket because it is reversible. (✔)
(我常穿這件夾克因為可以反過來穿。)

returnable 表『可退還的』, 如: The deposit of $100 is returnable. (一百元的定金可退。) reversible 表衣服等『可反過來穿的』。

revise

Forecasts of economic growth are being corrected downward. (✗)
Forecasts of economic growth are being revised downward. (✔)
(經濟成長率的預估正被向下修正中。)

revise 是逐步且局部地『修正』。revise sth upward(s)/downward(s)是指對成長值或獲利值的『向上/下修正』, 是商業英語用法。correct sth 指修正一般的錯誤。

riddle

See if you can guess at the riddle. (✗)
See if you can guess/solve the riddle. (✔)
(看看你是否能夠猜出這道謎語。)

guess at a riddle 是『猜謎語』的行為, 未必有猜中之意。guess/solve a riddle 表『猜中/解出』謎語。另外 speak/talk in riddles (恆用複數), 表『故弄玄虛』的講話, 如: Stop talking in riddles and tell me what's going on! (不要再故弄玄虛了, 告訴我怎麼一回事!)

R

right

The child is too young to tell the difference between the right and the wrong. (✗)

The child is too young to tell the difference between right and wrong. (✓)

(這個孩子年紀太輕了，還分不清是非對錯。)

right and wrong是『是非/對錯』的固定說法, 兩個名詞均為不可數。

They have decided to buy the film right to the novel. (✗)

They have decided to buy the film rights to the novel. (✓)

(他們決定要買這本小說的電影版權。)

指圖書、電視、電影的『版權』時, 限用複數形的 rights, 如: the rights to sth。另一種說法是 the copyright of sth。

right-handed

Sir Gawain is King Arthur's right-handed man. (✗)

Sir Gawain is King Arthur's right-hand man. (✓)

(高文爵士是亞瑟王的得力助手。)

a right-handed man 是一個『慣用右手』的男人。同理 a left-handed woman 是一名『慣用左手』的女人。但是 sb's right-hand man 是某人的『得力助手』。

ripe

The time is mature for his political comeback. (✗)

The time is ripe for his political comeback. (✓)

(他復出政壇的時機成熟了。)

mature 主要是指人在生理/心理方面的『成熟』或指『成熟期』的文藝作品。ripe 主要是指水果或其它農作物的『成熟』, 兼指時機的『成熟』。

risk

If your calcium intake is not sufficient, you'll take the risk of developing osteoporosis. (✗)

If your calcium intake is not sufficient, you'll run the risk of developing osteoporosis. (✓)

(如果你的鈣攝取量不足，將來就會有得到骨質疏鬆症之虞。)

take the risk of doing sth 表『決心要冒險做某件事情』, 如: I'm willing to take the risk of losing my life in order to see her again. (為了再見她一面, 我寧願冒失去性命之危險。) run the risk of doing sth 表『陷入/處於某種險境之中』。

roadwork

We had to make a detour because of some roadworking. (✗)

We had to make a detour because of some roadwork(s). (✓)

(因為部分道路施工，我們必須繞道而行。)

『道路施工』的英文說法是 roadwork (美式) 或 roadworks (英式)。

rob

Old Joe was robbed by gunpoint. (✗)

Old Joe was robbed at gunpoint. (✓)

(老喬被人用槍抵住行搶。)

R

be robbed by + 動作者, 如: The bank was robbed by three gangsters this morning. (這家銀行今早遭三名歹徒行搶。) be robbed of + 財物, 如: David was robbed of his wallet and gold watch. (大衛的錢包和金錶都被搶走了。) be robbed at knifepoint/gunpoint 是指『被人用刀尖/槍口抵住行搶』, 是固定用法。

rock

Their marriage is on the rock. (✗)

Their marriage is on the rocks. (✔)

(他們的婚姻岌岌可危。)

on the rocks (恆用複數) 有下列二義: (1) (婚姻/事業) 岌岌可危的 (2) (烈酒) 加冰塊, 如: I want my scotch on the rocks. (我的蘇格蘭威士忌要加冰塊。)

root

Buddhism has taken roots in this country. (✗)

Buddhism has taken root in this country. (✔)

(佛教已經在這個國家生根了。)

take root 本指植物『向下扎根』, 引伸為, 思想或制度的『生根』。表家族或文化的『根源』時, 恆用複數形的 roots, 如: The book is about the author's search for his roots. (這本書描述作者的尋根過程。)

rope

I'm a complete novice. Please show me the rope. (✗)

I'm a complete novice. Please show me the ropes. (✔)

(我完全是個新手，請告訴我訣竅吧。)

表『繩索』時 rope 兼有可/不可數的用法, 如: They are jumping rope. (他們正在跳繩。)。表『訣竅』時, 恆用複數形的 ropes。show/teach sb the ropes 表『告訴/教某人做事的訣竅』。learn/know the ropes 表『學會/知道做某事的訣竅』。

rote

Children still learn their times tables by memory. (✗)

Children still learn their times tables by rote. (✔)

(至今兒童仍用死背的方式來學九九乘法表。)

by rote 是『死背』的固定說法。

royalty

At the dinner party, they treated us like royalties. (✗)

At the dinner party, they treated us like royalty. (✔)

(在晚宴當中，他們待我們像是王室成員一般。)

royalty 表『王室/皇家成員』時是集合名詞, 不可數。複數形的 royalties 表出版書籍時作者所抽的『版稅』, 如: The writer gets 12% royalties on all his books. (這個作家所寫的書都抽取 12%的版稅。)

rubble

The earthquake has reduced the town to rubbles. (✗)

The earthquake has reduced the town to rubble. (✔)

(地震使這個小鎮淪為瓦礫堆。)

rubble 意為『瓦礫 (堆)』, 是不可數名詞。be reduced to rubble/ruins 表『淪為瓦礫堆/廢墟』, 其主詞通常是建築物。

A lot of rubble will have to be used in the roadwork. (✗)
A lot of gravel will have to be used in the roadwork. (✔)
(這段道路施工必須動用很多的碎石。)

rubble 是建築物倒蹋後所剩的『瓦礫』。gravel 是『碎石子』, 主要用於修/鋪路。

run

Never run through a red light! (✗)
Never run a red light! (✔)
(千萬別闖紅燈！。)

『闖紅燈』的正確說法是 run a red light。run through sth 表很快地『看/懂過某物』, 如: I just ran through the list but could not find my name on it. (我剛才匆匆看了一下名單, 卻找不到我的名字。)

Mom offered to put a bath for me. (✗)
Mom offered to run a bath for me. (✔)
(老媽提說要幫我放洗澡水。)

run a bath 是『放洗澡水』的正確說法。

runway

The plane started to taxi down the runaway. (✗)
The plane started to taxi down the runway car. (✔)
(飛機開始順著跑道滑行。)

runaway 作名詞時表『逃家/亡者』, 如: One of the runaways is her son. (她的兒子也是逃家者之一。) runway 有兩義: (1) 飛機起降的跑道 (2) 模特兒表演的伸展台 (相當於英式用法的 catwalk)。

The thief used a Benz as his runaway car. (✗)
The thief used a Benz as his getaway car. (✔)
(該竊賊利用一部賓士轎車以掩護其逃離。)

a runaway car 是一部『(失控) 車速過快的車子』, 猶如: a runaway horse 是一匹『脫韁之馬』。另外, a runaway success 表『比預期還要 (更快) 成功的人或事物』, 如: His new business is a runaway success. (他的新事業沒想到這麼快速成功。) a getaway car/vehicle 指的是『歹徒犯案逃走時利用的車輛』。

R

S s

S

sad

Sadly to say, their country is heading toward civil war. (✗)
Sad to say, their country is heading toward civil war. (✔)
Sadly, their country is heading toward civil war. (✔)
(不幸的是，他們的國家正邁向內戰之路。)

sad to say = sadly = unfortunately 皆可用來表示遺憾或惋惜。

safe

It's best to play it safely by boiling the water. (✗)
It's best to play it safe by boiling the water. (✔)
(最好把這水煮沸，不要冒險。)

play (it) safe 表『以安全為考量，不要冒險』，是固定用法。

safety

They walked for several days until they reached a safety. (✗)
They walked for several days until they reached safety. (✔)
(他們走了好幾天的路才抵達一個安全地點。)

表一個『安全地點』時，safety是不可數名詞。reach safety = reach a safe place。

sail

The Mayflower set sails for America. (✗)
The Mayflower set sail for America. (✔)
(五月花號啟航駛向美洲。)

表『船帆』時，sail 為可數名詞，如：hoist/lower the sails 即是『把船帆升起/降下』。但set sail (揚帆/啟航) 為固定用法。

sale

Do you have last year's sale figures? (✗)
Do you have last year's sales figures? (✔)
(你有我們去年的銷售額數據嗎？)

表販售貨物 (單一) 的成交/未成交，用 make/lose a sale，如：They lowered the price in order to make a sale. (為了做這筆生意，他們把價格降低了。) 表『總銷售額』時恆用複數的 sales。

I can afford to buy the digital camera because it is for sale now. (✗)
I can afford to buy the digital camera because it is on sale now. (✔)
(因為這台數位相機在特價中，我現在買得起了。)

for sale 表『出售中』，而 on sale 兼有『特價中』和『出售中』兩個意思。

salon

Kerri is now working at a beauty saloon. (✗)
Kerri is now working at a beauty salon. (✔)
(凱莉目前在一家美容院工作。)

saloon 相當於 bar，是『酒吧』之意，如：Henry stayed in the saloon all night. (亨利整晚待在那家酒吧裡。) 至於 salon 指的是一個『修剪頭髮/設計髮型』的地方。a

S

beauty salon/parlor 是一家『美容院』。

salvage

Some residents tried to rescue their belongings from the fire. (✗)
Some residents tried to salvage their belongings from the fire. (✓)
(有些居民試圖從大火中搶救出他們的財物。)

rescue 的用法以『搶救人員』為主, 如: Helicopters rescued more than 10 victims from the flood. (直昇機搶救了十幾名水患的災民。)『搶救 (沉船/火災等之) 財物』, 應該用 salvage 這個字。不過 rescue 這個字亦可用來表『搶救企業/公司』, 如: Henry has rescued an ailing business from near bankruptcy. (亨利將一個瀕臨破產的企業搶救回來。)

sanction

The Security Council will impose economic sanction on North Korea. (✗)
The Security Council will impose economic sanctions on North Korea. (✓)
(聯合國安理會將對北韓實施經濟制裁。)

表『批准』時, sanction 是不可數名詞, 如: War cannot be declared without the sanction of Parliament. (沒有國會的批准不得對外宣戰。) 表『制裁』時, 恆用複數形的 sanctions。

satisfying

The meal was not good enough, but it was satisfactory. (✗)
The meal was not good enough, but it was satisfying. (✓)
(這一餐雖稱不上精緻，但令人很有飽足感。)

satisfactory 用來說明事物『相當不錯, 因而令人滿意』。基本上, not good enough 和 satisfactory 並舉是矛盾的。satisfying 是『令人有飽足感的』。

saving

She was cheated out of her life saving. (✗)
She was cheated out of her life savings. (✓)
(她的一生積蓄都被人騙走了。)

saving 是可數名詞, 表『節省下來的一些錢/時間』, 如: Buying now makes a saving of $20. (現在買可節省 20 元。) 表『存款/積蓄』一律用複數形的 savings。

saying

The CEO has the final saying. (✗)
The CEO has the final say. (✓)
(執行長擁有最後的決定權。)

say 作名詞時表『發言/決定權』, 限為單數或不可數的用法。have a/no say in/on sth 表『對某事有/沒有發言 (決定) 權』。saying 是『諺語』, 如: As the saying goes, a penny saved is a penny earned. (有一句諺語這樣說:『省一分錢即賺一分錢。』

scan

All baggage has to be skimmed at the airport. (✗)
All baggage has to be scanned

S

at the airport. (✔)
(在機場所有的行李都要經過掃瞄檢查。)

表『略/跳讀』時, scan 和 skim 是相通的, 如: I only scanned/skimmed (through) the paper this morning. (今天早上, 我只是粗略地翻了一下報紙。) 表『(電波) 掃瞄』時, 限用 scan 這個字。進行『掃瞄』的機器是 scanner。

scene

I prefer to work behind the scene as a director. (✗)
I prefer to work behind the scenes as a director. (✔)
(我比較喜歡做幕後的導演工作。)

behind the scenes (恆用複數) 表『暗中』或『在幕後』。至於 at/on the scene 表『在 (事故/犯罪的) 現場』, 如: Five minutes later, the police arrived at the scene. (五分鐘後警方抵達現場。)

scholarship

The book is the result of her lifetime of scholarships. (✗)
The book is the result of her lifetime of scholarship. (✔)
(這本書是累積她一輩子的學問之成果。)

scholarship 表『學術/問』時是不可數名詞。表『獎學金』時則為可數名詞, 如: I was awarded a scholarship to attend Indiana University. (我獲頒獎學金就讀印地安那大學。)

scorched

It is very likely that our army will adopt a scorching earth policy. (✗)
It is very likely that our army will adopt a scorched earth policy. (✔)
(我軍很可能會採取焦土戰術。)

『焦土戰術/政策』英文的正確說法是 scorched earth policy。這種戰略是把一個地方的人員疏散, 帶不走的物資摧毀, 不讓敵人利用。scorching 表『非常炎熱的』, 如: Today is scorching hot, isn't it? (今天極為炎熱, 是不是?)

score

The NASDAQ scored 16 points yesterday. (✗)
The NASDAQ gained 16 points yesterday. (✔)
(美國科技股那斯達克昨天上漲了 16 點。)

score a point/two points 指的是球賽或考試的『得點/分』, 如: He scored another two points five minutes later. (五分鐘後他又再得兩分。) 指股票指數『上漲/下跌若干點』, 應該說 gain/lose...points。

scout

She was spotted by a star scout at the age of 17. (✗)
She was spotted by a talent scout at the age of 17. (✔)
(她十七歲就被一位星探發掘。)

scout 本義是『偵察兵』。a boy/girl scout 是一名『男/女童子軍』。而發掘演藝/運動界明星的『星探』之說法是 talent scout 或 scout。

scramble

In this exercise, the words in each

sentence are scattered. Rearrange them in the right order. (✗)
In this exercise, the words in each sentence are scrambled. Rearrange them in the right order. (✓)
(在這個練習中，每個句子的單字都被打散。請依正確順序重組。)

scattered 用來指東西四散或任意放置。指單字、句子的順序混亂應該用 scrambled/mixed up。

screen

We need a screening door to keep insects out. (✗)
We need a screen door to keep insects out. (✓)
(我們需要做個紗門以防止蚊蟲進入屋裡。)

screening 作為名詞用, 表『放映』或『甄選』。如: a screening of Steven Spielberg's new film 即是『放映史蒂芬・史匹柏的一部新片』。而 a screening committee 就是一個『甄選委員會』。『紗門』的英文說法是 a screen door。另外, 演藝人員的『試鏡』是 a screen test。

seam

The dance hall was bulging at the seam when excitement was at its height. (✗)
The dance hall was bulging at the seams when excitement was at its height. (✓)
(當大家興奮至最高點時，舞廳都已經快擠爆了。)

seam 指的是衣服的『接縫』, 或兩片木板/牆壁的『接合處』, 為可數名詞, 如: The seam at the back of my pants has split. (我褲子後面的接縫裂開了。) 但 be bursting/bulging at the seams(恆用複數) 表室內『人滿為患』, 好像快擠爆似的。另外, be coming/falling apart at the seams 是指某一個計劃或組織『快要解體』, 如:His business empire is falling apart at the seams. (他的企業王國快要解體了。)

search

Do you have a searching warrant? (✗)
Do you have a search warrant? (✓)
(你們有搜索令嗎？)

searching 作形容詞時, 表『追求真相/銳利的』, 通常用來形容某人的眼神或提出的問題, 如: I tried to avoid her searching look. (我試著避開她的銳利目光。)『搜索令/狀』的說法是 a search warrant。

The police have found nothing after searching for his house. (✗)
The police have found nothing after searching his house. (✓)
(警方搜過他的家後並沒有發現什麼。)

search for sb/sth 表『尋找 (不見的) 某人/物』。search sb/sth 表『搜 (某人的) 身』或『搜查一個地方』。

seating

Please be seating. (✗)
Please be seated. (✓)
(請坐。)

seat 當名詞時是『座位』, 當動詞時表『使 (某人或自己) 坐下來』, 是及物的用法, 如: The stadium will seat up to 20,000 people. (這座球場將可容納高達二萬人的座位。) 表『請坐』的正式說法有 (1) Please be seated. (2) Please seat yourself.

(3) Please sit down.。

The theater has a seated capacity of 600. (✗)

The theater has a seating capacity of 600. (✔)

(這家戲院可坐 600 人。)

a seating capacity of + 數字表『座位數』，是固定用法。

section

I enjoy reading the sports edition of the newspaper. (✗)

I enjoy reading the sports section of the newspaper. (✔)

(我喜歡看這家報紙的體育版。)

edition 是指印刷的一/再版等，如: It is a revised edition of the book. (這是這本書的修訂版。)。報紙的『體育/商業/旅遊版』應該說 sports/business/travel section。

security

If you won't leave, I'll have to call securities. (✗)

If you won't leave, I'll have to call security. (✔)

(如果你不離開，我就叫警衛。)

表『安全』或『警衛』時, security 是不可數名詞, 如: National security is our top priority. (國家安全是我們的第一優先。) 表『警衛 (人員)』時, security 是一個集合名詞, 差不多等於 security guards 的說法。複數的 securities 指『有價證券』。

sedentary

Some health problems are caused by our sedative lifestyles. (✗)

Some health problems are caused by our sedentary lifestyles. (✔)

(有些健康問題是我們久坐不動的生活方式所造成的。)

sedative 作為名詞時是『鎮靜劑』之意。sedentary 是形容詞, 表『久坐不動的』, 如: sedentary life/job/lifestyle 就是『久坐不動的生活/工作/生活方式』。

select

Only a selective few companies are allowed to compete for the contract. (✗)

Only a select few companies are allowed to compete for the contract. (✔)

(只有少數幾家公司被允許參加競標。)

selective 表『慎選的』, 如: We are very selective about what we wear. (對於所穿的衣物我們都很慎選。) a select few 表『少數的幾個人/物』, 是固定用法。

self-aware

Getting the job has increased my confidence, and I feel much more self-conscious. (✗)

Getting the job has increased my confidence, and I feel much more self-aware. (✔)

(得到這個工作使我信心大增，同時我也更加瞭解自己。)

self-conscious 表對某事物『忸怩不安』或『特別在意』, 如: He is pretty self-conscious about being short. (他對自已的個子矮小相當在意。) self-aware 表『認清自己的』。

S

selling

This car's main sale point is its installment plan. (✗)

This car's main selling point is its installment plan. (✔)

(這部汽車的主要賣點是可以分期付款。)

a selling point是讓人心動想買的一個『賣點』,為固定用法。另外, a selling price 是貨物賣出去的『售價』。

sense

I hope your brother will come to his sense and stop fooling around. (✗)

I hope your brother will come to his senses and stop fooling around. (✔)

(希望你的弟弟能夠醒悟,不再鬼混。)

表『感覺/官』時, sense 是可數名詞, 如: Everyone likes to create a sense of occasion at Christmas. (在耶誕節時大家都想營造出一種節慶的氣氛/感覺。) come to your senses 表『醒悟』,是固定用法。表『理性/道理』時, sense 是不可數名詞, 如: It makes sense to save money for a rainy day. (存錢以備不時之需是明智的。)

sensitive

Coral is very sensible to changes in water temperature. (✗)

Coral is very sensitive to changes in water temperature. (✔)

(珊瑚對水溫的變化極為敏感。)

sensible是『明智的』, 如: Keeping him at a distance is the sensible thing to do. (跟他保持距離是明智之舉。) sensitive是『敏感的』。

sentiment

There is no place for sentiments when you make an investment. (✗)

There is no place for sentiment when you make an investment. (✔)

(投資時不容感情用事。)

指某人的『想法/態度』時, sentiment 兼有可/不可數的用法, 如: It was a speech full of noble sentiments. (這是一篇充滿崇高理念的演講。) 或如: We should take account of popular sentiment. (我們應當考慮到一般大眾的想法。) 但是表『感情用事』時, sentiment 恆為不可數名詞, 其意義和用法相當於 sentimentality 這個字。

serial

The doctor is suspected of series killings. (✗)

The doctor is suspected of serial killings. (✔)

(這名醫生涉嫌連續殺人。)

指『連續性的節目/故事』時, series 差不多等於 serial, 不過 series 強調的是同一組人物的故事在固定的時段播出/連載, serial 則較不受限制。但 serial 可作形容詞用, 表『連續的』, 如: serial killings/murders。series 不能作形容詞。

We need to do a serial of tests first. (✗)

We need to do a series of tests first. (✔)

(我們需先做一系列的測試。)

表『一系列的……』時, a series of sth 是固定用法。

service

The hotel has built a reputation for an excellent customer service. (✗)

The hotel has built a reputation for excellent customer service. (✓)

(這家旅館已建立擁有一流客服的名氣。)

指商店/旅館/餐廳的『服務』時, service 為不可數名詞。指『服務業(者)』時, service 是可數名詞, 如: financial/insurance services 即是『金融/保險業(者)』。指一般性的『服務/幫忙』時, service 為單數或不可數的用法, 如: I'd like you to do me a serivce. (我要你幫個忙。) 或如: I'm at your service anytime. (我隨時為你效勞。)

Has your car been regularly served? (✗)

Has your car been regularly serviced? (✓)

(你的車有沒有固定維修?)

serve sth 通常表『提供食物/飲料』, 如: Dinner is served between 6 and 9. (晚餐於六點至九點間提供。) 作為動詞時, service sth 表『維修汽車或機器』。

serving

The new model is more fuel efficient and needs less serving. (✗)

The new model is more fuel efficient and needs less servicing. (✓)

(這款新車更省油而且較不需維修。)

serving (= helping) 是指食物的『客/份』, 為可數名詞, 如: These dumplings should make enough for five servings. (這些水餃應該夠五個人吃。) 而 servicing 是指汽車/機器的『維修』, 為不可數名詞。

settle

I think they are perfectly willing to solve out of court. (✗)

I think they are perfectly willing to settle out of court. (✓)

(我想他們十分願意在庭外和解。)

solve sth 是『解決』問題/困難等, 恆為及物用法。settle (sth)是針對法律糾紛進行『和解』, 兼有及/不及物的用法。an out-of-court settlement 為『庭外和解』名詞形式的說法。

sex

The young and pretty actress is full of sexual appeal. (✗)

The young and pretty actress is full of sex appeal. (✓)

(這名年輕貌美的女星極為性感。)

sex 和 sexual 經常結合名詞使用, 極易混淆。要之, 一切照字典規定使用。如: sex appeal/change/education/life/object/organ, 即『性感/變性手術/性教育/性生活/性感尤物/性器官』皆為固定說法。而 sexual abuse/harassment/intercourse/partner/relationship, 即『性虐待/性騷擾/性交/性夥伴/性關係』也是固定說法。

shade

Mike's brilliant academic performance really puts his older brother in the shadow. (✗)

Mike's brilliant academic performance really puts his older brother in the shade. (✓)

(麥克亮麗的學業表現真的使他哥哥黯然失色。)

shade 指『陰涼/暗處』是不可數名詞, 如: The tree gives pleasant shade. (那棵樹有涼快的樹蔭。) shadow 是『人/物影』, 如: I saw a man's shadow on the wall. (我看到牆上有一個人影。) 另外, put sb/sth in the shade 表『使某人/物黯然失色』, 是固定用法。

shake

He's no great shake as a writer. (✗)

He's no great shakes as a writer. (✓)

(他並不是很出色的作家。)

shake 兼有名詞和動詞的用法。作為名詞時, 表『搖動』, 是可數用法, 如: Give it a good shake before use. (使用前好好搖一搖。) be no great shakes 表『不是很出色』, 是固定的口語用法。

shame

The election was a complete shame. (✗)

The election was a complete sham. (✓)

(這回選舉完全是個騙局。)

作為『羞愧/恥』時, shame 是不可數名詞, 如: His Rolls-Royce puts my car to shame. (他那輛勞斯萊斯使我的車子相形見絀。) 作為可數名詞時 (恆用單數), a (crying/great/terrible) shame 表一件『令人惋惜之事』, 如: The election result was a great shame. (選舉的結果真是令人扼腕。) a complete sham 是一個『十足的騙局』。

shape

The idea began to take a shape in my mind two months ago. (✗)

The idea began to take shape in my mind two months ago. (✓)

(這個構想於兩個月前開始在我心中成形。)

表『形狀』時, shape 兼有可/不可數的用法。但 take shape 是固定片語。表『健康/身體狀況』時, shape 恆為不可數名詞, 如: Physical exercise will keep you in shape. (運動可以使你保持健康。)

share

My father owns a 20% share in that company. (✗)

My father owns a 20% shareholding in that company. (✓)

(我老爸在那家公司的持股率佔百分之二十。)

share 是『股票 (數)』, 如: She sold 10,000 shares this morning. (今天早上她賣掉了一萬股。) 又如: Share prices keep falling on the Tokyo Stock Exchange. (東京證券交易所的股價持續下滑。) shareholding 是『持股比率』。

shelter

We take a shelter in the basement when a tornado comes. (✗)

We take shelter in the basement when a tornado comes. (✓)

(當龍捲風來時，我們就在這地下室避難。)

表『避難處/庇護所』時, shelter 是可數名詞, The hut provided a shelter from the downpour for us. (那一間小屋為我們在大雨時提供一個庇護所。) 表『避難/庇護』的情況時, shelter 為不可數名詞, 如: take/seek/find shelter 就是在某個地方『找到庇護』。

S

shift

The thought of working night shift put me off taking the job. (✗)

The thought of working night shifts put me off taking the job. (✔)

(一想到要輪夜班，我就不想接受這份工作。)

shift 表『輪班』, 是可數名詞, 如: We work eight hours a day and in three shifts. (我們一天三班制工作八個小時。) 另外, shift 也可作動詞使用。shift attention/focus 就是『轉移注意力/焦點』, 如: The government has decided to shift the focus more toward internal affairs. (該政府已決定將其焦點多轉移一些到內政問題上。) 而 shift blame/responsibility 則是『推卸責任』之意。

shock

The soldier went into a shock through losing a lot of blood. (✗)

The soldier went into shock through losing a lot of blood. (✔)

(這名士兵由於失血過多而進入休克狀態。)

表令人『震驚』的情況/事件, shock 是可數名詞且通常以單數的形態出現, 如: His sudden death came as a shock to us all. (他的猝死令我們大家震驚不已。) 表身體的『休克』狀態, shock 為不可數名詞。

shoes

It'll be practically impossible to find someone to wear Peter's shoes. (✗)

It'll be practically impossible to find someone to fill Peter's shoes. (✔)

(要找人接替彼德簡直是不可能的事。)

『接替某人(的工作)』應該說 fill/step into sb's shoes, 是固定片語。

shoot

If you keep on going to work late, you'll shoot yourself in the leg. (✗)

If you keep on going to work late, you'll shoot yourself in the foot. (✔)

(如果你一直上班遲到，你會自找麻煩的。)

shoot sb in the back/head/leg/stomach 表用槍『射擊某人的背/頭/腿/腹部』, 是『如實』的說法, 如: The robber was shot in the back while trying to escape. (這名搶匪在逃離時背部中槍。) shoot yourself in the foot 表『自找麻煩』, 猶如『搬塊石頭砸自己的腳』這個說法, 是『比喻』的用法。

shooting

The robbery led to a shooting between the robbers and the police. (✗)

The robbery led to a shoot-out between the robbers and the police. (✔)

(這起搶案造成警匪之間展開槍戰。)

shooting 表『槍擊事件』時是可數名詞, a shooting 指的是某一方的人開槍, 對方中槍受傷或身亡的『一個槍擊事件』。如: The police believe that the shooting was gang-related. (警方相信這個槍擊事件和幫派有關。)" a shoot-out 是指兩方人馬的『一次槍戰』。另外, shooting 表『打靶/獵』時為不可數名詞, 如: I enjoy riding, fishing and shooting. (我喜歡騎馬、釣魚和打獵。)

shoptalk

I'm fed up with their shoptalks. (✗)
I'm fed up with their shoptalk. (✓)
(他們的工作經我實在聽不下去了。)

shoptalk 是 talk shop 的名詞說法, 表『工作/生意經』, 是不可數用法。

short

He is an outstanding politician, but a little short of tact. (✗)
He is an outstanding politician, but a little short on tact. (✓)
(他是一名出色的政治人物，但是圓滑稍嫌不足。)

be short of sth 主要表『物資方面的不足』, 如: We are short of clothing/food/money. (我們衣服/食物/金錢不足。) be short on sth 表『某種性質之不足』, 如: The mayor is long on speech but short on action. (這個市長講得頭頭是道, 可是卻遲遲未見實行。) 另外, be short for sth 表『某物為……之略』, 如:"Gym" is short for "gymnasium." (Gym 是 gymnasium 之略。)

For short, your boyfriend is a good-for-nothing. (✗)
In short, your boyfriend is a good-for-nothing. (✓)
(總而言之，你的男友一無是處。)

for short 表『簡稱』, 如: Her name is Elizabeth, but we just call her Lisa for short. (她的名字是 Elizabeth, 可是我們都叫她 Lisa 作為簡稱。) in short 表『總而言之』。

He stopped shortly in the middle of his speech. (✗)
He stopped short in the middle of his speech. (✓)
(他話講到一半就突然停止了。)

stop short = stop suddenly, 表『突然停止』, 是固定用法。shortly = soon, 表『不久』之意, 如: My mom will be back shortly. (我媽媽很快就回來。)

show

The time has come for a raise of hands. (✗)
The time has come for a show of hands. (✓)
(該是舉手表決的時候了。)

raise 作名詞時表『加薪』, 如: My boss promised to give me a raise. (老闆曾允諾給我加薪。) 不過, 作為動詞時, raise your hand(s) 表『舉手 (發問)』, 如: If you have any questions, please raise your hands. (如果有任何問題要問, 請舉手。) a show of hands 是『舉手表決』。

shred

The film has been torn to shred by the critics. (✗)
The film has been torn to shreds by the critics. (✓)
(這部片子已被影評人批評到一無是處。)

shred 意為『碎片』, 是可數名詞。tear sb/sth to pieces/shreds 本義是『將某人/物撕成碎片』, 引申為『把某人/物批評到體無完膚』。

S

sideline

Don't just stand on the sideline. You should get involved. (✗)
Don't just stand on the sidelines. You should get involved. (✓)
(不要只是袖手旁觀。你該介入了。)

on the sidelines (恆用複數) 本義為『在 (球場的) 邊線』, 如: He stood on the sidelines giving instructions to his team. (他站在邊線向他的隊員下達指示。) stand/stay/remain on the sidelines 亦可引申為『袖手旁觀』。另外, a sideline 表『一個副業』, 如: She is an accountant, but she sells insurance as a sideline. (她是一名會計, 不過她也賣保險當副業。)

sigh

We all breathed a sign of relief. (✗)
We all breathed a sigh of relief. (✓)
(我們大家都鬆了一口氣。)

a sign of sth 表『某物的符/信號』, 如: The red flag is a sign of danger. (那面紅色的旗子是危險的信號。) sigh 是『嘆息聲』。表『發出一 (……) 嘆息聲』用 breathe/let out/give/heave a sigh of sth。

sight

Many sights of UFOs have been reported throughout the world. (✗)
Many sightings of UFOs have been reported throughout the world. (✓)
(遍及全球已經有多起目擊幽浮的事件被報導。)

表『看見』或『視力』時, sight 是不可數名詞。複數形的 sights 指的是『景點』, 如: I enjoy seeing the sights of big cities. (我喜歡參觀大城市的景點。) sighting 是可數名詞, 表『目擊 (事件)』。

He looked around, but there was no one on sight. (✗)
He looked around, but there was no one in sight. (✓)
(他環顧四周，但沒見到一個人影。)

on sight 表『一見到就……』, 如: The commander ordered us to shoot any enemy soldiers on sight. (指揮官命令我們一見到敵軍就立即射擊。) in sight 表『在可以看到的範圍內』。另外, at first sight 表『第一次看到』, 如: I believe it was love at first sight. (我認為這就是一見鍾情。)

signal

The stars on the American flag signal the fifty states. (✗)
The stars on the American flag signify the fifty states. (✓)
(美國國旗的星星代表其五十州。)

signal 作為名詞時是『信號/號誌』, 作為動詞時表用信號向某人告知或示意, 如: The cop signaled me to pull over. (那名警察示意要我靠路邊停車。) signify sth 表『代表/象徵某物』之意。

signature

Many fans came to ask for the player's signature. (✗)
Many fans came to ask for the player's autograph. (✓)
(許多球迷前來要求該選手簽名。)

signature 指的是在文件上的『簽名』, 為可數名詞, 如: A document with two

S

signatures on it is missing. (一份上面有兩個簽名的文件不見了。) autograph 指的是影/球迷向影視紅星或運動明星要的『簽名』。另外, 表『簽署』時, signature 與 signing 相當, 為不可數名詞, 如: The contract is ready for signature. (這個合約已準備簽訂了。)

silver

It is Mary's job to polish the silvers. (✗)

It is Mary's job to polish the silver. (✔)

(瑪麗的工作是負責把銀器擦亮。)

表金屬『銀』或銀器時, silver 為不可數名詞。表運動會頒發的『銀牌』時, silver 為可數名詞, 如: She's got one gold and two silvers. (她已經獲得一金兩銀。)

size

Do you have these pants in size 10? (✗)

Do you have these pants in a size 10? (✔)

(你們這款長褲有 10 號的嗎 ?)

size 兼有可/不可數的用法。指人物/東西的『大小』時, in size 是固定說法, 如: The tumor has doubled in size in six months. (這個腫瘤在半年期間增大一倍。) 指衣物、鞋子的『尺寸』時,size 恆為可數名詞, 如: The coats come in three sizes. (這款外套有大、中、小三種尺寸。)

skip

It's not a good idea to skip over breakfast. (✗)

It's not a good idea to skip breakfast. (✔)

(不吃早餐並非是個好主意。)

skip over sth 是指略過某物, 不加以閱讀或討論, 如: Let's skip over the next few pages and go on to Chapter three. (我們略過下面這幾頁, 直接跳到第三章。) skip breakfast/lunch 是『不吃早/午餐』的固定說法。另外,『不去上學/課』也可說成 skip school/class。

slander

She's going to sue the newspaper for slander. (✗)

She's going to sue the newspaper for libel. (✔)

(她將控告那家報紙誹謗。)

slander 指的是口頭上的『誹謗』, 如: What he said about me is sheer slander. (他針對我所講的一切完全是誹謗。) libel 是文書上的『誹謗』。

slang

The "john" in the phrase is a slang. (✗)

The "john" in the phrase is a slang word. (✔)

(這個片語中的 john 是俚語。)

slang 表『俚俗語言』的總稱, 是不可數名詞。a slang word/expression 表『一個俚俗的用語/法』, 可數。(按: john 在美俚中表『廁所』)

slap

It was a real slap on the face when the bank turned us down. (✗)

It was a real slap in the face when the bank turned us down. (✔)

(被那家銀行拒絕讓我們覺得很難堪。)

a slap in the face 本義是『一巴掌打在(某人)臉上』,引申為『令人難堪』的情況,是固定用法。另外, a slap on the back 或 slap sb on the back 均表『友善地稱許某人』。

sleep

Let me sleep in it, and I'll give you my answer tomorrow. (✗)

Let me sleep on it, and I'll give you my answer tomorrow. (✓)

(讓我先想一個晚上,明天給您答覆。)

sleep on sth 表『考慮某事一個晚上』,是固定說法。

If you have a hangover tomorrow morning, get back to bed and sleep it away. (✗)

If you have a hangover tomorrow morning, get back to bed and sleep it off. (✓)

(如果你明早有宿醉現象,再回去睡一下讓它慢慢退掉。)

sleep sth away 有兩義: (1) 藉著睡眠以忘記憂慮/煩惱, 如: I'm sure she can sleep her troubles away. (我相信她睡一覺醒來, 煩惱就不見了。) (2) 睡掉一段時間, 如: Are you going to sleep the entire morning away? (你要賴床一整個早上是不是?) sleep sth off 表『藉著睡眠讓宿醉、疼痛或藥物作用等逐漸退掉』。

slip

Take care not to slide on the wet floor. (✗)

Take care not to slip on the wet floor. (✓)

(小心不要滑倒在潮溼的地板上。)

slide 表『滑行』, 如: Many children enjoy sliding on the ice in winter. (冬天有很多孩子喜歡在冰上滑行。) slip 表『滑倒 (在地)』。另外, skid 是指車輛失控『滑向一邊』, 如: My car skidded and ran onto the sidewalk. (我的車子滑向一邊後就衝上人行道。)

Since he has made the same mistake again and again, I won't let it slip this time. (✗)

Since he has made the same mistake again and again, I won't let it slide this time. (✓)

(既然他老犯同樣的錯誤,這回我不會坐視不管了。)

let sth slip 表『無意中說出某事』, 如: Jenny let it slip that she would sue her boss. (珍尼無意說出她要告她的老闆。) let sth slide 是『對某事坐視不管, 任其惡化』。因為 slide 可以表 (向下) 滑行如溜滑梯然, 所以亦可引申為『惡化/沉淪』。

slogan

What's the Democrats' campaign catchphrase? (✗)

What's the Democrats' campaign slogan/catchword? (✓)

(民主黨的競選口號是什麼?)

catchphrase 指的是某名流的『口頭禪』, 如: The mayor's catchphrase is "Wow, cool!" (這位市長的口頭禪是『哇, 酷!』) slogan 或 catchword 專指政黨競選或商業廣告中的『標語/口號』,是可數名詞。

S

smart

It takes smart and a bit of luck to succeed in show biz. (✗)

It takes smarts and a bit of luck to succeed in show biz. (✔)

(要在演藝界闖出一片天除要機伶外，還需一點運氣。)

smart 表『聰明伶俐的』，是形容詞, He was smart enough to play the innocent. (他很機伶,假裝不知。) smarts是『聰明伶俐』的名詞形式, 作單數使用。

smell

All police dogs have been trained to smell drugs and explosives. (✗)

All police dogs have been trained to smell/sniff out drugs and explosives. (✔)

(所有警犬都已接受訓練，能嗅出哪裡有毒品或爆裂物。)

smell sth表『聞(到)某物的味道』, 如: Do you smell gas? (你有沒有聞到瓦斯的味道?)。smell/sniff out sth 是『嗅出藏有某物的味道』。

soaked

We were caught in the rain and got soaking through. (✗)

We were caught in the rain and got soaking wet/soaked through. (✔)

(我們淋到雨，全身溼透了。)

soaking wet = dripping wet = sopping wet = soaked through = wet through 是『溼透』的幾種固定說法。

so-called

My uncle is really erudite. He is a so-called walking dictionary. (✗)

My uncle is really erudite. He is what is called a walking dictionary. (✔)

(我的伯父真有學問。他就是所謂的活字典。)

so-called 主要用於『不實的名稱』上, 如: The so-called scholar turned out to be a fake. (這名所謂的學者結果是假冒的。) 表一般『所謂的……』, 應該用 what is called 或 what you call 或 what is known as...。

society

Women are the most vulnerable members of the society. (✗)

Women are the most vulnerable members of society. (✔)

(婦女是社會中最容易受到傷害的一群。)

指一般的『社會』, society 是不可數名詞, 其前不加"a"或"the"。指特殊的『社會』時, society 是可數名詞, 如: They are a multicultural society. (他們是一個多文化的社會。)

solid

Your child is still too weak to eat solid. (✗)

Your child is still too weak to eat solids/solid food. (✔)

(你的孩子還太虛弱了，不能吃固體的食物。)

solid 兼有形容詞和名詞的用法。作形容詞時, 意為『固體的』; 作名詞時, 意為『固體』。但表『固體食物』時, 恆用複數形的 solids。

S

solve

Can you solve their secret code? (✗)
Can you crack their secret code? (✔)
(你能破解他們的密碼嗎？)

solve sth 表『解決 (一般性的) 問題』。『破解』一個密碼, 應該說 break/crack/decipher a code。

sore

Taking a hot bath can relieve your back sore. (✗)
Taking a hot bath can relieve your back pain/backache. (✔)
(泡個熱水澡可以緩和你的背痛。)

作名詞時, sore 表『因受傷或感染造成紅腫、疼痛的地方』, 如:The little girl is covered with sores. (這個小女孩渾身腫痛。) 這種紅腫疼痛不宜泡澡 (因易造成潰爛)。指『一般的腰痠背疼』應該用 pain 或 ache。

sound

Hush! The baby is soundly asleep. (✗)
Hush! The baby is sound asleep. (✔)
(小聲點！小寶貝睡得正熟。)

表『睡得很熟』的固定說法為 be sound asleep 或 sleep soundly。

spacious

Your office is quite specious. (✗)
Your office is quite spacious. (✔)
(你的辦公室相當寬敞。)

specious 表『似是而非的』, 如: It is at best a specious argument. (這充其量只是一個似是而非的論點。) 表『寬敞的』應該用 spacious。

speak

His wife's silence says volumes. (✗)
His wife's silence speaks volumes. (✔)
(他老婆的沉默不語意義深長。)

speak volumes 表『透露出很多訊息』, 是固定用法。

Now you are speaking nonsense again. (✗)
Now you are talking nonsense again. (✔)
(你現在又再胡說八道了。)

talk sense/nonsense 表『講道理/胡說八道』, 是固定說法。

You had better say the truth. (✗)
You had better speak/tell the truth. (✔)
(你最好說實話。)

speak/tell the truth 為『說實話』的固定說法。不過, 當你替人家斟酒時, 要說 Say when. (差不多時說一聲。) 而對方只要回答 When!一聲即表示『夠了！』

special

If you want to save money, just order today's specialty. (✗)
If you want to save money, just order today's special. (✔)
(如果你想省錢，就點今天的特餐。)

作為名詞時, special 是『特價供應的餐』。specialty 表某餐廳的『招牌菜』, 如: Their specialty is roast duck. (他們的招牌菜是烤鴨。)

specimen

Out of a random specimen of female office workers, about 15% said they had been sexually harassed. (✗)

Out of a random sample of female office workers, about 15% said they had been sexually harassed. (✓)

(從女性上班族的抽樣訪問中，有百分之十五說曾經被性騷擾過。)

表血液或尿液的『抽樣』, 用 sample 或 specimen 皆可, 如: They need to test a sample/specimen of your blood first. (他們要先檢驗你的血液採樣。) 對一群(特定)人士的抽樣調查/訪問, 限用 sample 這個字。

spice

To add spices to his life, Kevin has joined a few local clubs. (✗)

To add spice to his life, Kevin has joined a few local clubs. (✓)

(為了增進生活情趣，凱文參加了幾個當地的俱樂部。)

表『香料』時 spice 兼有可/不可數的用法, 如: Spices like cinnamon and aniseed are necessary for the recipe. (這個配方必需含有肉桂、八角等香料。) 表『趣味/刺激』時, spice 是不可數名詞。

spirit

Judging from the way she talked, she must have been in low spirit. (✗)

Judging from the way she talked, she must have been in low spirits. (✓)

(從她當時講話的方式來研判，她的心情一定很差。)

表『精神』時, spirit是不可數名詞, 如: My grandpa is 83, but he still feels young in spirit. (我爺爺都八十三歲了, 但精神上他仍覺得自己很年輕。) 或如: I can't come to your birthday party, but I'll be there in spirit. (我無法親臨你的生日派對, 不過我精神上參加。) 表『心情』時恆用複數的 spirits, 如: in high/low spirits。

spoil

Eating a lot of chocolate before dinner will destroy your appetite. (✗)

Eating a lot of chocolate before dinner will spoil your appetite. (✓)

(晚餐前吃太多巧克力會破壞你的食慾。)

destroy sth 是『徹底地破壞某物』, 如: The building was completely destroyed by the fire. (這棟大樓被大火完全燒毀了。)『破壞食慾』的固定說法是 spoil/ruin your appetite。另外, spoil sb 可表『寵愛/善待某人』之意, 如: His mother spoils him rotten. (他老媽徹底把他寵壞了。) 或如: Let's eat out and spoil outselves. (我們出去大快朵頤一番。)

sports

My son has been doing sports since he was 17. (✗)

My son has been playing

sports since he was 17. (✔)
(我兒子從十七歲開始就一直在從事運動競賽。)

do exercise (不可數) 表『從事 (體能) 運動』。play sports 表『從事運動競賽』。

She is a sport writer. (✗)
She is a sports writer. (✔)
(她是一名體育專欄作家。)

表與運動/體育有關的人事物, 恆用複數形的 sports 修飾其後之名詞, 如: sports fans/drinks 就是指『球迷/運動飲料』。另外, 當動詞時, be sporting sth 表 (以愛現的方式) 穿著某種衣物, 如: He was sporting a loud shirt. (他穿了一件俗麗的襯衫。)

spot

To be honest, I don't really want to visit the construction spot. (✗)
To be honest, I don't really want to visit the construction site. (✔)
(老實說，我真的不想去參觀那個工地。)

spot 通常指的是 (1) 景點, 如: It is an ideal spot for tourists. (這個地方是觀光的最佳地點。) (2) 發生地點, 如:The shoplifter was caught on the spot. (這名商店竊賊當場被逮。) 建築『工地』應該用 site。

spotlight

The prize-winning actress walked out onto the spotlight stage. (✗)
The prize-winning actress walked out onto the spotlit stage. (✔)
(這位得獎的女演員走上聚光燈所照的舞台。)

spotlight 兼有名詞和動詞的用法, 作名詞時意為『聚光燈』。in/under the spotlight 表某人/物『成為大眾或媒體關注的焦點』, 是引申的用法, 如: Nuclear waste is once again under the spotlight. (核廢料再度成為媒體關注的焦點。) 作為動詞時, spotlight 的過去式及過去分詞均為 spotlit, 後者表『為聚光燈所照的』。

stake

Lives of the flood victims are now at the stake. (✗)
Lives of the flood victims are now at stake. (✔)
(這些水患災民的生命岌岌可危。)

at the stake 是指『(被綁) 在火刑柱上』, 為古時酷刑的一種, 如: Joan of Arc was burned at the stake in 1431. (聖女貞德在一四三一年遭火刑燒死。) at stake 表『瀕臨危險』, 是固定用法。另外, pull up stakes (恆用複數) 是『搬家』之意, 如: I hate the thought of having to pull up stakes. (一想到要搬家我就心煩。)

staple

Our major diet is rice and noodles. (✗)
Our staple diet is rice and noodles. (✔)
(我們的主食是米飯和麵條。)

staple diet (= main food) 是『主食』的固定說法。

statistic

Remind him to drive carefully. I don't want him to become statistics. (✗)
Remind him to drive

carefully. I don't want him to become a statistic. (✔)
(提醒他得小心駕駛。我不可樂見他去鬼門關報到。)

become a statistic 是指某人出意外(尤指車禍), 為死亡名單再添一數字。statistics 表一般的『統計數字』, 接複數動詞; 表『統計學』, 接單數動詞。如: Their statistics are not reliable. (他們的統計數字不可靠。) 或如: Statistics is a branch of mathematics. (統計學是數學的一支。)

status

You did not mention your marital standing. (✗)
You did not mention your marital status. (✔)
(你並沒有提及你結婚與否。)

表社會/職業『地位』時, standing 和 status 互通, 如: People's jobs are an important measure of their social standing/status. (人們的職業是其社會地位的重要指標。) 表『婚姻狀況』時一律用 marital status。

steady

Julie has been going stable with her boyfriend for seven years. (✗)
Julie has been going steady with her boyfriend for seven years. (✔)
(七年來茱麗跟她的男友感情都一直很穩定。)

stable 表『穩定的』, 強調的是情況不再惡化或出差錯, 如: The patient in the ICU is in stable condition now. (這名加護病房的病人現在情況穩定了。) steady 強調的是『持續穩定的進展』, 如: Do you have a steady job/girlfriend? (你有穩定的工作/女友嗎?)

step

Watch your steps — the path is wet and slippery. (✗)
Watch your step — the path is wet and slippery. (✔)
(走路小心，這條小徑又溼又滑。)

watch/mind your step (恆用單數) 可用來提醒對方『走路』時或『言行方面』要小心, 如: You'd better watch your step — the boss is over there. (你最好謹言慎行, 老闆就在那邊。) 但表『採取步驟/措施』時則需用 take steps to do sth, 如: We should take immediate steps to pacify them. (我們應該採取立即措施來安撫他們。)

sting

It looks like you were bitten by wasps. (✗)
It looks like you were stung by wasps. (✔)
(看來你好像被黃蜂螫了。)

蚊子、螞蟻、蛇『咬人』, 用 bite。蜂、蠍子『螫人』, 用 sting。

store

When spring comes, she always puts her winter clothes in store. (✗)
When spring comes, she always puts her winter clothes in storage. (✔)
(春天來時，她總是會把冬衣收起來存放。)

in storage 表東西不用時被『存放』起來。in store (for sb) 表某件事情/意外將要發生, 如: We have no idea what lies in store (for

S

us). (我們不知道有什麼事情要發生。) 另外, in stock 表『有存/現貨』, 如: Do you have any newer models in stock? (你們較新的機種有沒有現貨?)

straddle

The town straddles between the US-Mexico border. (✗)

The town straddles the US-Mexico border. (✔)

The town straddles the border between the US and Mexico. (✔)

(這個小鎮跨在美國和墨西哥邊境的兩側。)

straddle sth, 是及物的用法, 本指『兩腳跨坐/騎在某物的兩側』, 引申為『某物坐落/跨在某地兩側』。另外, straddle sth 可兼指學術領域, 如: Her research straddles psychology and sociology. (她的研究跨及心理學和社會學的領域。)

straight

I'd like a pure whiskey. (✗)

I'd like a straight whiskey. (✔)

(我想來一杯純威士忌。)

straight 用來形容酒時表『不添加水或其它飲料的』。

straw

It seems that he is clutching at straw. (✗)

It seems that he is clutching at straws. (✔)

(他似乎狗急跳牆了。)

straw 表『稻草/麥稈』, 一般作不可數名詞, 如: The hat is made of straw. (這頂帽子是稻草做的。) 表『吸管』時, straw 是可數名詞, 如: She was drinking fruit juice through a straw. (她用吸管喝果汁。) clutch/grasp at straws (恆用複數), 表『狗急跳牆』, 是固定用法。另外, the last straw 或 the straw that broke the camel's back 表令人無法再忍受的『最後一件事情』。

stray

She said she'd take the astray dog home. (✗)

She said she'd take the stray dog home. (✔)

(她說她要把那隻流浪狗帶回家。)

astray 是副詞, 表『迷路地』, 如: One of the mountain-climbers went astray and got lost. (有一名登山客迷路走失了。) stray 是形容詞, 表『走失/偏離的』, 如: The man was hit by a stray bullet. (這名男子被一顆流彈打到。)

stress

Yoga can help relax your stress. (✗)

Yoga can help relieve/reduce your stress. (✔)

(瑜珈有助於減輕你的壓力。)

relax 表『放鬆』, 通常以『身體的部位』為主, 如: A full-body massage will relax your muscles. (全身按摩可以讓你的肌肉鬆弛下來。)『減輕某人的壓力』的說法是 reduce/relieve sb's stress。

strike

It was then that a good idea hit me. (✗)

It was then that a good idea struck/occurred to me. (✔)

It was then that I hit on a good

idea. (✔)
(就在那時我突然想到一個好主意。)

a thought/idea strikes sb = sb hits on a thought/idea, 表『某人突然想到一個念頭/主意』, 是固定用法。

He did not think he could strike a home run. (✗)
He did not think he could hit a home run. (✔)
(當時他並不認為自己能擊出一支全壘打。)

表『擊球』時, 用 strike/hit a ball 皆可 (strike 是較為正式的用法), 但擊出一支全壘打恆用 hit a home run。

They went on a strike to demand better working conditions. (✗)
They went on strike to demand better working conditions. (✔)
(他們為要求更好的工作環境而罷工。)

be (out)/go on strike 是進行『罷工』的固定説法。不過, strike 基本上是一個可數名詞, 如: The labor union is calling a strike. (該勞工聯盟正在呼籲罷工。)

student

My niece is a student of Yale University. (✗)
My niece is a student at Yale University. (✔)
(我的姪女是耶魯大學的學生。)

a student of sth 是指『對某學科極有興趣並勤加研習的人』, 如: He is a student of Chinese philosophy. (他喜歡鑽研中國哲學。) 表某校的學生, 需用 a student at...

stuff

Put the kitchen stuffs in order when you're done with cooking. (✗)
Put the kitchen stuff in order when your're done with cooking. (✔)
(烹飪完畢後請把廚具歸位。)

stuff 表『器材/材料』是不可數名詞, 不能加"s"。

stuffy

I hate to have a stuffed nose. (✗)
I hate to have a stuffy nose. (✔)
(我討厭鼻塞。)

stuffed 表 (1) 填飽的, 如: No, thanks. I'm stuffed. (不, 謝了。我填飽了。) (2) 充填的, 如: It is a stuffed toy. (這是一個充填的玩具。)『鼻塞』的説法是 a stuffy nose。

subject

The subject of the book is about American hegemony. (✗)
The subject of the book is American hegemony. (✔)
(這本書的主題是美國的霸權。)

不能説 the subject is about sth, 需説 the subject is sth 或 the book/article is about sth。

All the list prices are possible to change. (✗)
All the list prices are subject to change. (✔)
(所有的表列價格可能隨時更動。)

be subject to sth 表某物『極可能要受制於某情況』。

S

subscribe

I think I'll subscribe the newspaper. (✗)

I think I'll take/subscribe to the newspaper. (✓)

(我想我會訂閱這家報紙。)

『訂閱報紙/雜誌』應該用 take/subscribe to sth。

substitute

Vitamin pills are no substitution for a balanced diet. (✗)

Vitamin pills are no substitute for a balanced diet. (✓)

(維他命丸絕對無法替代均衡的飲食。)

substitution 是指『替換(人或物)』的動作或行為, 如: The substitution was made ten minutes before the end of the game. (在比賽結束前十分鐘做了換人的動作。) substitute 是指『替換的人/物』。

suffer

Our team suffered from two defeats last week. (✗)

Our team suffered two defeats last week. (✓)

(我們的球隊上週遭到兩次挫敗。)

suffer from + 疾病/貧窮/飢餓, 表『遭受』上述的痛苦, 如: The patient suffers from Alzheimer's disease. (這名病 人患有阿茲海默症。) suffer + 受傷/疼痛/損失/挫敗, 不搭配 from。

suicide

It was a suicidal attack, if I remember correctly. (✗)

It was a suicide attack, if I remember correctly. (✓)

(如果我沒記錯的話，那是一次自殺攻擊事件。)

suicidal 是形容詞, 表『想自殺的』, 如: The patient has suicidal tendencies. (這名病人有自殺的傾向。) a suicide attack/bombing/mission 表一個『自殺式的攻擊/轟炸/任務』, 是固定用法。

sunbathing

In the morning we did some sunbath on the beach. (✗)

In the morning we did some sunbathing on the beach. (✓)

(大清早我們在海灘上做了一點日光浴。)

sunbath 這個字並不存在。欲表達『做日光浴』, 須用 sunbathe 或 go sunbathing/do some sunbathing。

supply

A lot of medical supply will be sent to the war-torn country. (✗)

A lot of medical supplies will be sent to the war-torn country. (✓)

(有很多醫療補給品將被運至這個飽受戰亂的國家。)

表『補給』或『供應』的行為時, supply 是不可數名詞, 如: Oil is in short supply because of the war. (因為戰爭, 油 的供應減少。) 表『補給品』或『需用物資』時, 恆用複數的 supplies。

S

supporting

Will she take the supportive role in the film? (✗)

Will she take the supporting role in the film? (✓)

(她會接受這部電影的配角角色嗎？)

supportive 表『態度支持的』，如: My family was very supportive when I decided to join the army. (當我決定要從軍時, 我的家人都很支持我。) 表影視劇中的『配角』, 限用 supporting 來修飾。

surely

I'll surely stand up for you if anyone criticizes you. (✗)

I'll definitely stand up for you if anyone criticizes you. (✓)

(如果有任何人批評你，我一定會挺你。)

陳述你認為某事為真時, 可用 surely 或 definitely, 如: It is surely/definitely the stupidest thing she has ever said. (這肯定是她曾講過的最愚蠢的話。) 強調某事一定會發生時, 限用 definitely。

suspected

He was taken to the hospital with suspicious concussion. (✗)

He was taken to the hospital with suspected concussion. (✓)

(他因疑有腦震盪被送至醫院。)

suspicious 表 (1) (生性) 懷疑的, 如: She is suspicious of every stranger. (她懷疑每一個陌生人。) (2) 可疑的, 如: There's something suspicous about his leaving so soon. (他連忙離開, 有點可疑。) suspected 表『被懷疑 (染病/犯罪)時』, 如: The suspected arsonist was arrested. (這名涉嫌縱火者被逮捕了。)

swim

Let's go for swimming this afternoon. (✗)

Let's go swimming/for a swim this afternoon. (✓)

(今天下午咱們去游泳。)

『去游泳』的說法是 go swimming 或 go for a swim 或 take/have a dip。

swing

He waved the bat at the ball but missed it. (✗)

He swung the bat at the ball but missed it. (✓)

(他揮棒擊球但沒打著。)

wave sth 表揮舞著 (旗子/手) 等, 通常為了傳遞信號或引人注意, 如: She kept waving her hand to the soldiers. (她一直向那些士兵揮手。) 表『揮棒』打球應該説 swing a/the bat。

swipe

Scrape your card to get in. (✗)

Swipe your card to get in. (✓)

(刷一下卡片你才能進去。)

scrape sth 是 (不小心)『摩擦某物』在粗糙的表面上, 造成刮傷, 如: He scraped his car while parking it. (他停車時造成車身刮傷。)『刷 (信用/門鎖) 卡』, 限用 swipe 這個字。

S

sympathize

You need to sympathize with your children to be a good parent. (✗)

You need to empathize with your children to be a good parent. (✔)

(要當個好父母你需要對孩子有同理心。)

sympathize with sb 表『對 (苦難的) 人有同情心』, 如: I sympathize with her, but I don't know how to help. (我同情她但不知如何幫忙。) empathize with sb 表『對人有同理心』, 即能有『易身而處』的想法。

T t

T

table

Our team scored again and again and turned the table. (✗)

Our team scored again and again and turned the tables. (✓)

(我們的球隊一再得分，扭轉了形勢。)

turn the tables (恆用複數) 表『扭轉形勢』。另外, set/lay the table 表『將餐具排好在餐桌上』, 準備用餐。

tailor

These courses are all measured to the needs of individuals. (✗)

These courses are all tailored to the needs of individuals. (✓)

(這些課程都是為個人的需要量身訂做的。)

tailor sth to sth 表『為迎合某種情況而製作或改變某物』。是固定用法。

take

She asked if she could come to our party and take a friend with her. (✗)

She asked if she could come to our party and bring a friend with her. (✓)

(她問說是否可以帶個朋友來參加我們的派對。)

take sb/sth = go with sb/sth, 表『把某人/物帶離你目前的地點』, 如: Every time I go on vacation, I take a camera with me. (我每次去度假都帶一台照相機在身邊。) bring sb/sth = come with sb/sth, 表『把某人/物帶來你目前的地點』。

What's your taking on the election results? (✗)

What's your take on the election results? (✓)

(你對這次選舉的結果有何看法？)

sb's take on sth 表『某人對某事的看法或意見』, 是固定用法。

talk

The peace talk will be held next month. (✗)

The peace talks will be held next month. (✓)

(和平談判將於下個月舉行。)

表『談話』時, 用 have a talk, 如: We need to have a talk. (我們需要談一談。) 表『談判』時恆用複數的 talks。

taste

Your girlfriend has a good taste in clothes. (✗)

Your girlfriend has good taste in clothes. (✓)

(你的女友對衣服很有品味。)

表『品味』或『鑑賞力』時, taste 是不可數名詞。表『喜好』時, taste 兼有可/不可數的用法, 如: She has expensive tastes in clothes. (她喜歡買名貴的衣服。)

tasty

The furnishings in your living room are really tasty. (✗)

The furnishings in your living room are really tasteful. (✓)

(你家客廳的裝潢擺設真是有品味。)

T

tasty 表『美味的』, 如: The food your mother cooked was very tasty. (你媽媽烹調的食物很美味。) tasteful 是『有品味的』。另外, tasteless 是『沒品味/格調的』。

tax

He was charged with tax avoidance. (✗)

He was charged with tax evasion. (✓)

(他被控告逃漏稅。)

tax avoidance 指的是合法的『節稅』。tax evasion 是非法的『逃漏稅』。另外 tax dodge是合法或非法的『避稅』行為。

tedium

We solved the tedium of the long journey by reading. (✗)

We relieved the tedium of the long journey by reading. (✓)

(在那長途旅行中，我們以閱讀書報解悶。)

tedium是『沉悶無聊』的感覺。『解悶』的正確說法是 relieve the tedium。

teethe

These problems are nothing but teeth troubles. (✗)

These problems are nothing but teething troubles. (✓)

(這些問題不過是事情剛開始的小麻煩而已。)

teething 源於 teethe 這個動詞, 表嬰兒『初長牙』之意。因為嬰兒初長牙時會不舒服, 甚至發燒, 所以teething troubles/problems 引申為『事情剛開始的小麻煩』。這種麻煩很快就會過去。

tell

Beware of that man. He might tell against you. (✗)

Beware of that man. He might tell on you. (✓)

(提防那個人。他可能會打你的小報告。)

tell against sb (英式用法) 表『不利於某人取/贏得某物』, 如: I need the job badly, but my age would probably tell against me. (我非常需要這份工作, 可是我的年齡恐怕對我不利。) tell on sb 有二義: (1) 打某人的小報告 (如原例句) (2) 對某人有不良的影響, 如: When I turned 50, my age began to tell on me. (我一過五十歲, 就開始覺得身體大不如前了。)

temper

By temper, Arthur is a rather radical man. (✗)

By temperament, Arthur is a rather radical man. (✓)

(在性情上亞瑟是一個相當激進的人。)

temper 表『脾氣』或『一時的心情』, 如: My dad hardly ever loses his temper. (我老爸絕少發脾氣。) 或如: She seemed to be in a good temper then. (她當時似乎心情很好。) temperament是指一個人的『性情/格』。

tension

A patient of mine suffers from nervous tensions and insomnia. (✗)

A patient of mine suffers from nervous tension and insomnia. (✓)

T

(我有一位病患深受神經緊張及失眠之苦。)

表身心方面的『緊張』時, tension 為不可數名詞。表政治/社會/種族的『緊張』關係時, tension 兼有可/不可數的用法, 如: political/social/racial tension(s)。

term

The film is a huge success in term of its box office. (✗)

The film is a huge success in terms of its box office. (✔)

(就其票房而言，這部影片極為成功。)

表專門的『用字/説法』時, term 可依實際情況使用單數或複數的形式, 如: The word "anorexia" is a medical term. (『厭食症』是一個醫學用語。) in terms of sth 是固定用法, 表『就某方面而言』。其類似用法亦見於 in political/economic/historical terms 等。另外, on good/bad/friendly terms 等表『處於良好/不好/友善等關係』, 如: Sally is still on friendly terms with her ex-husband. (莎莉與其前夫仍保持友善的關係。)

terror

The 9/11 terror attack was a shocking experience for everyone. (✗)

The 9/11 terrorist attack was a shocking experience for everyone. (✔)

(九一一恐佈攻擊事件極為震憾人心。)

terror 表『恐懼』或『害怕』, 是抽象名詞。terrorist 是『恐佈分子(的)』。恐佈分子所從事的活動一律用這個字, 如: terrorist attack/activity/offence 等。

test

They don't know what's wrong with the patient. They'll take a blood test first, though. (✗)

They don't know what's wrong with the patient. They'll run a blood test first, though. (✔)

(他們並不知道該病人哪裡出問題。不過，他們會先進行驗血。)

take/do a test 是『參加考試』, 如: If you fail, you have to take the test again. (你如果不及格就要再考一次。) run/do a test 表(院方)做醫學『檢驗』。至於(病患)做醫學『檢驗』的説法是 have/undergo a test。

thanks

I really appreciate your timely help. Thanks a bunch! (✗)

I really appreciate your timely help. Thanks a lot! (✔)

(我真的很感激你的及時相助。非常謝謝。)

"Thanks a bunch." 主要用於『嘲諷對方』, 如: I could do without your help. Thanks a bunch! (我根本不需要你的幫忙。謝啦!) 表達真正的感謝應該説"Thanks a lot!"

theft

It was only a small theft. (✗)

It was only a minor/petty theft. (✔)

(這只是一樁小竊案。)

一樁『小竊案』的固定説法是 a minor/petty theft; 一起『重大竊案』的説法是 a serious theft。

T

throat

During the meeting, Tom and Alex were at each other's throat. (✗)
During the meeting, Tom and Alex were at each other's throats. (✔)
(開會時湯姆和亞力兩個人一直在吵架。)

be at each other's throats (恆用複數) 表兩個人『一直在吵/打架』, 是固定說法。

thunder

All of a sudden there was a great thunder. (✗)
All of a sudden there was a great clap of thunder. (✔)
(突然間來了一陣雷聲巨響。)

thunder是不可數名詞。表『一陣雷聲』應該說 a clap/crack/crash of thunder。而 a roll of thunder 表連續的『一連串雷聲隆隆』。另外, thunderbolt (閃電霹靂) 是可數名詞, 如: The trees must have been hit by a thunderbolt. (這幾棵樹一定是被一道閃電霹靂打到。)

tick

Twenty minutes ticked off and we still could not reach a decision. (✗)
Twenty minutes ticked away and we still could not reach a decision. (✔)
(二十分鐘過去了，而我們仍無法下決定。)

指時間一分一秒的『經過』, tick away/by 是標準說法。tick sb off 表『激怒某人』, 如: Her behavior is really ticking me off. (她的舉止真的惹我生氣。)

tie

Japan's economic tie with Taiwan will remain strong in years to come. (✗)
Japan's economic ties with Taiwan will remain strong in years to come. (✔)
(日本和台灣的經濟關係在未來幾年仍將維持強勢。)

表『關係』時多用複數形的 ties, 如: economic/diplomatic/personal ties 即為『經濟/外交/人際關係』。表比賽『不分勝負』, 用 end/finish/result in a tie, 如: The game ended in a tie. (這場比賽以平手作收。)

tie-in

Because the film's popularity keeps soaring, its peripherals have enjoyed brisk sales. (✗)
Because the film's popularity keeps soaring, its tie-ins have enjoyed brisk sales. (✔)
(因為這部影片受歡迎的程度持續升高，它周邊的產品也一直熱賣。)

peripheral 指的是電腦的周邊設備如『印表機』等。tie-in指的是某部(熱門)電影的周邊產品,如:『玩具』、『T恤』、『書籍』等。

time

I forgot to wear my watch. Do you have time? (✗)
I forgot to wear my watch. Do you have the time? (✔)
(我忘了帶錶。請問現在幾點？)

T

Do you have time? 是詢問對方『現在有沒有空』。詢問『現在幾點』應該說 Do you have the time? (美式用法) 或 Have you got the time? (英式用法)。

timer

Set the clock on the microwave oven for two minutes. (✗)
Set the timer on the microwave oven for two minutes. (✓)
(將微波爐的計時器設定兩分鐘。)

clock 是一般的『時鐘』。(電子) 鍋爐的『計時器』是 timer。

timetable

By the way, do you have a train times table? (✗)
By the way, do you have a train timetable? (✓)
(順便問一下，你有火車時刻表嗎？)

times table = multiplication table 是『乘法表』, 如: a nine times table 即為一張『九九乘法表』。火/汽車等的『時刻表』是 timetable。

tiring

These naughty children are rather tiring. (✗)
These naughty children are rather tiresome. (✓)
(這幾個調皮的孩子相當令人厭煩。)

tiring 表『令人疲憊的』, 如: Looking after small children can be very tiring. (照顧小孩子有時挺累人的。) tiresome 表『令人厭煩的』。

toast

I had a toast and an egg for breakfast this morning. (✗)
I had a slice of toast and an egg for breakfast this morning. (✓)
(今天早上我吃了一片土司和一個雞蛋作早餐。)

toast 表『土司麵包』時為不可數名詞, 需用單位來表達, 如: a loaf/slice of toast 就是『一條/片土司』表『敬酒』時, toast 為可數名詞, 如: I proposed a toast to the bride and groom. (我向新郎新娘敬酒。)

token

The army met with only some symbolic resistence. (✗)
The army met with only some token resistence. (✓)
(這一支軍隊只是遭遇到一些象徵性的抵抗。)

symbolic 表『具有某種 (重要) 象徵意義的』, 如: A wedding ring is symbolic of eternal love. (結婚戒指象徵永恆的愛。) token 意為『象徵性的』, 是指『略帶假裝』或『意思意思一下的』行為。

T

toll

The tolls in the bomb explosion could rise to over twenty. (✗)

The toll/casualties in the bomb explosion could rise to over twenty. (✔)

(這起炸彈爆炸事件的傷亡人數可能會超過二十人。)

表『傷亡人數時』恆用單數形的 toll 或複數形的 casualties。

topping

What ingredients would you like for your pizza? (✗)

What toppings would you like for your pizza? (✔)

(你的披撒要放什麼料?)

ingredient 表『混在一起烹煮的食物材料』, 如: Flour and egg are the most important ingredients. (麵粉和雞蛋是最重要的配料。) topping 專指加在蛋糕/披撒上面的『配料』, 是可數名詞。

tour

She works as a tourist guide in Beijing. (✗)

She works as a tour guide in Beijing. (✔)

(她在北京當導遊。)

『一名導遊』的正確說法是 a tour guide。a tourist attraction 是『一個觀光景點』。

trace

They have disappeared without a track in the mountains. (✗)

They have disappeared without a trace in the mountains. (✔)

(他們在深山裡消失得無影無蹤。)

trace 是人或物留下來的『痕跡』, 兼有可/不可數的用法。disappear/vanish without (a) trace 表『消失得無影無蹤』, 是固定用法。track 可表『足跡』或『軌跡』, 又可指『小徑』, 如: There is a dirt track leading to his farm. (有一條泥土小路通往他的農場。) 另外, be on the right/wrong track 表『做 (或想) 對/錯某事』, 如: It appears that we are on the wrong track. (看來我們好像做錯了。)

trade

These two countries became trade partners in 1995. (✗)

These two countries became trading partners in 1995. (✔)

(這兩個國家在一九九五年成為貿易夥伴。)

trading nation/partner 是『貿易國/夥伴』的標準說法。但『貿易赤字』的說法是 trade deficit。

traffic

They were stuck in a heavy traffic for almost an hour. (✗)

They were stuck in heavy traffic for almost an hour. (✔)

They were stuck in a traffic jam for almost an hour. (✔)

(他們卡在車陣當中將近一個小時。)

T

traffic 可表『來往於道路的所有車輛』，是不可數名詞。『交通壅塞』的說法是 heavy traffic 或 a traffic jam。另外，traffic 表『非法交易』時亦為不可數名詞，如: He was arrested for traffic in drugs. (他因販售毒品而遭逮捕。)

trap

Many victims are still caught in the burning building. (✗)

Many victims are still trapped in the burning building. (✓)

(許多災民仍被困在火燒的大樓中。)

be caught in sth 表突然『遭遇到某種難以擺脫的不愉快狀況』，如: We were caught in a heavy rain on our way there. (在前往那裡的途中，我們突然遇到一陣大雨。) be trapped somewhere 表『被困在某個地方』。

The agency deals mainly with business trip. (✗)

The agency deals mainly with business travel. (✓)

(這家旅行社主要是做商務考察的業務。)

travel 是『旅行』最一般性的用法，通常作不可數名詞。trip 指的是短暫的『旅行』，是可數名詞，如: We'll take a trip to Tokyo. (我們將至東京旅行。) journey 表較費時/勁的『旅行』。voyage 是海上/太空的『旅行』。tour 是觀光『旅行』。

treat

The doctor will soon be here to heal your head injury. (✗)

The doctor will soon be here to treat your head injury. (✓)

(醫生很快就來處理你的頭部外傷。)

heal 用來表達傷口『痊癒的過程』，如: It'll take about two weeks for your wound to heal. (你的傷口大約需兩個星期才能痊癒。) 傷口的 (即時)『處理』應該用 treat 這個字。

trial

They promised to give me a raise after the trying period. (✗)

They promised to give me a raise after the trial period. (✓)

(他們允諾在試用期後給我加薪。)

產品或員工的『試用期』是 a trial period。trying 表『難熬的』，如: We all had a trying day. (我們都度過難熬的一天。)

trouble

Thank you for making a lot of trouble to help us. (✗)

Thank you for taking a lot of trouble to help us. (✓)

(謝謝你煞費苦心幫忙我們。)

make trouble 是『製造麻煩』之意。take the/a lot of trouble 表『不厭其煩/煞費苦心』去做某事。另外，spell trouble 表『將有麻煩的問題發生』，如: If you keep driving so fast, it may spell trouble. (如果你一直開這麼快，可能就會有麻煩要發生。)

try

The next time I go jogging, I'll try on my new running shoes. (✗)

The next time I go jogging, I'll try out my new running shoes. (✓)

(下次慢跑時，我要穿新的跑步鞋出去試

試看。)

try on sth 指的通常是 (在鞋/衣服店) 試穿某物, 如: Try it on before you buy the shirt. (買這件襯衫前先試穿一下。) try out sth 表『試試某物的成效/品質如何』。)

tune

You don't have to dance with his tune all the time. (✗)

You don't have to dance to his tune all the time. (✓)

(你不必老是跟著他的音樂起舞。)

dance with sb 表『與某人共舞』, 但 dance to sb's tune 表『(事事) 遷就某人』, 是固定用法。另外 sing in/out of tune 表唱歌『唱得字正腔圓/荒腔走板』。

Stay tuning for the late-night weather report. (✗)

Stay tuned for the late-night weather report. (✓)

(請繼續收看/聽本台的深夜氣象報導。)

作動詞時 tune 表『調頻道』。tune in 表『收聽/看 收音機/電視之節目』, 如: Millions of people will tune in to watch the game. (數百萬人將會收看這場比賽。) stay tuned 表『不要轉台, 繼續收看』之意。

turn

We'll take a turn carrying the suitcase. (✗)

We'll take turns carrying the suitcase. (✓)

(我們將輪流提手提箱。)

take a turn doing sth 表『輪到某一個人做某事』, 如: Would you like me to take a turn driving the car? (要不要換我來開車?)

take turns doing sth 表兩人或以上『輪流做某事』。

Each of the contestants will give a five-minute speech by turns. (✗)

Each of the contestants will give a five-minute speech in turn. (✓)

(每一名參賽者將依序發表一段五分鐘的演講。)

by turns 表『時則……時則……』, 如: She is by turns kind and cruel to her children. (她對自己的孩子時則仁慈時則殘忍。) in turn 表『依序』做某事。

twenty

The bar is very popular with the twenties. (✗)

The bar is very popular with twentysomethings. (✓)

(這一家酒吧很受二十幾歲的年齡層歡迎。)

the twenties 可指 (1)『二〇年代』, 即一九二〇年至一九二九年這十年的期間, 如: This song was very popular in the twenties. (這首歌在二〇年代頗為流行。) (2) 氣溫的『二十幾度』。指『年齡』時應該說: in sb's twenties, 如: He made a lot of money in his twenties. (他在二十多歲這段期間賺了不少錢。) twentysomething 兼有 (可數) 名詞和形容詞的用法, 表『二十幾歲年齡層(的)』。另外, thirtysomething/fortysomething 等用法亦同。

twist

From here, the path tosses and turns up to the summit. (✗)

From here, the path twists and turns up to the summit. (✓)

(從這裡開始, 這條小徑一路盤旋到山頂。)

T

toss and turn 表某人『翻來覆去睡不著』，如: Sometimes I'll toss and turn all night. (有時候我會整晚翻來覆去睡不著。) twist and turn 表道路/河流『盤旋/蜿蜒』。

type

Mary is a good girl, but she's not my like. (✗)

Mary is a good girl, but she's not my type. (✓)

(瑪麗是個好女孩，可是她並非我喜歡的典型。)

sb's like 表『像某人這樣的 (好) 人』，如: We won't see his like again. (像他這種人我們再也見不到了。) sb's type 表『某人喜歡的典型人物』。

U u

U

ultimate

The hotel is the last in luxury. (✗)
The hotel is the ultimate/last word in luxury. (✓)
(這一家飯店可以說是奢侈豪華的極致。)

表『某物的極致』應說 the ultimate/last word in sth。the last 表『最後 (一次)』, 如: He showed up sometime last month, and that was the last I saw of him. (他上個月有出現過, 那也是我最後一次看到他。)

unconscious

The boy was knocked unaware in a fight. (✗)
The boy was knocked unconscious in a fight. (✓)
(這個男孩在一場打架中被打成不省人事。)

表『對某事不知情』時可用 be unaware/unconscious of sth, 如: Fred was unaware/unconscious of the trouble he had caused. (弗瑞德根本不知道他已闖禍。) 但『被 (人) 打成不省人事』只能用 be knocked unconscious 來表達。

under

For further information, see under. (✗)
For further information, see below. (✓)
(想要更進一步的資訊，請看下面的部分。)

see below 為『請看 (文章) 較後面的部分』之固定說法。指少於或不足某數量/年齡時可用 and/or below/under..., 如: Children aged 12 or below/under must be accompanied by an adult. (十二歲或以下的小朋友必須有一大人陪同。)

The doctor and the nurse were still talking when I found myself going below. (?)
The doctor and the nurse were still talking when I found myself going under. (✗)
(醫生和護士都還在討論時，我已經不省人事。)

go below 是『走到下面去』。go under 表『不省人事』。

understanding

Luckily, the actress has a very understandable husband. (✗)
Luckily, the actress has a very understanding husband. (✓)
(幸好這名女星有一位善解人意的丈夫。)

understandable 是指『可以被理解的』, 如: His strong language was understandable in the circumstances. (在那種情況下, 他的措詞強烈是可以被理解的。) understanding 兼有名/形容詞的用法, 作名詞時表『瞭解』, 作形容詞時表『善解人意的』。

uninterested

Most of the people here are disinterested in politics. (✗)
Most of the people here are uninterested in politics. (✓)
(這裡的大多數人對政治不感興趣。)

disinterested 是『公正無私的』, 如: We need to invite a disinterested political commentator. (我們需邀請一位公正無私的政治評論家。)。表對某物『不感興趣的』, 應該用 uninterested 方為正確。

unique

In fact, every person's DNA is unusual. (✗)

In fact, every person's DNA is unique. (✔)

(事實上每一個人的 DNA 都是獨一無二的。)

unusual 表『不尋常的』或『奇怪的』如: You must admit it was a most unusual experience. (你不得不承認那是一個極為不尋常的經歷/遭遇。)。unique 表『獨一無二的』。

unisex

All the leisure wear we are selling is neutral sex. (✗)

All the leisure wear we are selling is unisex. (✔)

(我們現所賣的休閒服都是中性系列的。)

unisex 是形容詞, 表『中性的』, 即男女兩性皆可用/穿的。neutral 表『中性』時意指 (化學) 酸鹼度的平衡, 如: This plant prefers a neutral soil. (這種植物性喜中性的土壤。) 另外, 指 (衣服) 顏色時, neutral colors 表不太亮麗也不太暗沉的『中性顏色』。

united

The three political parties will form a united government. (✗)

The three political parties will form a coalition government. (✔)

(這三個政黨將籌組一個聯合政府。)

『聯合政府』的正確說法是 a coalition government。『聯合陣線』是 a united front, 如: The opposition parties will present a united front. (反對黨將結合形成一個聯合陣線。)『聯合國』的說法是 the United Nations (簡稱為 the UN)。

universal

English is the universal language. (✗)

English is the international language. (✔)

(英語目前是一種國際性語言。)

a universal language 是『一種全世界共通的語言』。英語雖然在全球很多人使用, 但還沒有到達上述的地步。比喻而言, 我們可以說: Music is a universal language. (音樂是一種全球共通的語言。)

unrest

You can sense her unrest from the way she talks. (✗)

You can sense her anxiety/uneasiness from the way she talks. (✔)

(你可以從她說話的方式感受到她的焦慮不安。)

unrest 指的是政治/社會的『動盪不安』, 如: The capital city is facing increasing political unrest. (該國首都正面臨越演越烈的政治動盪不安。) anxiety/uneasiness 是個人心理的『焦慮不安』。

update

The dictionary has been revised and upgraded. (✗)

The dictionary has been revised and updated. (✔)

(這本字典已經被修訂並更新其內容。)

upgrade sth 表『使 (電腦/機器等系統) 升級』, 如: The system must be upgraded to meet customers' needs. (這種系統必須升級才能迎合顧客的需求。) update sth 表『更新某物的內容』以趕上時代。

U

urban

My parents don't like to live in urbane areas. They prefer living in the countryside. (✗)

My parents don't like to live in urban areas. They prefer living in the countryside. (✔)

(我父母不喜歡住都市地區。他們寧可住在鄉下。)

urbane 表『溫文儒雅的』, 如: He has an urbane manner. (他的舉止溫文儒雅。) urban 表『都市的』, 其相對的字是 rural, 意為『鄉村的』。

V v

V

vacancy

This strongman's sudden death created a power vacancy. (✗)

This strongman's sudden death created a power vacuum. (✓)

(這名政治強人的猝死造成一個權力真空現象。)

vacancy 專指旅館的『空房』或職場的『空缺』, 如: "Sorry, we have no vancacies," said the hotel manager. (旅館的經理說:『抱歉, 我們沒有空房了。』) 或如: There are several vacancies to fill in the Marketing Department. (行銷部還有幾個空缺待補。) a political/power vacuum 是指沒有人來領導的『政治真空』或『權力真空』。

valid

The round-trip ticket is effective for six months. (✗)

The round-trip ticket is valid/good for six months. (✓)

(這張來回票的有效期限為六個月。)

effective 表『有效果/力的』, 通常指的是藥物或方法, 如: These drugs are just as effective as those you used. (這些藥物和你之前使用過的藥物一樣有效。) 票券、執照的『有效』應該用 valid/good。

valuable

The prince is the most valuable bachelor in Europe today. (✗)

The prince is the most eligible bachelor in Europe today. (✓)

(這名王子是歐洲目前最有身價的單身貴族。)

valuable 可表 (1) 值錢的 (東西), 如: The antique is very valuable. (這個古器物很值錢。) (2) 有實用價值的, 如: I think he'll provide valuable information for us. (我想他會提供寶貴的資訊給我們。) eligible 用來形容某人時, 表某人的『身價/行情』很高, 是異性夢寐以求的結婚對象。

value

Each employee's performance is valued once a year. (✗)

Each employee's performance is evaluated once a year. (✓)

(每位員工的表現一年評估一次。)

value sth 表 (1) 重視某物, 如: We value your knowledge and experience. (我們重視你的知識和經驗。) (2) 估算某物值多少, 如: These famous paintings were valued at $3 million. (這些名畫被估三百萬美元。) evaluate sth 是『評估』某人/物的能力/效果等。

vantage

The whole thing looks stupid from my vintage point. (✗)

The whole thing looks stupid from my vantage point. (✓)

(從我的觀點來看，這整件事情似乎是愚蠢的。)

vantage point 本指某人所處的『有利位置』, 亦可引申為某人的 (特殊)『觀點』, 相當於 viewpoint 這個字。vintage 本指『釀酒用葡萄的收成 (期)』, 亦引申為『某年份所釀的美酒』, 如: What vintage is this wine? (這瓶酒的年份為何?) 另外, a vintage car 是指一部『名貴的古董車』, 是引申的用法。

variable

Temperature is a variation in this experiment. (✗)

Temperature is a variable in this experiment. (✔)

(氣温是這項實驗的一個變數。)

variation 表某物的『變化形式』, 如: Our new plan is a slight variation of the original one. (我們的新計劃是將原先的計劃稍作改變而已。) variable 作為名詞時, 是指會對事物產生影響的『變數』。另外, variety 強調的是『多樣性』, 如: Variety is the spice of life. (五花八門可使人生饒富情趣。)

vary

Eating habits change from country to country. (✗)

Eating habits vary/differ from country to country. (✔)

(飲食習慣各國不同。)

change 表 (本質上) 全面或局部的『改/轉變』或『調整』, 如: The signal changed from red to green. (號誌從紅燈轉成綠燈。) 或如: You should change your lifestyle. (你應該調整一下你的生活方式。) vary 強調的是多樣性的『變化』。

vegetarian

In fact, my older sister is a vegetarian. She doesn't even eat eggs or cheese. (✗)

In fact, my older sister is a vegan. She doesn't even eat eggs or cheese. (✔)

(事實上我老姊吃全素。她甚至連雞蛋或乳酪都不吃。)

vegetarian 不吃魚肉, 但偶而吃點蛋類或乳製品。相較之下, vegan 的自我要求更為嚴苛, 非但連蛋類、乳製品都不吃, 有人甚至連動物製品如皮帶/鞋都不用。所以 a vegan 相當於 a strict vegetarian。

vent

He used to give a vent to his anger by beating his children. (✗)

He used to give vent to his anger by beating his children. (✔)

(他過去時常打小孩來發洩他的怒氣。)

作為『通風/出氣孔』解時, vent 是可數名詞, 如: There is a small air vent in the ceiling. (天花板上有一個小小的排氣孔。) give vent to sth 表『發洩某種強烈的情緒』, 不加冠詞, 是固定用法。

verbal

How could you stand his oral abuse? (✗)

How could you stand his verbal abuse? (✔)

(你怎能忍受他的粗魯謾罵呢?)

oral 表『口説/服的』。verbal 兼指『口説或使用文字的』, verbal abuse 表『粗魯的謾罵』, 是固定説法。

vested

The project will face strong opposition from vested interest. (✗)

The project will face strong opposition from vested interests. (✔)

(這項計劃將會面臨既得利益者的強烈反對。)

V

a vested interest 表對某事物『強烈的興趣並關切』, 主要是因為有利益可期, 如: He has a vested interest in seeing the incumbent re-elected. (他極為關切現任者的再次當選。) vested interests 指的是『獲利團體』或『既得利益者』。

virtuoso

V

The virtual pianist gave a brilliant performance last night. (✗)

The virtuoso pianist gave a brilliant performance last night. (✔)

(這名大師級的鋼琴家昨晚做了一場亮麗的演出。)

virtual 表『簡直就是……的』, 如: All his servants live like virtual prisoners. (他所有僕人過的日子簡直就像囚犯一樣。) 另外, virtual reality 表電腦所創造出來的『虛擬實境』。virtuoso 表『名家/大師/巨匠的』。

vision

My son doesn't wear any glasses. He has a twenty-twenty vision. (✗)

My son doesn't wear any glasses. He has twenty-twenty vision. (✔)

(我的兒子沒戴眼鏡。他視力正常。)

表『視力』時 vision 為不可數名詞。twenty-twenty vision 表『視力正常』。表『想像/幻想 (畫面)』時, vision 為可數名詞, 如: I had visions of being attacked by a pack of wild dogs. (我曾經幻想到被一群野狗攻擊的畫面。)

voice

Could you please turn down your voice? (✗)

Could you please lower your voice? (✔)

(麻煩你們小聲點好嗎?)

turn down sth 表調低 (電視、音響等) 音量, 如: Turn down the music/radio/volume, will you? (請把音樂/收音機/音量關小聲點, 可不可以?)『降低講話的聲音』應該說 lower your voice。

When it comes to the problem of pay, the workers speak with one sound. (✗)

When it comes to the problem of pay, the workers speak with one voice. (✔)

(說到薪資問題時，這批員工則口徑一致。)

speak with one voice 表某些人對某問題『有同樣的看法或意見』, 是固定說法。

vocabulary

Considering he is so young, he has a lot of vocabulary. (✗)

Considering he is so young, he has a wide vocabulary. (✔)

(要是考慮到他還如此年輕，他懂的字彙算相當多了。)

vocabulary 表『字彙』, 是某人所懂的單字之全部。have a limited/wide vocabulary 表某人『擁有字彙有限/頗豐』, 是固定說法。另外, 表『擴充/增加』你的字彙可說 enlarge/expand/increase/build up your vocabulary。

vote

Let's have an election on where to go for our vacation. (✗)

Let's have a vote on where to go for our vacation. (✓)

(針對去哪裡度假我們來投票表決好了。)

election 主要是針對 (公職) 人選作投票選舉。vote則兼有對人選或議題作投票表決。

I think I'll drop a vote for the young and vigorous candidate. (✗)

I think I'll cast a vote for the young and vigorous candidate. (✓)

(我想我會投一票給這位年輕有勁的候選人。)

cast a vote/ballot for sb 是『投票給某人』的固定說法。drop sth (into...) 則表『投入/下某物』，如: I dropped a coin into the vending machine. (我投入一枚硬幣在那自動販賣機裡。)

V

A Quick Note

W w

W

wad

The man pulled a stack of 100-dollar bills out of his pocket. (✗)
The man pulled a wad of 100-dollar bills out of his pocket. (✓)
(那個男士從他的口袋裡抽出一疊百元美鈔。)

a stack of sth 通常是『一疊/堆』書報、唱盤等, 如: On her desk is a stack of CDs. (她的書桌上有一疊 CD。)『一疊鈔票』應該說 a wad of bills/banknotes (英式說法)。

wage

Tony earns a daily salary of $75. (✗)
Tony earns a daily wage/pay of $75. (✓)
(東尼每天的工資是 75 美元。)

salary 指的是按月/年給的『固定薪水』, 如: The CFO receives an annual salary of a million dollars. (這位財務長的年薪為一百萬美元。) wage 是指每小時/天/週的『工資』。

wait

Since we don't have an umbrella with us, let's stay here and wait for the rain. (✗)
Since we don't have an umbrella with us, let's stay here and wait out the rain. (✓)
(既然我們沒有帶傘，我們就留在這裡等雨過去吧。)

wait for sb/sth 表『等候某人/物來到』, 如: What are you waiting for? (你在等什麼啊?) wait out sth 表『等候某種 (不愉快的) 情況過去』。另外, wait up (for sb) 表『熬夜不睡等候某人回來』, 如: I'll be back very late tonight, so don't wait up (for me). (我今晚會很晚回來, 所以早點睡, 不用等我。)

walk

These volunteers are people from all walk of life. (✗)
These volunteers are people from all walks of life. (✓)
(這些志工都是來自社會的各個階層。)

from all walks/every walk of life 表『來自社會的各階層』, 是固定說法。

walking

My grandpa is very erudite. He's a living dictionary. (✗)
My grandpa is very erudite. He's a walking dictionary. (✓)
(我的爺爺很有學問。他是一部活字典。)

a walking dictionary/encyclopedia 指的是一個『很有學問的人』, 活像一部字典或百科全書似的。另外, a living legend 指的是一個『現仍活躍的傳奇性人物』, 如: The Harry Potter series has made its author a living legend. (哈利波特系列的書籍已使該作者成為一個傳奇性人物。)

warfare

Intelligence operations play a very important role in the modern warfare. (✗)
Intelligence operations play a very important role in modern warfare. (✓)
(情報活動在現代戰爭中扮演一個極為重要的角色。)

warfare表『戰爭的型態』,是不可數名詞,如: chemical/nuclear/jungle/guerrila warfare 就是指『化學/核子/叢林/遊擊戰』。war表『戰爭(行為)』兼有可/不可數的用法, 如: It's a war that neither side will win. (這是一場雙方都不會贏的戰爭。) 或如: We had no choice but to declare war. (我方別無選擇, 只好宣戰。)

warm-up

Always have warm-up before you do any strenuous exercise. (✗)

Always have a warm-up before you do any strenuous exercise. (✔)

Always warm up before you do any strenuous exercise. (✔)

(做任何激烈的運動之前總是先要暖身一下。)

warm-up 表『暖身』,是可數名詞, 其動詞的說法是 warm up。

warrant

The DVD player is still under warrant. (✗)

The DVD player is still under warranty. (✔)

(這一台數位光碟機仍在保證期限內。)

warrant 是法院開出的搜索/逮捕『令狀』, 如: The court has issued a warrant for his arrest. (法院已對他發出逮捕令。)』warranty 是某家公司產品的『保證書』。under warranty 表『在保證期限內』。

wash

Tell the small children to do the wash before they eat. (?)

Tell the small children to wash up before they eat. (✔)

(孩子吃東西前先叫他們去洗手。)

the wash = the laundry 表『待洗的髒衣服』或『剛洗好的衣服』。do the wash = do the laundry. 是『洗衣服』之意, 如: I'll have to do the wash tomorrow. (明天我必須洗衣服了。) wash up 是『洗手/臉』之意(美式說法)。另外, wash up 在英式的說法裡則表『洗碗盤』,相當於 do the dishes 的說法。

washed-up

You must admit that she is already a washed-out actress. (✗)

You must admit that she is already a washed-up actress. (✔)

(你必須承認她已經是個過氣的演員。)

washed-out 表衣服『褪色的』, 如: Never wear those washed-out clothes again. (不要再穿那些褪色的衣服了。) washed-up 指演員或明星『過氣了』。

waste

The authorities should find ways to end the dumping of industrial wastes into rivers. (✗)

The authorities should find ways to end the dumping of industrial waste into rivers. (✔)

(政府當局應該想出辦法來制止傾倒工業廢棄物進入河川的行為。)

W

表『廢棄物』時 waste 是不可數名詞, 如: household/industrial/chemical waste 就是指『家庭/工業/化學廢棄物』。表『浪費』的行為時, 經常使用 a waste of sth, 如: What a waste of time! (多麼浪費時間啊!)

water

Does anyone want a water? (✗)
Does anyone want a drink/glass of water? (✔)
(有人想喝杯水嗎？)

water 指『生水』或『飲用水』時均為不可數名詞。因此 water 經常搭配單位使用, 如: a gallon/liter of water 即是『一加侖/公升的水』。但指一大片的『海/水域』時則恆用複數形的 waters, 如: Our ship is sailing into Caribbean waters. (我們的船正駛進加勒比海域。)

Cutting onions always makes me cry. (✗)
Cutting onions always makes my eyes water. (✔)
(切洋蔥時總是會讓我流眼淚。)

make sb cry 是『使人哭泣』之意。難道切洋蔥時會讓人想起若干傷心往事? 因風沙或切洋蔥引起某人流眼淚時, 需說: make sb's eyes water。另外, make sb's mouth water 表 (某食物)『令某人想吃而流口水』。

way

Jeniffer is in the lead, with the other runners very behind. (✗)
Jeniffer is in the lead, with the other runners way behind. (✔)
(珍妮佛目前領先，其他跑者則遠遠落後。)

very 不能用來修飾與介詞相關的副詞。這種情況需用 way 來修飾, 如: way ahead/behind/beyond/over 等。

weakness

Peter has weakness for chocolate. (✗)
Peter has a weakness for chocolate. (✔)
(彼德偏愛巧克力。)

表『虛/疲弱』的狀態時, weakness 為不可數名詞, 如: the weakness of the dollar 就是指美元的『疲弱不振』。表『弱點』或『偏愛』時, weakness 是可數名詞, 如: It's important to know your own strengths and weaknesses. (知道自己的優點和弱點是重要的。) have a weakness for sth 用於表達『偏愛某物』,have a soft spot for sb 則為『偏袒某人』。

wear

Don't wear your welcome. (✗)
Don't wear out your welcome. (✔)
(不要待太久惹人厭。)

wear sth 表『穿戴衣物』, 如: She's wearing a pink dress to the interview. (她穿一件粉紅色的洋裝去參加面試。) wear out (sth) 表 (因長期使用)『磨破某物』, 如: My shoes have worn out. (我的鞋子已經磨破了。) wear out sb's welcome 為引申的用法。

There will be a range of leisure wears on sale as of tomorrow. (✗)
There will be a range of leisure wear on sale as of tomorrow. (✔)
(從明天開始有一系列的休閒服特價出售。)

表『衣服』時 wear 為不可數名詞, 如: casual/leisure/sports wear 即為『便/休閒/運動服』。另外, 表『磨損』時, wear 亦為不可數名詞, 如: He wanted me to check the machines for wear and tear. (他要我檢查這些機器的損耗情形。)

weather

Cold weathers will continue through the weekend. (✗)

Cold weather will continue through the weekend. (✔)

(寒冷的天氣將持續至週末。)

weather (天氣) 一般為不可數名詞, 但 in all weather(s) 則兼有單複數的用法, 如: Jeff goes out jogging in all weather(s). (傑夫不論天候如何都出去慢跑。)

weave

A motorcycle wove in and out of traffic. (✗)

A motorcycle weaved in and out of traffic. (✔)

(有一部摩托車在車陣裡穿梭而行。)

表『編織』時, weave 的過去式為 wove, 過去分詞為 woven, 如: She sat there and wove a garland. (她坐在那裡編花圈。) 表汽/機車的『穿梭/蛇行』時, weave 的過去式及過去分詞均為 weaved。

weight

He has been lifting weight since he was 17. (✗)

He has been lifting weights since he was 17. (✔)

(他從十七歲就開始練舉重。)

表『重量』或『體重』時, weight 是不可數名詞, 如: The doctor often reminds people to watch their weight. (這位醫師時常提醒人們注意自己的體重。) 表『重物』時, weight 是可數名詞, 如: Can you pull such a heavy weight? (這麼重的東西你拉得動嗎?) life weights 為『舉重』固定說法。

Fruit and vegetables are usually sold in weight. (✗)

Fruit and vegetables are usually sold by weight. (✔)

(水果和蔬菜通常是論斤兩販售。)

in weight 表某人/物的『重量為何』, 如: I'm about 70 kilos in weight. (我體重大約七十公斤。) by weight 表『按重量』來計算價格等。

well

Hans is doing pretty good at college. (✗)

Hans is doing pretty well at college. (✔)

(漢斯目前在大學的表現相當好。)

do well 是『表現良好/優異』的固定說法, 其中的 well 是副詞。嚴格來說, good 只有形容詞和名詞的用法。do (sb) good 意為(對某人) 有好處/用處, 如: I'll go borrow money, but it won't do any good. (我會去借錢, 不過這沒什麼好處。)

wheel

The bus driver must have fallen asleep on the wheel. (✗)

The bus driver must have fallen asleep at/behind the wheel. (✔)

(這名公車司機一定是開車時睡著了。)

W

wheel 可表『車輪』或『方向盤』。at/behind the wheel 表(某人)坐在方向盤後面『開車』。on wheels 表『裝有輪子的』, 如: We need to buy a TV table on wheels. (我們需要買一張裝有輪子的電視座台。)

wide

"Open widely," said the dentist. (✗)
"Open wide," said the dentist. (✔)
(牙醫說:『(嘴巴)張開大一點。』)

wide 兼有形容詞和副詞的用法, 均表實際(可見)的寬敞/大, 如: Leave the door wide open. (讓那扇門敞開著。) 或如: Tom sat on the sofa, with his legs wide apart. (湯姆坐在沙發椅上, 兩腿敞開著。) widely 表『廣泛/普遍地』, 如: The drug is widely used in the treatment of cancer. (這種藥被廣泛使用在治療癌症上。)

wild

The fans grew wild when Louis scored another goal. (✗)
The fans went wild when Louis scored another goal. (✔)
(當路易再進一球時, 球迷們都沸騰起來。)

grow wild (副詞) 表植物『野生』, 如: A variety of flowers grow wild on either side of the mountain track. (在這條山路的兩旁有形形色色的野生花朵。) go wild (形容詞) 表人們因興奮而『沸騰』起來。

win

The British won on three points. (✗)
The British won by three points. (✔)
(英國隊贏了三分。)

win on points (不搭配數字) 表『取得最/較多的分數獲勝』, 如: In the playoff the French won on points. (法國隊於延長賽中取得較多分獲勝。) win by two/three/four points 表『以二/三/四分的差距獲勝』。

I do hope this meeting will help create a two-win situation for us. (✗)
I do hope this meeting will help create a win-win situation for us. (✔)
(我鄭重希望這個會議將有助於我們營造雙贏的局面。)

a win-win situation 表一個『大家/雙方都贏的局面』, 是固定說法。另外, a no-win situation 則表一個『怎麼樣都不討好/成功的局面』。

wink

Just before I gave a presentation, my boss blinked at me knowingly. (✗)
Just before I gave a presentation, my boss winked at me knowingly. (✔)
(就在我上台說明之前, 我的老闆心照不宣地對我眨了一眼。)

blink 是不自覺的『眨眼』, 而 wink 則是故意『眨眼』以示意。wink 亦可作名詞用, 如: I didn't get a wink of sleep last night. 或 I didn't sleep a wink last night. (我昨晚沒闔過一眼。)

wipe

Give your little sister's face a mop, will you? (✗)
Give your little sister's face a wipe, will you? (✔)
(幫你的小妹妹臉擦乾淨, 好嗎?)

mop 作名詞時是『拖把』,並沒有『擦拭』之意。作為動詞時, mop 除可表『拖地板』之外, 亦可像 wipe 用來表『擦拭』臉上的(汗水等), 如: It was so hot that he kept mopping/wiping his face. (天氣真熱, 所以他一直擦拭臉上的汗水。) give sth a wipe 表『給某物擦拭一下』, 是固定用法。

wise

He is a wise guy, so he can give really good advice. (✗)

He is a wise man, so he can give really good advice. (✔)

(他是一個智者, 因此可以給人很好的建言。)

a wise guy 是指一個『自作聰明的人』, 為嘲諷的用語。一個『智者』應該說 a wise person/man。

wish

We all wish you lucky. (✗)

We all wish you luck. (✔)

(我們大家都祝你好運。)

表『祝福』時應該用 wish sb sth (名詞形式) 的句型, 如: I wish you a happy New Year. (我祝你新年快樂。)

wonder

It's a small wonder that you were fired. (✗)

It's small wonder that you were fired. (✔)

(難怪你會遭到解雇。)

表『難怪……』固定說法是 (it's) no/small/little wonder (that)...。但表『驚訝』時則須用 it's a wonder (that)..., 如: It's a wonder that nobody got hurt. (居然沒人受傷, 真是奇蹟。)

Proper exercise can sometimes make wonders. (✗)

Proper exercise can sometimes do/work wonders. (✔)

(適當的運動有時會有意想不到的效果。)

do/work wonders (恆用複數) 表『有意想不到的效果』, 是固定用法。

word

I give you my words that I won't do it again. (✗)

I give you my word that I won't do it again. (✔)

(我向你保證我再也不會做那種事了。)

表『文字』或『一段談話』時, word 為可數名詞, 如: Can I have a word with you? (我可否跟你講一下話?) 或如: Tell us in your words what happened. (以你自己的話告訴我們發生了什麼事。) 表『承諾/保證』或『消息/資訊』時, word 為不可數名詞, 如: My friend is a man of his word. (我朋友是個信守承諾的人。) 或如: Word of the riot spread quickly. (發生暴動的消息傳的很快。)

When you see the general, say a good word for me. (✗)

When you see the general, put in a good word for me. (✔)

(當你見到將軍時, 替我美言幾句。)

put in a (good) word for sb 表『替某人美言幾句』, 是固定說法。

work

If Dad is not at home, he may be still in work. (✗)

W

If Dad is not at home, he may be still at work. (✔)
(如果老爸不在家，他或許仍在公司忙。)

in work (英式用法) 表『就業』, 是『失業』 out of work 的相反情況, 如: After she got divorced, she was back in work. (她離婚後又回去就業。) at work 表『在上班的地方』工作。另外, in the works 表某事/物『正在被計劃/發展中』, 如: The construction of a new incinerator is in the works. (興建一座新焚化爐的工作目前正被籌劃中。)

W

worse

If worse comes to worst, we'll sell our house. (✗)
If worst comes to worst, we'll sell our house. (✔)
(假如情況壞到極點，我們就賣掉房子。)

if (the) worst comes to (the) worst 表『如果情況壞到極點』, 是固定說法。其中加"the"的是英式用法。另外, go from bad to worse 表『每況愈下』之意。

wrap

Be sure to cover each dish with a plastic wrap. (✗)
Be sure to cover each dish with plastic wrap. (✔)
(務必用保鮮膜把每一道菜包好。)

表『包裝紙』或『保鮮膜』時, wrap 是不可數名詞。wrap 表『披肩/圍巾』時相當於 shawl, 是可數名詞。另外, wrapper 表已包好在貨物周圍的『包裝紙』, 是可數名詞。而 wrapping paper 則指專門用來包裝禮物的『包裝用紙』。

write

Lend me a pen—I have nothing to write. (✗)
Lend me a pen—I have nothing to write with. (✔)
(借支筆吧，我沒有東西好寫字。)

I have nothing to write. 用來說明『我沒有信件/文章/報告等要寫』。write with sth 表『以某物來書寫』。同理, I have nothing to write on. 表『我沒有紙張/簿本來寫字』。

writing

I like the T-shirt with Japanese writings on it. (✗)
I like the T-shirt with Japanese writing on it. (✔)
(我喜歡那件印有日文的 T 恤。)

表書寫/印刷的『文字』時, writing 為不可數名詞。writings 是指某個作家的『(全部)作品』, 如: I'm very interested in Kafka's writings. (我對卡夫卡的作品深感興趣。)

wrong

Follow the recipe and you can't go wrongly. (✗)
Follow the recipe and you can't go wrong. (✔)
(參照這食譜你絕錯不了。)

worng 和 wrongly 均可作副詞用, 但 go wrong 表『出差錯』, 是固定用法。表『錯誤地』時用 wrongly, 如: My name is wrongly spelt. (我的名字被拼錯了。)

X x

X-ray

You had better go to the hospital for X-ray. (✗)

You had better go to the hospital for an X-ray. (✓)

(你最好去醫院照個 X 光片。)

X-ray 表『X 光線』或『照 X 光檢查』, 為可數名詞。另外, X-ray 亦可作 (及物) 動詞用, 如: I was advised to have my lungs X-rayed. (有人建議我去做肺部 X 光檢查。) 或如: All baggage will be X-rayed in the airport. (在機場所有的行李都要經過 X 光檢查。)

X

Y y

yawn

I managed to prevent a yawn and look interested. (✗)

I managed to stifle a yawn and look interested. (✓)

(我設法抑制住一個呵欠然後表現出很感興趣的樣子。)

『抑制一個呵欠』的正確說法是 stifle/suppress a yawn。

young

You look really young at your age. (✗)

You look really young for your age. (✓)

(以你的年齡來看，你真的很年輕。)

be/look young for your age 表某人『比自己的實際年齡要年輕』。be young at heart 表某人『人雖老但心不老』。

youth

The fire was set by a gang of youth. (✗)

The fire was set by a gang of youths. (✓)

(這火是一幫不良少年放的。)

youth 作為不可數名詞有二義: (1) 青春 (時期), 如: In my youth, I often fought with my siblings. (我年輕時常跟兄弟姊妹吵架。) (2) 青少年 (總稱), 如: The youth of today seem less happy. (今天的青少年似乎比較不快樂。) 但作為可數名詞時, youth 通常是指『不學好的少年 (男子)』。

Z z

z's

I'm going home to catch some zs. (✗)
I'm going home to catch some z's. (✓)
(我要回家睡個覺。)

catch/get some z's 是『睡覺』的俚俗說法。

zap

In the future, there will be more and more channels to zip. (✗)
In the future, there will be more and more channels to zap. (✓)
(將來會有越來越多的頻道供人切換。)

zip 表『拉 (衣服、皮包等) 拉鏈』。zap 表利用遙控器來『切換』頻道等。『拉鏈』的說法是 zipper (美式用法) 或 zip (英式用法)。『遙控器』的說法是 zapper 或 remote control。

Z

zero

Water freezes at zero degree Celsius. (✗)
Water freezes at zero degrees Celsius. (✓)
(水在攝氏零度時結冰。)

表『零度』恆用複數形的 zero degrees。其原因是:『零』對『負數』而言為無限大。另外, zero in on sth 表『集中火力/注意力於某物』, 如: The newspapers all zeroed in on her private life. (各家報紙爭相報導她的私生活)。

zone

The island is located in an earthquake area. (✗)
The island is located in an earthquake zone. (✓)
(這個島位於地震帶。)

area 表一般的『地區』, 如: urban/rural area 就是指『都市/鄉村地區』。zone 表有特殊現象的『區域』或『地帶』, 如: war/battle zone 是『戰區』。time zone 是依地球經度劃分的『(標準) 時區』。另外, 按緯度劃分有 the Frigid/Temperate/Torrid Zone, 即『寒/溫/熱帶』。

國家圖書館出版品預行編目資料

用字正典 / 李端編著 / --初版.
臺北市：常春藤有聲, 2005 [民 94]
面：　　公分-- (常春藤全民英語硬底子系列；E17)

ISBN　986-7638-64-6 (精裝)

1. 英國語言 -- 字典, 辭典

805.13　　　　94007171

常春藤全民英語硬底子系列 E17

用字正典

編　　著：李　端
編　　審：賴世雄・Bruce Bagnell・Joe Roberts
校　　對：常春藤中外編輯群
封面設計：黃振倫
電腦排版：朱瑪琍・劉濰崢・蕭佩真
顧　　問：賴陳愉嫺
法律顧問：王存淦律師・蕭雄淋律師
發行日期：2005 年 10 月　初版/三刷

出 版 者：常春藤有聲出版有限公司
台北市忠孝西路一段 33 號 5 樓
行政院新聞局出版事業登記證
局版臺業字第肆捌貳陸號

服務電話：(02)2331-7600　　服務傳真：(02)2381-0918
信　　箱：臺北郵政 8-18 號信箱
郵撥帳號：**19714777**　　常春藤有聲出版有限公司
定　　價：**475** 元
＊如有缺頁、裝訂錯誤或破損　請寄回本社更換

常春藤有聲出版有限公司

讀者回函卡

✍感謝您的填寫，您的建議將是公司重要的參考及修正指標！

我購買本書的書名是		編碼	
我購買本書的原因是	□老師、同學推薦 □家人推薦 □學校購買 □書店閱讀後感到喜歡 □其他		
我購得本書的管道是	□書攤 □業務人員推薦 □大型連鎖書店 □書店名稱＿＿＿＿＿＿ □其他		
我最滿意本書的三點依序是	□內容 □編排方式 □雙色印刷 □試題演練 □解析清楚 □封面 □售價 □促銷活動豐富 □信任品牌 □廣告 □其他		
我最不滿意本書的三點依序是	□內容 □編排方式 □雙色印刷 □試題演練 □解析不足 □封面 □售價 □促銷活動貧乏 □廣告 □其他		
我有一些其他想法與建議是			
我發現本書誤植的部份是	□書籍第＿頁，第＿行，有錯誤的部份是 □書籍第＿頁，第＿行，有錯誤的部份是		

✍我的基本資料

讀者姓名		生　日		性別	□男 □女
就讀學校		科系年級	科 年級	畢業	□已畢 □在學
聯絡電話		E-mail			
聯絡地址	＿＿ ＿＿ ＿＿(郵地區號)				

請您填寫完後寄至：

台北市忠孝西路一段33號5樓　常春藤有聲出版有限公司　出版部收

填寫日期：西元＿＿＿年＿＿＿月＿＿＿日